PRAISE FOR JOSEPH FLYNN AND HIS NOVELS

"Flynn is an excellent storyteller." — *Booklist*

"Flynn propels his plot with potent but flexible force."
— *Publishers Weekly*

The President's Henchman
"Marvelously entertaining." — *ForeWord Magazine*

Digger
"A mystery cloaked as cleverly as (and perhaps better than) any John Grisham work." — *Denver Post*

"Surefooted, suspenseful and in its breathless final moments unexpectedly heartbreaking." — *Booklist*

The Next President
"*The Next President* bears favorable comparison to such classics as *The Best Man, Advise and Consent* and *The Manchurian Candidate*."
— *Booklist*

"A thriller fast enough to read in one sitting."
— *Rocky Mountain News*

The Echo of the Whip

A JIM McGILL NOVEL

Joseph Flynn

Stray Dog Press, Inc.
Springfield, IL
2016

ALSO BY JOSEPH FLYNN

The Jim McGill Series

The President's Henchman, A Jim McGill Novel [#1]
The Hangman's Companion, A JimMcGill Novel [#2]
The K Street Killer A JimMcGill Novel [#3]
Part 1: The Last Ballot Cast, A JimMcGill Novel [#4 Part 1]
Part 2: The Last Ballot Cast, A JimMcGill Novel [#4 Part 2]
The Devil on the Doorstep, A Jim McGill Novel [#5]
The Good Guy with a Gun, A Jim McGill Novel [#6]
The Echo of the Whip, A Jim McGill Novel [#7]
McGill's Short Cases 1-3

The Ron Ketchum Mystery Series

Nailed, A Ron Ketchum Mystery [#1]
Defiled, A Ron Ketchum Mystery Featuring John Tall Wolf [#2]
Impaled, A Ron Ketchum Mystery [#3]

The John Tall Wolf Series

Tall Man in Ray-Bans, A John Tall Wolf Novel [#1]
War Party, A John Tall Wolf Novel [#2]
Super Chief, A John Tall Wolf Novel [#3]
Smoke Signals, A John Tall Wolf Novel [#4]

The Zeke Edison Series

Kill Me Twice, A Zeke Edison Novel [#1]

Stand Alone Novels

The Concrete Inquisition
Digger
The Next President
Hot Type
Farewell Performance
Gasoline, Texas
Round Robin, A Love Story of Epic Proportions
One False Step
Blood Street Punx
Still Coming
Still Coming Expanded Edition
Hangman — A Western Novella
Pointy Teeth, Twelve Bite-Size Stories

Published by Stray Dog Press, Inc.
Springfield, IL 62704, U.S.A.

First Stray Dog Press, Inc. printing, August, 2015

Visit the author's web site: *www.josephflynn.com*

Flynn, Joseph
The Echo of the Whip / Joseph Flynn
378 p.
ISBN 978-0-9908412-7-2
ISBN eBook 978-0-9908412-4-1

Printed in the United States of America

PUBLISHER'S NOTE
This is a work of fiction. Names, characters, places, and incidents are either the product of the author's imagination or are used fictitiously; any resemblance to actual persons, living or dead, events, or locales is entirely coincidental.

Book design by Aha! Designs
Cover photo courtesy of iStockPhoto.com

DEDICATION

For Catherine once more.

ACKNOWLEDGEMENTS

Catherine, Cat, Anne and Susan do their level best to catch all my typos and other mistakes, but I usually outwit them. Please be kind. Even Ty Cobb didn't get a hit every time at bat.

CHARACTER LIST

[in alphabetical order by last name]

Ah-lam, wife of Tyler Busby
Eugene Beck, assassin/thief, formerly U.S. military
Abra Benjamin, Special Agent, FBI
Gawayne Blessing, White House head butler
Ellie Booker, Independent news producer
Philip Brock, Democratic Congressman from Pennsylvania
Tyler Busby, fugitive billionaire wanted by FBI
Edwina Byington, the president's personal secretary
Hugh Collier, CEO of WorldWide News media empire
Celsus Crogher, retired Secret Service SAC
Byron DeWitt, Deputy Director of the FBI
Deirdre "Didi" DiMarco, WWN news show host
Darren Drucker, billionaire co-founder of ShareAmerica
Carolyn [McGill] Enquist, first wife of Jim McGill
Jordan Gilford, whistleblower, murder victim
Erna Godfrey, federal prisoner, woman who killed Andrew Hudson Grant
Patricia Darden Grant, President of the United States, second wife of Jim McGill
Andrew Hudson Grant (deceased), philanthropist, the president's first husband
Bahir Ben Kalil, (deceased) personal physician to the Jordanian ambassador to the U.S.
Dr. Hasna Kalil, twin sister of late Dr. Bahir Ben Kalil
[SAC] **Elspeth Kendry**, head of the Presidential Protection Detail
Carina Linberg, novelist, formerly a colonel in USAF.
Donald "Deke" Ky, Jim McGill's personal Secret Service bodyguard
Leo Levy, Jim McGill's personal driver
Wallace MacDuff, LAPD detective
Jim McGill, president's husband, *aka* The President's Henchman

CHARACTER LIST

[Continued, in alphabetical order by last name]

Roger Michaelson, (formerly Senator D-OR) Patti Grant's one-time political nemesis

Galia Mindel, White House chief of staff

Jean Morrissey, Vice President of the U.S.

Thomas Winston Rangel, conservative intellectual

Joan Renshaw, former director of The Andrew Hudson Grant Foundation

Putnam Shady, head lobbyist of ShareAmerica, Sweetie's husband

Margaret "Sweetie" Sweeney, McGill's longtime friend and police partner; Putnam's wife

Edmond Whelan, chief of staff to House Whip

Welborn Yates, the president's personal (official) investigator, Air Force captain

Eloy Zapata, LAPD detective

CHAPTER 1

Pacific Palisades, California, Friday, March 13, 2015

The whistling man approached the rear entrance of the fertility clinic just off Sunset Boulevard dressed in a tan janitorial jumpsuit, a Los Angeles Dodgers baseball cap and wraparound sunglasses. Both his fingerprints and his sneakers' tread pattern had been altered by applications of adhesives that could be removed with hot water and soap.

The color of his complexion might have been that of a Latino, Asian or light-skinned African-American. The blurring of his ethnic lines was intentional, the product of artfully applied cosmetics. The makeup also served to camouflage his age, though gray hair at the temples, peeking out from his baseball cap suggested he was at least middle-aged.

Still, the spring in his step as he pushed a covered, wheeled trash can to the rear door suggested that he possessed the vigor of a younger man. Though there was no one about to hear him in the first rays of daylight, he continued whistling a show tune. Both personal experience and psychological studies proved this exercise to be disarming. What evil intent could someone whistling "My Favorite Things" from *The Sound of Music* have?

It would be as farfetched as suspecting Julie Andrews of being an assassin.

Upon reaching the keypad that would provide entrance to the clinic, he tapped in the seven-number code smoothly, as if he'd done it countless times before. The door clicked open and he pushed his trash can into the building ahead of him. At that early hour, the only other person in the building was a private security officer named Mindy Crozier. A recent graduate of Cal State Fullerton with a BS in criminal justice, she had an application in to join the LAPD.

She was surprised to see the guy in custodial garb. The cleaning crew usually worked right *after* office hours. She might have reached for her sidearm if he hadn't been whistling, stopping just long enough to smile at her.

She was just about to say, "Hey, what's up? You got a special job to do?"

Only in the moment she'd been lulled into a false sense of security, the guy pulled a C2 Taser — she recognized the model at a glance — out of a pocket and shot her. The 50,000 volt charge lit her up like a Beverly Hills Christmas tree. Her eyes rolled up in her head and with a moan she crumpled to the floor.

Whistling once more, the man in the Dodgers cap took a hand-held vacuum cleaner out of his trash can and meticulously sucked up every last anti-felon ID tag, confetti-like bits of material stamped with bar codes that would identify the taser that had dispersed them.

He gave just a moment's attention to Mindy. Her respiration appeared to be rhythmic and without distress. There was really no telling how long she might remain unconscious. It would be best if he worked quickly. He didn't want to kill her if he didn't have to.

A second keypad protected the room where the embryos were kept in cold storage. The whistler knew the code for that keypad, too. He entered the room. Tanks of liquid nitrogen were used to store the embryos of the men and women who had reason to bank their most personal assets. A liquid known as cryptoprotectant was added to the tanks to safeguard the embryos during freezing. Not all embryos survived freezing and thawing, but the man in the Dodgers cap was determined that none would be lost due to his activity.

He'd been drilled on how to handle the matter. He had the equipment he needed in his trash can. Barring some staffer or doctor making an unexpectedly early appearance, he should have more than enough time to complete his task.

He set about his work with complete focus. He'd stolen a number of things over his career, but he'd never heisted potential human beings before. When he'd been told what his objective was, he'd been struck by a thought that had never occurred to him until that moment: *What would it be like to become a dad?*

He decided he should know whose embryos he was stealing.

So he made a point of finding out, after meticulously completing his primary assignment.

The girl security guard, bless her little heart, stayed lights out throughout. No need to spill any of her blood. Chances were the brief look she got at him, at the likeness he'd wanted her to see, would be as scrambled as a plate of eggs when she woke up.

The whistler had the trash can stored securely in the back of his van within minutes. He was driving away from Pacific Palisades before most of the locals had gotten out of bed. Good for him, a shame for them. It was yet another beautiful morning in SoCal.

Made him keep right on whistling. "My Way," now.

He'd decided to keep one of the embryos for himself.

CHAPTER 2

Washington, DC, Friday, March 20, 2015

On the first day of spring, President Patricia Grant was impeached.

In an exclusive one-on-one interview with Ellie Booker, she was asked how she felt.

"I'm tempted to say I'd rather be in Philadelphia, but I'll leave that line to W. C. Fields. What I can tell you is that a political assassination is preferable to a real one."

For the sake of propriety and political cover, the House of Representatives had followed the procedures for impeachment in fine detail. The Judiciary Committee took up the question of whether there were grounds to impeach the president. Their focus was on the president's authorization to transfer Joan Renshaw to the Federal Correctional Institution at Danbury, Connecticut and the prison cell holding Erna Godfrey.

Erna was the woman who had killed the president's first husband, Andrew Hudson Grant.

Within the first hour of her incarceration there, Joan Renshaw had choked Erna Godfrey to death. The murder was captured on video, as was Renshaw's declaration: "I sure hope this was Patti Grant's idea, putting me in here."

It was actually Margaret "Sweetie" Sweeney's idea.

But President Patricia Grant had made it happen.

"You know what the Republicans are saying about that," Ellie Booker told the president.

"I do."

"That you knew how Joan Renshaw would react when put within arm's reach of Erna Godfrey.

"I didn't know; no one knew."

"Nonetheless, they're saying you wanted revenge for what Erna did to Mr. Grant."

Patti Grant reminded Ellie and by extension the American people, "I issued a grant of clemency to Erna Godfrey, commuting her sentence to life in prison when I could have let her be executed, if what I wanted was to see her die."

"The reply to that is you regretted that decision, that it ate at you and you could abide it no longer. So you sent Joan Renshaw into Erna Godfrey's cell in the hope that she would do just what she did."

"No, that was not the reason. I hoped Joan Renshaw would talk to Erna Godfrey and resolve the matter of whom Joan Renshaw had worked with in the planned attempt on my life at Inspiration Hall."

"The people who voted to impeach you today claim that's just a pretext for what you did."

The Judiciary Committee, where questions of impeachment originated, had sent a resolution to the full House stating there was reason to impeach the president.

A small group of cooler heads in the House leadership decided that first degree murder, requiring malice aforethought, was too much of a reach, but second degree murder, under the assertion of depraved indifference, deficient moral sense and recklessness would do just fine.

Murder-2 also fit neatly under the Constitution's "other high crimes and misdemeanors" grab-bag of impeachable offenses.

"There was no pretext," the president said. "There was no depraved indifference. Joan Renshaw had no history of physical violence. It was also unimaginable to think that Erna Godfrey would offer no attempt to defend herself when she was attacked. And I have no record of seeking vengeance against anyone. I was simply trying to learn who was involved in the plan to kill me, but it went tragically wrong."

"And yet the House voted to impeach you," Ellie said.

The Rules Committee had set the terms of the debate and the vote on the question of whether to impeach the president. The ayes had it, 258-177. The GOP and True South voted unanimously for impeachment. They were joined by three Democrats.

White House Chief of Staff Galia Mindel had silently vowed to make the lives of those three turncoats miserable until the days they died.

With the article of impeachment approved by the House, the process would move to the Senate. The president would be tried there. The chief justice of the United States, Craig MacLaren, would preside. A two-thirds vote of guilty by the Senate was required for conviction.

By all present expectations, Joan Renshaw would not be available to testify. She'd suffered a psychotic break shortly after killing Erna Godfrey. The psychotherapists attending her wouldn't even hazard a guess as to when or if she might regain mental competence.

In the event she did, however, a voluntary manslaughter charge against her was pending.

Ellie pointed out the political lay of the land to the president and the country. "The coalition of the Republicans and True South, caucusing together, took control of the Senate in the midterm election. But they don't have the two-thirds majority necessary to convict you. Do you think they'll be able to persuade enough Democrats to vote with them for conviction?"

The president offered a thin smile. "I won't say anything that might be misconstrued as an improper attempt to influence the Senate."

That wrapped up the president's interview.

When Ellie managed to get a moment on camera with James J. McGill, he was far more blunt.

He told her, "You know what might be just the thing to straighten out this town? A good punch in the snoot. At least one for every troublemaker working in the federal government."

The implication that a large number of those miscreants occupied seats in Congress could not be missed. Within minutes of the airing of McGill's sentiment, the Capitol Hill Police were flooded with protection requests from worried senators and representatives. The thrashing McGill had once given former Senator Roger Michaelson had quickly come to mind.

McGill Investigations, Inc. — Georgetown

"You can't talk like that," Galia Mindel told McGill as she sat in his office.

In the six-plus years of Patricia Grant's presidency, the White House chief of staff had never visited the offices of McGill Investigations, Inc before that day. She'd been warned from the start to keep her nose out of McGill's private sector business. That had rankled her in the beginning, but she'd come to see that McGill kept his nose out of government business as much as possible, and his restraint had made things easier for her.

Reciprocity mattered to Galia.

Then there was the fact that McGill had saved her life, endearing him ever after to Galia's sons and grandchildren. Crossing the president's henchman would risk causing a family rift. The very thought of that was enough to make Galia tread lightly.

"You mean I shouldn't give any warning?" McGill asked. "Just punch anyone who gets out of line."

Margaret Sweeney and Special Agent Deke Ky were in the room with McGill and Galia.

Neither of them looked like they took McGill's words as jest.

To the contrary, they might join in any brawl he initiated.

"I'm serious, Mr. McGill. The president's immediate well being and her place in the history of our country depend on many things going right. We can't afford any unnecessary distractions. I do not want to see her convicted by the Senate."

Hearing that idea expressed aloud set McGill back in his seat.

"You think there's a real chance of that?" he asked.

Galia gave him the numbers. "The GOP and True South hold fifty-four seats in the Senate; they need sixty-seven to convict. Persuading thirteen Democrats to vote with them might seem like a reach, but fourteen of them are up for reelection in 2016. Four of those fourteen looked like losers before the president was impeached. I expect them to defect shortly."

McGill would have cursed if Sweetie wasn't there.

Instead, his face grew red and he looked as if he might ask Galia for the names of the four would-be traitors. The better to rearrange their facial features sooner rather than later. But he took a deep breath and let his anger dissipate as he exhaled.

"Even if those four change sides, that means the other side would still have to get nine out of the ten Democrats up for reelection to get to the two-thirds majority," McGill said.

Galia nodded. "The thing you have to remember is the president has been a Democrat for a very short time. She doesn't have a lot of long-standing friendships in the party. She doesn't have a history there to rely on. And as you no doubt know any politician's first loyalty is to keeping his or her seat."

McGill's face went slack. "You *truly* think Patti might be convicted?"

"I think it's within the realm of possibility … but I also think the other side might push for and be satisfied with a resignation."

"Like Nixon," McGill said.

"Yes."

McGill asked Sweetie and Deke to step out. They left without objection.

"Galia, you don't have to say a word. I'm just going to look you in the eye. I'm going to see whether you have a plan to prevent both a conviction by the Senate and any chance that Patti will be forced to resign."

The chief of staff kept her face impassive, but her eyes burned fiercely.

Telling McGill: *Damn right I do. Good thing you saved my keister.*

McGill nodded, satisfied.

"One more thing, sir."

"What's that?" McGill asked.

"I have a case for you to work, in California."

McGill's Hideaway — The White House

"Looking on the bright side," the president told her husband that evening, "you've been wanting to get out of Washington for some time now."

McGill had just lit a fire in the last remaining wood-burning fireplace in the executive mansion. The night outside was as cold and dark as his mood. Satisfied that he'd done a good job getting the blaze alight, he turned to look at Patti. She sat on his long leather sofa and extended a glass of Italian brandy to him. Oak aged, very smooth and mellow. Had a soft, fruity aroma.

Even at this stage of McGill's life in the White House, it was far from his usual drink.

But it didn't seem like the time for a beer.

McGill accepted the glass and sat next to his wife, close enough that their shoulders, hips and legs touched. That was the kind of warmth McGill needed. After a sip, though, he had to admit the brandy wasn't bad either.

"Are you talking about Galia sending me off to the West Coast or the prospect of the both of us finding new lodgings?"

Taking a moment to consider, Patti said, "Both, I suppose."

McGill looked his wife in the eye. "You seem to be handling the adversity of the situation with uncommon grace. Even for you, I mean."

Patti nodded. "I'm trying to come to terms with the situation. Looking at the worst that might happen."

"Being removed from office."

"That and, who knows, facing possible criminal prosecution, if I get booted out of here."

McGill's jaw dropped. That idea had never occurred to him. It had been Attorney General Michael Jaworsky's opinion that there had been no way for the president or anyone else to have foreseen the tragic events that took place in Erna Godfrey's prison cell and, therefore, there was no criminal liability. Jaworsky's disinclination to prosecute had spurred the House to begin its impeachment proceedings.

So how could —

Patti told McGill how. "Erna Godfrey died on federal property, giving the federal government jurisdiction. There's no federal statute of limitations on homicide. Even though Attorney General Jaworsky saw no criminal liability for me or anyone else, if the next president comes from one of the parties that want to remove me from office, the new attorney general might take a different view of things."

The very idea left McGill speechless.

"Take a sip of brandy," Patti told him. "It's not likely that will happen, but I'd be foolish not to be ready for the possibility. You know, just in case."

"Yeah," McGill said. He knocked back the brandy like it was a shot of cheap booze.

The president forced a smile. "Maybe we could contact Tyler Busby's travel agent."

The billionaire fugitive, wanted in connection with the would-be attempt on the president's life at Inspiration Hall, had been on the run for a year now, and all the police, military and espionage assets of the United States and its allies had yet to find him.

"It'd be just our luck that she's retired," McGill said, playing along.

He poured more brandy for Patti and himself, limited his consumption to a sip.

"There's the man I love."

"The one who'd best serve you by beating it out of town."

"Well, Galia gave you a case to work, right?"

McGill nodded. "There's a turn of events I never thought I'd see."

"Why not? Galia can't know someone in need of help?"

"Of course, she can. I just thought … well, we have made peace more than I ever thought we would, Galia and me."

"I hear you're getting on well with Celsus these days, too."

Celsus Crogher was the former head of the presidential security detail, now retired from government service and doing well in the private sector providing executive security services.

"Far from bosom buddies," McGill said, "but we share a measure of mutual respect."

"No doubt owing to your personal charm and professionalism."

"No need to butter me up," McGill said. "I've already said yes to Galia." He took another sip of brandy and studied his wife. "But you were sure I would, weren't you?"

"To a near certainty, yes."

McGill studied Patti Grant's face, an exercise he never found tiring.

"There's more to this case than Galia told me, isn't there?" he asked.

"I certainly hope she gave you only the basics. Your discussions with the White House chief of staff aren't privileged. Conversation with your dear wife, however, is legally protected."

"Damn right. So what's the nitty-gritty here?"

"You start. Tell me what Galia told you, and I'll fill in the rest."

"She said a person or persons unknown made off with the frozen future family of a friend when a fertility clinic in a high-end L.A. neighborhood was robbed. The friend, Mira Kersten, was a former protégé back when Galia managed campaigns for New York pols."

"It's Ms. Kersten's fervent hope that the stolen embryos have been kept viable."

"Understandable. Why'd she bank them? She was facing medical treatment that would result in infertility?"

"Not that I've heard, no. My understanding is she wanted to take advantage of youthful ova, ones more likely to produce healthy children, until she was … at a better time in her life to bring them to fruition."

"You're kidding," McGill said.

Patti shook her head. "Such planning is far from uncommon these days, but Ms. Kersten was ahead of the curve by several years."

That raised the obvious question for McGill. "Her husband, boyfriend or whoever was on board with that?"

Patti put her brandy glass down. "With your charming aversion to the nuts and bolts of Washington politics, you don't know who Edmond Whelan is, do you?"

McGill shook his head.

"You do know the function of a legislative whip, though, right?"

"Sure, vote counting is something they teach in Chicago kindergartens. The whip is the guy who counts the votes for pending legislation and gets the troops to fall into line with the party boss's desires. Threatens dire consequences when necessary."

"Exactly. Only the fragmentation of the political right in Congress has made it hard to truly scare people, especially in the House. Committee assignments aren't the plums they once were; ideological purity reigns. But if anybody can bring order to the mob —"

"Hold on a minute," McGill said. "If this guy Whelan is a big elected poobah, even I should have heard of him."

Patti smiled. "That's the thing. He's never been elected to any office. He's the chief of staff for the House whip. They call him the echo of the whip because he supposedly mouths whatever his boss says. In reality, it's the other way around. Whips come and go, but Ed Whelan stays in place. He's a master strategist. The other guys just read the lines he writes for them."

"Sonofabitch," McGill said, "that's some system we've got."

"Yes, well, the Founders couldn't think of everything. Or they had more moral fiber in their diet back in the 18th century. Anyway, can you now guess who was married to Mira Kersten?"

McGill knew how to respond to a spoon-fed line. "Whelan. He's the dad. Half of the stolen genetic material is his. Does that mean he has equal legal rights to the stolen goods?"

The president sighed. "That would be subject to any legal agreement between the two parties, I think. But the kicker is Mira's stored ova weren't fertilized exclusively by Mr. Whelan. I think those of different paternity are the embryos she'd most like returned."

McGill put his glass down now. He didn't want any more alcohol fuzzing up his ruminations. Patti waited him out in silence.

"There's still more to this, I think," he finally said. "If Whelan is such a schemer for the other side, and he wants to ruin your life, well hell, maybe he stole the frozen goods out in California because ... Mira Kersten has something he wants. Getting her embryos back is the quid pro quo."

Patti Grant nodded. "Just what she suspects."

"Could Whelan be the mastermind behind the effort to impeach and convict you?" McGill asked.

"Maybe not *the* mastermind, but he probably is at or near the top of the cabal."

"And he's hard at work right now," McGill said.

Patti shook her head. "Actually, no. He's taken a leave of absence. He hasn't been seen in Washington for over a week."

McGill said, "Maybe that's putting a crimp into the opposition's plans. In any case, finding out how the opposition plans to try their case in the Senate would be useful."

"We can only hope."

"And Mira Kersten doesn't have whatever it is Ed Whelan wants from her?"

"According to Galia, no. And Galia's very good at hearing words that don't ring true."

In the chief of staff's job, she had to be, McGill knew.

"So the real job here for me is to find both the kids on ice and whatever it is Whelan wants."

"Yes."

"You could have just come to me, you know," McGill said.

"Galia's intercession is your cover."

"Yeah, but you could have whispered the story into my ear."

"I wasn't sure I wanted you involved at all."

A rueful grin crossed McGill's face. "But then I threatened to beat up all of Congress, if necessary, and things changed."

The president nodded. "Yes, I took that as a sign."

CHAPTER 3

The Verizon Center —
Washington, DC, Saturday, March 21, 2015

Jean Morrissey, the vice president of the United States, wore an ice hockey uniform from her alma mater, the University of Minnesota. She'd outbid everyone else for it in a silent auction. While the uniform was new, her skates were the ones she'd worn during her collegiate playing days. Some women concerned themselves with keeping the same dress size from their younger years; Jean contented herself that her skates still fit. Her dress size, no big deal to her, had actually gone down a notch.

She'd lined up a half-dozen pucks on the blue line, facing an open net. The Washington Capitals, the NHL team in town, had graciously agreed to let the vice president rent an hour of ice time whenever they were on the road. The blue line was 64 feet from the goal line; the puck centered in front of the goal net was the shortest and most direct shot. The others to the right and left were longer shots with more oblique angles.

Jean started her rush, skating full speed, out of the opposite end of the rink. In college she had played defense, but she'd patterned her game on that of Bobby Orr. He'd not only won eight straight Norris Trophies as the NHL's best defenseman, he was also the only defensive player ever to win two scoring championships.

He'd accomplished his all-around excellence with great skating speed and nearly magical stick-handling ability.

When she was an adolescent player, Jean had wanted to marry Bobby Orr. As she matured, she realized that was just a fantasy, but she always wore the same number he did — 4 — in his honor. Word of that had apparently gotten back to Orr. After a game against Wisconsin in which Jean had scored a hat trick — 3 goals — she'd gotten a note from Boston.

Jean, you're too cool for school. — Bobby

The future vice president immediately had the message framed.

It hung on a wall of her office in the White House.

Zipping past the only other skater on the ice, Jean hit the puck on the right end of the blue line with a resounding slap shot. The black disc became a blur rocketing through the air. It hit the upper left inside corner of the net. Not pausing to admire the shot, she skated backward to the next puck, flicked a wrist shot just inside the right post of the net. Working her way down the line of pucks, she alternated slap shots and wrist shots. All of them found the back of the net.

Adding a twist, she took the last shot backhanded.

It, too, flew into the goal.

FBI Deputy Director Byron DeWitt glided up to Jean. Not possessed of an athletic uniform, he wore hockey skates, blue jeans and a sweatshirt with the Bureau's logo and the legend: *G-men never sleep. We keep the bad guys up all night.*

He said, "I think you might have a gift for this ice hockey stuff, Ms. Vice President."

"Yeah, well. It's harder when there's a goalie in front of the net and and a lot of other people flying around between you and her."

"Your scoring record leads me to believe otherwise."

DeWitt smoothly skated away, backward and smiling.

Jean laughed and followed him. "You move like a figure skater."

"Should I get that other kind of skates?"

She closed the distance between them. "You do and it's over between us."

"Not before I get you on a board out on the Pacific."

They'd come to an agreement sports-wise: The deputy director would learn to ice skate; the vice president would learn to surf.

"A deal's a deal," she agreed. Then she frowned. "Although I'll probably get some grief from the Secret Service about that."

"Really?" DeWitt asked.

"I'm not saying they can stop me. It's just that …"

The deputy director understood the need for people is high government posts to keep their secrets, especially when you were just a heartbeat away from the Oval Office. He extended an arm to Jean Morrissey, saying, "If pairs skating won't ruin your image."

"There are agents watching us, you know."

"Yes, I know."

The Secret Service people were in the stands, at every entrance to the seating bowl and surrounding the exterior of the building.

"Oh, what the hell," Jean said. she took his arm.

Hanging on to her stick with the opposite hand.

They skated leisurely around the perimeter of the rink.

DeWitt said, "Not that you have to tell me, but is there any reason the security cocoon will get any more oppressive than it already is?"

She gave him a look. "The FBI hasn't heard that the president's been impeached?"

The rhetorical question brought DeWitt to an abrupt halt. "The president is going to resign?"

Having also stopped, Jean said, "What? No. Never, I hope."

DeWitt heaved a sigh.

"Is that the sound of relief?"

"Yes, I voted for the president twice."

They resumed skating. Their relationship had taken on more than a professional dimension after the vice president had asked the deputy director to be her escort at a state dinner. She'd filled in for an absent Patricia Grant and needed a date. DeWitt had obliged.

He'd been cleared for one of the highest jobs at the FBI, but the

Secret Service examined his life all over again. Nothing personal. Just due diligence. That and the guys who labored for the Treasury Department — the Secret Service — didn't entirely trust the people at the Justice Department — the FBI.

DeWitt had come out squeaky clean, but the process had turned up one thing Jean Morrissey hadn't known. So she'd asked her date for the evening, "How do you get away with having a portrait of Chairman Mao on your office wall?"

"The Bureau is short of linguists. As to having Westerners with at least a partial grip on the culture over there, we are few and far between. Me and a few Mormons who studied for and got turned down on their request to do missionary work in China."

Later in their burgeoning relationship, DeWitt had added, "I think the Bureau's going to lose one of its China specialists."

"Who?"

"Me. I'm burning out. When I wrap up the cases on my desk, I think I'm going home."

"California."

"Yeah," DeWitt said with a smile.

"That's a damn shame," Jean told him. "I've been thinking of proposing."

He'd given her a look. "You mean marriage?"

"It helps to be married when you run for president."

"And Bobby Orr's not available?" He knew a few of her secrets.

She'd given him an elbow. Intended for his ribs. As a matter of reflex, DeWitt met it with the palm of his hand.

"You make me hot when you do that, you know? Protect yourself so casually. Like you were just passing the salt at the dinner table."

"Kung-fu parlor trick," DeWitt said.

They'd gone on to discuss whether the vice president's attraction to the deputy director was more than a matter of political convenience. Both allowed that they shared similar social and cultural points of view. Senses of humor as well. As to physical interactions … well, they were certainly physical. And from the way they both took care of themselves it was likely to continue that way for a long time.

From there, discussions evolved. Was a bicoastal relationship feasible both personally and politically? The conversation was on-going, the outcome to be determined.

Meanwhile, the vice president asked as they skated along at the Verizon Center, "You think they have any directional mikes aimed at us?"

"Your people do, but my people are jamming them."

The vice president's eyes widened. "You're kidding, right?"

DeWitt gave a minimal shake of his head.

"You've got a mole in your security detail. I thought I'd pass the word along today."

Jean Morrissey bit back a reply but points of red burnished her cheeks.

The arm-in-arm skating had been loosely held, but now DeWitt found himself pulled close. The second most powerful woman in the world whispered to him. "The president is going to relinquish a good bit of her daily calendar to me, and you know what I'm going to do with it?"

DeWitt didn't miss a beat. "Kick some ass?"

"Lots of it. You know who the mole in my security detail is?"

He nodded and gave her the name.

The vice president said, "Okay. So …"

DeWitt bided the moment in silence, expecting to hear one thing but getting another.

"I'm going to use that sonofabitch. Get the opposition looking the wrong way and cut their legs out from under them. Better yet, I'll let them do themselves in."

Classic Sun-Tzu, DeWitt thought. "The supreme art of war is to subdue the enemy without fighting." He'd given Jean *The Art of War* to read, and she'd actually done it. Not bad for a hockey player.

Of course, that didn't mean she couldn't kick the opposition once they were down.

"I think someone's here to see you," Jean said.

She inclined her head to her left. Standing behind the protective glass was James J. McGill.

"How do you know he's here for me?" DeWitt asked.

"When he wants me he uses a wolf-whistle."

The deputy director laughed, gave the vice president a wink, and skated off to the bench area adjacent to where McGill stood. Before either man said a word to the other, they turned to watch Jean Morrissey in action. She had more pucks lined up on the opposite blue line.

This time she banged out nothing but slap shots, each one dead on target.

Carmel-by-the-Sea, California

The house Edmond Whelan was calling home for the moment had nine bedrooms, eleven bathrooms, a wine cellar, sculptured gardens, a waterfall, stunning ocean views and, best of all, an encircling stone wall artfully hidden behind a stand of local trees and other greenery. The place was a fortress with the creature comforts of a palace.

Normally, the security staff and the household help brought the population of the property to double digits. Whelan had given everyone who'd otherwise have catered to his needs an indefinite paid furlough. Not that any of the money for the service people or the house itself would come out of his pocket. That wasn't the way Whelan worked.

He flew first class, but always for free and under the radar.

Under a string of pseudonyms, too.

There would be no official record of his presence in California. He was simply a guest of the house's owner. A friend welcomed to partake of the fresh ocean air and unwind from the pressures of his job as a senior staffer in the House of Representatives. Nothing wrong with that. As a working stiff, not an elected office holder, Whelan could plead that he was in no position to return the favor to his host. It wasn't like he could direct, say, a Department of

Defense contract that could pay for a subdivision of homes such as the one in which he'd found shelter, to a preferred CEO's company.

Oh, no, he couldn't do that.

But he could push his nominal boss, the House whip, to do it. With a list of explicit reasons why a specific contractor should be chosen. Should anyone ask. Which rarely happened.

Such an inquiry should be even less likely now that Jordan Gilford, that whistle-blowing bastard, had been taken care of. Shot dead on the National Mall. Whelan liked that. Should have a nice chilling effect on any other do-gooder who might be tempted to step forward.

It was somewhat worrisome that the shooter, Jerry Nerón, had been caught. The man clearly hadn't lived up to his reputation. Still, Nerón didn't know who had hired him.

Other potential problems included the greedy fools of The Tabulation Team, the gang of Armed Services committee members in the House and Senate who'd taken to the wholesale looting of the defense budget. Wesley Tilden, GOP House member from South Carolina, had the good grace to get gunned down on his front lawn by an unknown party. That was a help. But Tanner Rutledge, a True South member from Texas, was in FBI custody and supposedly singing to beat the band. That could produce some very unfortunate results.

But not fatal for either Whelan or the House leadership. He'd reined in their more impetuous notions, made sure they personally steered clear of legal jeopardy. Kept them on the right side of the House rules, too. Pointed out repeatedly that playing it straight still left plenty of room to cull fat, easy retirements for themselves. All the golf, gin and Cialis they could ever want.

The irony of Ed cautioning his nominal superiors to mind their ways was he had finally stepped across the line. Hired a thief, through a cutout, to steal his ex-wife, Mira's, frozen embryos. He felt sure he'd get away with it, but he couldn't deny it had been an act of desperation, and he hated the idea that he'd been forced to put himself in *any* potential jeopardy.

There were people in Washington who knew his real power and they'd like nothing better than to gut him and watch buzzards eat his entrails.

Galia Mindel would be right up front, rubbing her hands in glee.

As with so many men in Washington, sex had put Whelan in peril. Specifically, developing an irresistible letch for Mira Kersten. She was a stunner, yeah, but so were a lot of women in DC. The chump who had said politics is show business for ugly people hadn't included the supporting cast in his evaluation.

Legislative and executive branch staff, lobbyists and even a good number of the academics who came and went in Washington could match head-shots with any other industry in the country, including show biz. By and large, they were smarter than other pretty faces, too. At the top of the pyramid, of course, was Patti Grant. She'd made it in both modeling and acting, and had left those *glamour* jobs to become the most powerful person in the world.

Whelan, with his Boston Yankee father and his sugar magnolia mother, had always thought he looked like what Andy Griffith's kid on his TV show should have been. A mop-top of chestnut brown hair over a cherubic face. That and the wised-up eyes of some smart guy out of a George V. Higgins novel. Like he was going to take over Mayberry after "Paw" retired, run it his way.

Only Whelan had set his sights higher than a hick town in North Carolina.

Ambition as well as sex had drawn him to Mira Kersten. Sure, he wanted to jump her from the start, but more than that he wanted to lead her over to his side of the political divide. Not make her see the light of good governance. He was too cynical for that. He wanted her to do things his way just to please him.

What he hadn't realized until later was she'd been playing her own game. She was interested in the sex, too, but what really made things special for her was when one of the candidates she and Galia Mindel backed beat one of his people. That was when she couldn't get enough of him. Rub it in. In the most personal way possible.

They'd lasted ten years together, before things got old for both of them.

Long enough to put a dozen embryos on ice.

Only there were *nineteen* of them in the shipment he'd received. Mira must've kept stocking up over the years. All of the frozen embryos were coded. No names, no conception dates. Not even a "best by" time stamp. Whelan would have preferred spoiling some other guy's specimen, but he couldn't take the time to decipher the code.

He picked one at random, let it thaw. Photographed the spoiled results with a throw-away phone and routed the image around the world on the Internet to Mira. With the photo he sent the message: *An embryo is a terrible thing to waste. Give me what I want. Fast.*

He knew she'd verify what it was the photo showed.

He truly hoped someone else was the dad, if that was possible to tell.

If it turned out to be his would-be kid, she might not give a damn.

J. Edgar Hoover Building — Washington, DC

Not just anyone could park on Pennsylvania Avenue outside the building housing FBI headquarters. Even slowing down in a suspicious manner, not keeping up with the flow of traffic, would bring a swift and unforgiving response. The Bureau had realized immediately after 9/11 that its headquarters would make a propaganda-rich target for terrorists. The gotcha value of setting off a car-bomb there, killing staffers and damaging the structure would be enormous.

Many countermeasures had been taken.

McGill, though, had called ahead, mentioned that he'd have Deputy Director DeWitt with him and would, please, like to use the VIP drop-off for just a minute or two. The combined weight of the president's husband and one of the Bureau's own top people cleared the way — once their bona fides had been verified.

"I'm sorry, Mr. McGill," DeWitt said. "I really don't have the time to help you. I shouldn't even have been at the Verizon Center, but the vice president insisted that I speak with her there."

"And you just happened to have your skates with you?"

McGill had seen the two of them gliding along hand-in-hand. Thought it was sweet. He'd heard through both the Secret Service and the White House staff grapevines that Jean Morrissey and Byron DeWitt were getting to be an item.

"The vice president suggested I might enjoy skating with her for a few minutes."

McGill had also heard the vice president was going to run for the presidency.

Made him wonder if DeWitt knew what might lie ahead for him.

As if reading his mind, the deputy director asked McGill, "Would you mind if I asked you a question, Mr. McGill?"

Guessing what that question might be, McGill said, "It's tough enough right from the start and it only gets harder. I think Mexico might have things right, limiting their presidents to one six-year term."

DeWitt nodded. "That was only part of what I've been wondering. Do you think it would be possible to be married to the president and not live in Washington?"

McGill chuckled. "The president once asked me if I'd like to continue to live in Illinois and have a commuter marriage. I told her I'd prefer to keep my sweetheart close."

"So you opened your business here in Washington."

"Yeah."

"But there must be many times when the press of the president's schedule keeps the two of you apart."

McGill sighed. "That's another thing that gets really old. We're both looking forward to life after the White House. We'll probably keep the loyal family retainers with us, though."

He nodded toward Leo and Deke seated in the front seat of his armored Chevy sedan.

Deke cleared his throat.

"Oh, that's right," McGill said. "Special Agent Ky is in line to take over the Washington office of my little shop."

"And you've got one in Paris now, too, right?"

McGill smiled. "Yeah, I came to Washington thinking I'd be Philip Marlowe and I'm turning into Allan Pinkerton. If you're considering a return home, what do you have in mind for your next job?"

"I thought I'd teach at UCSB, but maybe I could just do guest lectures, hold seminars when the president is out of the country or otherwise occupied."

"A part-time commuter marriage? Patti and I never thought of that. Might work."

"I just had another idea, though," DeWitt said.

"What's that?"

"Have you ever thought of opening a third office? The case you told me about is in California. Why not set up a shop out there? Seems like there could be a lot of business."

McGill looked at DeWitt. "Would you be interested?"

"I think I might. Working for you, lecturing at the university, getting back to DC as needed: that'd seem like part-time work compared to my current grind. I bet I could even find the time to go surfing."

McGill laughed. "Okay, I'll think about it. Meanwhile, I still need a fed to keep me company out west. Aside from Special Agent Ky, whose focus has to remain on keeping my precious hide from getting perforated."

"You want someone who's smart, tactful, able to interact with local law enforcement and not raise their hackles, should you cross their path. That's what you told me, right?"

"Right," McGill said. "How about your colleague, Special Agent Benjamin?"

"She's on an overseas assignment. What about your unofficial protégé, Captain Yates?"

"Welborn and Kira are out of the country, too. Introducing their twins to the English royal family, I think."

DeWitt laughed. "Bully for them."

"Hell, Mr. Deputy Director, can you recommend anyone?"

DeWitt gave it a moment's thought. Then he grinned and nodded.

"Who?" McGill asked.

"Someone I believe you've met. He's the Co-director of the BIA's Office of Justice Services, and he'd fit your requirements perfectly. His name is —"

John Tall Wolf," McGill said. "I remember meeting him."

CHAPTER 4

Punta del Este, Uruguay, Sunday, March 22, 2015

United States Representative Philip Brock (D-PA, 9th District) woke from a long, deep slumber and needed a moment to reorient himself, remember just where he was. He rubbed the sleep from his eyes and as his hands grazed his face he felt his emerging beard. That brought his circumstances back to him in a rush.

He'd been forced to retreat to his refuge on the Pacific Coast of Costa Rica. The panicky feeling that all of his schemes were about to collapse had made flight imperative. The FBI might finally connect him to the death of Senator Howard Hurlbert, the founder of the True South party. Dr. Hasna Kalil most likely considered him suspect number one in the murder of her brother, Dr. Bahir Ben Kalil. Last but far from least, Tyler Busby was still at large and might implicate Brock in the assassination plot to kill President Patricia Grant at Inspiration Hall.

When Brock had returned to Costa Rica, he'd learned that a traveling priest had visited his property, accompanied by a lieutenant of the *Fuerza Pública* — the National Police. The padre had heard the confessions of everyone who worked on Brock's estate and then had provided all the food and drink for a grand fiesta. He'd even provided new clothes for the little ones.

"You all had a good time?" Brock asked his majordomo.

"Sí, muy bueno."

"Did this wonderful priest spread his blessings on any other nearby properties?"

"No sé." The man didn't know.

Brock quickly found out. His property was the only one the priest had visited. Several of his servants had photos of themselves with the man, and they knew his name. It was a famous one, Inigo de Loyola. Ignatius Loyola in English.

Aside from belonging to one of the Catholic church's better known saints, the name also identified a Central American priest who had moonlighted as a guerrilla fighter. After things had gotten too hot for him in his native territory, Loyola had decamped for *El Norte* and was thought to be working among the poor in a major American city, possibly New York or Washington.

So sayeth Wikipedia.

Brock felt sure the online font of knowledge had most of its facts right this time. His money said the priest was living and spreading his gospel of economic redistribution in Washington. Meaning he'd come to Costa Rica to do whose dirty work? Looking at the worst case scenario, Brock settled on James J. McGill.

That SOB would certainly want to know who had tried to kill his wife.

With a pang of regret, Brock knew he'd have to leave Costa Rica. He wouldn't even be able to sell his beautiful 500 acres of land on the Pacific Coast. If he tried that, his pursuers — and he was sure they would be many — would only have to follow the money to find him. So his first hideaway was a write-off.

He was grateful that he had money to spare and a second place to hide. He drove to Panama City, using a counterfeit New Zealand passport, and flew to La Paz, Bolivia. The charm of one of South America's two landlocked countries was that its government despised the United States. The socialist leadership there would never extradite him.

The drawback: Bolivia was not a hub of high Western culture and gracious living. Brock quickly concluded he did not want to spend his remaining years there. He came to that realization in the time it took for his new beard to thicken. He streaked both his hair and the beard with gray dye. He bought a Land Rover and drove south, leaving behind another property.

He was taking a bath in the real estate market.

The distance between La Paz and Buenos Aires via the *Ruta Transchaco* was 2,081miles or 3,350 kilometers. This time Brock traveled on a Maltese passport. It was a grinding drive, but any pursuer would have to wonder where he might have left the road; maybe he'd had a light plane or helicopter waiting for him.

In Buenos Aires, he broke out his last passport, this one Canadian. The logic behind it was any U.S. citizen with a brain should be able to fool a South American into thinking he was from Vancouver. That and Canadians had far fewer natural enemies than Americans.

Operating from Buenos Aires, using his Canadian identity and a local real estate agent, Brock bought a modest — 10-room — but comfortable home across the Rio de la Plata in Punta Del Este, Uruguay.

Uruguay was ranked first in Latin America in democracy, peace, press freedom, proportional size of the middle class, prosperity, lack of corruption and quality of life. It ranked third in South America for innovation, infrastructure and income growth. Overlooked by Brock, it also ranked third in the *world* for percentage of the population using the Internet.

Besides all that it had a mild climate and great beaches.

All in all, there wasn't much for an anarchist to rail against, but Brock thought maybe he should put that part of his life behind him. About the only complaint he had was the driving distance from Buenos Aires to Montivideo: 594 miles. Ten-and-a-half hours. If you took the ferry crossing the mouth of the river, though, you cut travel time to a mere two hours and twelve minutes, and you cruised in relative comfort. Providing the seas were calm.

They were and, except for an excursion to the bar for a soft drink and a potty visit, Brock spent the sea cruise in his Land

Rover with a view of the water. His decision to be reclusive proved lucky. As the ferry came abeam of a super-yacht making little or no headway, Brock saw a figure that looked familiar on the yacht's helicopter pad.

He got his binoculars out of the glove box just in time to make a positive identification. The hair color was different and the man was wearing sunglasses, but Brock had no doubt of whom and what he was observing.

Tyler Busby was helping an ill-looking, very pregnant Asian woman into the aircraft. A moment later, it lifted off with Busby and the woman aboard and banked in the direction of Buenos Aires. What a gift, Brock thought.

Busby was the FBI's most-wanted man. Handing him to the feds might count for … something, should Brock feel an unexpected urge to surrender. He used his phone to photograph the yacht, capturing its name. *Wastrel.* That made him laugh.

Even when Busby was in hiding, he couldn't help but announce himself.

But should Brock make contact with, say, the U.S. embassy in Montevideo immediately? Help in the capture of Busby before he could hope to get away. How could Brock do that, though, without taking the risk of exposing himself? On the other hand, if he waited to make sure he was safe, who knew where else Busby might run off to and hide.

In the end, Brock decided self-preservation had to come first.

He drove off the ferry and to his new home, met the real estate agent, shook his hand and took the keys.

As things worked out, Brock needn't have worried about Busby eluding him. They were to become neighbors. A fact he'd learn before Busby did.

McGill Investigations, Inc. — Georgetown

"Sorry to ask you to give up your Sunday morning," McGill said, extending his hand.

John Tall Wolf shook it. The two men stood in McGill's office. Tall Wolf had two, maybe three inches of height on McGill. Standing next to Deke Ky, the BIA man and the Secret Service agent were a real Mutt and Jeff act.

Tall Wolf said, "No problem. I had time to have breakfast with my fiancée and see her off to the airport."

McGill smiled. "You're getting married? Congratulations."

"Thanks."

"I'm not taking you away from any wedding planning, am I?"

Tall Wolf smiled. "Rebecca is a lieutenant in the Royal Canadian Mounted Police. We've got a *lot* of planning to do to get things right. Our exchange of vows is certain but not imminent."

Another commuter marriage, McGill thought. Maybe it was a new trend.

He offered Tall Wolf a seat, asked if he'd like something to drink. Within a minute, Dikki Missirian, the building owner, delivered two bottles of San Pellegrino, introduced himself to Tall Wolf and bowed out. Deke stepped into the outer office.

Sweetie, an observant Catholic, was spending the morning at church and a family brunch.

McGill raised his glass and Tall Wolf did likewise.

"Here's to a productive relationship," McGill said.

"Getting the job done." After taking a sip of his sparkling water, Tall Wolf added, "I've heard about your basketball game with Senator Michaelson. Would have liked to see it. But were you serious about punching out members of Congress?"

McGill nodded. "At the time I spoke, yeah. I can be very defensive when it comes to the president. Upon reflection, it'd probably be better if I let one of them take a poke at me first."

"Probably best not to tussle with a female member at all."

McGill laughed. "Yeah, good point."

"I'm not here on a quid pro quo basis, I'm happy to help, but Deputy Director DeWitt said if I help you out maybe you could ask the president to keep an eye out to recruit Native American candidates for Congress. People who are suitably qualified, of course."

McGill gave Tall Wolf an assessing look.

"Is that a suggestion someone asked you to raise?"

"No, it's my idea. Seems like every other ethnic group is making sure they have a seat or ten on Capitol Hill. Why not the people who got here first?"

McGill nodded. "Sounds like a great idea. If you don't mind, though, I'd like to put a little spin on it." He opened a desk drawer, took out a business card and gave it to Tall Wolf. "You've heard of Cool Blue, right?

"The new political party, sure." Tall Wolf smiled. "They won *ten* seats in the mid-term."

"Nine in the House, one in the Senate. Took four seats from the Democrats, five from the GOP and one from True South. You ask me, they're the coming thing. The guy whose name is on that card is the man to talk to; you can tell him I sent you."

"Putnam Shady. That's some name."

"Yeah, but he's a good guy. Whip smart. Got a real eye for the future. He's also married to my partner, Margaret Sweeney."

Tall Wolf nodded and slipped the card in a coat pocket. "Thanks."

The preliminaries taken care of, McGill got down to business.

He told Tall Wolf about Mira Kersten's stolen embryos.

"From an L.A. clinic," Tall Wolf said, "and you don't want any hassle with the LAPD."

"Right. Them or any other law enforcement agency."

"I know a couple of retired officers from LAPD. They should be able to help me find someone to talk to before we arrive."

"That would be good," McGill told him. "I don't want to step on any toes, and I'm happy to give any credit for a positive outcome to the local police."

"That'd be a start."

"Yeah, but if the city cops get territorial, I'm not going to stop."

"So, that's where I come in. Being a fed of some standing, they can't muscle me."

"Exactly ... and I thought of an angle to make federal involvement inevitable, if they really get cranky."

"What's that?"

"Well, not that I particularly agree with the point of view, but there's any number of people these days who would argue that personhood begins at conception. You see where I'm going?"

Tall Wolf smiled. The man had a cunning turn of mind that almost reminded him of Marlene Flower Moon. "I do. If being a person begins at conception, those embryos are people, and stealing them isn't just theft of property, it's kidnapping."

"Right," McGill said.

"You're a pretty devious thinker, Mr. McGill. But the FBI usually handles kidnappings."

"True. Thing is, we know who some but not all of the fathers who helped create those embryos are. It's possible to think one of the dads might be —"

"Native American. I take it back. You are a very devious thinker, sir."

Even Coyote would have enjoyed McGill's guile.

"Thanks, but call me Jim. I'll call you John, if that's all right."

Tall Wolf nodded.

"There's something else I have to tell you," McGill said. "I have reason to think that the embryos were taken to be ransomed not used for gestation. Only money isn't what will be demanded. It will be another commodity considered more valuable."

McGill's vague description registered with Tall Wolf.

"You don't want to tell me what that commodity is, do you, Jim?"

"Not yet. Maybe not at all."

Tall Wolf thought about that, remembering who McGill's wife was.

Just like Byron DeWitt, Tall Wolf had also voted for the president twice. Was well aware that she had just been impeached. Tall Wolf had the feeling he was about to plunge into deep political waters. It could be to his advantage not to know too much. Should he ever be hauled in front of a judge or a congressional committee.

"Okay," Tall Wolf said. "You'll let me know if and when I should know more."

McGill nodded. "Absolutely."

McGill's office phone rang. Mira Kersten was calling.

She tried to remain composed, but her voice was tremulous. She asked for McGill's e-mail address. She had something she needed to send him.

"What's that?" McGill asked.

"A photograph of a thawed …" Her voice cracked. "An unviable embryo. That bastard killed one of my babies."

WWN Studio — Washington, DC

WorldWide News lured Didi DiMarco away from MSNBC with a huge contract and the promise of more airtime than any of its other reporter-personalities. WWN boss Hugh Collier had two reasons for making the talent raid. Didi was a genuine audience draw, and he wanted to have another powerful woman on board to give him leverage over Ellie Booker.

Ellie's trump card had always been her threat to hook up with another network if Hugh didn't see things her way. Her streak of independence had begun to seep like a toxic waste spill among WWN's on-air reporters and, more important, the top producers behind the cameras. If Hugh didn't put a stop to this spread of personal liberty … well, he could imagine his uncle, Sir Edbert Bickford, the network's founder, laughing at him from some toasty corner of hell.

Hugh had killed his uncle, inherited his network and would no doubt burn right next to him eventually, but that was a worry for another day.

Ellie had scored another coup, interviewing both the president and McGill in the wake of the impeachment vote. Hugh would give an arm and a leg — someone else's — to get video of McGill actually punching a member of Congress in the nose, but as far as he knew that had yet to happen.

In the meantime, he'd scored a big "get" for Didi DiMarco's new Sunday morning show: *First Thing*. As in the first thing you did to keep up with the world, you watched Didi's show. As her premiere guest, Didi had another scrappy character, Vice President Jean Morrissey.

Who knew? By the next time Ms. Morrissey appeared on the show, she might be sitting in the Oval Office running the country. Wouldn't that be a lovely coup to put Ellie Booker and the rest of the rabble back in their places?

Hugh watched from the control booth as his new show went on the air.

Didi gave the viewing audience a polite smile and got right down to business.

"Good morning. I'm Deirdre DiMarco and this is the first show of the program we call *First Thing*. The focus here will be to bring you the most important news stories of the upcoming week in a substantive but succinct manner. Our first guest is the vice president of the United States and the former governor of Minnesota, Jean Morrissey. Good morning, Ms. Vice President."

Jean's stylist had set her up with a well-coifed but not overly severe look.

Feminine but not concealing the VP's athletic muscle tone.

"Hello, Didi."

"Will you tell our audience, Ms. Vice President, how you think President Grant's impeachment will affect her, the Grant administration, our country and you yourself?"

"Of course," Jean said, "and I should let you know that in accepting your invitation to appear this morning, the president and I discussed what the country might like to know about the situation and I'm authorized to tell you the following: The president will continue in her role of commander-in-chief of our armed forces and as the chief architect of our foreign policy without any diminution of those responsibilities."

"I'm sensing a 'but' coming next," Didi said.

"You're right about that. As a matter of practical politics, the president has to prepare to defend herself in the matter of her trial in the Senate. She also doesn't want to be seen as conducting any political disputes outside of the context of that trial."

"For fear it might work against her?" Didi asked.

"Because it's neither the time nor the place for her to do so."

"And where does all this leave you, Ms. Vice President?"

"The same place it always does, a heartbeat away from the presidency. However, with the extraordinary demands currently being placed on President Grant, I've been asked to step up to first place in making sure there's continuity in the president's domestic agenda."

A small smile played on Didi's lips. "With the hostility between the majorities in Congress and the president, and adding in the spectacle of the trial in the Senate, do you think you can get anything accomplished in that area?"

"Well, you're right about the hard feelings. It used to be we had opposition parties in this country, and that's a good thing. Ideas should contend and compromises should be worked out. But in the past several years, and especially since Patricia Grant became president, the members of Congress on the other side have become more like *enemy* forces. Doing whatever they can to destroy Patti Grant politically has become the order of the day. The impeachment is just the latest example."

Didi, one smart cookie, felt something good, something big, was coming from Jean Morrissey. She did her best to ask her next question with a straight face. "How do you, with your enhanced responsibilities, intend to respond to such a harsh political environment?"

"Well, you're right that Congress isn't going to pass any law that the administration favors. So that leaves only one tool to use: executive action. I'll set the tone and the direction for the country that the executive branch has within its purview. The president, of course, will have the final word on any proposal I put forward."

A tingle ran down Didi's spine. She reached for self-restraint, and missed.

"Forgive me, Ms. Vice President, if I'm getting off-track here, but you were a star hockey player during your college days."

Jean Morrissey responded with a straight face. "Yes, I was."

"You excelled at both defense and scoring."

"I did fairly well, yes."

"In fact, you were named an All-American for your playing prowess, but what comes to mind is a certain game against Great Lakes State."

Jean only nodded.

Didi said, "The star player of the opposing team hit your face with her hockey stick right after you scored a goal."

"In the game, it's called a cross-check," Jean said. "The stick is held in both hands and used as a blunt instrument. It's against the rules. In my case, my nose was broken, and the infraction was ruled a major penalty."

"But that wasn't the end of the matter," Didi said.

"No, it wasn't. Even though I was bleeding profusely, I was still conscious. I dropped my hockey gloves and retaliated. I knocked out the opposition player with one punch."

In a quiet voice, Didi asked, "Should Congress take any lesson from that incident?"

The vice president smiled. "I'm not James J. McGill, and I think he was kidding about punching people. I'm certainly not going to hit anyone. But in the coming days Congress will see just what they'll be getting if the Senate convicts Patricia Grant."

In the control booth, Hugh Collier rubbed his hands with glee.

Dupont Circle — Washington, DC

As a place to live in the capital, Dupont Circle had just about everything going for it. The area had a Walk Score of 98, meaning there was no end of shops, restaurants and entertainment venues within easy walking distance. The streets there were safe, too. Crime was 60% lower than the city average. Of course, all the benefits came at a price. The median cost of a row house came in at $600,000.

Having moved to DC from the San Francisco Bay Area, Craig MacLaren, chief justice of the United States, was unfazed by the property costs. Bay Area housing prices were even higher and rising faster. His fellow member of the Supreme Court, Associate Justice Daniel Crockett, on the other hand, had paid only one-fifth of the price of his nearby row house for the four-bedroom home he owned in Tennessee.

Neither man, however, was thinking of real estate or what it cost to become a homeowner in Washington at the moment. Sitting in the chief justice's den, they'd just finished watching Didi DiMarco interview Jean Morrissey.

"I think we just saw our next president introduce herself to the American public," MacLaren said.

Crockett steepled his hands. "Possibly, Chief, but you never know what might happen."

"Are we having a partisan moment here, Daniel?"

Both men had been appointed to the high court by Patricia Grant. MacLaren, a Democrat, had been the chief judge of the U.S. Ninth Circuit Court; Crockett, a Republican, had been a U.S. Senator from the Volunteer State. The chief justice had been confirmed by little more than a bare majority vote of the Senate; Crockett had been approved overwhelmingly.

Once seated on the court, though, those numbers became meaningless.

The chief was the chief. He was considered the senior justice, regardless of length of service on the court. He chaired the conferences in which cases before the court were discussed and voted on. He spoke first in those meetings, setting the tone and direction. Likewise, he set the agenda at the weekly meetings where the justices decided whether to accept or reject petitions for the court to hear a case. Again, in these meetings, he spoke first.

When voting with the majority, the chief justice also had the power to assign the justice who would write the Opinion of the Court, including the option of doing so himself. This perquisite gave the chief the opportunity to influence the historical record, pinning a decision to language that would clearly define a decision and make it more daunting for a future court to nitpick or overturn.

Last but far from least, the chief presided over the impeachment trial of a president.

Regarding the matter of partisanship, Associate Justice Crockett told the chief, "Maybe just a small moment. I think Ms. Morrissey, as the sitting vice president, will certainly be the favorite for her party's nomination."

"You think there's someone on your side of the aisle who can beat her? Or do you dislike her chances because you think the American people won't elect a second consecutive woman?"

"There is a bit of a gender issue, but heaven help any fool on my side, as you call it, who would bring that up. The backlash would be immediate and immense. Independent and moderate women would flock to defend their gender."

"So, what are you thinking, Daniel?"

"Well, there are two things. If the Senate actually were to convict Patricia Grant, that would make Jean Morrissey the president, and it would also enrage the partisans on your side of the debate. Ms. Morrissey would be much harder to beat as a sitting president, and God help us all with the divided government we'd have then. But the one thing I think could stop Ms. Morrissey is her own … forceful personality, shall we say. I think she could come on *too* strong. Put off a lot of those same women in the middle."

"What you're suggesting is a double standard, Daniel. A man has to be seen as strong to become president, but a woman advancing the same positions in the same words and tone might be seen as overly strong, according to your judgment."

"Just my humble opinion, Chief. It's been wide of the mark before."

MacLaren laughed. "But not too often."

"Kind of you to say."

The question Crockett hadn't answered was who he thought might defeat Jean Morrissey. There were two possibilities he could think of, one of whom was him. The problem with that, though, was his time on the court had made the idea of getting back into the melee of electoral politics less than enticing. Today, anyway.

As that line of thought rambled through Crockett's mind, he and the chief were interrupted by what the associate justice thought was a rudely loud knock at the door to the room.

"Allow me, Chief," Crockett said, rising.

Before he could reach the door, though, the chief's houseman, Denton, opened it.

"I'm sorry, sir, but they insisted."

They were the Supreme Court Police in the persons of head of protective services, the aptly named, John Law, and his first assistant, Emily Ringwald.

"Very sorry to intrude, Mr. Chief Justice," Law said, "but a threat against your life, believed to be highly credible, has been relayed to us by the FBI. We can't afford to take any chances."

MacLaren and Crockett looked at each other.

"Just me or the court as a whole?" the chief asked.

Law said, "You specifically, Mr. Chief Justice. As pertains to your role in the trial of President Grant. To be careful, we're extending extra protection to the associate justices also. You'll all have to follow a new security protocol, sir."

That might well be, but there was another Sunday morning news show both justices wanted to see. MacLaren asked if they might linger for thirty minutes.

His appeal was denied.

Law said he'd have a recording made. As things stood, he couldn't let either of them sit in a room with a window looking out on the street. They had to relocate.

Now.

U.S. Capitol — Washington, DC

The television program the two justices of the Supreme Court wanted to see was on MSNBC. Ellie Booker, having learned of Didi

DiMarco's interview of Vice President Morrissey, had decided to strike back against Hugh Collier, and fast. She was doing a stand-up interview on the West Front of the Capitol with former Senator Roger Michaelson.

The guy James J. McGill had pounded to a pulp in a one-on-one basketball game.

That was where Ellie started.

"Senator, your confrontation on a local basketball court with the president's husband has become something of a Washington legend. Can you tell me now how much of the story is real and how much is exaggeration, taking a simple story and embroidering it into something bigger and more dramatic?"

Michaelson offered a thin smile. "I'll put it simply: Mr. McGill beat the crap out of me."

"If that was the case, why didn't you file a criminal complaint against him?"

"Because I was doing my best to beat the crap out of him." Michaelson's smile broadened and warmed. "I was happy to learn not too long ago that I managed to inflict a good deal of pain on Mr. McGill. That made me feel much better, still does."

"Are you saying that you and Mr. McGill still harbor ill feelings?"

"I don't. I can't speak for him."

"What was it that caused the confrontation in the first place?"

"Patti Grant, President Grant, was my political nemesis from the first time we ran against each other for a House seat in Illinois. She won, beating me out of a seat I thought would be mine. Once she reached the White House and I'd won a seat in the Senate, I decided to make her political destruction my life's goal. Mr. McGill, not unreasonably, took offense."

"So he set you up for a confrontation in the guise of a basketball game?"

Michaelson laughed. "Yeah, he did, the SOB. I'm just glad dueling had been outlawed. I probably wouldn't be here otherwise."

Ellie said, "Despite all that, when you needed the services of a private investigator, you turned to Mr. McGill's firm."

"I did. Whatever the differences between us, I was in a bad spot, having been accused of playing a role in an assassination plot against the president. With my background, I made a pretty good patsy. I needed someone to help clear me. I turned to Jim McGill because he has a history of getting results. I did so despite any differences I had with him."

"But Mr. McGill turned you down," Ellie said.

"He did, but his partner, Margaret Sweeney, didn't — after she got the go-ahead from the president. That Patricia Grant could decide to provide me with help after the way I'd behaved toward her all those years ... it was enough to make me a changed man."

"Do you believe, Senator, that the president sent Joan Renshaw into Erna Godfrey's prison cell with the idea that Ms. Renshaw would cause Mrs. Godfrey harm?"

Michaelson shook his head. "No. That would be completely inconsistent with the generosity she showed me. I never wanted to cause Patricia Grant any personal harm, but I did want to destroy her politically. The idea that she could forgive me but scheme to cause harm to Erna Godfrey is absurd."

Ellie gave Michaelson a look of assessment. She'd known many blue ribbon BS-artists in Washington, and prided herself at being able to see through their lies. But she didn't see any deception in Michaelson's eyes.

It was almost enough to nick her armor of cynicism.

"So where do you go from here, Senator?"

"I'm going to be spending a lot of time right here at the Capitol. As a former senator, I still have access to the Senate floor. I'll be speaking to many of my colleagues."

"On the president's behalf?" Ellie asked. "Even in the face of her coming trial?"

Michaelson gave the question a firm nod. "Especially because of that. I'm a prime example that Patricia Grant is far more inclined to mercy than vengeance."

"Have the president's lawyers decided to call you to testify for her?"

"Not yet, but if they do, my answer will be yes."

38,000 Feet Above West Virginia — Westbound

McGill closed his laptop. Sitting in the chartered Gulfstream G450, he and John Tall Wolf had just finished watching Ellie Booker interview Roger Michaelson, and Didi DiMarco's talk with Jean Morrissey before that. Nobody had intruded on them with a demand they be moved to a more secure setting.

Tall Wolf was armed, as were Deke Ky and Leo Levy, the latter two sitting in the rear of the cabin. For all McGill knew, the pilot, co-pilot and two cabin attendants were also packing heat. He was probably the only one who'd left his sidearm at home.

He didn't have a permit for concealed carry in California.

The federal officers aboard didn't need one.

That wasn't the reason McGill was frowning, though.

"What's the matter," John asked, "you thought Senator Michaelson was putting on an act?"

McGill deflected the question back to him, "Do you think he was being honest?"

"As a matter of fact, I do." John offered a small grin. "If the man can lie that well, he'd probably still be in office."

That brought a smile to McGill's face. Made him think that working with the BIA man was going to work out.

"Yeah, he probably would. It's just hard for me to wrap my head around it, the way things can change. Erna Godfrey and Roger Michaelson were people I counted on to be lifelong enemies, and now … I have to reevaluate, to say the least."

Tall Wolf said, "The Great Spirit moves in mysterious ways."

"Ain't that the truth?"

"Something else is bothering you, isn't it?"

McGill nodded. "It occurred to me that it wouldn't look good if something bad were to happen to Roger Michaelson. What with Erna Godfrey dying as the result of a well-intended effort, losing

Michaelson, too, would be really bad optics, as they like to say in Washington."

Tall Wolf looked closely at McGill.

"You think that's a real possibility?"

"If Michaelson works the Senate floor on Patti's behalf and shifts the vote in the president's favor, that will change the arc of history. Be pretty damn ironic, too. I have no doubt any number of people would hate to see a not guilty verdict."

"So, if you and I weren't flying off to California, you'd —"

"No, not me," McGill said. "But I know someone I can ask to make sure Michaelson keeps on breathing for the foreseeable future. Allow you and me to focus on our jobs."

McGill took out his phone and called Celsus Crogher.

Amsterdam, Netherlands

FBI Special Agent Abra Benjamin sat on a park bench in the Bijlmer area of Amsterdam. The temperature was in the low 40s, but a steady wind from the north made it feel a good ten degrees colder. Benjamin had the collar of her trench coat up and her hands in its pockets. She did her best to relax, not shiver, but the cold was sinking into her bones and the man she was supposed to meet was already fifteen minutes late.

A woman out on her own in Bijlmer, one without Benjamin's law enforcement training, might have been trembling for other reasons. The place's reputation wasn't the best, at least the section where she sat. Described in some tourist literature as "vibrantly multicultural," Bijlmer could also be thought of as sketchy.

In fact, the more forthcoming visitor's guides warned that the area was not infrequently the scene of violence and drug dealing. Home to illegal immigrants who lived off the books. A place best avoided unless accompanied by "a trusted local."

On top of all that, a light rain began to fall from a slate gray sky.

Never known as someone with a passive demeanor or boundless patience, Benjamin was about to get up and leave. Return to the U.S. embassy and send a message to Washington that the Dutch were jerking her around. She had suggested a Monday morning meeting with a cop from the intelligence division of the KLPD, the national constabulary. No, no, she'd been told. Let's do it Sunday afternoon.

The joker she was supposed to meet, one Bram Dekens, was probably sitting down to Sunday dinner, maybe having a second helping, not worried about the American woman sitting out in the cold and wet. Yeah, well, screw him, too. After she checked in at the embassy, she'd be going to her hotel for her own dinner and a hot bath.

Tomorrow, she'd tear Dekens a new one.

Before that could happen, though, some jerk with a Middle Eastern mug decided he had to get in on the act. He walked right up to the bench where she sat and stopped directly in front of her. He was about her height, five-eight. He had a stocky build and appeared not to shave or bathe more than once a week. He gave her the stink-eye. As if that was supposed to terrify her.

Benjamin smiled at him.

That threw him off balance. "You are a whore?"

Benjamin shook her head but kept smiling.

"Why are you here?"

"Taking in the scenery."

Despite the newly greening grass and a few spindly trees, the park was never going to be featured on a post card for beautiful Amsterdam. The guy was just smart enough to know he was being mocked. He didn't like it, especially coming from her.

"You *are* a whore. Worse, you are American."

"Jewish, too," Benjamin added. "Don't overlook that."

Benjamin took her hands out of her pockets and crossed her arms.

The guy paid no attention to that. He was staring at her face with all the contempt he could muster. To his credit, the amount was plentiful.

He never had a moment's thought that she might be any threat to him.

"You will leave this place now or I will beat you."

Benjamin let her smile vanish and replied, "Fuck off."

The guy drew back an open right hand to smack Benjamin senseless. Knock her off the bench and onto the wet pavement. After that, who knew, he might even have some stomping in mind. Only Benjamin was already in motion by the time he cocked his arm.

Her own right hand was in striking position, and in it was the metal baton she'd withdrawn from her pocket. It sprang into its extended position. Moving quickly to her right, Benjamin whipped a back-handed blow to the thug's left knee cap. She felt as well as heard the bone shatter.

The man howled in agony. Not one to leave a job half-done, Benjamin brought the baton streaking back in a forehand strike. She caught the guy's left wrist squarely. More bones fragmented. The man collapsed in agony, shrieking louder than ever.

A blare of police sirens added to the cacophony. The cops, three carloads of them, had arrived. Far too quickly not to have been lurking nearby all along. A tall guy in civilian clothing with a bit of a gut, blue eyes and a walrus mustache led the charge.

He came to a halt within spitting distance of the asshole writhing on the pavement.

He told the uniformed cops, "Take Mr. Kasim away, gentlemen."

Once that had been done, he turned to Benjamin and said, "Special Agent Benjamin? I am Inspector Bram Dekens of the National Police. So sorry to be late for our appointment."

Benjamin sneered. "Yeah, bullshit. You set me up."

Pacific Palisades — Los Angeles

Jim McGill, John Tall Wolf and Deke Ky met two LAPD detectives from the Commercial Crimes Division in the parking lot of the fertility clinic that had been robbed. The facility was closed on that Sunday afternoon. The detectives' names were Eloy Zapata and

Wallace MacDuff. With them were the clinic's owner, Dr. Danika Hansen, and its security guard — now on medical leave — Mindy Crozier.

McGill introduced himself and his companions. With a nod to the car in which they arrived, he added, "My driver is Leo Levy. He's federally licensed to carry a firearm."

The cops nodded and shook hands with simple professional courtesy.

Young Ms. Crozier looked slightly starstruck.

Dr. Hansen also seemed pleased to meet McGill and Tall Wolf.

McGill focused on the detectives. "Thank you for taking the time to meet with Co-director Tall Wolf and me, gentlemen. We'll do our best to be good guests in Los Angeles and cooperate with your investigation in every way we can."

The L.A. cops were both twenty-year veterans.

They knew a charm offensive when they saw one.

"Not just cooperate in every way period?" Zapata asked.

McGill said, "There may be aspects of client confidentiality I have to observe."

Dr. Hansen nodded and said, "I'd also like this matter to be handled discreetly. The less said publicly the better."

MacDuff took no notice of her concern. He said to McGill, "I get it that a man in your position needs a Secret Service guy. I'm surprised you have only one, in fact. But a bigwig from the Bureau of Indian Affairs? Wasn't expecting that."

McGill turned to Tall Wolf. "John?"

He asked the detectives, "You've spoken with Ron Ketchum and Keely Powell?"

"Yeah, we have," Zapata replied. "Don't know them personally, but we've heard of them. Good people, both. Makes us feel a little better about the two of you being here."

MacDuff picked up the thread. "What we'd like is for you gentlemen to remember who has primary responsibility for solving this crime and making the arrest."

McGill nodded. "Of course. What I hope Co-director Tall

Wolf and I can accomplish is the successful retrieval of Ms. Kersten's embryos while they're still viable."

"As do I," Dr. Hansen said.

"Yeah. How exactly is that a federal responsibility, Mr. Co-director?" Zapata asked.

Tall Wolf explained McGill's notion that if embryos were people, the crime they were looking at was kidnapping not robbery. Then he added, "Normally, that'd bring the FBI in on the case, but you know how that would go. They always want to be the lead dog. Wouldn't leave much for LAPD to do. On the other hand, I'm more of a low-key guy. Happy to give the credit to others. You can check my record on that. But if you want to go by the book, I can call FBI Deputy Director Byron DeWitt right now."

He took out his phone.

Zapata and MacDuff got the message: McGill and his pal were the guys with the clout. If the local cops tried to muscle them, *they'd* be the ones out in the cold.

Not wanting to put any noses out of joint, however, McGill played the nice guy.

"Listen, gents, I was a cop, too. I know how you feel. I'll also be happy to see you and LAPD get the credit here. All I want is to get my client's embryos back."

If something additional, of benefit to the president, also came to hand, well, so much the better, but the cops didn't need to know about that, McGill thought.

"So we'll all be one big happy family?" MacDuff's tone said he didn't believe in such fairy tales.

McGill responded, "I can tell you right now that Ms. Kersten believes her ex-husband, Edmond Whelan, is behind the theft."

"Not that he did it, though, right?" MacDuff asked.

"No," McGill said, "from what I've heard, he delegates."

Zapata smiled, "Delegates, that's good. Chicago cops talk like that?"

Letting McGill know they'd done at least some homework on him.

"Not much," he said. "I've picked up a bit of polish living in the White House."

Letting them know just how much power he had backing him.

Turning back to the matter at hand, MacDuff asked, "Did Ms. Kersten say why Mr. Whelan would steal the embryos?"

"Hard feelings," McGill told him. "They didn't part happily. I'm sure you've seen that before."

The expressions on the two cops' faces said they'd lived that experience.

McGill showed them the image on his phone of the spoiled embryo Mira Kersten had sent him. Forwarded it to both of the cops' phones. Literally a picture of cooperation.

"We want to talk to the lady," Zapata said, "but she said she wants to meet with you first."

McGill suggested, "I can call her, ask if she's ready to see the whole crew of us."

The cops didn't like the idea of being co-opted into anyone's crew, but they saw that McGill was making an effort to bridge their differences. That or he was being one slick SOB working a set piece. Not that they could say so to his face. They queried each other with a silent look and came to an agreement with a nod.

"Yeah, that'd be good," MacDuff conceded.

"Okay," McGill said, "but let's see what we might learn here first."

Dr. Hansen was all for that. As they proceeded into the clinic, Mindy Crozier provided a voluble narrative of what she remembered happening. Trying to impress the LAPD guys, but the men from Washington more.

Both McGill and Tall Wolf had the same thought. The young security guard might be their most valuable source of information — into the workings of the fertility clinic and what, if anything, the LAPD detectives came to discover there.

***

Amsterdam, Netherlands

Inspector Bram Dekens owned up to his ploy over dinner at a restaurant called Guts & Glory that was currently featuring chicken. Not the fried kind that came in a bucket. The whole roasted free-range bird. With wine and dessert, it was almost enough to make Special Agent Benjamin forgive Dekens for using her as a patsy.

"I couldn't use one of my own people," the inspector told the American visitor. "The criminal element here has almost a sixth sense for recognizing police personnel."

"That or they've got an inside source," Benjamin said.

Dekens put a hand to his mouth, as if suffering a tickle in his throat.

He coughed and Benjamin thought she heard a camouflaged, "Possibly."

She wasn't rude enough to ask him to repeat himself.

"I could never take the chance of using a civilian" Dekens added. "A display of anxiety would be a certain giveaway. Spoil the whole plan. Maybe cause the loss of an innocent life."

Benjamin said, "But a hardass American cop, someone who could stand up to a creep, would be an acceptable risk."

"Yes, exactly. I have to admit, though, I thought the FBI would be sending a man when the idea occurred to me. When I heard a woman was coming, I paused to reconsider. Then I said to myself, 'Now, Bram, don't be a sexist. Women can be formidable.'" He raised his glass to Benjamin. "You more than justified my faith."

Benjamin laughed. "You're so full of shit. Does that kind of BS really work on women over here?"

Dekens produced a devilish grin. "For me, quite often, yes."

"Okay, I'll drink to that bit of honesty."

She raised her glass and they both drank.

"So that creep I smacked, why did you want him so bad?"

"Tariq Kasim was an efficient but non-political drug dealer. He never touched any product or dirty money himself, but he manipulated others brilliantly. We've pruned any number of limbs from his organization but they quickly grow back. Him, we've never been able to uproot."

"Can't just send him back to where he came from?"

"He was born in Amsterdam. Legally, he's as Dutch as I am."

"So he's been a pain in your ass for a long time. But something had to change. Top guys don't go threatening people on park benches with physical harm."

Dekens said, "In your American idiom, Kasim got religion. In truth, it was forced on him."

"By guys with beards who curse the decadent West?" Benjamin asked.

"Yes. We police weren't able to catch up with Kasim, but our intelligence people tell us he was given a rather thorough talking to by people who told him if he wanted to keep his head he'd have to become far more devout in his faith and donate the majority of his earnings to the cause."

"But it was fine to keep selling addictive narcotics to the infidels."

"Yes, of course."

"These terrorists have a name?"

Dekens told her and offered a suggestion. "You should let your DEA know of this partnership."

Benjamin nodded. "So what did I do for you today? Park my backside in a reserved seat? Interrupt a meeting Kasim was supposed to have with a supplier?"

"Exactly," Dekens said.

"Well, that explains why he was so testy. By any chance were Kasim's new business partners watching from a distance? Them and the other guy's people, of course. You can't be too careful in this kind of thing."

Dekens smile was one of admiration this time. "You are a credit to the FBI."

"Yeah, I'm going places in the Bureau, something for you to keep in mind. Anyway, having all those people see Kasim attempt to assault me and get taken down by both a woman and the cops, his professional future can't look bright at all. So, now that you've got him on the crime of attempting to assault a woman, how much do you think you can get out of him?"

Another hint of Dekens' nature filled his eyes; the guy could be merciless.

The inspector said, "He'll tell us everything. Otherwise, we apologize to him for an improper arrest and let him go."

"And if he gets lucky he'll be gunned down. Not so lucky, he does lose his head."

"Either way, he would not be missed," Dekens said.

He turned his attention to his meal. The chicken was delicious. Benjamin liked that, a guy who could think of throwing someone to the wolves and not let it spoil his appetite. Picking up her own knife and fork, she wished Byron DeWitt could have been more like that, ruthless, professionally and otherwise.

When the white burgundy arrived as the digestif, Dekens turned his attention to Benjamin's professional needs. "And now that you know how much you've helped me, how may I be of service to you?"

"I'm looking for Tyler Busby," she said.

Dekens smiled. "Your fugitive, phantom billionaire. He's been gone quite some time now, hasn't he?"

"Over a year."

"Telling you that he still has quite a bit of money he's managed to hide from your government. Otherwise, you'd have found him by now."

Benjamin said, "We came to that conclusion some time ago, and there are a great many people looking for Busby's money as a way to find him. There were also quite a few military personnel looking for him in the jungles of the Philippines. They've concluded he was not taken prisoner by the local guerrillas."

Dekens sipped his wine. "You're not here to revisit what hasn't worked; you've thought of something new."

That compliment hit home. Benjamin smiled. "When following the money doesn't work, you need another trail to explore. Tyler

Busby, it's well documented, just can't do without women. Lots and lots of them."

"A common failing," Dekens said with a straight face.

"Yeah, but rare among his class, he didn't mind being seen and photographed in public with women who were known to be high-end prostitutes. No one really called him on it because the business end of the relationships with the ladies was handled discreetly."

"And, no doubt, because anyone who might dare to be so gauche would also have his private life examined. By the media or Busby's private detectives," Dekens said.

"That, too. So my idea is: If following the money doesn't work, follow the nookie."

Benjamin saw that nookie was a new word to the inspector, but he made the correct inference and smiled. No doubt adding the term to his vocabulary. He nodded his approval.

"Your thought is Mr. Busby, wherever he might be hiding, wants to keep his sex life robust with the same type of women he previously … entertained."

"Exactly."

"That is brilliant."

"Imaginative anyway."

"And you've come to see me in Amsterdam because we know a thing or two about international sex tourism," Dekens said.

"More than just the girls in street-view windows. I'm told you know about the high-end trade, the kind Busby and other big spenders like."

A new, guarded look appeared on Dekens' face. "Possibly."

Benjamin didn't like his sudden reluctance. "Don't get cold feet on me, Inspector. I don't give a damn about any European big shots who don't mind paying for sex, but I think this is the way I can nail Busby."

Get a promotion to assistant deputy director, too, but Benjamin didn't need to share that.

For his part, Dekens now saw that he was dealing with a woman who would thrash him professionally as mercilessly as she'd broken Kasim's bones. That she was American didn't lessen the threat. Just protesting the way he'd used her to his superiors would sting.

If the FBI were to look at the KLPD as uncooperative, well, his job would be sacrificed before the government's relationship with the Americans would.

The problem was, many of the "European big shots" who paid for their carnal pleasure were members of neighboring governments. Embarrassing them would also not be good for him. But on balance …

"Of course, I'll help you," Dekens told Benjamin, "but my inquiries will have to be discreet and singularly focused."

"Sure, those considerations are fine, but don't try to drag things out, hoping I'll go away. I won't. That's not who I am."

She took her iPad mini out of her purse. Showed the inspector photos of women who'd been Tyler Busby's escorts at public functions in New York and Washington. Told him the FBI had tabbed the ladies as prostitutes.

She said, "We don't know if Busby has called on any of these women in the past year, but if their faces haven't wrinkled or their figures sagged, maybe he has. If not, we'd like to know if others of their type with the same professional connections have traveled to out of the way places. Locales that women like them wouldn't normally visit. You understand what I'm saying?"

"I do," Dekens said. Still hedging his bet, he asked, "Would any of the women I might locate be required to testify in American courts?"

Benjamin shook her head. "We don't care who they screw or if any of them banged Busby. All we want to do is find the SOB. We've got enough to hang him as it is."

Shock filled Dekens' voice. "The United States still hangs people?"

Benjamin, a lawyer as well as a federal officer, had to check her memory. "New Hampshire allows it by choice of the corrections officials; Washington state allows it by choice of the condemned person. But I was speaking figuratively. The federal government wants to lock him up for the rest of his miserable life. How's that?"

"Much better. I will begin my inquiries first thing tomorrow."

"Terrific. Just so you know, you prove helpful to the United States in this matter, we'll see that you, the KLPD and your government get full credit. Or we won't say a word. Your choice."

"Yes, it's always good to have choices."

Dekens chose to gulp his aperitif, put Benjamin in a cab to her hotel and call it a night.

Walter Reed National Military Medical Center — Bethesda, Maryland

By the whim of irony and the dictate of political necessity, Joan Renshaw, following her psychotic break, had been transferred from the federal correctional institution in Danbury, Connecticut to a secure ward in the same military medical facility where Reverend Burke Godfrey had taken his last breath.

Burke Godfrey, of course, had been the televangelist husband of Erna Godfrey, the woman Joan Renshaw had choked to death. When Renshaw's change of address had made the news, there had been public gatherings of people praying for the late preacher to wreak supernatural vengeance on his wife's killer. Thinking just the opposite, the government had moved the prisoner with thoughts of greater security and a higher quality of care.

Thus far, mass supplication for supernatural payback had yet to make it to the top of the Almighty's to-do list. Even so, the nature of Renshaw's continued existence didn't rise beyond simple respiration and being fed and drained through various tubes. Her condition was described as Kahlbaum Syndrome, motionless catatonia.

She exhibited what was called waxy flexibility. Placed into a given posture, she would hold it indefinitely. Her position in the bed which formed the boundaries of her world was changed regularly to avoid the development of bed sores.

Available treatments included anti-psychotic medications and electro-convulsive therapy. Both of those avenues were fraught with risks and adverse effects. A conservative approach — intravenous feeding, hydration and close monitoring — was the chosen approach for the patient.

Just in case she made a spontaneous recovery, though, her bed was wired to an alarm that would sound if her weight was removed from it. Four cameras also watched her 24/7. The monitors receiving the feed from those cameras were what a duty nurse happened to glance at and see the first sign of motion from Joan Renshaw since she'd been admitted.

Renshaw smacked her forehead with her right hand.

The nurse blinked. Now, the patient was back in her normal supine position: arms at her sides. The video feed was recorded; the nurse played it back. Watched Renshaw slap herself three times.

Looked like physical self-criticism for making a really stupid mistake.

Like: *Dummy, how could you have done that?*

Now, though, she was back to imitating a mannequin.

The nurse took one more look at the blow and then called people well above her pay-grade to figure it all out. Had it just been a moment of catatonic excitement or was the patient finally waking up? Boy oh boy, wouldn't that cause a ruckus?

Carmel, California

Edmond Whelan sat on the veranda of his borrowed estate and looked out at the darkening Pacific Ocean. The sun had just about set and … there, in the wink of an eye, the top arc dipped below the horizon. Thing was, there was still light in the sky. Would be for a few minutes. Whelan had liked that phenomenon from the first time he'd seen the lingering light when his parents had brought him to California as a young boy.

He'd asked his mother and father how the sun's light could remain after it had disappeared. Neither of them had a scientific explanation, but his father had given an answer that had helped to mold Whelan's life. "Powerful things leave their mark."

Resting on Whelan's lap was the only printed copy of his masterpiece: *Permanent Power*. The volume was hand-bound in claret leather with its pages edged in gold leaf. Originally intended to be Whelan's doctoral thesis at Georgetown University, the document had become something far more valuable: his passport to greatness.

Not to fame, though. Far from it. His overt achievements, by design, would leave him remembered only as a minor functionary of a widely despised institution, the Congress of the United States. Whelan's intellectual inquiry had begun with a simple question: *Under our current form of federal government, how might one of the two major political parties achieve either actual or virtual permanent power?*

Up until leaving for Washington, Whelan's background in politics had been entirely academic. He'd never stuffed envelopes or hustled votes for any candidate at any level of government. The nuts and bolts of practical campaigning — shaking the nose-picking hands of perfect strangers, good God — had always struck him as too grubby to consider.

Even when local pols had dropped by his parents' Beacon Hill home only his mother's endless childhood lessons in etiquette had compelled him to behave graciously. Those people were nothing more than well-heeled beggars. If allowed into the Whelan house at all, he thought, they should have entered through the kitchen door with the rest of the tradespeople.

When he expressed that opinion to his banker father, he was told, "Ed, it might be people like us who possess large sums of money, but it's people like them who have the power to *print* it. Try not to forget that."

That was Whelan's first lesson in political reality.

It was also the day he decided to forgo becoming a banker. Through the good offices of one of the "beggars" who solicited funds from his father, he went to work at the clerical level for a

Boston congressman who would eventually rise to become speaker of the House. Dad had told him to keep his head down and let the quality of his work speak for itself. That was the right way to attract attention.

It took only two months for his father's advice to prove correct. The future speaker stopped by the desk where Whelan was laboring, grinned at him and said, "I've shaved with straight razors that aren't half as sharp as you, young man. Come into my office and let's talk a bit."

Whelan followed and once seated was offered a huge cigar.

Taking it, he said, "I don't smoke, sir, but if you don't mind, I'll keep this as a memento."

The congressman laughed and said, "Damn, boy, you're a natural. Charm, good looks and family money. You could run for office next year, and I'd back you."

"Thank you," Whelan told him, "but I don't see that as my ambition."

Surprised, the pol asked, "No, how do you see your future then?"

"More as a trusted adviser. Someone well-read, versed in the important issues, aware of political directions and crosscurrents."

"A plotter and a schemer when necessary?"

Whelan, truthfully, had yet to think of himself in those terms, but once they were suggested, he said, "I suppose things could come to that for the right cause."

"And what cause might that be?"

The younger man shrugged. "Keeping the right people in office, what else?"

"Damn right, starting with me," the congressman said.

He made Edmond Whelan his deputy chief of staff when he was just twenty-four years old. There was no doubt he would have bumped his nominal superior, the chief of staff, out of the top spot had he elected to stay with the congressman, but he felt his thinking needed more intellectual depth. So he applied to the doctoral program in government at Georgetown University.

Besides the stellar grades from his undergrad and master's level programs he brought with him, and his practical experience of two years' work in the congressman's office, Whelan also added to his Georgetown application the beginning of the treatise he was writing on how either the Democrats or the Republicans might become the dominant political party for an indefinite, but certainly decades-long, period of time. He called his burgeoning collection of thoughts on that subject *Permanent Power.*

The first and only person to read his application and his strategy for one-party government was Thomas Winston Rangel of The Maris Foundation, a Washington non-profit and ostensibly non-partisan think tank. T.W. Rangel, on a voluntary basis, helped Georgetown University screen it's Ph.D. in Government candidates.

When he'd read Edmond Whelan's application and especially his nascent notions on permanent power, he arranged an interview. Meeting in a private room at a Washington club, Rangel asked Whelan first thing, "Young man, is there any chance you're as ruthless as you are smart?"

"Might well be, sir," Whelan replied, "as I don't yet know how smart I am."

Rangel sat back and offered a skeptical look.

Whelan told him, "Honestly, I keep thinking one day I'll walk into a room where everyone is smarter than me."

"Not likely in this town or any other I know. How many times have you entered a room where *anyone* was smarter than you?"

"It's happened once or twice, and my father has a gift for encapsulating thoughts I feel I should have come up with long before hearing them from him."

Rangel smiled. "My compliments to your father. Be sure to show him your appreciation at regular intervals."

Whelan already did, but he promised to do so anyway.

Never hurt to butter up your elders; everyone knew that much.

Rangel told Whelan. "I'm going to recommend you for admission to the doctoral program. You should give it a try, see if it suits you. If you feel less than completely satisfied, call me and we'll talk again."

"Regarding what, sir?"

"Regarding whether you do possess the necessary measure of ruthlessness."

"To do what, exactly?"

"To put your ideas in *Permanent Power* into practice. In other words, to make your mark in this world."

Make his mark, Whelan thought. Leave his light to linger even after he'd vanished.

He wondered if Rangel had talked with his father before meeting with him. He decided it didn't matter. The man intuitively understood him, knew just how to seduce him. *Put his ideas into practice?* What more could a thinking young man want?

Whelan withdrew from Georgetown before his first month at the university had elapsed. T.W. Rangel had him working on Capitol Hill by the following week. His second day on the job, he received a handwritten note from his old boss, the man who would become speaker.

Never figured you for a traitor, Ed. Meaning that Whelan would join the GOP.

Hell, the old man hadn't known the half of what he'd eventually become.

Whelan had learned earlier that night that Mira had hired James J. McGill to find her damn embryos. The man had a record of cracking the toughest nuts. Just look at the havoc he'd wreaked on the gang looting the budget at the Department of Defense.

Those fools had been warned by Whelan and others to cease and desist.

Soon they'd all be in court or on the run. Setting his plan back years.

Worse, he hadn't counted on McGill coming after him personally. He should have, though. He'd long known of Mira's connection to Galia Mindel. The White House chief of staff must have been the one to sic McGill on him.

Sitting in the dark now, Whelan decided there was only one

thing to do about that.

Increase McGill's historical profile. Make him the first presidential spouse to be murdered. Whelan sent a message to the Whistler. Nobody questioned his ruthlessness these days.

CHAPTER 5

Monday, March 23, 2015 — Pacific Palisades, California

By the standards of the neighborhood, the house on Avenida de Cortez was more than modest but less than opulent; more than a million dollars but not quite two. Four bedrooms, four-and-a-half baths, a small pool, nicely landscaped with mountain views but no ocean vista.

McGill led a party of five to the front door and rang the bell. With him were John Tall Wolf, Deke Ky and the two LAPD detectives looking for the malefactor who had made off with Ms. Kersten's frosted tots, Eloy Zapata and Wallace MacDuff. Mira answered the door dressed in a sleeveless white top, khaki shorts and flip-flops.

Her limbs were toned and tanned, her finger and toenails painted, but McGill thought her face, well formed and symmetrical, looked too lined and hard for a woman in her forties. He kept that thought off his mug and to himself. He extended a hand and said, "Jim McGill."

She smiled, the expression igniting a glow and warming her features. "Yeah, I recognize you. Mira Kersten. Come in, I've got a big kitchen table where we all can sit."

She led them through the house to the kitchen at the rear. Without being obvious about it, McGill, Tall Wolf, Zeke and the two local cops all surveyed points of entry where an intruder might break in. Without looking back at any of them, Mira said, "This place is wired wall-to-wall and floor-to-ceiling, best security system money can buy. Armed response time is less than two minutes. I don't keep much cash here and the only jewelry I own is a watch and a few pairs of earrings."

She looked over her shoulder at the men following her. "Just in case any of you were wondering."

Tall Wolf asked, "What about trade secrets?"

She looked up at Tall Wolf. "And you are?"

He introduced himself. She already knew the cops' names from phone calls they'd made to her. That and checking them out once she'd heard they'd be working her case. The Secret Service guy's role was obvious.

"The Bureau of Indian Affairs?" Mira asked. "Well, that's intriguing." She looked to McGill for elucidation.

"Co-director Tall Wolf is an exceptional investigator and he carries the authority of the federal government with him," McGill said.

A smart cookie, Mira understood just what that meant.

McGill wasn't going to let himself get bullied by the LAPD. She liked that. She got everyone except Deke seated at a large circular table. The Secret Service agent said he'd keep a roving patrol outside the house. Mira didn't object.

She offered her seated guests a choice of orange juice or coffee. McGill and Tall Wolf went with the OJ; the cops took the coffee. Mira brought their beverages and provided herself with a glass of a dark green liquid supporting a foamy head. None of the others asked if they might have a sip.

Mira turned her attention to Tall Wolf.

"To return to your question so you won't have to ask it again, I shredded all the paper-and-ink records of my previous incarnation as a political campaign manager and saw the confetti go into a paper pulper. I would have burned the stuff only that wouldn't have been environmentally friendly."

"What about photographs and videos?" Tall Wolf asked.

Mira smiled and said, "You do have an interesting mind. They've also been disposed of as responsibly as possible, with a few hundred thousand exceptions owned by media outlets and a handful of peculiar paparazzi."

McGill said, "So you've retired from politics? If that's the case, how do you spend your time?"

Mira nodded to the LAPD duo. "Gentlemen?"

Zapata said, "She's a talking head."

"Dispenses wisdom on TV for most every local and state election anyone might give a damn about," MacDuff added.

"And?" Mira prompted.

"She's right more often than a lot of those dopes," Zapata conceded, "about who's going to win and by how much. If she handicapped horse races, people'd be lining up to buy her tip sheet."

"How sweet," Mira said. "I'll have to remember that line at my next contract negotiation." She told McGill and Tall Wolf. "Running political campaigns is a young person's game. You stay in it too long, it will literally kill you. You hit forty, you start thinking about doing a TV gig."

"Or become White House chief of staff?" McGill asked.

Mira beamed. "There's only one Galia Mindel. She's my second mom. So, are all you fine gentlemen going to help me become a mother before it's too late?"

McGill said, "Each in his own way. As guests in town, John and I thought it would be polite to let the detectives speak to you first."

Zapata and MacDuff did want first crack.

They weren't crazy, though, about the idea that McGill was doing them a favor. That and he'd hear their line of questioning. They did their best to adapt to circumstances without audible complaints, knowing they'd get more information with good manners this time around.

Zapata said to Mira, "The gentleman from the BIA raised a good point a moment ago but maybe he didn't take it far enough. Do you know of any video of you in other hands that might jeopardize your new line of work?"

Mira's jaw clenched. Then she made a conscious effort to relax.

"If you mean, does anyone have a sex tape of me ..." She thought about that. "It's possible, I suppose, but if one exists, it was made without my knowledge. It also would have been made after I was divorced and single."

"You sure about that, Ms. Kersten?" MacDuff asked.

"Positive, I'm very good at keeping my calendar. Between being genuinely interested in my ex-husband, physically, in the early part of our marriage, way too busy in the middle years, and not wanting to give him any edge in our divorce near the end, I was faithful to him for the duration of our marriage. After we split, there were other men, men only, and I practiced all the precautions I'd preached to my candidates: no outdoor frolics, nobody more than ten years younger and nothing more than a handshake for anyone coming out of rehab."

McGill glanced at Tall Wolf. Both kept straight faces while smiling inwardly.

For their part, the detectives appeared to buy Mira's answers. They seemed to be disappointed, though. They'd been hoping for a crime grounded in more familiar territory. Who the hell had ever heard of embryos being held for ransom?

"Why are you so sure your former husband is behind this theft?" MacDuff asked. "We've heard from Dr. Hansen at the fertility clinic that your ex wasn't the only man involved in creating those embryos."

Mira tensed again and this time she clung to her displeasure.

"Did she tell you who they were?"

Both LAPD cops shook their heads.

Zapata said, "No, ma'am. No names or even how many. Just that your ex wasn't the only man in the picture here."

That appeased Mira somewhat.

Until MacDuff added, "The doctor said she couldn't breach her confidentiality obligation, at least not without a court order. But you, you can just tell us. Because we need to know who to question."

Both L.A. cops looked to McGill and Tall Wolf to see if they'd object.

They didn't.

Mira looked at McGill, too.

He said, "That's a legitimate line of inquiry. You should tell them." Then he turned to Zapata and MacDuff. "And you guys should see to it that there are no leaks coming out of LAPD."

The good will McGill had earned a moment earlier from the detectives by telling Mira to cooperate vanished after he'd delivered his warning. The guy had some balls telling them what they should do. Then again, he'd been on the job. He knew all the angles a cop could play. Still …

Zapata pushed back, telling Mira, "We need to speak with the other men before you do."

Now, she smiled. "Too late. I've already called them. You can waste your time if you want but it's not any of them."

"How do you know?" MacDuff asked.

"I've spent more than twenty years inside electoral politics. I know a lie when I hear one."

No one at the table chose to argue with that. Zapata and MacDuff got the names and phone numbers of the other embryo co-creators. After a glance at McGill, they requested that Mira not call the men again, not before they had the chance to talk to them.

Mira looked to McGill for confirmation.

He said, "That's reasonable."

His approbation once again caused mixed feelings for Zapata and MacDuff. McGill had done the right thing, as before, but it chafed more than ever that they needed his approval. They left before their tempers got the better of them, saying they had all they needed for the moment.

Mira took the first sip of her noxious-looking drink.

"Soylent green," she told McGill and Tall Wolf. "Made from the bodies of candidates I've defeated."

"Good thing you waited for the cops to leave before saying so,"

Tall Wolf said.

McGill smiled. Kidders, the both of them. Well, so was he, but it was time for Tall Wolf and him to get down to business.

"Okay, Ms. Kersten," he said, "the LAPD didn't get around to asking you the obvious question, what the thief wants in return for your embryos. Why is that?"

"When I spoke to them on the phone, I mentioned I was gathering all the cash I have."

"And let them make the obvious inference," Tall Wolf said.

"Yes."

"Cops don't like being misdirected," McGill told her.

Mira shrugged. "Ed Whelan thinks I stole something he treasures."

"You didn't?" McGill asked.

"No."

"Do you know who did?" Tall Wolf asked.

"No."

"What does Whelan want?" McGill asked. "Please be specific."

"Well, in part, Mr. McGill," she said, "it's an explanation of why your wife was impeached." Before McGill could ask for an elaboration, Mira added, "Galia Mindel could give you chapter and verse but she knows it'd be safer if I tell you privately."

Tall Wolf got to his feet. He looked down at McGill.

"You want me to go?"

McGill looked him and then at Mira, took a moment to consider. "No, stay."

He rarely worried about his own well-being, but if things got dicey, he wanted someone else who knew the story to be able to carry on. Make sure things turned out right for Patti.

Saint Aloysius Church — Washington, DC

Margaret "Sweetie" Sweeney sat at the rectory's kitchen table with a cup of green tea in front of her. Seated across the table was Father Desmond Nkrumah, the pastor of St. Al's parish for the past two years. Sweetie had befriended him within days of his arrival. After taking a sip from his own cup of tea, the priest steepled his hands and said, "I'm sorry, Margaret, I simply can not forgive you for this act because I do not consider it to be a sin."

Sweetie had attended morning mass, after Putnam had taken Maxi off to school.

Then she'd collared Father Dez after the service and asked him to hear her confession.

He'd asked, "Is this about what we've been discussing for quite some time now, Margaret?"

She'd nodded, and he'd said, "Let's have a cup of tea in the rectory."

He put a do not disturb sign on the kitchen door and brewed the tea himself.

"You've heard that the president has been impeached, haven't you, Father?" Sweetie asked.

The priest nodded, "I have, yes. I was sorry to learn of this, but it does not change the purity of your intentions. You've done nothing wrong. We are all subject to the possibility that even our best plans might go amiss."

"Amiss, Father? Erna Godfrey died, was choked to death, because of a plan I set in motion."

The priest reached across the table and grasped both of Sweetie's hands, his own warm from clasping his cup of tea.

"Margaret, the White House chief of staff and the president herself, women far more versed in politics than you, were unable to foresee the tragic outcome. You really must … pray for a moment of grace to see that you are only human. *You* need to forgive yourself. Otherwise you will be unable to be the mother and wife that your daughter and husband both deserve. Now, that would be a sin."

Father Dez had learned from the start how devoted Sweetie was to her family.

Tears came to her eyes, and she bobbed her head. "You're right. The president and Galia Mindel have people to help them.

Jim McGill for a starter."

Sweetie's mind searched for other important allies.

The priest said, "If I've read the newspapers correctly, the chief justice, who will preside at the president's trial in the Senate, was nominated by the president. Perhaps he is sympathetic."

Sweetie marveled at Father Dez's political discernment. He was an immigrant who had been in the country less than five years. But that was a Jesuit for you. Those guys studied the lay of the land wherever they went.

"Many of the chief justice's rulings in his earlier postings were quite close to the president's own positions on the issues, weren't they?" the priest elaborated.

Sweetie didn't have a clue; she tended to avoid the workings of the courts.

Unless they affected the way cops got to do their jobs.

That brought Sweetie back to the sorest point of what she felt was the worst mistake of her life. "Father, the reason I find it so hard to forgive myself is that I was an experienced police officer for a long time. I still think of myself that way. I was the one who should have foreseen better than anyone else the possibility of violence occurring within a prison."

"Quite possibly," Father Dez agreed. "Maybe this terrible misjudgment should tell you something. It may even have done so, scaring you badly, and that's why you are so troubled."

Sweetie knitted her brow.

"What do you mean?" she asked.

"Well, would you have made this tragic mistake ten years ago or even a year before it happened?"

Without any hesitation, Sweetie shook her head. "No way, Father. No way."

"Well then," the priest said, "perhaps the lesson to be learned here is that you should no longer think of yourself as a cop or even as a private investigator. Perhaps all your discomfort is a sign you should move on to something else."

Sweetie's mouth fell open. See herself as something other than some kind of cop? The idea had never occurred to her. Even so, she couldn't think of a word of rebuttal.

And then a totally new self-concept entered her mind.

The Hay-Adams Hotel — Washington, DC

President Patricia Grant rented the Abraham Lincoln, George Washington and John Adams Rooms, connecting meeting spaces on the top floor of the luxury hotel near the White House. All three rooms had views of the Executive Mansion. The gathered media throng was openly chattering about the reason the president had chosen to speak to them and, by extension, the American people from a private setting.

Was she about to —

The president entered the room, not with Vice President Jean Morrissey, Chief of Staff Galia Mindel, any member of her cabinet or hand-picked senators or members of the House. The woman accompanying her was Jacqueline Dodd, the new director of The Andrew Hudson Grant Foundation, the charitable organization established by the president's late first husband.

The president stepped to the lectern and looked out at the two hundred or so members of the domestic and global media. Ms. Dodd stood just behind the president and to her right. Both Ellie Booker and Didi DiMarco had snagged front row seats.

Everyone stood until the president asked them to be seated.

Patricia Grant made sure her notes were in order and then looked out at the crowd and the cameras and smiled. She said, "Before I get to my reason for asking all of you to be here this morning, I'll answer the question I'm sure is uppermost in all your minds. No, I am not going to announce my resignation from the presidency. I have no plans to resign. I intend to serve out my full second term as president."

She could see that to a person the newsies could barely restrain themselves. Questions of how she planned to fight for her political life during her trial in the Senate were all but erupting from them.

But the one person from the White House staff who was present, Press Secretary Aggie Wu, was staring death rays at the newsies.

Silently telling them anyone who misbehaved, showed the president the least bit of disrespect, would soon be covering the White House from Guam.

Patricia Grant said, "I'm here today to announce what I'll be doing after I complete my second term of office. For the first time since becoming president, I recently asked to see the books of the Andrew Hudson Grant Foundation. In addition to helping many deserving people in our country and around the world, the foundation must accrue capital to sustain itself. I'm happy to say that the investment holdings supporting the foundation have been brilliantly managed despite often difficult economic conditions.

"The result is that the foundation's assets are currently valued at just over $20 billion." The president smiled and said, "Anywhere outside of the U.S. budget, that's considered big money."

Aggie Wu grinned, giving the crowd permission to chuckle.

The president continued, "Deciding how to make the best use of such a sum is a tremendous responsibility. To accomplish that goal in the future, I've decided that half of the foundation's investment holdings — $10 billion — will be allocated to a new fund called Committed Capital.

"The purpose of Committed Capital is twofold. It will invest in high-tech start-up companies that will keep the United States at the forefront of both science and commercial applications. As a condition for the funding the new companies receive, they will be obligated to train and hire American workers. None of their technical or design jobs will be outsourced to any other countries. Manufacturing jobs for products to be consumed in the United States must also be based in our country.

"More often than not technological disruptions have thrown people out of work in our country. Add in competition from low-wage countries and these forces have devastated the middle class in the United States. It's long past time we turned this situation around.

"We can harness the power of American ingenuity to benefit more than the lucky few who get in on initial public stock offerings. If you are a person who has a great idea for a new product or service and need seed money to get it off the ground, Committed Capital will be there to help. Just so long as you are willing to extend a helping hand to your fellow countrymen and women.

"I'm happy to announce that after contacting other venture capital firms from coast to coast, we have attracted another $10 billion dollars to be made available to our effort. Once my term of office is completed and a new president is inaugurated, I will become the chief executive officer of Committed Capital.

"Ms. Jacqueline Dodd, head of The Andrew Hudson Grant Foundation, will be happy to answer any questions you may have about how things will unfold as we move forward. Jackie?"

The president waved Dodd to the lectern, but Ellie Booker, ignoring any possible retribution from Aggie Wu, jumped to her feet.

"Madam President, how much will you be paid to do your new job?"

Not batting an eye, Patricia Grant answered, "One dollar per year." She smiled and added, "I have a bit of money in my own accounts."

Not to be outdone, Didi DiMarco stood and piped up. "Madam President, was Committed Capital your idea or someone else's? Say, Joan Renshaw's?"

"Or Jim McGill's?" Ellie offered.

Aggie Wu looked like she was going to pummel both of them.

But the president held up a restraining hand.

"I wish I could claim credit for it," she said, "but I can't. Neither can Joan Renshaw. Nor my husband. But it did originate within our family. At a lunch with Abbie and Kenny McGill, we started tossing ideas around about what Mr. McGill and I might do next. I'm not sure whether it was Abbie or Kenny who first offered the notion for investing in both the country's technological and human capital; I'd have to give credit to both of them."

Emboldened by his competitors, a reporter from the *Wall Street Journal* asked, "Do you think your late husband, Mr. Andrew Hudson Grant, would approve of this idea?"

"I do," the president said. Recalling her first husband, in front of the crowd and its cameras, tears misted the president's eyes. "Andy had such a good heart. I know this would make him happy."

Pacific Palisades, California

"The crazy part is, Ed really believes this is a good thing for the country," Mira told McGill and Tall Wolf as the three of them sat on the outdoor deck at Gladstones, a seafood restaurant on the beach opposite the western terminus of Sunset Boulevard.

Deke Ky made sure nobody was seated within fifteen feet of them. The waitress had brought their lunch orders and departed. The surf rolled in loud enough to obscure their conversation from any directional microphone that might be pointed their way. Not that Mira thought that anyone was actively snooping on her, but why take chances?

"I've sometimes wondered if maybe his brain blew a circuit," she added.

"He's advocating a one-party state?" McGill asked. "That's the definition of tyranny."

Tall Wolf nodded. "Yes, but whether that's a good or bad thing depends on if *your* party is the one in power."

McGill had long thought the country would have been far better off if Patti had gotten more of her ideas passed into law. He could see the temptation of what Tall Wolf had said, but Patti wasn't going to be president forever — thank God. Who knew where things might go under the next chief executive?

Mira nodded. She knew just what McGill was thinking. "Right. What if a saint is followed by a solid-gold SOB? I tried to make Ed see that for half the time we were married."

"He refused to be enlightened?" Tall Wolf asked.

"Persistently, but I was the one who didn't believe he could make his cockamamie scheme work. The magic in our relationship had pretty well waned, and it fit with my exit plan to see him as a loser in as many ways as I could. But the truth is he was entirely practical in his means and methods. if not always exactly on the mark."

McGill said, "Take us through it again, how Edmond Whelan intends to make the United States a country with a permanently conservative governing majority."

Before she could, their waitress came and asked if they'd like something for dessert.

They settled for another round of ice tea.

Once the waitress brought their drinks and departed, Mira resumed.

"Ed told me if you want to build something, you need a foundation. He said the way to consolidate power at the federal level is by controlling state governments. You worked your tail off to get your people elected to state legislatures and governors' offices. When census time rolled around and new legislative maps were to be drawn, your side gerrymandered the other guys out of as many seats in the federal House of Representatives as possible."

"You control half of Congress," Tall Wolf said, "nobody can ever pass a law you don't like."

"Right," Mira said, "but there are other advantages, too. As I said, Congressional maps are redrawn every ten years. So you get *five* House elections in a decade. The advantage a one-term House incumbent has over a challenger with no federal government experience is enormous. With each reelection, that advantage continues to grow. Your power becomes entrenched. In the 2014 House elections, forty-one members retired; only nineteen lost their re-election attempts. So the odds are better than two-to-one you'll get sick of the job rather than get booted out. Also, voters prefer governors to legislators as presidential candidates."

"So what's to keep the Democrats from wising up and competing harder at the state level?" McGill asked.

"Nothing, but again, they'd be fighting uphill. There are 31 state legislatures in GOP control," Mira said. "If turning that around were a betting proposition, where would you put your money?"

Tall Wolf held up a hand. "Wait a minute. What about the demographic shift that's going on? Isn't that supposed to work against the right wing?"

Mira said, "On the national level, yeah. But not necessarily in state elections. Especially, in the ones that are trying to tilt things the other way with voter registration laws that discourage Democratic voters: minorities, younger voters, people who are only marginally interested. The big things liberals have going for them are rising resistance to income inequality and a growing sentiment that everybody should get a fair shake, including gays and immigrants."

McGill sat back and took a sip of his drink, thinking about what he'd heard.

"Tell me how the president's impeachment fits into Whelan's plan," he said.

"Well, electing a president is unlike anything else. It's the only election, coupled with the election of a vice president, where the whole country gets to vote on the same office. Also, there's more public interest. People who aren't totally disengaged think they *should* vote for who they want to be president."

"Even if they don't know anything more about the candidates than what they see in campaign commercials," Tall Wolf said.

Mira Kersten grinned. "Not everybody reads the *New York Times*, Mr. Co-director. Not even in the old days when you could get it for free online."

"Meanwhile, back at the impeachment," McGill said.

"Yes, back to that. Well, let's look at what happened to Bill Clinton, after Ross Perot helped him beat Poppy Bush. Clinton got slimed from Day One. Accused of everything up to and including the murder of Vince Foster. More than one official investigation ruled Foster's death a suicide. That didn't stop the smear campaign. There's no end of people today who will tell you to this day that the Clintons had the man killed. And then there were all the old

Arkansas scandals and the bimbo eruptions. All that set the stage. So when the special prosecutor said Billy Boy had perjured himself and obstructed justice by denying under oath that he got a blowjob from a White House intern, the Republicans in the House impeached him."

"As you say, it's all part of a process," Tall Wolf said. "If the other party's candidate wins the White House, you de-legitimize him."

"Or her," McGill said.

Mira nodded. "Yes, exactly. If you prosecuted every politician in Washington, including more than a few women, who lied about having sex with someone other than a spouse, you'd have time for nothing else. But in Patricia Grant's case you have a president who puts the woman who murdered her husband into a prison cell with the woman who kills her.

McGill said, "There's never been another case like that."

"No there hasn't," Mira agreed.

"It's about more than de-legitimizing the president this time, isn't it?" McGill asked.

"Yes," Mira said. "Patricia Grant left her old party, spurned it and then won reelection by one electoral vote that many people still think was stolen. This time they want revenge."

"Does that figure into Whelan's master plan, too?" McGill asked.

Mira sighed. "That's the hell of it; I don't know. I read Ed's original treatise in its traditionally published form: ink on paper bound in leather. Damn handsome presentation for some truly ugly ideas. But the thing is, he kept revising and amending his work to keep up with the times. What I've heard is the latest edition is a digital file, an e-book. That's what he thinks I stole."

"But you said you haven't," McGill said.

"So why does Whelan think otherwise?" Tall Wolf asked.

Mira looked sheepish and took a sip of her ice tea. "I was part of a televised panel discussion, me and three other talking heads, and the topic of the 2016 presidential election came up. We all agreed Jean Morrissey as the sitting vice president would get the Democratic nomination. The others debated whether the GOP would unite with True South behind a single candidate this time or split the vote again like they did in 2012. When it came my turn to opine, I said, 'I sure would like to know what Edmond Whelan has up his sleeve.'"

McGill recognized the significance of that. "I'd never heard of Whelan until a day or two ago. My guess is most of the American public never has either. You were outing him. Revealing him as a power behind the scenes. He wouldn't have liked that."

"He didn't," Mira said. "I heard from him directly for the first time in years. He started cursing me and I replied in kind." She sighed. "I told him it was time I threw a monkey wrench in all his finely calibrated plans. You see why I'm sure Ed is behind the theft of my embryos?"

McGill and Tall Wolf looked at each other.

Not saying a word, they agreed with Mira's assessment.

McGill turned to his client and said, "Guys like Whelan don't do their own dirty work. Do you have any idea of who might have pulled off the theft for him?"

Before she could reply, Tall Wolf added, "One more thing to think about: If you'd wanted to steal his e-book, how might you have done it?"

She answered Tall Wolf's question first, albeit with some reluctance.

"I hate to admit it, but I've kept loose tabs on Ed over the years. I told myself it was for my own protection, in case I ever wanted to use one of the embryos we created together. Truth was, there was more to it. I wanted to see if he'd crash and burn without me. So I can give you a list of the people he associates with most closely. And I know some of the places he likes to spend his personal time. If I'd wanted to steal his book, I would've tried to subvert someone near if not dear to him."

"Your list will be a good start," Tall Wolf said.

Turning to McGill, Mira said, "Ed was never in the military, but he's one of those guys who's a big fan of the men and women who are. Always makes sure to advocate for big budgets for the Pentagon. I don't know of anyone in particular Ed might have used, but the military trains people to have all sorts of interesting skills, don't they?"

"They certainly do," McGill said.

He knew right then he would have to intrude on Welborn Yates' holiday in England.

Austin, Texas

The unofficial motto of the capital of Texas was: *Keep Austin Weird.*

Eugene "Gene" Beck certainly did his part. Three days a week he laced up his running shoes with the intention of running a marathon distance: 26 miles, 385 yards. Didn't matter what the weather was. The only thing that could stop him was … a woman, a bar, a broke-down car. Anything that might become the lyric for a country-and-western song.

Gene collaborated with a dozen musicians who called Austin home.

He didn't read musical notation or play an instrument, but when he handed over a page of verses and a chorus he'd whistle the way he thought the tune might go. Sometimes his collaborators would confess they didn't share his vision, and that was okay. But nobody ever tried to rip off one of his songs. Claim it as their own creative product.

The reason for hewing to straight deals with Gene was people invariably got the feeling he was the kind of guy, if you got him mad, he might take you out into the hills and grill your liver over a campfire. Eat it while you had just enough life left to watch him do it.

Not that he'd ever threatened such a thing. It was just a feeling people got, should they ever do anything to displace his usual genial nature. His normal good spirits were evinced by the way he'd whistle merrily as he strode mile after mile on Travis County blacktop.

Local motorists would wave to him as they passed by. They weren't bothered by the sight of the gun holstered at the small of his back or the knife in the sheath on his right calf. That was just a man exercising his Second Amendment rights as well as his body. Nothing weird or scary about that for Texas.

In fact, more than a few women, young and old, blew him kisses as they motored by. He'd written a song about them. Called it "Highway Honeys."

Beck was an Air Force vet, had planned to get trained in aircraft maintenance and take his skills into the private sector when his hitch was up. But that plan, while practical, failed to engage his imagination. He decided he wanted something with more sex appeal. Something you could tell the ladies and, eventually, your grandkids about and make them all say, "gee whiz."

He applied for training as a Combat Controller, one of the USAF's special ops positions.

Among other things, Combat Control Teams seized enemy airfields for use by American forces. They also pinpointed enemy targets for U.S. pilots and ground commanders. To achieve some of their goals they might become "bike chasers." Airmen tossed dirt bikes out of cargo planes, and the combat control guys followed. Chutes popped for both the machines and the men and they hit the ground rolling.

How cool was that? Enough to fire Beck's jets, that was for sure. He aced the FAST, fitness and stamina test. He was lean but strong as a "wild animal," according to his evaluation. He could run forever and stay awake and functional for days on end. Better yet, he seemed to inspire other men to find unsuspected reserves of the mental toughness the job required.

Soon enough, Beck was pegged not just for his desired posting but also for an officer's commission and a leadership role.

Until, that was, it was pointed out to him that in certain battlefield environments complete stealth was called for and the way he whistled while he worked would be a dead giveaway, death being the fate special ops warriors were tasked to deliver not absorb.

"Yes, sir," Beck told his training instructor. "I'll just switch the music to internal mode in those situations."

"Come again," the instructor ordered.

Hearing Beck's explanation, the instructor sent him to visit a medical officer, in this case a psychologist. The doctor asked Beck, "You say you always hear music, actually *hear* it, and that's why you frequently whistle?"

"Yes, sir. For a long time, I thought everyone was that way. I was halfway through elementary school before I learned different. Later on, I was told some people always hear a ringing in their ears."

"Yes, that's called tinnitus," the doctor said.

"Must be awful, but me I hear music, and I love it."

"The music never stops?"

"When I sleep, I suppose."

"But when you're awake?"

"It's always there."

"Is the music from songs you've heard on the radio or elsewhere?"

"Sure, that's some of it, but I hear a lot of tunes that just come to me, too."

"So you whistle along with what you hear?"

"Yes, sir. It makes me feel good." Beck hesitated before adding, "Like I'm part of a big band."

The psychologist paused to reflect. Then he asked, "Have you ever heard of an artist having a muse?"

At that point, Beck hadn't, so the psychologist explained the idea.

There were nine Greek goddesses who ruled over the arts. They inspired poets, musicians and others. The muse of music was called Euterpe. Beck found the idea that he might be tuning into a goddess even cooler than chasing a dirt bike out of an airplane.

Unfortunately for reaching his goal as a combat controller, the psychologist also raised the possibility that Beck might be in an incipient stage of schizophrenia, a condition in which auditory hallucinations were common. He was washed out of special ops training and separated from the Air Force with a medical discharge.

This swift reversal of fortune might have been crushing except for the immediate appearance of a man in civilian clothes who identified himself as Nicholas Wicklow and told Beck, "I'm from the Defense Intelligence Agency, the DIA. I'm told you could be a musical prodigy or a budding madman. Either way, I might have a job for you, if you're interested."

Having no other immediate prospects, Beck was.

He was taught a multitude of skills the Air Force hadn't covered, including: how to speak Russian with a Swiss-German accent, how to alter his appearance to blend in with six different ethnic groups and fourteen ways to kill without using a firearm or edged weapon. In short, Beck became a bilingual, versatile, elusive assassin.

The really good part, from the DIA's point of view, was that Beck worked off their books. If it ever became necessary to disavow a killing that went wrong, there'd be no documentary link between him and the Pentagon. Better yet, the jukebox in Beck's head provided him with a mental condition that would make it child's play to paint him as a delusional loon.

What Nicholas Wicklow and the boys at the DIA hadn't counted on, though, was that even with his aberration Beck had his head screwed on straight. He realized his position was far from secure. So he gave himself the ultimate safeguard. He said no to any hit he didn't like. What the hell could anyone do about that?

Zip was what. Wasn't like he had a contract they could hold him to. They might have threatened him with physical harm or maybe even a fatal accident. Only they'd helped to make him harder to kill than Godzilla. In fact, Beck was about the biggest bad-ass in the DIA's out of bounds playground. If you went after him and messed up, he was going to be vengeful.

He didn't care much about money either, so threatening to cut off his monthly wire transfers didn't carry any weight. Beck had told Wicklow if he ever needed another gig he'd head for Nashville and write songs. He suspected there were a lot of people there who always heard music in their heads.

On the other hand, if approached in a fair-minded way, he could be entirely reasonable. If you made an objective case that some foreign asshole represented a real threat to the country and the agency had a practical plan for disposing of said asshole, Beck would take the job. Assuming his payday was proportionate to the risk he'd have to take, of course. That wasn't greed, just common sense.

His favorite role was playing a corrupt Russian ex-military man who was selling advanced hardware out the back door. None of his terrorist marks had any trouble believing that because it was really happening. You paid off the big wheels of the kleptocracy in the Kremlin, you were good to go.

Beck had promised to deliver artillery, armored vehicles, and anti-aircraft systems — and that was just the first letter of his imaginary inventory. He thought it might be pushing credulity to say he could put his hands on a nuclear sub, but he did sucker one wannabe jihadi with the irresistible idea that he could finagle cosmonaut training for the chump, get him a ride to the international space station and let him blow up outer-space infidels from around the world over the skies of the Great Satan.

The guy took it hard when Beck told him the truth and put a bullet between his eyes.

After a number of variations on that con, the real crooked Russian arms dealers caught on that some SOB was damaging their brand and dispiriting their customer base. They sent teams out to hunt him down and kill him in the most gruesome way possible. Tough as Beck was, he still thought it was time to beat a tactical retreat.

He relocated his money and himself, not bothering to notify Wicklow or anyone else at the DIA. He fetched up in Austin under a new name and started writing lyrics for the better songs in his head. He also took some private sector outlaw jobs to keep from getting bored.

He limited himself to property crimes. High-end theft. He didn't want to leave a trail of blood that some smart tracker could follow back to him. More than that, he told himself the only bastards he'd killed had all been enemies of his country. In his heart, he still saw himself as a special ops guy.

If he started acing people for money, he'd become just another gun thug.

He didn't want that. But murder was just what the guy who'd hired him to steal the frozen embryos requested. Not just kill any poor sap either. He wanted James J. McGill hit.

The president's henchman, for Christ's sake.

There was no way Beck was going to do that.

But it was kind of interesting to think about how he *might* do it.

As he ran down the road outside Austin whistling.

Bel-Air, California

"How's her majesty?" McGill asked, his phone on its speaker setting.

From London, Captain Welborn Yates replied, "Fit and chipper. Might be planning a *coup d'état.* Retake the throne. Maybe reclaim the colonies. She sends her regards."

"Right back at her," McGill said.

"She also told me she's confident you'll work something out to spare the president any embarrassment. She has great faith in you."

"I'll try not to let either her or Patti down."

McGill sat on a silk sofa in what had formerly been the presidential suite of the five-star hotel tucked snugly into a cozy canyon in L.A.'s snootiest neighborhood. Taking everything in from an opposing armchair was John Tall Wolf.

The BIA man had arched his eyebrows at the mention of royalty.

Shifting the discussion to business, McGill mentioned that he had company in the room and introduced Tall Wolf. "Kira and the girls aren't in the room with you, are they?"

"Aria and Callista are tucked in for the night. Kira put them to bed and has yet to return to me. She's probably trying to accommodate herself to the idea that we can't afford our own palace on an Air Force officer's salary."

McGill laughed and Tall Wolf grinned.

"Yeah, let's hope she can dispel that sorrow," McGill said. "Listen, is your schedule over there tied down tight? If you've got any free time, I could use some help scaring a little cooperation out of the brass hats at the Pentagon."

"I'd be working under presidential authority?"

"Unofficially. It'd be better if you could create that impression without coming right out and saying so."

"But if I were to find myself in a corner?" Welborn asked.

McGill thought about that. "Give them Galia's name."

"Oh … kay."

The note of doubt in Welborn's assent was unmissable. In most cases, short of acts of war, the White House chief of staff's backing would have prompted swift Pentagon compliance. With the president about to go on trial in the Senate, though, the top brass and civilian leadership at the Department of Defense might want to hedge their bets.

"You're right," McGill said, agreeing with Welborn's unspoken misgiving. "What I'll do is call Jean Morrissey, see if I can get her in on the act."

That would still give Patti some cover, McGill thought, and the woman who might well be the next commander-in-chief would get compliance from any officer or bureaucrat who valued his job.

"I think that would do it," Welborn agreed. "Getting back to your question, we've met all the high-and-mighty on our schedule over here. All that's left is the shopping. I can tear myself away from that, and gladly. What do you need from me?"

McGill told Welborn about the stolen embryo caper.

"So what I'd like," he said, "is for you to look for a connection between Edmond Whelan, the chief of staff to the House Majority whip, and anyone in the military possessing burglary skills and a willingness to misapply them."

A moment of silence followed, long enough for McGill to ask, "You still there, Welborn?"

"Yes, I was just thinking. If things go very badly for me, I might be given political asylum over here. The queen is very fond of my girls."

After McGill ended the call, John Tall Wolf told him, "I could probably hide out with the Tarahumara tribe down in Mexico, my mother's relatives, if things come to that."

"I thought you said you were getting married to a Mountie."

The BIA man shrugged. "Never met a Canadian who didn't appreciate a winter getaway."

McGill grinned. "I really don't think any of us will have to flee the country."

"Not until Whelan's crew takes complete control," Tall Wolf said deadpan.

"Yeah, well, if it comes to that, I've heard good things about New Zealand. Meanwhile, I was wondering whether you think we've got Detectives Zapata and MacDuff sufficiently grounded in the political realities of this case."

Tall Wolf gave McGill a look. "You mean do I think they won't try to lean on you if I'm not around? I wouldn't count on it."

"Me either, but I'm going to chance it."

"My services are no longer required?" Tall Wolf couldn't remember the last time he'd been booted off a case. Truth was, it had never happened.

McGill wasn't about to change that. He had another idea.

"Oh, I still want your help, no question about that. But you and Welborn both raise a good point. There could be political fallout from this case, the extent of which I can't even guess. I've got two solid pensions, an expanding business and a rich wife. I'll be okay whatever happens. But I can't make that promise to anyone else. If you want to bow out, I'll understand."

Tall Wolf shook his head.

"Not a quitter, huh?" McGill asked.

"Never."

"Good. So what I'm thinking is this: You look at the list of people Mira Kersten gave you, the ones she said she'd have turned to if she had wanted to subvert Whelan, and see what they might have to tell you."

"Sure, I can do that. What about the 'handful of peculiar paparazzi' who might have video clips of Ms. Kersten? That tidbit struck me as a bit odd. Almost a throwaway line, but who knows?"

McGill agreed. "That 's worth a look, too. Your choice whether to look at the names on the list or the unspecified tabloid people first."

"Probably won't take long to run down the list."

"You think Ms. Kersten gave us those names just for appearance's sake, Mr. Co-director?"

"That idea did occur to me. With your friend Captain Yates searching for military malefactors, what will you be doing?" Tall Wolf asked.

"I'm going to take a closer look at my client," McGill said.

Talk with the security guard at the fertility clinic, too.

But he kept that to himself.

Number One Observatory Circle — Washington, DC

Vice President Jean Morrissey sat hip to hip and holding hands with FBI Deputy Director Byron DeWitt in the living room of her official residence. Logs burned in the fireplace. The curtains were drawn. The Secret Service had been instructed to keep a discreet distance.

Things were as cozy as they ever got for two top-tier government poobahs.

Well, with the exception of the private quarters at the White House.

"So what do you think?" DeWitt asked.

"It's not quite the marriage proposal I've always dreamed of," the vice president said, "but it might work."

"I promise to make my ice skating skills more macho," DeWitt said.

Jean smiled. "While you're out in Santa Barbara? I don't think so."

"I'll be back here whenever you need me or I get, you know, lonely."

That earned him a kiss and a question. "You mean you won't always be *lonely* when I'm not around?"

"Sure, I will, but I've heard from the world's only authority on the issue that being the president's husband can mean sharing the woman you love with the world."

"Jim McGill said that?"

"In his own words, yeah," DeWitt said.

"And you and me, do we really love each other?"

"Just what I asked myself earlier, on the way over here. I told myself that we're both too old for our feelings to be simple teen-age lust. I mean, I admire your mind, too."

Jean laughed. "I want to give you an elbow, but I know you'd just block it."

"See, we're already getting accustomed to each other's habits. Really, though, I'd be on hand any time you need me. Might even pester you sometimes when you don't. But I've got to get out of Washington at least part of the time and my old home calls out to me."

Jean leaned in closer. "I know what you mean. I have the same kind of feelings. Would you be up for a Christmas or nine in Minnesota? We could skate on a frozen pond."

"Sure, just as long as we make it to East Beach by New Year's Eve."

Both of them were thinking they could make it work, juggle a commuter marriage, separate careers, maybe one of them being the presidency, and write a happy ending to it all. But if Patti Grant was convicted by the Senate, and Jean served out her predecessor's last year and two of her own terms ... Jeez, she'd become the longest-serving president since FDR. What marriage could survive that kind of an ordeal?

That was when Jean had the damnedest idea of her political career.

Before she could spring it on DeWitt, though, his cell-phone rang. He looked at the caller ID screen and sighed. Showing it to Jean, he said, "See what I mean. Business never lets up."

The display read: *Spec Ag A. Benjamin.*

As part of their growing intimacy, Jean and DeWitt had shared stories about their pasts, and the people who had populated them. The VP knew that Abra Benjamin had once been DeWitt's lover, had been impregnated by him and had given up their child for adoption. Despite all that, they'd maintained an effective working relationship. Benjamin had been neither shuffled off to a remote posting nor promoted beyond merit.

That was important to Jean because either vindictiveness or favoritism would have made DeWitt look bad if his relationship with the vice president went public, and the media started snooping into his personal life, as they inevitably would. A prospective mate had to be an asset not a liability.

Fortunately for Jean, as she was truly sweet on the guy who'd just, sort of, proposed to her, he'd handled the situation as well as it could be. Even to the point of agreeing to allow his biological son to be adopted by two solid citizens.

There was one thing left for Jean to do: get a good look, a fix, on the other woman.

Make sure there were no lingering feelings that might screw things up.

"Take the call," she told DeWitt.

"You sure?"

"Yes, you're not out on the beach yet."

DeWitt nodded. He accepted the call by saying: "You have news?"

Jean liked that. Right down to business with a positive tone.

DeWitt listened for a moment. "That's good, very good. Yes, by all means, follow up. Let me know what resources you need and I'll see that you get them."

DeWitt's enthusiasm was infectious. Jean put a hand on his near arm and asked, "What's happened?

The deputy director told Benjamin, "Hold on, Special Agent." He put a hand over the phone and said, "Benjamin had a very smart thought on tracking down Tyler Busby, and it may have produced a lead. She's just returned from Amsterdam."

"Catching Busby would be wonderful," the vice president said.

Not only would Busby's apprehension be great news for the president at a time when she badly needed a win to bolster her public standing, heading into her trial in the Senate, but if DeWitt were to play a prominent role in Busby's capture that would elevate his public profile.

Nothing to boost a presidential candidate's standing like marrying a law enforcement hero.

Jean immediately had mixed feeling about that thought. It was unworthy of a guy for whom she had real feelings. Then again, politics wasn't a pretty business. That only reinforced the idea she'd had a moment ago concerning her political future.

Jean had thought she might follow in Patricia Grant's footsteps in more ways than one.

It had occurred to her a moment ago to change political parties. See if Cool Blue, the new progressive party, would have her as its standard bearer. Serve out the remaining year of Patti Grant's term, if necessary, and pledge to serve only one term of her own. She thought that she and DeWitt could endure four or five years in the White House.

"Please tell the special agent to come over as soon as possible," the vice president told the deputy director. "I'd like to hear all the details of what she's discovered."

DeWitt gave Jean a look, and then nodded. "Yes, ma'am."

He thought it was bound to happen sometime, the two of

them meeting.

Wrapping the introduction in good news might be the way to go.

Just in case, though, he answered Jean's earlier question. "Yes, I do think we love each other. In fact, I'm certain that's the way I feel."

Before Jean could respond, he told Benjamin to join them at the vice president's house.

The Oval Office — The White House

The president said, "Yes, Jim, I'm fine."

McGill had called from California to ask the missus how she was holding up. His call was encrypted. Not even the NSA or Chinese hackers could eavesdrop. Supposedly.

For legal purposes, though, their conversation was a hundred percent shielded under spousal privilege. On a practical level, the president's secretary, Edwina Byington, had left her desk for the day. Word had been passed to all other personnel that the president was not to be disturbed for anything less than a national or familial emergency.

The sole exception was Chief of Staff Galia Mindel.

She sat on a sofa opposite the president's desk, wearing earbuds.

Listening to a report from her political spy network, unable to hear anything else.

"How are things going on your end?" Patricia Grant asked.

"I think John Tall Wolf will be a big help." McGill told his wife of Tall Wolf's request to recruit Native American candidates for Congress. "I gave him Putnam Shady's name. I'll call Sweetie about it in the morning."

"I think that's a good idea. A Native American voting bloc could bring a fresh perspective on national priorities. Wish I'd thought of it," the president said.

McGill grunted. "How much free time have you and I had the last six-plus years? Not a lot that I recall. What I'm saying is, you can't think of everything."

"You don't want me to resign, do you, Jim? We'd have a lot more free time."

McGill thought of Mira Kersten's political assessment: The other side wanted revenge. McGill was sure a resignation wouldn't satisfy them. They'd demand legal action after Patti had left office. Maybe, as Patti had suggested, even get an indictment if a president from the GOP or True South was elected next year.

The only sure way for Patti to avoid possible prosecution would be for Jean Morrissey to give her a blanket pardon just as Gerald Ford had done with Richard Nixon.

McGill said, "No, that would blight your entire record." Talk about delegitimizing a president. Edmond Whelan would be dancing a jig. "We've got to fight it out in the Senate and win."

The president took that moment to tell McGill about the threat to Chief Justice MacLaren's life.

"Damn, that's awful," he said. "The Supreme Court has its own cops, doesn't it?"

"Yes, they've stepped up the security for all the justices, and the FBI is working with them to investigate the threat."

"Any leads yet?"

"Only the original message. To wit: 'Do the right thing with Patti Grant or you die.' No specificity about what the right thing might be."

McGill said, "Makes it harder to narrow the suspect pool that way. Could be a threat from either side of the political divide. On the other hand, it's not instructive about what the bastard actually wants."

"The FBI is working primarily on the assumption it comes from the other side politically, as Chief Justice MacLaren and I tend to agree on questions of Constitutional interpretation more often than not."

"That'd be my hunch, too, but it might also be a political ally telling MacLaren not to go weak in the knees at exactly the wrong moment," McGill said.

"The FBI said a follow-up message might be coming to provide clarity."

"Maybe," McGill said, "but that would also increase the risk of the creep's identity being discovered."

The president sighed. "One way or another, Jim, we will both get through this."

"Yes, we will. I saw your YouTube video on Committed Capital. That's a great idea, too. Maybe McGill Investigations, Inc. can start a security division and protect your new offices."

Patti laughed. "Only if you have the low bid."

"Hugs and kisses as needed. That's all I ask."

"You just won the contract. You are so good for me."

"Works both ways," McGill told her.

They spoke about the kids and plans for vacations they swore they would take.

Then McGill sprang a surprise on the president, asked if by any chance Galia was nearby. He was happy to hear she was. McGill asked Patti to leave the connection live and lay her phone on her desk. Give him ten minutes before she returned to the Oval Office.

Without asking a question or even saying goodbye, the president did as requested.

It didn't take five seconds before Galia picked up the phone.

Number One Observatory Circle — Washington, DC

A Secret Service uniformed officer knocked on the living room door and after receiving permission to enter from the vice president ushered Special Agent Abra Benjamin into the room and departed. Ever the gentleman, Deputy Director Byron DeWitt made the introductions. Better yet, he did it without becoming tongue-tied and got both women's names right as he acquainted his former lover with his present one.

He discreetly kept to himself his marriage proposal to the VP.

For her part and to her credit, Benjamin kept her tone professional and respectful.

"Ms. Vice President, it's an honor to meet you."

Both women possessed firm handshakes, but neither overdid it.

"Good to meet you, too, Special Agent. The deputy director tells me you might have good news regarding the hunt for Tyler Busby. Why don't we all sit down?"

Jean Morrissey sat alone on the sofa. DeWitt and Benjamin took arm chairs facing her. The deputy director gestured to Benjamin. The stage was hers.

She explained her follow-the-nookie concept, phrasing it as politely as possible.

It still drew a laugh from the vice president. "That's a wonderful insight, Special Agent. And you're saying it paid off almost immediately?"

Benjamin was smart enough not to over-promise, even as she felt her body temperature warm from the praise. "Up to a point, yes ma'am. With the help of the national police in the Netherlands, we located the … *broker* who handles the very top-end *talent* for some of the world's —"

"Richest horny old bastards?" Jean interjected. "It's okay to say pimps and hookers in front of me, Special Agent."

"Yes, ma'am, thank you. In any event, we managed to speak with one woman, an Australian, who sexually serviced Busby on a yacht called *Shining Dawn* when it cruised off the coastline of Malaysia last year."

That news made DeWitt sit up straighter in his chair.

Jean noticed but didn't comment.

Benjamin continued, "The Australian woman was one of six hookers aboard at the time. Despite the variety of sexual partners available to Busby, all of the working girls thought he was pining for a senior female member of the yacht's crew, a Chinese woman named Ah-lam."

"She *wasn't* available to Busby?" DeWitt asked.

"I think that was a note of skepticism in the deputy director's voice, Special Agent," Jean said. "I have to say, given the context, I share it."

"As do I, Ms. Vice President, The consensus of the hookers aboard was that Busby just hadn't met her price."

The vice president looked at the deputy director. It was the time for his two cents.

DeWitt started ticking off points of information on his fingers. "Tyler Busby leased the *Shining Dawn* from Donald Yang, CEO of Asia Global Liability, the insurance company that issued coverage for the forged paintings Busby sent to Inspiration Hall."

"The place where the president was supposed to be killed," Jean said.

"Right." DeWitt continued his count. "Busby put a senior female member of the *Shining Dawn's* crew off the yacht near the Philippine island of Mindanao. Shortly after that, a bar girl who refused to give her name called the FBI office at the U.S. embassy in Manila. She said Busby had been kidnapped by Abu Sayyaf guerrillas and spirited away into the jungle. I think we can all connect the dots here."

Jean Morrissey said, "Busby met Ah-lam's price. But where is he now?"

Benjamin was happy to answer, to the extent that she could. "The Australian hooker was called by her pimp last week and asked if she'd be up for a repeat performance with the gentleman she'd gone cruising with off Malaysia. On another super-luxury yacht. This time somewhere in the western hemisphere. That was as specific a location as she got."

"That covers a lot of ocean," DeWitt said, "but I can't believe Busby would risk coming anywhere near North America. He'd have to stay somewhere south of Panama, in either the Atlantic or Pacific."

"Why did he start using prostitutes again?" the vice president asked. "He got tired of his formerly special sweetheart?"

DeWitt said, "From everything I've read about the man, he's not the type to look for a soulmate."

"Or," Benjamin suggested, "maybe Ah-lam got pregnant."

She and DeWitt both knew from experience that not even the pill worked 100% of the time.

"And what?" the deputy director asked. "She lost her figure and sex appeal at the same time?"

Benjamin shrugged. "Maybe it was her choice. She wanted to keep the baby but didn't want to be bothered with sex. Could have told Busby he should get his action elsewhere."

DeWitt was uncertain about that scenario, but the vice president said, "I can see that, but how do we narrow the search?"

"Wait to see where the world's top hookers flock to," Benjamin said.

The vice president nodded but turned to DeWitt for a recommendation. He felt like he was being tested. It might have been annoying if he hadn't already come up with his own idea.

He said, "Two points to consider. One, the man apparently likes old favorites, e.g. revisiting a particular sex partner. Two, he probably has other appetites. Do some research and find out what he likes to eat. Not just gourmet stuff but also snack food. Maybe snacks especially. Munchies you can get in the U.S. but not abroad. Look at brands of beer and soft drinks, too. See if any or all of those things are being shipped to an anchorage somewhere in South America."

The vice president liked that. She told Benjamin to get right on it.

Let her know as soon as she found anything.

The Oval Office — The White House

"This conversation never happened, Galia," McGill told the chief of staff.

"Of course not. Only the president is authorized to use this phone."

"Right. I need to know everything you can tell me about my new client, Mira Kersten.

"I already gave you a full briefing, from her college days to the present."

"You didn't tell me she works on television."

"That's post-politics. She blathers to earn a living. It's nothing of substance."

"So you're saying, what? She doesn't put her heart into her work?"

Galia hedged. "No, I wouldn't say that."

"How about being ambitious? You think she's left that behind her?"

"No, I'd never say that about Mira."

"So, as pleasant as being a TV celebrity in Los Angeles might be, the big action in televised political punditry is in —"

"Washington and New York," Galia said.

"Uh-huh, and even the LAPD detectives working the case know that Mira has already outclassed the local competition."

"What are you getting at, Mr. McGill?"

"An unspoken if not successfully hidden agenda on Ms. Kersten's part."

"What could that possibly be?" Galia was starting to get nervous.

"It might be as simple as personal ambition. Say a network TV contract in New York. Maybe a weekly column in *The Times*. Who knows? Maybe a book deal with movie possibilities attached. You know, something along the lines of 'All the President's Men.'"

"All that?" Galia asked, incredulous.

But her mind whirled as she considered McGill's speculation.

"Come on, Galia. You know where I'm going here."

Called on the question, Galia had to admit that she did. Not that the idea had occurred to her before that very moment. Not that she necessarily agreed with McGill's conclusion either. But she had to consider it was possible.

Galia said, "You think there's a chance Mira is setting up both you and me. She either does possess Edmond Whelan's latest grand plan for the right wing's domination of the government or she knows who does. She's going to feed you enough crumbs to lead you to a patsy or, I hope, some muckety-muck on the right."

"Could be one person playing both roles," McGill said, "or it could be something else entirely. She denied knowing who stole Whelan's book of schemes, but I'm not sure I believe her."

"What do you think she could be doing?" Galia asked.

"Let's say Mira has reached the conclusion Whelan's side is going to win the White House next year and keep both Houses of Congress, and that will be only the start of a very long hold on power. Maybe she just wants to be on the winning side."

"You think Mira is going to sell out?" Galia asked in disbelief.

"Why not? Dick Morris went from Bill Clinton's White House to Fox News."

"But if that's the case, why bother to involve you in … what? A bogus theft? And would she really risk the viability of her embryos? I can't imagine that."

"Maybe I'm just getting paranoid," McGill said, "but if the Senate trial goes against the president, and Jean Morrissey gives Patti a blanket pardon, what's left for the other side to do?"

"Trash the president's legacy. Make her look as bad as possible in retrospect."

"Right. Maybe through me. Say, catch me doing something shady while I'm investigating an important Republican staffer. That might be worth a book deal in itself."

Galia wanted to tell McGill that he was letting his imagination get the better of him.

Only she couldn't argue with the political logic. If McGill was caught doing something underhanded, who would be accused of putting him up to it? The president, who else?

There was still one thing, however, that kept Galia from buying into McGill's scenario.

She said, "I know for a fact that whatever Mira's other ambitions are she is determined to get pregnant and soon. I just can't see her risking those embryos for any other consideration."

McGill told Galia, "When Ms. Kersten and I first met, she gave me a very warm smile. My ego said it was a product of meeting the president's husband. But I should have recognized the way she looked sooner than I did."

"What do you mean?"

"She reminded me of Carolyn on three very special occasions."

"You mean —"

"Yeah, she had the same glow my ex-wife did each time she told me we were going to have a baby."

"You think Mira is *already* pregnant?"

"I'd bet on it," McGill said. "She's playing some kind of game."

CHAPTER 6

Tuesday, March 24, 2015 — Los Angeles, California

John Tall Wolf found his way to a locked door on Melrose Avenue between Fairfax and Crescent Heights. It was situated between a hair-styling salon on one side and an art gallery on the other. Just inside the door, a stairway led up to a second-floor suite of offices. Before pressing the doorbell, Tall Wolf gave the pane of tinted material in the door a light rap: polycarbonate resin not glass. The door's frame was heavy-gauge brushed steel.

Stylish and very secure. Made Tall Wolf wonder if the area had a *serious* burglary problem. He pushed the button to announce his presence.

"Yeah?" The voice came from a speaker above Tall Wolf's head.

He instinctively looked up. Saw the camera lens that just got a good look at him. Tall Wolf gave it a cheery smile and a wave.

He said, "Keely Powell sent me. John Tall Wolf to see Jeremy Macklin."

"Hold on."

Tall Wolf looked at his watch to time the wait.

Seventy-five seconds. Long enough to make a phone call confirming his referral.

Even so, the voice said, "Show your ID to the camera."

"No."

"*No?* Then get lost."

Tall Wolf stayed right where he was, took out his phone and made his own call. "Keely? It's John. This guy Macklin you sent me to is being a dick. You might want to let all your police contacts in L.A. know. What? Okay. I'll give it a minute."

John looked back at his watch. This time the response took twenty-nine seconds.

The door buzzed open and Tall Wolf stepped inside. He walked up twenty-five steps. As he arrived at another door, a twin of the one at street level, he heard a buzz and a click. He pushed the door open. Confronting him was an open laptop computer sitting on an otherwise bare desktop. The image of a man's face twitched nervously on the screen.

There was no question the guy was scared.

"Jeremy Macklin?" Tall Wolf asked.

The head bobbed. "Why wouldn't you show me your ID?"

The BIA Co-director sighed and took out his badge and photo identification.

"People can fake these things, you know," he said. "A referral from someone you already know and trust is far more credible."

Ignoring Tall Wolf's point, the man asked him, "What's your tribe?"

"Homo sapiens."

"Come on, damnit. You know what I mean."

"Yeah, I do. Northern Apache and Navajo."

"Where'd you go to college?"

"St. John's, Santa Fe. That's the last question I'm answering. Now, here's a question for you, one I hadn't even planned to ask: What the hell's scaring you? You want me to call LAPD?"

"No."

Another buzz and click admitted Tall Wolf to an inner office. The face of the man who'd been on the computer looked even more frightened in person. He sat behind another desk, this one supporting multiple uneven stacks of paper as well as a desktop computer. Macklin, if that's who he was, had his right hand in a desk drawer.

"If you're holding a gun," Tall Wolf said, "you'd do far better to shoot yourself than a federal officer. The pain would be over much faster. And, hey ..." He held up an open right palm and put a solemn expression on his face. "I come in peace, pale face."

Despite whatever trouble he was facing, Macklin let a nervous laugh escape him.

He closed the desk drawer and showed Tall Wolf an empty hand.

"Was it you or your favorite dog whose life was threatened?" Tall Wolf asked.

"I don't have any pets," Macklin said.

"So you then. Was it something you did or something you're not supposed to do?"

"I just got a phone call telling me I'm not supposed to stay in business."

"Huh. Keely told me your little website is called *The Scandal Sheet*, and you deal in what you call 'the unedited truth.' You finally touch a nerve you shouldn't have?"

Macklin didn't reach for the drawer where he might have had a gun, but he did look in that direction, until Tall Wolf shook his head.

"I really am no threat to you. I'd say honest injun, only that'd be politically incorrect."

Macklin laughed again, and this time he couldn't stop. Until he started to sob. That went on until a sense of embarrassment overtook the man. He blew his nose in a Kleenex and said, "I'm sorry. You know, I've been threatened by a lot of people: politicians, actors, producers, cops, crooks and creeps. None of them ever scared me."

"What was different this time?" Tall Wolf asked.

"This SOB not only threatened to make me disappear, he said he had the law behind him to make it happen."

Tall Wolf's guts tightened as the words *covert rendition* came to mind.

"So you're worried about the federal government disappearing you, and I'm a fed."

Macklin's head bobbed uneasily.

"Don't worry," Tall Wolf told him. "I may be moving to Canada soon."

Buenos Aires, Argentina

Watching from a car parked at the port in Buenos Aires, Tyler Busby saw his most recent super yacht, *Wastrel*, get under way to Perth, Australia. The distance between the capital of Argentina and the city Down Under was 6,803 nautical miles. The vessel could cruise 6,000 miles at 17 knots without refueling. Throw in time to refuel and re-provision and the trip could be made in two-and-a-half weeks.

In fair seas. Without any medical emergencies. Or time to island hop and relax.

The party to whom Busby had leased *Wastrel*, though, was unlikely to be in any such hurry. Señor Juan Lopez — Spanish for Mr. John Smith — had leased the vessel for a year. It had been whispered to Busby by his leasing agent that Lopez was being set up to take the fall for the recent murder of a special prosecutor who'd been looking into charges of corruption against Argentina's president, a woman with a reputation for spite and shifting blame.

So Lopez had done the smart thing. He stole as much money as he could going out the door and fled on a vessel that could hide him in comfort for quite a while. Long enough, he hoped, for some other sucker to pay for the sins of his superiors.

If Lopez eventually did appear in remote Perth, there was the vast Western Desert of Australia to hide in, should he still be the object of pursuit. A better choice, though, would be to get on another pleasure craft and head out onto the even greater expanse of the Indian Ocean.

Alternating landlocked and floating hideaways had worked well enough for Busby — until recently. Until the completely unexpected happened and Busby fell in love. Not with Ah-lam, but with the son she'd given him.

Jonathan Kwan Busby.

The fugitive billionaire had never become a father before. Not to his knowledge anyway. When he'd learned that Ah-lam had become pregnant, despite taking every reasonable precaution she'd said, he'd thought of it as a mere annoyance. He'd even checked with the physician aboard and was assured the man knew how to perform an abortion.

That would have been that, if Ah-lam had not insisted on having the baby.

Busby told her, "If you think that will earn you a dollar more than we've already agreed upon, you couldn't be more wrong."

Ah-lam slapped his face, something no one had done since his nanny had delivered a blow for pinching her bottom. Busby hadn't known whether to laugh or have Ah-lam thrown overboard. Instead of doing either, he listened to what she had to say.

"Think, you old fool. This child has already beaten formidable odds just by forcing its own conception. With the cunning and ruthlessness he will inherit from us, what will be the limits on his achievements? He might well rule the world."

Busby doubted that. There were too many other ambitious parents and kids. Too many cross-cultural barriers to surmount. Still, discarding the hormonal bias of a pregnant woman, he could see a little critter with his genes and hers growing up to leave a hell of a mark on the world, if not rule it.

If his sperm hadn't succumbed to the defects of age, that was. He was in his seventies. Hell, his best jizz must have been produced and expended decades ago. That thought led uneasily to other foreboding ideas. What if the kid was handicapped or something? Forget about dreams of glory. How about if the whelp couldn't tie his own shoe laces?

Ah-lam read the misgivings on Busby's face like it was a billboard.

"Our son will be perfect," she told him with all the arrogance of vigorous youth.

Wanting to believe not argue, Busby's only other question was, "How do you know the baby will be a boy?"

"Wait and see. You will learn that I am right about everything."

Then she took him to bed one last time. After that came a period of abstinence longer than any other since he'd laid the nanny who'd once smacked him. The period of self-denial might have gone on indefinitely if Ah-lam hadn't said she would procure for him again. In due time.

"You need the pleasures of a woman to remain strong," she told him. "You need to be strong to set a good example for your son."

Busby had smiled inwardly upon hearing that.

Talk about a liberated woman.

Or one who didn't want to be bothered anymore.

Ah-lam was endearing, maddening and more than occasionally frightening. For all that, he thought he was coming to truly value if not love her. He was sure that she would outlive him, eventually possess all of his money and …

Damn if a shipboard sonogram didn't prove her right.

They were going to have a boy. You could see his little nub of a wienie clear as day.

In that moment, Busby felt a sense of fulfillment that all his money, power and carousing had never brought him. He'd have to do his best to keep up with Ah-lam. Not let her be the only one to influence their son's development. Busby knew better than to think he should be imperious with the child; that would only bring rebellion. He'd charm the little bugger. Let Ah-lam be the bad cop.

The mere thought of cops brought Busby up short, made him think as rich and slick as he was, the United States government and all its well-armed minions were looking for him. Eventually, they were going to find him. Lock his ass up for the handful of years he still had left, maybe even execute him outright.

Put him on the Tim McVeigh fast-track express to a date with a lethal injection.

So the question now was: What the hell could he do to jump

off that train?

The answer, in some measure, was to do what Juan Lopez had in mind. Stay out of sight until another tethered goat could be slaughtered. Only Busby would do more than hope for another victim; he would provide the fall guy.

U.S. Representative Philip Brock.

Nothing satisfied the public ire like punishing a politician.

First, though, he needed to go to the hospital and pick up little Jonathan and Ah-lam. Then they would be off to the ferry for the short trip to Uruguay. If the president of Argentina learned he'd been mucking about in her country's internal affairs, helping Lopez make his getaway, there might be a price to pay. Better to go to stable, peaceful Uruguay.

He'd already purchased a modest 14-room house in Punta del Este.

It was perfect.

Who'd ever think to look for Tyler Busby in a housing development of McMansions?

The White House — Washington, DC

Vice President Jean Morrissey stepped to the lectern in the James S. Brady Press Briefing Room. The newsies knew enough to come to their feet just as they would for the president. They were all well aware that Patricia Grant had said her number two would step up to handle domestic matters of state until her fate had been decided by the Senate. The prevailing assumption, though, was that the VP would handle things quietly, off-stage so to speak.

Her appearance before an overflow media contingent in the White House was a surprise. Press Secretary Aggie Wu had given the newspaper, Internet and TV people only 45 minutes notice. The stern look on the vice president's face and the taut posture of her body said a big story was about to break; this wasn't just a PR move by the administration.

"Please be seated," the vice president said. Once everyone

was settled and quiet, she began. "After a long and meticulous investigation, the Department of Justice has concluded that Congressman Philip Brock conspired to assassinate President Patricia Grant during a visit to Inspiration Hall in 2013. A warrant for the congressman's arrest has been issued, but the FBI has been unable to locate him at either his Washington condominium or his home in Pennsylvania.

"Congressman Brock also owns a large property in Costa Rica. At the request of our government, Costa Rican authorities went to that property to take the congressman into custody and begin extradition proceedings. But they didn't find him there either. Workers on the property in Costa Rica told the local authorities that Congressman Brock had been there recently but left after only one night in residence.

"It is the opinion of the FBI that the congressman knows of his legal jeopardy and is fleeing prosecution. The DOJ has been in touch with Interpol. Congressman Brock is now a wanted person by the international law enforcement community. Relevant authorities are searching to see if there are records of any other real estate purchases the congressman might have made abroad.

"In another matter of great concern, the FBI has arrested six members of the United States House of Representatives and four United States senators."

Rumor had spread through the Washington press corps that the FBI was looking for Brock, but not that he'd been connected to the plot to kill Patti Grant. So that was shocking enough. The second bombshell that ten members of the legislative branch had been arrested left the newsies goggle-eyed. What the hell was going on? When had the country become a banana republic?

Jean provided elucidation. "The six representatives and four senators are all members of their respective bodies' armed services committees. They are being charged with several counts of massive fraud that amount to looting the federal treasury of billions of dollars. Also under consideration is the question of whether they should be charged with complicity in the killing of Jordan Gilford who was employed by the Department of Defense in its inspector general's office."

Someone in the back of the room said, "Holy shit."

Jean gave the reporter a pointed look: *Do that again and you're out.*

Everyone else in the audience got the message, too.

"The man who shot and killed Mr. Gilford, Geronimo "Jerry" Nerón, has pled guilty to the crime and is cooperating with the Department of Justice to help investigators determine who was directly involved in hiring him to assassinate a decent and brilliant man whose job it was to make sure the taxpayer's dollars are spent honestly and efficiently. Once those individuals directly involved in the crime are identified, a determination will be made as to how far the legal liability for Mr. Gilford's death extends."

The vice president paused for a breath. Aggie Wu handed Jean a bottle of water. She took a sip and gave the bottle back.

"Our government has known the taint of scandal almost from its first days," the vice president said. "In a way, that's understandable. We're all human; we're all imperfect. We make mistakes. But the idea of settling our political differences with violence or enriching ourselves through massive acts of theft goes beyond simple personal flaws. Such boundless ambition speaks of a hunger for power and wealth that is destructive to democracy, and it must stop.

"In the near future, the Senate will be examining the motives of the president regarding the question of whether her actions were intended to result in a woman's death. As you've just heard, four members of that body are themselves now facing criminal prosecution, as are six members of the House of Representatives that impeached the president. It seems to me that this moment of crisis is also a time of opportunity. We have to set things right for both the executive and legislative branches of our government.

"Doing only half the job would be insufficient."

Jean Morrissey took a breath and lowered her head for a moment.

When she looked up there was a grim smile on her face.

"I might as well announce now that I intend to run for the presidency in 2016. It is my fervent hope that I will not take office until Inauguration Day 2017. If I should arrive in the Oval Office before then, I guarantee the American people I will do my best to see that they have a federal government, in all three branches, in which they can take pride."

Jean left the room without taking any questions.

The Oval Office

Patricia Grant and Galia Mindel looked up from the iPads on which they had just finished watching the vice president speak. The chief of staff asked the president, "Did you hear what I heard? Did the vice president just declare war on Congress?"

A contemporary take on Mona Lisa's smile etched itself on the president's face. "That and tell them her housecleaning, so to speak, is what she'll use to run for the presidency next year."

The president laughed and clapped her hands in approval.

"You didn't know this was coming, did you?" Galia asked.

The president shook her head. "No, I didn't."

"Do you approve of what she said, what she's planning?"

The president laughed again. "Approve? Galia, I'd pay to see what Jean is going to do next. I'm almost tempted to … No, I can't do that."

"What?"

"For just a moment, I thought how pleasant it would be to leave all this." Patricia Grant spread her arms to encompass the White House in particular and Washington in general. "Leave it to Jean and let her carry on the fight."

"You mean resign?" the chief of staff asked.

"Come on now, Galia, be honest. Wouldn't you like to get away, too? Do nothing but rest and read good books in a sunny place for a year or so. Recharge and then find something useful to do that doesn't require endless political battles and swarms of Secret Service agents to keep all the violent loons in the world from killing you."

"You put it that way …" The scenario the president had painted began to take root in Galia's imagination. She had to shake herself to bring her focus back to the present moment. "You said you couldn't do it, resign. Why not?"

"Jim thinks it would put me in the company of Richard Nixon."

Galia nodded. "He's right."

"I might even make Tricky Dick look good after the other side gets done smearing my reputation."

"They'd never stop doing that," Galia said. "You'd become the political gift that keeps on giving. Whether it was your politics or your gender, you'd become the right's perpetual piñata. Look how long they bashed Jimmy Carter."

"Quite a while, as I remember. Until Bill Clinton came along to be the whipping boy."

"Yeah, despite the booming economy and the first budget surplus in 50 years," Galia said. "So we stay but we don't do anything to inhibit Jean Morrissey?"

The president laughed one more time. "Hell, no. Maybe we'll have the guys in the kitchen make some popcorn for us. We'll put our feet up and enjoy the show."

Sure beat dwelling on the idea the Senate might convict her.

Austin, Texas

For just a moment, Gene Beck, uncredentialed government assassin, thought he was imagining things. He'd been running along a stretch of Bee Cave Road when he saw the first of a series of billboards that seemed to be addressed specifically to him. He blinked hard to clear his vision, make sure neither his eyes nor his mind were playing tricks on him.

The first sign said: *Clean Gene …*

Followed by: You're not invisible …

Time to get to work …

Before your world turns miserable.

Beck didn't think for a minute that someone was trying revive Burma Shave jingles. The SOB who wanted him to kill James J. McGill was telling him that not only had he been found — right down to knowing the routes he liked to run on a given day — he was also threatening Beck with dire consequences if he didn't play ball.

To his credit, Beck didn't break stride or otherwise call attention to himself, and by the time he'd passed the final billboard an indignant rage burned with him. Did this asshole know who he was fucking with? He'd rip the guy's throat out with a claw-hand grab right there in public if he had the chance.

Of course, the bastard knew enough not to come within arm's reach.

Still, he might be watching. Observing whether Beck was smart enough to understand his message or had even noticed the signs. If Beck ignored the threat, the guy might feel he had to get closer to make his point. Come within hands-on range. Maybe not, though. He might just make good on the warning. Drop a ton of shit on Beck from 30,000 feet, move on and get some other sap to do his dirty work.

Beck turned around well short of his intended destination. He zigged and zagged on the way back to his rental house, hoping to catch a glimpse of someone following him. Thinking about things as he ran, Beck decided that his recruiter and handler, Nicholas Wicklow, wouldn't be stupid enough to try to blackmail him.

Wicklow had accepted Beck's vetoes of legitimate jobs he hadn't wanted to do. He'd had to. If Beck ever went public with what he was doing for the government, Wicklow would go to prison, too. Well, that would be Wicklow's fate if someone higher on the DIA's organizational table didn't kill Beck's handler first to give the military spook shop plausible deniability.

Hey, the big-timer could say, I didn't know Wicklow had gone renegade.

Still, Wicklow must have told his superiors about the jobs Beck had accepted, the ones that had worked out just fine. From the Pentagon's point of view anyway. The bastards Beck had killed wouldn't have agreed.

Maybe Wicklow wasn't feeling so good about things these days either. What if some DIA muckety-muck had Wicklow killed preemptively, *before* Beck had been tasked with knocking off the president's husband? That would eliminate any link between Beck and the DIA, and if Wicklow was already dead from some innocuous cause, say a fall off a ladder, it would look a lot less suspicious than if he died after Beck had made an accusation against the DIA.

With Wicklow the victim of an accident, any charge Beck might make against the military's spy shop would be dismissed as a paranoid delusion, publicly accepted as such, and after a suitable length of time Beck might suffer his own mishap. No, that *would* look suspicious. It'd be better if he just disappeared.

Of course, Beck knew, he wouldn't be safe even if he somehow managed to kill James J. McGill. If you agreed to play the part of Lee Harvey Oswald, you could be sure Jack Ruby was waiting in the wings. At that moment, Beck couldn't see any good way out for himself.

The best he could do was buy time.

He at least had to *look* like he was going to kill McGill.

Los Angeles

McGill took Mindy Crozier, the security guard from the fertility clinic, to breakfast at Canter's Deli on Fairfax. He'd once taken his younger daughter, Caitie, there when he'd gone to visit her during a movie shoot she was doing at Paramount, not far away on Melrose. Both of the young women had chosen the deli because it offered breakfast 24 hours a day.

It was closer to lunch time but Mindy ordered the banana pancakes. She'd had to keep a dental appointment before meeting with McGill. He went with a BLT and kettle chips. Deke Ky, sitting alone at a table opposite McGill's booth and keeping an eye out for any menace greater than a plate of high cholesterol, asked for a cup of coffee which he didn't touch.

Nobody working at the deli kvetched about such a stingy order taking up a table. They remembered McGill and the tip he'd left from his last visit. More than one staffer asked where his cute daughter was, and mentioned that they were still behind the president. McGill's heart warmed on both counts.

Once they were left alone with their meals, Mindy said, "It must really be something, being married to the president, huh?"

McGill noticed Deke tilt his head ever so slightly, the better to hear the response.

He said, "Being married to my wife is the highlight of my life; her being the president is another matter entirely."

"Yeah, but the two of you never would have met if she hadn't gotten into politics, right?"

McGill gave the young woman a look. Her eyes looked tired from being up all night, but otherwise she was the picture of youth and health. Clear complexion, freshly polished teeth, trim figure but not a workout fiend. A Girl Scout just coming into full bloom.

In some ways, she reminded him of his older daughter, Abbie.

She responded to McGill's silent examination by saying, "Sorry, I didn't mean to get personal. I just thought I should read up on you a little, after you said you'd like to talk with me. Hope that's all right."

McGill smiled. "It's more than all right. It's what any good cop would do, check out the other guy before you put yourself into an uncertain situation."

"Thanks, but I'm not so sure about becoming a cop anymore."

"No?"

"Unh-uh. I'm not so sure I'm even going to keep working security much longer."

"Because of what happened at the clinic," McGill said.

"Yes. The paramedics who came to take me to the hospital? The older one said getting hit by a taser is the closest thing to knowing what it's like to be struck by lightning."

"You check that out, too?" McGill asked.

She nodded. "I did the research, if that's what you mean. A taser packs 50,000 volts. Lightning, they think, could go as high as a billion."

"Amazing anyone survives that."

"Sure is. Even a 50K jolt like the taser can mess with a person's memory or keep her from thinking straight. But I'm clear-minded enough to know I don't ever want to get tased again. Or shot either."

"Perfectly sensible," McGill said.

"Kind of chicken-hearted, too." Mindy made a couple of clucking sounds. Her eyes brightened when McGill laughed. "I read that you and the special agent over there have both been shot, and you both stayed on your jobs."

"Sure, but everyone knows women are smarter than men."

"I don't know about that. We make mistakes, too. We just usually keep ours more private." She grimaced and shook her head. "Only a few of us cartoon characters get their heinies zapped when they're supposed to be holding down the fort."

McGill grinned. He liked Mindy's spirit "Don't be too hard on yourself. You were set up."

That assertion changed her mood in a hurry. "What do you mean?"

"Dr. Hansen told me you need to correctly hit a seven-key sequence to open the door the thief used to enter the clinic."

"That's right."

"Well, that'd mean there are 5,040 different possible combinations just using the numbers on the keypad. But there are two more keys, an asterisk and a pound sign. So now we're talking hundreds of thousands of combinations."

Mindy saw where McGill was going. "But whoever zapped me got it right on the first try."

"Someone tell you that?" McGill asked.

She shook her head. "I checked the digital log."

"Good for you. Does the log keep a record of when people hit the wrong keys and have to start over?"

"Yes, it does. You get only two tries to get it right or someone inside has to let you in. Usually, that happens only when there's been an office party and somebody had a little too much to drink at lunch."

"So what does it say that the thief got it right the first time, other than he hadn't been drinking?" McGill asked.

"He knew the code and practiced," Mindy said. "It wasn't his first time; he's a pro."

"Right. Now, the code for the keypad, how often is it changed? Regularly, I hope."

"Yes, first of every month."

"Does the new code come from someone in the clinic or someone at the security company that installed the system?"

Mindy blinked twice. "I don't know."

"You think you could find out, discreetly?"

She thought about that. "Yes, I think I could."

"The LAPD is going to look into the source of the code, too. They'll investigate to see how many people had access to it."

"Then why do I need to look? Just to help you?"

"Pretty much. But I think the thief is most likely not an Angeleno. If he lives outside the city, that'll mean the LAPD will have to get another police entity involved. Who knows how much importance they'll place on the theft? The whole thing might go into a figurative deep freeze, and the guy who zapped you can rest easy."

Mindy frowned. She didn't like that idea.

McGill had another unhappy thought for her.

"You should be prepared to have Detectives Zapata and MacDuff consider you as a suspect, a person who knew the code and might have provided it to the thief."

"Me? But I got —"

"Your heinie zapped? Yeah. What could be better cover for an accomplice? You're young and healthy. Chances were you wouldn't be permanently hurt."

"How do you know how healthy I am?" she asked.

McGill let her work it out.

"You checked up on me, just like I did with you."

He nodded. "I even looked at your extracurriculars in high school and college. No drama club or acting classes. Some people can lie effectively without any training, but I don't think you're one of them. I don't think you were in on the theft either. I can't say how the local cops will feel about that, though."

Deke caught McGill's eye. "Here comes the LAPD now."

Zapata and MacDuff had just entered the deli. They spotted McGill and headed his way.

Deke got to his feet, screening McGill and Mindy from the cops.

"You don't have to help me if you feel uneasy about it," McGill told Mindy, slipping her one of his business cards. "But if you'd like to lend a hand, I'd appreciate it. You don't have to say anything to the cops about that, but otherwise play it straight with them. Okay?"

She nodded and slipped his card into a pocket.

"Will you stick around if they start asking me questions?" Mindy asked.

"Sure," McGill said, "if that's what you want."

"I do."

Santa Monica Municipal Airport

John Tall Wolf told Jeremy Macklin they could wait in the SMPD substation at the airport, but the tabloid reporter opted for the observation deck instead. The day was clear and the Santa Monica mountains stood out in sharp relief. Palm fronds rustled in a light breeze. The beach and the ocean were a short drive to the west.

"I appreciate what you're doing, believe me," Macklin said, "but, damn, I'm going to miss this place."

"Picture postcard day," Tall Wolf agreed. "Feel free to change your mind."

Macklin laughed. "Like I have a choice. Besides, I already paid for the charter flight and the landing fee here at the airport."

"Yeah, you might as well go."

Back at Macklin's office, Tall Wolf had explained to the reporter that he needn't fear being locked up in some grim foreign prison for years.

"Why not?" Macklin asked.

"Because it would be so much simpler just to kill you."

The reporter's mouth fell open, but he remained speechless. Couldn't find a word to rebut Tall Wolf's point. Eventually, though, he managed to ask the obvious question: "What do I do now?"

Tall Wolf said he had an idea, and that led the two of them to the airport.

They were awaiting the arrival of an executive jet.

Seemed an unnecessary risk to Tall Wolf to expose themselves to public view and conceivably a sniper shot, but he didn't see any vantage point where a shooter might set up. Besides, nobody knew they were going to the airport, and he hadn't seen anyone following them from Macklin's office. In the real world, bad guys needed time to work out their plans like anyone else. They didn't just step out of a shadow for the convenience of the script.

The only person Tall Wolf had ever met who didn't appear to be bound by the shackles of mundane reality was Marlene Flower Moon. She seemed able to come and go with the ease of a breeze. She also often knew things without having a perceptible source of information.

Then again, Tall Wolf thought his co-director at the BIA might be the human manifestation of a supernatural being known to Native Americans as Coyote.

He wondered if he should ask Marlene for help sorting out this new situation.

Not yet, he decided. He didn't want to owe Coyote a favor.

He told Macklin, "I never got around to asking you about Mira Kersten."

"The political talking head? What about her?"

Tall Wolf decided how best to order his questions. He took

out his phone, set it to audio record and asked, "Do you know of any paparazzi who've taken an interest in her? If so, who are they and what's the attraction? Is there any special man in Ms. Kersten's life? If so, who is he? Is there any dissonance between Ms. Kersten's public persona and her private behavior?"

That last inquiry drew a laugh from Macklin. "You mean is she two-faced? Hell, in this town or any other, what public figure isn't?"

"So you do know a thing or two about her?" Tall Wolf asked.

Macklin nodded. "Look, paparazzi suck the blood of celebrities who sell tabloids in supermarkets. Ms. Kersten, from the photos I've seen of her, isn't bad looking but she's no movie star, model or even TV newsbabe. She gets people elected to offices most other people don't think about twice a year, if that. Or she used to. Now she *talks* about getting people elected to those same boring jobs."

"So why would any paparazzo bother with her?" Tall Wolf asked.

"Well, here's the thing, if one half of a couple is a cipher to the general public maybe the other half isn't. If that's the case, you might have a Cinderella story going."

"Okay, who's playing Prince Charming here?"

"That's the reason a handful of the more enterprising ambush jockeys have been sniffing around her. They want to know, too. So far, no one has found out, but the rumor persists. Of course, Kersten might just be screwing with their heads for her own laughs."

"Okay, but what's the speculation about who the man might be?"

"Someone who shares her liberal views, someone in show biz with the good looks to prove it, and someone who is a more than a bit younger. That's one of the big hooks: the reversal of the older man, younger woman roles. It plays right into the fantasies of the supermarket shopper."

Tall Wolf wouldn't argue with that but he pursued another angle. "Could there be any tangible benefit to Ms. Kersten? Any way such an association might advance *her* career?"

Macklin laughed. "Everybody looking out for number one is another universal truth. If the lady was an actress there might be a bump in the number of roles she landed, if her sweetheart has that kind of juice. But, hell, what I've heard is the TV station that airs Ms. Kersten's political talk show is going to pull the plug any day. Its audience is smaller than what you get with infomercials. I don't know *anyone* who has the pull to keep it on the air."

Both men turned their heads as they heard the approach of jet engines.

A sleek executive jet started to make its descent into the airport.

"Your ride," Tall Wolf told Macklin.

"Your sure this is going to work?" the reporter asked.

John had called his cousin, Arnoldo Black Knife, president of the tribal council of the Northern Apache reservation in New Mexico. With just a bit of dickering they'd worked out an agreement to stash Jeremy Macklin in a cabin that featured both electricity and indoor plumbing for at least a month and no more than a year. Macklin would pay a market rate rent and would serve as volunteer editor on the newspaper of the rez high school.

Arnoldo would also see to it that no one from outside the rez would be allowed to arrest Macklin. Would even hide him if the feds pressed their case. The FBI had exclusive jurisdiction on reservations for charges of murder and certain other serious crimes. How an interpretation of a shadowy violation of the Patriot Act might be resolved was anybody's guess.

But if Arnoldo said Macklin would be safe for a year, Tall Wolf trusted him to keep his word. Macklin bought in because he had no better choice.

Tall Wolf saw Macklin onto the plane, exchanged an embrace and a few words with Arnoldo and then returned to his car. He called McGill first thing and mentioned that he'd gone to see a tabloid Internet reporter.

Then he told the president's husband, "I tried to call you earlier. Got sent to your voice mail three times. You haven't checked your messages, I guess."

"No," McGill said. "I was interviewing the security guard from the fertility clinic, and then at her request I kept her company while the detectives from LAPD questioned her. I'm pretty sure they've eliminated her as a suspect in the clinic robbery."

"How about you?" Tall Wolf asked.

"I've definitely eliminated her."

"Because?"

"It'd be out of character with everything I've learned about her, and there's been no recent legal or medical crisis in her life that would cause her to commit a crime out of desperation."

Tall Wolf was tempted to ask what sources McGill used to glean his information, but he decided he'd rather not know if the man could tap into law enforcement or national intelligence databases.

He only said, "Your relationship with LAPD remains amicable?"

"Zapata and MacDuff were annoyed that I got to sit in on their interview and that it was conducted in a deli instead of their office, but I made a point of telling Ms. Crozier to cooperate fully with the police."

"And you had Special Agent Ky nearby," Tall Wolf said.

"Yes, I did," McGill replied. "Anyway, I had my phone off for a couple of hours. So what'd I miss?"

Tall Wolf told him the details of his interview with Jeremy Macklin.

"The man received two phone calls that scared him badly. One threatened him with a government covert rendition if he published information he said he'd received only minutes earlier. The first call frightened him, too."

"What'd the first caller say?" McGill asked.

"He said someone is on his way to kill you."

McGill fell silent for a moment.

Allowing Tall Wolf to add, "I imagine someone in your position has received more than one death threat, but for the time-being I think you probably should leave your phone on."

The White House — Washington, DC

Unlike her predecessor, Celsus Crogher, Elspeth Kendry, the Secret Service special agent in charge of the presidential protection detail, was known to sleep at night. She'd even snatch cat-naps in her office after having pulled an all-nighter. With Holly G. — the president's code name — having been impeached by the House and about to be tried by the Senate, every homicidal loon in the country with a political axe to grind seemed to think he now had license to announce that he was going to save the country the time and expense of going through the Constitutional remedy for removing a wayward president.

By God, he was coming to get her.

And there were droves like that.

Many of the threats were sent directly to the White House and signed with real names. Some of the criminally indignant were so certain they were acting on God's orders they included their home addresses. Those were the easy ones to arrest. The attorney general made his own public statement: Anyone who threatened the life or well-being of the president would be tried and if convicted would serve a very long sentence in a federal prison.

Testing that warning, Destin E. Conden, the owner of a wholesale plumbing supply company and proud possessor of a messiah complex, posted a YouTube video showing him with his AK-47. He said, "I'm gonna shoot that damn woman and anyone who tries to stop me."

Just what woman he meant was made clear by the photo of Patricia Grant with a bull's-eye superimposed atop her face. The picture was affixed to the wall behind Conden. On the wall next to the picture was a copy of the Great Seal of the Commonwealth of Virginia, featuring the state motto: *Sic Semper Tyrannis*. Thus Always to Tyrants. John Wilkes Booth's cruel farewell to Abraham Lincoln.

The second visual reference might have been an attempt at misdirection, though not much of one as Conden was a resident of neighboring Maryland. It might also have been he didn't think his home-state motto *Fatti maschil, parole femine* — Manly Deeds, Womanly Words — carried the same sense of theatrical menace.

Whatever the case, Conden was so cocksure of the righteousness of his cause that he put his money where his mouth was. "Now, I know I'm not alone in gunning for this horrible woman, but I've got $10,000 that says I get her before any of you other boys do. If you do beat me to the draw, though, I'll pay you that money gladly."

Conden was arrested less than thirty minutes after his video was posted. The video was taken down but not before the FBI received a call asking if the bounty would still be paid even if Conden, you know, got himself arrested. The FBI told the caller to drop by and they'd see what they could work out.

Jesus, Elspeth thought when she got that report, thank God so many of these fools were so stupid. Problem was, they weren't *all* morons. Some of them had the smarts to match their malice. They were the ones who kept Elspeth awake most nights.

She was just about to catch forty winks on her office couch when her phone rang. She might have let it go through to a duty officer but she saw Holmes' name come up on the caller ID. James J. McGill, as much of a pain in the ass as he might otherwise be, never called frivolously. He took the president's safety very seriously, even if he was cavalier about his own.

She answered the call.

"SAC Kendry, sir. How may I help?"

McGill said, "I've just been informed about a possible threat to my life." He provided the details. "This one might be serious, Elspeth. Much as I hate to do it, I think I'd better ask for someone to back up Deke. Just one special agent, someone good, but I don't want a brigade."

"Yes, sir. I'll get right on it."

She went immediately to Galia Mindel and the two of them proceeded to the Oval Office.

The president listened closely to what her husband had told

the SAC.

For her part, Elspeth asked that a brigade be sent to protect McGill.

The president vetoed that.

She sent Elspeth instead.

Carmel, California

Ed Whelan had once been in love with Alfa Romeo Spiders, ever since seeing Dustin Hoffman and Katharine Ross in "The Graduate." But after he and his leading lady, Mira Kersten, got divorced, he switched to Porsche Boxsters. He'd briefly considered stepping up to the Porsche 911 for its quicker acceleration and greater cachet, but he decided the Boxster was as far as he could go and still pretend that he held nothing more than a middling position in Washington's pyramid of power.

The pretense of being something less than he was, though, had worn thin.

So had the hair at the crown of his scalp, damnit. He'd never been vain about his appearance before because he'd effortlessly held on to his small-town-boy good looks. True, he'd first noticed the incipient bald spot when he'd celebrated his fortieth birthday, six years ago. But noticing it had been a fluke, an unexpected alignment of two mirrors had provided a glimpse.

He couldn't say he deliberately avoided looking at dual mirrors from then on, but even his hair stylist didn't show him his haircut from the rear view any more, and he didn't have to ask why. He certainly didn't *request* to see the extent of the defoliation back there.

What really grated on him was the more hair he lost the more he wanted a 911. Maybe even a Tesla Model S. Zero to 60 in just over three seconds. He wouldn't stop with just a fancy car either. He'd need high-end houses, at least two, a summer home in Newport and a loft in Manhattan. Possibly a villa somewhere warm and fashionable as well.

Owning an executive jet would probably be a hassle, what with needing a place to base it, upkeep and having pilots on the payroll, but he could see signing up for a good lease.

He could also see that he was feeling a powerful need to compensate not just for losing his hair but coming to acknowledge that his grand plan for conservative political dominance wasn't as foolproof as he'd thought in years gone by. He'd seriously underestimated the willingness and ability of the liberals to fight back.

Patricia Grant had fallen more or less into a defensive crouch, as he'd thought she would, but he hadn't anticipated the emergence of a bare-knuckle brawler like Jean Morrissey. Then again, Patti Grant might be playing things just right. She was the one who'd picked Morrissey to be her new vice president and had given her unprecedented say over domestic policy.

The president must have had, at the very least, an idea how her number two would respond to being given the opportunity to strike back at a Congress threatening to remove her boss from office. After all, Jean Morrissey hadn't been the captain of her school's debate team; she'd been the enforcer and the high scorer on the ice hockey team.

He probably shouldn't have been surprised at Morrissey's fighting spirit.

For just a moment, Whelan wondered what the VP would be like in bed.

He quickly decided to push that thought aside.

The damn woman was scary enough fully clothed. She had Whelan's nominal boss, House Whip Carter Coleman of Oklahoma scared shitless. Him and Speaker Peter Profitt of North Carolina.

Both men had spoken to Whelan shortly before he'd decided it was time to scoot down the road from Carmel. In what he now thought was a totally inadequate Boxster. Profitt had been even more wrought up than Coleman.

"You can see how this might play out, can't you?" the speaker asked.

Whelan could foresee several scenarios, but he asked, "What

do you have in mind, sir?"

"Well, goddamnit, Jean Morrissey already has half our caucus soiling their britches. They've read between the lines of her statement from the White House. If we're out for the president's blood, she'll be out for ours. And with those goddamn fools on the Armed Services Committees in both chambers looking like they've stolen billions, there's good reason for all of us to be scared.

"Of course, if we go ahead and convict Patti Grant, that'll make Jean Morrissey president. The first thing she'll do is pardon her predecessor, just like Jerry Ford did with Nixon. That's bound to raise calls in the House for the new president's impeachment."

Whelan couldn't help but add color to that picture.

"And you'd be next in line for the Oval Office, Mr. Speaker."

"If you think I'd take the job that way, Ed, you're not the genius we all hope you are. If Jean Morrissey becomes commander in chief and we try to take her down, too, she'd probably have the military round us all up and pack us off to Guantanamo."

"Or beat all of us to death with a hockey stick." That popped out before Whelan could stop himself. He was mildly pleased that the joke drew two nervous laughs.

Still, the speaker and the whip's fear was real. Things were going exactly the opposite of the way Whelan had predicted they would. His side was getting weak-kneed and queasy and liberals were the ones acting like they had brass balls. Even the women.

"We're counting on you to get things turned around, Ed," the speaker said, as if he'd been reading Whelan's mind.

And somewhere in the back of Whelan's mind he heard his old boss, a previous speaker, laugh and tell him, "Serves you right, being in this fix, you turncoat bastard."

Feeling a sense of defiance toward the ghost of his past, Whelan said, "Gentlemen, you can count on me." He left things there.

Scanning his smart phone as he headed south on the Pacific Coast Highway, Whelan found the locations of two stops he wanted to make. Stop one was a high-end hair stylist. His first request was beneath the talents of artists working there: Shave his head.

He wasn't going to fight the damn bald spot; he would embrace it.

Whelan's second appeal called for artistic judgment, and all three stylists working in the shop offered their considered opinions on the question: What type of facial hair should Whelan grow to balance his newly denuded pink scalp. The consensus was a modified goatee. To the classic lines of the beard covering the upper lip and chin, he was advised to add a razor thin line of growth extending along the jaw line on either side of the face to the mandible and up to the points opposite his earlobes.

Whelan had his doubts. Then they showed him the look on a computer illustration and he thought, "What the hell?"

His only misgiving was he probably should have grown the beard first.

At the moment, his head looked a bit egg-like.

That didn't stop him from going to a Tesla dealership a mile away.

When a fine-looking saleswoman greeted him with a non-judgmental smile and asked if she might be of help, Whelan said, "I'd like to buy a Batmobile."

She laughed and replied, "Oh, we can do much better than that."

Florida Avenue — Washington, DC

When Sweetie returned home from dropping Maxi off at school, she found a black limo parked at the curb out front. Looked like it could be either Thing One or Thing Two, the presidential Cadillacs. But the faces of the Secret Service agents standing athwart the steps leading up to her front door were unfamiliar. She knew most of Patti's protection detail.

These people belonged to someone else.

And she was unknown to them.

"Please keep moving, ma'am," the guy with the most gray in his hair said.

Sweetie replied, "I would only you're blocking my front door."

"Your name, please?" the guy asked, his tone softening slightly.

Sweetie gave him her full legal name: "Margaret Mary Sweeney Shady."

He tapped it into his smart phone. Sweetie's image came up, above a list of information, including, it seemed, where she might have been just now.

"You took your daughter to school, ma'am?"

"I did, and then I dropped in on an old friend, the president of the United States."

She smiled to let the guy know she was kidding, but also to remind him she worked with Jim McGill and was, in fact, a friend of the president.

"Of course, ma'am."

"Who's inside my house that dragged all you people along for the ride?"

"The vice president called to ask if she might have a moment with Mr. Shady. Must've have happened after you left home. They shouldn't be long."

"They can take their sweet time, and it'll be fine by me. I'm going inside. It's my house."

The senior special agent made the wise choice. "Of course, I'll see you inside and advise the vice president that you've returned home."

Sweetie could live with that. She gestured to the guy to lead on. Another agent, without needing to be told, trailed after Sweetie. She didn't complain.

A moment later, she even smiled when she heard her husband, Putnam, call out, "We're in the kitchen, Margaret. Come on in and join the party."

Putnam and Jean Morrissey appeared to be having tea at the kitchen table. Green tea and honey, using the good china, with a plate of Mint Milanos as a grace note. Jean Morrissey got to her feet as Sweetie entered the room. Putnam stood, too, and gave his wife a wink.

The vice president extended a hand and said, "Ms. Shady, a pleasure to meet you."

Jean gave a nod to the agent who'd walked Sweetie in and he left, taking his subordinate with him.

"Good to meet you, too, Ms. Vice President."

The two women, both tall, blonde and strong, took each other's measure. Sweetie was maybe five years older. The resemblance was not quite strong enough for sisters, but cousins to one degree or another might have been a possibility.

"Cup of tea, my dear?" Putnam asked his wife.

"Thanks, but I don't want to intrude. I'll just get back to my knitting."

Jean Morrissey laughed. "Please stay. I'd like my conversation with your husband to remain confidential for now, but I'm sure you know how to keep a secret or two, working with Jim McGill and being a friend of the president."

Sweetie nodded. "I value my privacy, and I respect other people's privacy."

Putnam pulled out a chair at the table and filled a cup for his wife. Once everyone was seated and Sweetie was served, Putnam looked at Jean Morrissey. "May I, Ms. Vice President."

"Please speak freely," Jean said.

Putnam looked at Sweetie and said, "The vice president came to ask my opinion of whether Cool Blue would support her running for president on our party's ticket in 2016. I told her we weren't considering a presidential campaign so soon, but it is a wonderfully intriguing idea."

"It's more than that," Sweetie said. "It's an opportunity that's too good to miss." Turning to Jean, she said, "I'd already decided you'd be my first choice even before you made your announcement."

The vice president beamed. "That's great to hear, but you don't know what my plans are."

"Me neither," Putnam said.

Before Jean could say anything, Sweetie looked at her and said, "You're going to kick some serious backside once you're in office, aren't you?"

Jean laughed and asked Sweetie, "Did you ever play hockey? No, it doesn't matter. I'm sure the two of us are kindred spirits."

"Maybe in more ways than anyone knows," Sweetie said.

Putnam asked, "What do you mean, Sweetie?"

She took a deep breath, looked at Jean and then at Putnam, "I mean, after much thought and counseling, I've decided to stop being any kind of a cop. Maybe it wasn't my fault that Erna Godfrey is dead, but it was my idea that led to her death. I still want to be of service, though, so I've decided to —"

"Run for some sort of office," Jean said with a tone of certainty. "You intend to go into politics."

Sweetie looked at the vice president and they both felt an intuitive connection.

"Only in a very small way," Sweetie said, "but since I live in Washington now and this is where Putnam and I will be raising our daughter, I thought maybe I could run for a city council seat." She turned to look at her husband.

Putnam Shady thought he had heard it all in Washington.

Nothing could surprise him — until just now.

He told Sweetie, "Maybe we should talk about this later."

"Sure," Sweetie said.

"Or I could get out of your way right now," Jean suggested, getting to her feet.

Putnam stood and extended a hand. Jean shook it.

"Ms. Vice President, it's been a pleasure meeting you. Cool Blue intended to wait and see how well we fared in the near term before putting up a presidential candidate, but I like the idea of your joining the party at the top of the ticket. I'll speak with Darren Drucker about it, if you'd like me to do that."

"I would," Jean said. "But let's keep this from going public for the time being."

"Right. Before you go, I'd like to get your take on another interesting idea that came my way quite recently. How would you feel about Cool Blue recruiting Native American candidates to run for

Congress?"

The vice president nodded. "Seems like a natural to me. Only I've heard from some indigenous people that they preferred to be identified by the names of their tribes or bands."

"Learn a new thing every day," Putnam said.

Confirming his point, he turned to look at Sweetie.

The Sails Marina — Fort Lauderdale, Florida

Carina Linberg had just finished a day's writing when her phone rang. Had that happened even a minute earlier, she would have let the call go to voice-mail. In fact, she was a bit surprised she hadn't muted the ring tone. She didn't like to be disturbed when she was working.

As it was, she picked up the instrument and said, "You have good timing."

It wouldn't be just anyone, however. The software for the system rang through only pre-approved numbers. The caller had to be one of a select few business contacts or one of an even smaller number of people who interested her personally.

That was when she saw the caller's name on the ID screen: Yates, Capt. Welborn.

She added merrily, "Stuck in rank, are you?"

"By my own choosing," Welborn replied.

"Is that so?"

"I had to fight off a promotion to major."

"Of course. You should be a colonel by now."

"And how are you Carina? I kept looking for your TV show, 'Woman in Command,' but I couldn't find it, not even on Netflix."

She sighed. It was only fair that he should jab her after she'd been so catty with him. "I'm afraid that project sank after Sir Edbert Bickford took his fatal plunge. I did get paid, though, quite a bit of money for handing in one ne'er-to-be produced script."

"So do you still have your boat?"

"*Irish Grace* and I are inseparable. It's where I do all my work."

"That work being?"

"Under the guise of a pen name, I write novels, the naughty kind ladies are ashamed to admit they love." She told him her *nom de plume.*

"That's you? I'm surprised poor old *Grace* isn't your dinghy these days."

"I'm faithful 'til the end, though I wouldn't hold it against you if you weren't."

"Kira and I just took the twins to meet the queen at her palace in London."

"Swell, but what are you doing for fun on Saturday night?"

Welborn laughed. "Come on now. As a glamorous woman with a huge and growing fortune, you must have no end of gentlemen admirers."

"The money looks fine and gets more appealing all the time, but I've gotten way too much sun on my boat the past few years."

With a note of concern, Welborn asked, "Skin cancer?"

"Not quite that bad, but my wrinkles are hideous. Though there are a few spots I've kept shielded if you'd care to take a look. Or did you call just to remind me how much younger you are?"

Welborn chose not to comment on the offer of a peep show. "I called because I need a bit of help from someone who might know how military spooks work, and I thought a former Air Force intelligence officer who worked at the Pentagon might be a good place to start."

"I used to have some knowledge of that kind of thing, but what they're up to these days I really couldn't say. I'm not even supposed to say what was going on way back when."

"Might be something here you could use for a book, if you make a few judicious changes."

"Ooh. You remember when I said I wished you had a bit of the rascal in you?"

"I do, but we're not talking about that kind of personal failing here," Welborn said.

"Damn. Still, you're not just leading me on about the story

material, are you?"

"No. If you have some contacts from either your military or reporting days who might be willing to chat, you could say you're researching the idea on your own."

That was another reason Welborn had called: to keep himself at a careful distance.

Carina recognized that immediately and laughed. "First, you'll have to promise you'll come visit me in prison."

"How about I promise you won't go to prison, not for helping me anyway."

"You know what?"

"What?" Welborn asked.

"I think you are a rascal in your own way, and I'd feel better about all this if you were a colonel."

"But —"

"Unh-uh,"Carina said. "If you expect me to believe you can keep me out of the pokey, show me you can manage another good trick. Like a big jump in rank, overnight."

"You want me to become a colonel by tomorrow?"

"Yeah, let's see what you can do."

"I may have to look elsewhere for help."

"Okay, maybe a captain is all you were ever meant to be."

"I'm thinking of moving my family to Los Angeles and writing for television."

After a moment of silence, Carina said, "That would rankle, if you succeeded at something I couldn't. All right, I'll tell you what. Become a major by tomorrow, since you say that rank was already offered to you, and that will show me that you're still wired into the powers that be."

Welborn sighed. "The things I do for my country."

The Supreme Court Building — Washington, DC

After hearing a polite knock at his office door, Chief Justice of the United States Craig MacLaren said, "Come in."

Associate Justice Daniel Crockett entered the chief's inner sanctum and closed the door behind him. "Celia said it'd be okay to drop in. I caught her just as she was heading for home. Otherwise, she'd have buzzed and announced me. I said I didn't think we needed to stand on formality."

"If this is just a casual call, Daniel, you won't mind if I offer you a drink," MacLaren said.

Crockett grinned. "There are times when I'm sitting on the bench that I wouldn't mind a drink."

The chief nodded. "Every judge's dirty little secret. You still drinking that Van Winkle stuff?"

"It comes from Kentucky," said the former senator from Tennessee, "but I'll choke down a glass anyway."

"Very hospitable of you." The chief went to his liquor cabinet, found the right bottle and poured two fingers for each of them. He handed Crockett a glass and retook his seat. "So you simply dropped in to chat, Daniel? Shoot the breeze about your minor aches and pains or how the kids are doing in their new professions?"

"Sorry to disappoint, Chief. No physical miseries to report. My offspring are cruising along like fate doesn't have any nasty tricks in mind for them." Crockett put his glass down and steepled his hands in divine supplication on the latter point.

"Good. So then, what brings you around?"

Crockett reclaimed his glass. "I don't know if any our brethren or …" For a moment, Crockett looked stumped. "What's the female equivalent of brethren?"

"The girls," MacLaren said with a laugh.

Crockett chuckled. "Oh, yeah, that'd win the hearts of the female members of the court."

"We'll keep it our secret. I have the feeling you're here to speak confidentially anyway."

"Yes and no. I was asked by our colleagues to let you know they're already chafing under the increased security that's been imposed upon us as a result of the threat on your life. The others would like to know if the Court Police and the FBI have made any progress with their investigation. Justice Kern said there are cops everywhere but under her robe with her."

"They'd like to be there, too," MacLaren said, "but I told them our spouses might object."

Crockett ignored the jest and focused on the point. "Has Mrs. MacLaren objected?"

"Not to the increased security. She wants more, if anything. What she's raising hell about is the idea that things have come to this state of affairs. It's understandable, she feels, that the president needs massive protection, but the president is a singular figure. A lightning rod, if you will. But the court is equal in number to the starting lineup of a baseball team."

"And we don't even appear in a pack of trading cards with a sheet of bubble-gum included," Crockett said with a grin. "Where that analogy breaks down, though, Chief, is your office is as unique as the president's."

MacLaren downed his drink. "It is, and here I thought it was a great honor. To answer your question, I don't know how close our minders are to setting us relatively free."

"How real does the threat feel to you, Chief?"

"It seems real, unreal and surreal. Having all the cops crowding us tells me they think it's serious, and they'd know far better about such things than you or me. Even so, there are moments when I have to shake my head and say, 'Come on, this can't be happening.' And then there are brief periods when I feel like I'm an actor in a movie, only I don't know if I'm a character who survives or gets it in the head."

Crockett grunted. "That last possibility is worrisome. You might be a survivor and the poor sap next to you gets shot by mistake."

MacLaren laughed.

"That's funny?" Crockett asked.

"You just brought an image to mind, Daniel. My sitting alone hearing arguments with eight cardboard cutouts of my colleagues joining me. See what I mean about surreal?"

The associate justice grinned. "That is sort of funny. So is the idea, no disrespect intended, that you'll play a pivotal role in the trial of the president. You administer oaths or affirmations to the senators who will decide the innocence or guilt of the president. Otherwise, you'll sit there and look solemn.Your role is more ceremonial than judicial. That and to make sure the president *pro tem* of the senate — the vice president of the United States, one of those nasty politicians — doesn't get to preside."

"In this case the president *pro tem* would be Jean Morrissey," MacLaren said. "Wouldn't that be interesting, to see her as the ringmaster of this circus?"

"That's a colorful characterization — circus — isn't it, Chief?" Crockett asked.

MacLaren got up and fetched the bottle of bourbon, poured each of them another drink.

He left the Pappy Van Winkle on his desk, as if the bottle might be tapped yet again.

"You're a constitutional scholar, Daniel. Tell me what happened in the matter of the Senate trial of President Andrew Johnson, a Democrat, in 1868. Not the outcome, but how the Republican majority in the senate interacted with Chief Justice Salmon Chase."

Crockett knew the answer but felt uneasy about where MacLaren might be going.

"Chase claimed the authority to decide procedural questions on his own. The Senate majority overruled him twice."

"Right. Jumping ahead to the 20th century Senate trial of President William Clinton, Democrat, what happened when Chief Justice Rehnquist decided *he* could rule on procedural questions?"

"The Republican majority neither objected to nor overruled the Republican chief justice."

MacLaren sipped his drink. "Funny how those things can work out, isn't it? You'd almost think political calculations were at work. What would you guess might happen if I started to issue rulings in the trial of Patricia Grant, what with my being a Democrat like the president, and the senate having a Republican-True South majority?"

Crockett sipped from his own glass. "Chief, I think they'd bat your rulings right back in your face."

"So do I." MacLaren put his glass down and lowered his head for a moment. When he looked up at Crockett, his eyes were filled with blue-steel resolve. "Daniel, I'm not going to ask you if you think the president is guilty of the charge the House has filed against her."

"No, sir. That would be improper."

"I won't tell you how I feel about the matter either."

"Very wise, Chief."

Leaning forward, closing the distance between them, MacLaren said, "But I will tell you this: If the people on either side of the aisle expect me to sit mute and let this matter become a political show trial, they are in for the surprise of their lives."

Crockett would dearly have loved to know the specifics of what MacLaren had in mind, but he knew better than to ask.

He finished his drink, put his glass down and offered MacLaren a wry smile.

"I'm sure it'd be must-see TV, Chief, if we allowed a camera in the court."

The associate justice was about to get up when the chief gestured him back into his chair.

"Hold on a minute, Daniel. Allow me to do a bit of research here."

The chief scooted his chair over to his desktop computer and tapped a flurry of keys. Crockett couldn't see what appeared on the screen, but he saw the chief nod. He was satisfied with what he'd found.

Turning back to his colleague, he said, "Daniel, the feminine equivalent of brethren is — no kidding — sistren."

"Never heard of it."

"My dictionary tells me the word fell out of common usage until just recently. It was revived by feminists. So, you see, you can put a new spin on old customs."

Crockett understood the chief had more than a dusty locution in mind.

Dumbarton Oaks — Washington, DC

White House Chief of Staff Galia Mindel's house sat in one of the capital's highest-end neighborhoods, and had what was sometimes known in real estate parlance as a media room: a place where even the largest of flat screen televisions wouldn't seem out of scale. The space had been constructed for the children of the original owner as a small theater, complete with a stage.

The stage had made way for HD productions of ever denser arrays of pixels. The old plush velvet seats had yielded to sleek leather designs. As before, though, there were parking spaces for sixty derrieres.

Galia stood at a lectern up front as her guests filed into the room. Her deputy chief of staff greeted the arrivals. He'd also overseen the security arrangements. Galia had reached into the private sector to keep the guests and her property safe that evening. No government cops would be on hand, and the only people in the room would be the parties directly involved.

Herself and the forty-six senators who would decide the president's political fate.

James J. McGill had asked her if she had a plan to save Patricia Grant from her political enemies. With just a look, she'd assured him she did. In a matter of moments, she was about to execute a part of the strategy she had in mind.

Until that morning, she had two unresolved questions in mind concerning the meeting that was about to take place. Should she invite only the fourteen Democratic senators who would be up for reelection in 2016 or the whole caucus? And what time of day should she hold the meeting?

She chose to invite every Democratic senator, thinking it would be better for all of them to see how ruthless a discipline was about to be enforced from above. She was pleased that not a single one of the senators had tried to beg off. They were already anxious about what they might hear.

She also decided on an after-office-hours time for the gathering so nobody would have the press of business as a convenient excuse for not coming. Beyond that, she wanted them to carry her words fresh in their minds as they lay down in bed that night. She hoped to inspire more than a few nightmares. The truly awful ones that would conjure images of the ends of political careers and the beginnings of prison sentences.

Galia's deputy, who'd been keeping a running head count even as Galia watched the seats fill, gave her a thumbs-up, stepped out and closed the door behind him. Nobody was left standing at the back of the room. The senators had heeded Galia's instructions, and nobody had tried to slip a senior staffer or two in with him or her. They'd been told that what she had to say was for their ears only.

Galia wasted no time with small talk.

"You are the people who will decide how Patricia Grant's presidency will be remembered. I'm one of the two people who will decide, in no small measure, how each of you will be remembered. The other person will be Jean Morrissey, our vice president."

At the back of the room, the junior senator from Georgia, Randall Pennyman, got to his feet and called out, "Bullshit. To hell with you, Galia, if you think you're going to scare me into doing what you say."

Galia had anticipated someone might take an immediate stance of confrontation.

In fact, she was counting on it.

In a monotone freighted with menace, Galia said, "It's been nice knowing you, Senator."

Already on his way to the door, Pennyman's step faltered. He stopped and saw Galia staring daggers at him. Every eye in the room focused on him. He leaned back slightly in the direction of his seat. Then he realized how bad it would look for him to sit back down. He would literally have been put in his place. He'd brand himself as a man who could be cowed.

Problem was, Pennyman had remembered too late how it was he had sneaked into office as a Democrat in a deep red state. On the eve of the election, the news broke that his opponent, a married man, would soon become an out-of-wedlock father, with a first cousin, and had tried to get her to end the pregnancy. When he got to Washington, Pennyman had quietly joked with Galia that she must have arranged that.

Galia had nothing to do with the illicit romance, but she had found out about a closely held secret and let the news leak at just the right time. Looking at Galia now, he realized that she was the person most responsible for his being elected. He started to skulk back to his seat.

Before he could get there, though, Galia said, "Too late."

Pennyman realized he'd just been made an example. There was nothing left for him to do but leave the room. He mustered the grit to do that without trying to plead for mercy.

Once he was gone and Galia's deputy had re-closed the door, she looked at her remaining guests. "I guess my reputation for being a scary broad has some merit. But if you want to know where your real political danger lies, look to Vice President Jean Morrissey. She told me, and asked me to pass the word along to all of you, that she considers the House's impeachment to be a declaration of war against the president.

"This will be two Democratic presidents in a row the other side has impeached. It's not hard to imagine voters coming to think there's no point in voting for a progressive politician to be president if the other side controls Congress because he or she will be impeached. The vice president is not going to stand for that. She's going to fight back hard. The members of the armed services committees in both the House and the Senate are going to be investigated back to their moments of conception. Indictments are anticipated.

"You've probably already suspected as much, but here's what all of you should keep in mind. The vice president has told me to inform you that she feels we can't have a viable two-party system if progressive members run for cover at the first perceived threat to their own seats. You are, of course, free to vote your consciences, but if you vote against the president for political self-interest … well, let's hope *you* haven't stepped across any legal lines.

"Because, if you have, the chances are you'll also be hearing from the Department of Justice. And while the FBI may not know everyone's dirty little secrets in this town, I pretty much do. You and Senator Pennyman have just seen how ruthless I can be.

"If anyone here tonight votes to convict President Grant, I won't be happy, and neither will you."

Walter Reed National Military Medical Center — Bethesda, Maryland

Midnight approached and the secure wing of the hospital was quiet.

Joan Renshaw was alone in her private room. The nurse on duty had checked on her only moments earlier. Her vitals were stable and she appeared to be resting as comfortably as … any other piece of furniture in the room.

Only the slight rise and fall of respiration differentiated her.

Until Joan opened her eyes. There was no scheme behind the timing of that, no secret plan for an escape about to be launched. Her lids simply opened. She looked straight ahead, to her right and left and then back to center. Then her lids closed again.

The whole sequence was over in seconds.

It would have been the easiest thing in the world to miss.

Only there were video cameras focused on this patient 24/7.

They caught the event and were programmed to alert the staff.

CHAPTER 7

Wednesday, March 25, 2015 — Los Angeles, CA

L.A. was the kind of place, most times, where only the tourists ever thought to pester the celebrities with inane requests for autographs and photos. The locals, people who'd been around a couple years or more, were too cool for such nonsense. People who'd actually been *born* in town kept hoping for the arrival of some new sort of natural disaster that would displace every immigrant who hadn't been in the city at least as long as the Dodgers had — since 1958.

None of the local folkways, however, kept almost every patron in the diner on Sunset Boulevard from peering at the large group having breakfast at the shoved-together tables in the back corner of the joint, a few feet from the swinging doors to the kitchen. The public attention became so persistent and obvious that management brought out folding screens that formed a visual barrier and helped to muffle voices.

Special Agent Deke Ky stood watch to discourage anyone from creeping too close to eavesdrop or commit a more nefarious act.

"Probably should have ordered room service," McGill said. "I thought people were more sophisticated around here."

"They are," Detective Zapata said, "if all they have to deal with is movie or music stars."

"But a retired cop turned PI gives them goosebumps?" McGill asked.

"You know better than that," Detective MacDuff said.

McGill did. People fixated on him that morning because he was married to the president, and she was fighting for her political life and legacy. Add in the fact that he was sitting among a group of people who all looked like they were carrying guns — and they were — and it would have been suspicious if someone wasn't looking their way.

The two LAPD cops were enjoying McGill's discomfort. They were both Angelenos by birth. Would be happy to see McGill climb aboard the first plane leaving LAX.

He wasn't about to indulge them.

McGill told the detectives, "I thought it would only be good manners to introduce the new visitors to town to the local cops working the fertility clinic robbery investigation. I guess from now on I'll just email you any updates."

"You know our email addresses?" Zapata asked, a note of suspicion in his voice, as if McGill had been snooping on them.

He shook his head. "I'll just send any bulletins in care of the chief of police."

Reminding them of the pull he had.

As if the arrival of the two new women, a Secret Service big shot and McGill's PI partner, hadn't made it clear they weren't going to be able to muscle him. They'd been wracking their brains trying to find some angle that would let them do just that. Now, it looked hopeless.

The best they could do now was try to ignore McGill.

Find the asshole who had burgled the fertility clinic before he did. Only they were coming to think McGill's resources were probably a lot greater than theirs. The guy probably had half the federal government behind him. He'd get the answers first and they'd look like mopes to everyone in the LAPD.

Neither of the detectives liked the situation confronting them.

But they couldn't do dick about it.

Except not let the SOB pretend he was a good guy who wanted to be their friend. They'd declined his offer to buy them breakfast, accepting only a cup of coffee each. Which they hadn't touched.

The new Secret Service broad, Kendry, was giving them the evil eye. It was a pretty good one, too, they'd later come to agree. She looked like she had some foreign blood, maybe Middle Eastern, and would happily slit their throats if they tried to get up in McGill's face.

The other woman, the big, good-looking blonde, Sweeney, looked like she'd be a handful, too, if they tried to enforce their role as the primary investigators in this damn case. If all that wasn't bad enough, and it was, Zapata and MacDuff had done their due diligence on McGill himself.

The bastard knew how to take care of himself in a fight. They'd watched the YouTube videos of him kicking that militia dimwit's ass on the National Mall. Walking right up to the guy and his armed rabble and planting the SOB in the grass like he was some snot-nosed kid.

Zapata got to his feet and MacDuff followed.

"Thanks for the introductions," Zapata said. "We'll await any future news on further troop movements. You know, when we're not trying to solve the crime that interests all of us."

"I'd be perfectly happy if you did," McGill told him. "I'm not looking to take any credit here."

Both of the LAPD detectives offered smirks of disbelief. Headed out without saying goodbye. Elspeth Kendry stood and said, "I'll walk the gentlemen out, have a word with them."

McGill thought to object, but decided not to.

He looked at Sweetie and John Tall Wolf, both of whom had remained silent throughout the meeting. Tall Wolf told McGill, "I don't think they believed your message of good will."

McGill sighed. "Me either. How about you, Margaret?"

"I used to think we'd cornered the market on cynics in Washington, but apparently not."

Tall Wolf got to his feet and extended a hand to Sweetie. "A pleasure to meet you, Ms. Shady. I think I'll go make sure SAC Kendry isn't terrifying the locals."

Zapata and MacDuff weren't quaking in their Prada loafers, but they were on the receiving end of a blunt message from Elspeth. "You guys are assholes."

Before Zapata could reply, Elspeth shook her head.

"Just shut up and listen or you'll find out how miserable I can make your lives. My only job in this town is to make sure Mr. McGill stays alive and well. He tried to be a nice guy with you just now. He honestly doesn't care about claiming any credit here. If you'd just been polite, and he was the one to solve this case, he would have handed all the credit to you two jackasses. He still won't look for the limelight. But none of that matters to me. What does matter is if by some misbegotten chance he and you get into a shooting situation with some bad guys, you two will *not* draw your weapons. If I see you attempt to do so —"

That was too much for Zapata. "What? You think —"

"I *know* you don't like the man. So what I'm saying is, if things get hairy, you two pricks don't do anything but duck and cover."

"Bullshit," MacDuff said. "This is our town. You don't tell us —"

"I'll tell you this right now. You fire your weapons and, say, Mr. McGill *accidentally* gets hit by friendly fire, Special Agent Ky and I will make sure you bastards don't leave the scene alive. You got that?"

"I know I'd take it as gospel," John Tall Wolf said.

Nobody had noticed his arrival. His imposing size and affirmation of Elspeth's position told both cops further argument would not be a good idea. They looked at each other and all but growled.

"Fucking feds," Zapata said. He stomped off as noisily as you can in $800 loafers.

MacDuff followed, shoulders hunched, both hands clenched.

Tall Wolf glanced at Elspeth. "I wouldn't want your job."

"I'm beginning to have my own doubts," she said.

***

"I'd vote for you," McGill told Sweetie. He'd picked up the tab for the meals that had been ordered and had left a substantial tip. At the moment, he and Sweetie were finishing their breakfasts and Deke was enforcing their privacy. "Only I'm going to do my damnedest to get Patti to move far from Washington."

When Sweetie had arrived that morning with Elspeth, McGill had been surprised to see her. Elspeth, too, to a lesser degree. It had been easy for him to infer that Patti had sent the chief of her own security detail because she trusted Elspeth to do a better job than anyone else, save Deke. McGill wasn't surprised, though, to hear that his long-time friend and colleague in police and investigative work was leaving that part of her life behind. He knew Sweetie still held herself responsible for Erna Godfrey's death. He'd tried to disabuse her of taking the rap for that, but he knew, in the end, she was the one who'd have to make peace with herself.

The idea, though, that she wanted to go into politics, that did catch him off guard.

Until Sweetie explained that she saw it as a move into public service.

With anyone else, save Patti, he'd have seen public service as a euphemism. For Margaret Mary Sweeney Shady, he saw it as a vow. She would work for the well-being of the people she represented. She probably hadn't realized it yet but most of the people living in her neighborhood were already pretty well set up, i.e. monied and connected.

Well, it wasn't his place to burst any bubbles. Sweetie would likely soon understand that she'd need to cast a wider net to help the less fortunate. Become mayor of DC? McGill could picture that.

Sweetie had her own speculative thoughts.

"Have you thought about where you and Patti might live next?" she asked.

McGill raised his hands and let them fall. "Don't know. Abbie's going to graduate from Georgetown in a couple months. Kenny, God love him, just heard from Stanford saying he's been admitted."

Sweetie beamed and slapped McGill's shoulder. "That's great. That was an amazing essay he wrote about getting a second chance at life. Brought tears to my eyes."

McGill nodded. "Mine, too. So did the way he raised his grades and test scores. Anyway, that's two out of three kids who'll be well launched."

"And Caitie? She's still intent on conquering show biz?"

"Yeah, but not in the way we all thought."

"What's new?"

"You ever hear of *La Fémis?*"

"No."

"It's also known as *L'École Nationale Supérieure des Métiers de l'Image et du Son.*"

"Okay, I caught the national school part, and I'm thinking it must be in Paris."

McGill nodded. "Right on both parts. Caitie decided an actress's career is too short. So she thought directing would be the way to go. Learning the craft from the French would be the pluperfect way to go. I've put a call in to Yves Pruet to see what she'd need to do to qualify."

Sweetie laughed. "Just be Caitie, that's all she'll need to do."

"Yeah, well. I'm insisting on great schoolwork in this country until she's ready to apply, a demonstrated ability to manage her money and mastery of the basics of Dark Alley. We'll see how much she really wants it."

"You'd better get Patti to teach you French so you can see Caitie's movies without the subtitles."

McGill grinned. "Yeah, I guess so. But I still don't know where Patti and I will live next."

"You'll figure it out. Until then, you're stuck with me."

"While I'm still in Washington?"

"Right here, right now. This'll be our last case working together."

McGill gave Sweetie a look. "Who cooked up that idea, you or Patti?"

"We both just knew it was the right thing to do, but Patti told me to tell you it's either me or a brigade of Elspeth's people."

"You," McGill said.

Sweetie smiled. "That wasn't hard, now was it?"

Beverly Hills, California

With the arrival of Sweetie and Elspeth, Leo had to upgrade McGill's ride to a Secret Service Chevy Suburban. The passenger load also included John Tall Wolf, Deke and Leo. The vehicle was roomy, comfortable, as solid as Fort Knox and, McGill suspected, armed with everything from a .50 caliber machine gun to surface-to-air missiles.

Heaven help the —

Before McGill could complete the thought, Leo said, "Lotsa cops up ahead, Boss. Puttin' on a light show and blockin' the road."

They were taking Sunset west, heading out to Pacific Palisades. McGill wanted to have another chat with Mindy Crozier, the security guard who'd been moved to the day shift. He also wanted to speak with the fertility clinic's owner, Dr. Danika Hansen.

Sweetie had put that thought in his head.

"You ever ask yourself where the guy who stole Mira Kersten's embryos is keeping them, assuming the numbnuts was told to preserve their viability."

"Somewhere cold," McGill said.

"Okay, but how about getting a little more specific?"

Tall Wolf watched the two of them work, enjoying what he saw.

Elspeth was taking an interest, too.

"You've been giving this some thought, Sweetie?" McGill asked.

"Putnam and I have discussed the possibility of maybe having one more child, the home-grown kind."

McGill knew science was extending the horizons of fertility, and found it understandable that his friend might want to explore more than one dimension of motherhood.

"So what have you learned?" McGill asked.

"Well, among other things, if you want to give yourself the best chance of embryo viability, you don't just stick your future generation in the freezer at home next to the gelato and salmon filets."

McGill didn't need long to chew on that clue.

"Of course not," he said, "you'd use another fertility clinic where the preservation equipment was state of the art and the people were trained professionals."

Tall Wolf nodded and added, "All you'd need to do would be change the name on who provided the embryos and they'd be just one deposit among many of the same type. Perfect camouflage."

Everyone liked that, and Elspeth took things a step farther.

"There's something else to consider, too," she said. "The closer the other facility is to the one that was robbed, the shorter the exposure for the thief. You cut your risk of discovery and arrest."

Everyone thought that was worthy of investigation, too.

So they'd ask Dr. Hansen where her nearest competitors were located and whether she thought they might be less than conscientious about taking on some off-hours inventory. Fudging the names of the depositors.

Then Leo informed them of what appeared to be a police blockade of Sunset Boulevard ahead, and now added, "Another whole bunch of cops is comin' up from behind." He asked McGill, only half-kidding, "You want me to lose 'em, Boss?"

McGill said, "They're LAPD, right?"

"Yeah."

He looked out the window and saw a street sign; they were just passing North Rexford Drive. He knew what that meant. Where they were.

"Stop right here," McGill said.

Leo did just that, with a look that said McGill was spoiling all his fun.

Elspeth told Deke, "Stay here with Holmes. I'm going to have a little talk with the locals."

"I'll go with you," Tall Wolf said.

"No," McGill told both of them. "Everyone just sit tight. Sweetie and I need to chat for just a minute."

He turned to his old friend and said, "How do you see all this, Margaret?"

"Lots of ticked-off coppers out there," she replied.

"Things could get out of hand quickly, couldn't they?"

"Without a doubt."

"What makes cops angrier than anything else?"

"Losing one or more of their own," Sweetie said, "or the threat of the same."

"Did you or I do or say anything like that?"

Sweetie shook her head.

McGill looked at Tall Wolf and Elspeth.

"John, we've only recently met, but I'm pretty sure naked aggression isn't your style."

Tall Wolf said nothing and kept an impassive demeanor. McGill turned to Elspeth.

"Elspeth, I know your job is one of the hardest in the world, especially when you have to deal with me. I also know Detectives Zapata and MacDuff were acting like bullies who got their bluff called. Even so, I want to know what you said to them after they left the diner."

Everyone in the SUV could hear the Secret Service SAC grind her teeth.

Then she admitted, "I said if things ever came to a shootout in this investigation of yours and one of them just happened to accidentally shoot you, I'd gun them down."

Sitting up front, Deke Ky nodded his head.

He not only agreed, he'd do the same. No orders from above necessary.

McGill turned to Tall Wolf. "Did you have anything to contribute?"

"I said the cops shouldn't doubt SAC Kendry's sincerity."

"Boss," Leo said, redirecting McGill's attention.

A tall uniformed man with a single star on his collar and nicely styled gray hair stood at the front of the line of patrol units. Using the P.A. speaker on the nearest car, he said, "Everybody step out of the vehicle with your hands on top of your heads."

Just then a helicopter flew overhead.

Looking out a window, Tall Wolf said, "Air support, LAPD chopper."

Then Deke said, "Two more aircraft approaching. Looks like TV station birds."

"Step out of the vehicle now!" the police commander ordered.

McGill sighed. He extended a hand to Leo and received the microphone for the SUV's PA speaker. "Hold on a minute, Commander. I'm calling in federal air assets so we can have a balance of power here."

The man instinctively looked up and retreated. Several other cops stuck their heads out of their cars and gazed skyward.

McGill added, "You might want to order the civilian aircraft to back off, Commander, to avoid any chances of an unfortunate accident."

The TV choppers took a beat to absorb that message and then darted away.

McGill handed the microphone back to Leo. He leaned back and said to Sweetie, "Did Patti or I ever introduce you to Sheldon Silverman?"

"No, who's he?"

"He's the mayor of Beverly Hills, a big supporter of Patti's. Will you please give him a call? Say I told you to call and tell him he might want to send his chief of police to our location because the LAPD is intruding on his jurisdiction big time." McGill pulled up the mayor's number on his phone.

Sweetie chuckled and said, "Right away."

McGill looked at Elspeth. "May I have your phone, please?"

"Why?"

"To run a bluff. Maybe get all of us out of here with no damage done to either flesh-and-blood or anyone's career."

Elspeth handed her phone to McGill.

He told everyone, "I'm going out there to talk to that cop. See if we can't come to a peaceful resolution."

Deke said, "I'm going with you. Nobody's going to put cuffs on you."

"I'm sure I could make bail," McGill said, "but it probably wouldn't look good. Okay, Deke, you but no one else."

McGill and Deke got out of the SUV. Neither of them had his hands on his head. They closed ranks and strolled to within twenty feet of the amassed police cruisers. McGill smiled, took a deep breath and said, "Lovely day, isn't it?"

The LAPD commander, knowing he had to look good in front of his troops, stepped forward, stopping within ten feet of McGill and Deke. The name tag on his uniform read Marsden.

He said, "I gave everyone in your vehicle a lawful order to step out with their hands in a position of surrender. I expect it to be followed right now."

McGill ignored that and asked, "Is this about Detectives Zapata and MacDuff?"

"It's about a direct threat to the lives of two LAPD officers."

"That's a serious allegation," McGill said. "Who made the threat?"

"A member of your Secret Service detail."

McGill hooked a thumb at Deke. "Special Agent Ky?"

"No."

McGill arched his eyebrows in mock surprise. "*SAC Kendry?* The head of the *presidential* security detail?"

Marsden said, "We have a recording."

"What a coincidence," McGill said, "so do I. Makes me wonder if your recording was edited. To be more inflammatory. This is SAC Kendry's phone. Now, if your recording —"

McGill and Marsden both looked up, hearing the roar of approaching aircraft.

Two military attack helicopters, AH-64D Apaches, arrived and took up station just aft of the hovering police chopper. They looked like a pair of Dobermans about to pounce on a chipmunk. Must've scared the airmobile cops shitless. The din of the three aircraft was all but overwhelming.

McGill had to hold his temper. Elspeth had taken his line of BS and made it real. She must have used the SUV's radio to contact an Air National Guard unit, undoubtedly invoking the president's name and voilà. Must've had the good timing to reach a command with birds already in the air.

The only thing left for McGill to do was make the best use of the situation.

He yelled to Deke to stay where he was and stepped forward and put an arm around Marsden's shoulders and led him to the side of the road. He shouted, "Now, listen to this."

He played Elspeth's recording for Marsden.

Unable to hear it clearly himself, he nonetheless yelled to the commander, "Does that clear things up for you?"

Marsden looked as if he might ask for a replay or worse want to take possession of the phone, but at that moment another cop stepped forward. This one was wearing a Beverly Hills PD uniform with a badge labeled CHIEF OF POLICE. The chief's name tag read BRIDGER.

He served just that function for McGill and Marsden. Reminded the commander that LAPD was out of its jurisdiction in Beverly Hills. Suggested to McGill that the director of the Secret Service might want to contact the chief of the LAPD and maybe the two of them could smooth things over.

McGill said he'd recommend just that to the president. That was good enough for Bridger, leaving Marsden to either agree or look like a dick. All the more so once McGill extended his hand to him. The commander shook on the deal.

Five minutes later, McGill and company were once more heading toward Pacific Palisades.

That night, the near collision between federal and local law enforcement would be the lead story on all the national news shows. The news choppers had stayed within camera range. Got some nice video of McGill confronting all those L.A. cops.

It wasn't drama on a par with the guy in Tiananmen Square stopping the tank.

But it went viral anyway. The whole country saw it. Most of the rest of the world, too.

Pacific Palisades, California

Hours before McGill saw his level of global notoriety rise — at a time when he was supposed to be working behind the scenes — he handed Elspeth's phone back to her. The westbound Chevy Suburban was quiet enough for all six people inside to hear their hearts beat and their blood circulate. Everyone, save McGill, was waiting to see if he intended to chew Elspeth's ass for threatening to kill LAPD detectives.

After an eternity of at least five minutes, Elspeth could take the pressure no more and opened her mouth to speak. McGill raised a hand to stop her. He turned and looked at Sweetie.

"Margaret, from what you've seen of Detectives Zapata and MacDuff, if they had either suspiciously or recklessly caused my death during an exchange of gunfire, what would you do?"

McGill knew he was putting Sweetie on the spot, but she didn't hesitate to answer: "I'd become so distraught that my own marksmanship would suffer fatal errors. Exactly *two* such errors. Then, of course, I'd have to go to confession, explain what I'd done, beg for absolution and pray for forgiveness."

The subtext was clear to everyone.

McGill turned to Elspeth. "Thank you for doing your utmost to protect me, SAC Kendry. Celsus Crogher would be proud of you. As for me, I hope you'll be a bit more subtle in the future."

Letting her know she still had a future in the Secret Service.

Assuming she wanted one.

"Yes, sir. Thank you," Elspeth said.

If she wasn't as tough as nails, she might have shed a tear.

They rode the rest of the way to the fertility clinic in further but more comfortable silence. The tension level rose when they saw an LAPD patrol unit parked at the curb in front of the building. As they pulled into the parking lot, though, the two cops inside the unit stayed right where they were. Neither of them even radioed in their sighting of the demonic PI from Washington and his federal minions.

At least not while McGill was in a position to see them.

Before getting out of the Suburban, McGill told Leo, "Feel free to look at the cops, but don't stare at them."

"I'll just keep an eye out for pretty girls," Leo said.

"That's the spirit."

With Deke leading the way and Elspeth bringing up the rear, McGill, Sweetie and Tall Wolf entered the clinic. Two young couples and a pair nearer to middle age waited in the reception area. They all looked at McGill and his entourage, but being the cool California natives that they were, they didn't seem impressed. They went back to their reading and their conversations.

McGill told the receptionist, "Jim McGill to see Dr. Hansen and Ms. Crozier. I called yesterday and asked for a bit of their time."

The girl behind the desk, obviously new to town, did look awe-struck.

Then an expression of disappointment creased her face.

"I'm sorry, sir, Mindy is no longer with us."

"No?"

She shook her head.

McGill felt there would be no point in asking for particulars.

He'd either get a canned answer or a declaration of ignorance.

He said, "Is Dr. Hansen available?"

The clinic's owner must have been nearby, possibly even listening in to the conversation, because she opened a door and stepped into the reception area as if hearing a cue. Her features were pulled taut into a mask of firm resolve.

She was not going to be helpful.

But she did extend a hand and McGill shook it.

"I'm so sorry, Mr. McGill. I just had a call from my attorney.

He'd spoken with the chief of police. The LAPD would prefer to have the investigation handled solely by their own people."

The three couples waiting in the reception area all leaned forward.

Now they were interested, and Dr. Hansen noticed.

"Nothing to worry about," she told them. "Everything's fine. We'll be with all of you in just a few minutes."

Besides being unimpressed by celebrity, cool Californians were natural skeptics.

Especially if they worked in any area of show business.

They knew something was up and didn't buy Dr. Hansen's happy talk.

Well, two out of the three couples didn't.

After McGill politely said, "Sorry to be a bother, Doctor," and left the building, they followed him out to the parking lot and asked what was going on.

McGill answered truthfully. "I'm investigating the theft of my client's embryos from this clinic."

The younger woman and the two men cursed; the older woman gasped.

"I can't provide my client's identity," McGill said, "but as you might imagine, there's a great deal of concern."

"We're going to get our embryos out of there right now," the older man said.

"And we're going to use another clinic," the younger woman said.

Her significant other nodded.

The older woman got teary-eyed. "What kind of a monster would do such a thing?"

McGill told them all, "That's what I'm trying to find out. Can any of you tell me the names of any other clinics you considered before coming here?"

"Why?" the younger woman asked. "You think this might happen again somewhere else?"

McGill shook his head. "It's probably a one-off crime directed at a specific person."

The older man, showing some savvy, followed up. "If that's the case, why do you want to know about other facilities?"

"I'm considering the possibility there might be a receiver of stolen goods somewhere nearby," he said. "A place with the necessary equipment and personnel to maintain the viability of the embryos."

All four of them nodded their heads. The older woman who'd most taken the bad news to heart suggested, "You might also want to check with some of the universities in town. They could have the right people and refrigeration, too."

McGill bobbed his head. "You're right, thank you, I should have thought of that."

The two couples gave him the names of four other clinics in town and two in Orange County.

He'd probably gotten as many leads as he would have from Dr. Hansen.

When everybody got back in the Suburban, Tall Wolf had another suggestion. "This being California, I wouldn't be surprised if there are facilities for cryogenic preservation close by. You know, places where people have their remains frozen until they can be thawed out when science discovers a cure for being dead."

McGill grinned. "I like that. Seems like the ethics at places like that would be fairly flexible."

"Could be a simpler choice, too," Sweetie said. "Like a small town morgue with a vacant cold chamber. Those things can be set to really cold temperatures."

McGill frowned. "Now it's starting to look like there are too many possibilities. Maybe an industrial refrigerator at a meatpacking plant would work."

"Or a refrigerated rail car," Tall Wolf added. "The way to look at things might be to see if Edmond Whelan or any of his colleagues has a link to a place that deals in cold spaces."

McGill gave Tall Wolf an appreciative look. "Yeah, that could be a good approach."

In the meantime, he told them, they'd see if Mindy Crozier could be found and was willing to talk with them.

Dumbarton Oaks — Washington, DC

White House Chief of Staff Galia Mindel did something that she indulged in maybe once a year: She played hooky. Called in sick to work when she was feeling fine. Physically fit, that was, but she was more than a little on edge psychologically. Jim McGill's suggestion that Mira Kersten was already pregnant was eating at her.

She'd tried to tell herself that McGill was overrating his instincts on the matter. What man was so perceptive that he might know if a woman was newly with child just by looking at her? An obstetrician perhaps, someone professionally trained and experienced in the matter. But someone who'd spent his working life as a policeman of one sort or another?

She didn't think …

Trouble was, she did think so. James J. McGill was a smart man, and no slouch at paying attention to small details. To be honest, Galia couldn't remember how she'd looked when she became pregnant with her two sons. Couldn't identify a particular smile she might have shown that said, "Hey, look at me. I'm going to be a mom."

What she did remember quite clearly was the way she had felt each time she'd learned she was carrying another life inside her. There was joy and worry and maybe, peculiar to ambitious women like her, a sense of great power. She would deliver into the world a child who would grow up to become someone important. A person who would affect many other lives for the better.

Quite possibly even someone of historical significance.

Her two sons, good men both, a computer engineer and a professor of musicology, were devoted husbands and fathers. Both gave of themselves to their children's schools and other community organizations. It was quite likely, though, that neither of them would ever have as high a public profile as their mother.

Still, more than a few people's lives would be better for having known them.

What more could a mother want? Just thinking of her boys, Joshua and Aaron, made her smile ... and that was when the memories returned to Galia. Yes, she had smiled exactly the way she was doing now when she'd been young and pregnant, anticipating what sort of wonderful little person she was nurturing within her body.

So why should she doubt for a minute that Jim McGill, the father of three, hadn't seen much the same expression of bliss and wonder on the face of the mother of his children? If he felt sure Mira Kersten was already pregnant, chances were very good he was right.

That being the case, why had Mira come to her and asked for McGill's help in finding her stolen embryos? The simple answer might be that she'd like to have more than one child. But if that had been the case, why wouldn't Mira have just said so? Something along the lines of, "Galia, I'm pregnant, and I'm so happy. But my embryos were stolen, and that makes me so sad and angry. I want to have more than just one child."

Galia would have understood that jumble of feelings perfectly. Jim McGill would have, too. But all Mira had talked about was being victimized.

So she was hiding something, a scheme of which Galia likely would not approve.

Galia felt sure the plan must be political. Mira and Galia had always been attuned to the same philosophy: Be progressive but practical. Even so, people had been known to change their views. It could be that Mira had gone so far as to think it might be fun to *use* Galia to achieve her own goals.

The protégé twitting her mentor.

It might have worked, if McGill hadn't noticed the fabled glow of the expectant mother. For the first time in her career in politics, Galia wondered if she might have lost a step. Perhaps it was a good thing her tenure in the White House would soon be at an end. Until that day came, though, she would do her utmost to protect the president and her own legacy as well.

An ironic smile formed on Galia's face as she realized she'd also need to protect the way history would remember James J. McGill. How was that for a turnaround? If someone was plotting to make the president's henchman look bad, she was going to cover McGill's backside.

Balance the ledger for his rescue of her.

Galia began to make phone calls. Her spy network was about to be put into overdrive. She was going to find out, first, if Mira Kersten truly was pregnant. If so, she'd find out who the father was. Hell, she was going to find out all the details.

Right down to whether either party to the conception murmured, "Was it good for you, too, honey?"

The Residence — The White House

"I'm calling you from my bath," the president said.

"Didn't Lyndon Johnson do that?" McGill asked from his California hotel suite.

"I believe he might have spoken from the porcelain throne a time or two."

"Ah, well, he was a good deal more rustic than you."

"And didn't have nearly the svelte figure I do."

McGill laughed. "Are we going to talk dirty? Is this a secure call?"

"Heads will roll if it isn't. No, wait. I think my head-rolling powers might be suspended these days."

"That can't be any fun. I'll tell you what: Leave a letter of resignation pinned to your pillow and meet me in Vegas. They say that what happens there stays there."

"No, no," Patti said. "The only thing that stays there is the money of people who think they can beat the house."

"Yeah, maybe that's it. I don't suppose you —"

"Happened to see the guy I love face down legions of armed and dangerous men, backed up only by his trusty sidekick? Really, Jim, I thought getting you out of town was supposed to *lower* your public profile."

"Celebrity seems to seek me out," McGill said.

"We'll have to put an end to that."

"Can't happen soon enough. Tell me more about your bath."

"It's hot, deep and lonely, but let's get back to business for just a minute."

McGill said, "I look forward to putting an end to that, too, but go ahead."

"Secretary of State Kalman came to see me today."

"You're not taking the country to war, are you?"

"The old wag the dog trick? No. Secretary Kalman heard from the Jordanian ambassador today inquiring whether any progress has been made in solving the murder of Bahir Ben Kalil, his late personal physician."

"Isn't that one of the things keeping Byron DeWitt up nights?"

"It is. State talked to the FBI. The director talked with DeWitt. He feels that fugitive member of Congress Philip Brock is the culprit responsible for Ben Kalil's death, but the Bureau doesn't have the goods on him for that quite yet."

"Nor do they have Brock himself," McGill pointed out.

"Correct. The FBI thinks Brock might also have killed Senator Howard Hurlbert."

"Damn," McGill said, "and he's already on the run for his part in the plan to assassinate you at Inspiration Hall."

"Beyond even that, he was one of the people pushing hardest for a new Constitutional Convention."

McGill asked, "What the hell did the guy have in mind, chaos?"

"Quite possibly. Tear everything down and you get to start again from scratch."

"After who knows how many people die or have their lives ruined in the meantime."

Patti sighed. "Getting back to the inquiry from Jordan, I was wondering, unofficially of course, whether you as a law enforcement hero to the masses have an opinion on whether I should share with the Jordanians the FBI's suspicion of Brock as being Dr. Ben Kalil's killer. "

A moment of silence ensued on McGill's end.

Then he said, "The Jordanians have to be aware of the Interpol wanted bulletin on Brock, don't they?"

"I would think so, yes. They have quite a sophisticated security apparatus."

"Well, then they know why the FBI wants Brock, too. For his role in the planned assassination of the U.S. president. Maybe what the secretary of state should do is tell the Jordanians if they were to assist in the effort to catch Brock and were the ones to actually nab him, both countries would be greatly pleased."

Patti said, "You're a pretty subtle thinker for a former Chicago flatfoot."

"Devious is the word," McGill said. "I think it comes from drinking Lake Michigan water."

"And here I spent all those years chugging the bottled stuff. You wouldn't have a suggestion up your sleeve where an interested party might find Brock, would you?"

"Well, he could be anywhere. He's got some personal wealth, doesn't he?"

"Not like Tyler Busby, but Brock does have millions."

"Okay, let's start there," McGill said. "He's likely accustomed to a certain level of comfort. Human nature being what it is, he's probably not going to want to spend the rest of his life hiding in a hut in a swamp or on top of a mountain. He had that spread in Central America."

"Costa Rica," Patti said, "hundreds of verdant acres, ocean views, beach access."

McGill wasn't surprised by Patti's detailed knowledge.

Presidents got briefed on *everything*. The good ones remembered what was important.

"So," McGill said, "Brock lost that little corner of paradise, and he probably wouldn't want as flashy a place for his next hideout. But ..."

"But what, Jim?"

"Does Brock speak Spanish?"

Patti did a quick mental dip into Brock's file. "Yes, he does."

"Okay. If he's fluent in the language and comfortable in a Latin culture that could narrow the list of places he might have absconded to. Of course ..."

"What?"

McGill said, "I've never studied Portuguese, but it's always seemed similar to Spanish to me."

"Both are Romance languages."

"Right. So, if Brock speaks Spanish, it might not be much of a jump to learn Portuguese. If he did that, he might go to Brazil, and from what I've read that's a pretty big place."

"About 85% of the size of the U.S.," Patti said.

"Had that info top of mind, did you?" McGill asked. "You know what would be fun?"

"We're not still talking about bathing here, are we?"

"No, we'll get back to tub games when we can play them. Your knowing the relative size of Brazil made me think it would be great if you could get a panel of former presidents on 'Jeopardy.' Maybe I'll get in touch with Alex Trebek, as long as I'm here in L.A."

Patti laughed. "You know what would be even better? Get *presidential* candidates to play 'Jeopardy' instead of having debates. You could see who really knew their stuff then. Meanwhile ... "

"Right, back to catching Brock. So Brazil is really big and it's got that enormous Amazon wilderness area, jungles and all. A guy could hide out there a long time."

"But you said Brock's not likely to rough it."

"I did, didn't I? Well then, if you're looking for consistency, he'd probably buy a condo on a trendy beach filled with cute girls getting too much sun while they gossip in Spanish. Whatever language is being used, though, the crooked rich guys I've known all needed to be fawned over. So there will probably be at least a small group of people who surround Brock, even if they don't know his true identity. Is any of this blather helpful?"

"Definitely. How is your investigation proceeding? Well, I hope."

McGill told Patti of his suspicion that Mira Kersten was already pregnant.

She thought about that for a moment and replied. "If Mira is pregnant, it must have happened before the theft of her embryos occurred. Maybe she really likes being a mom-in-waiting and simply has all the more reason to feel aggrieved after the break-in."

There was a beat of silence before McGill said, "Have I ever mentioned that you're really smart?"

"A time or two."

"Well, think about this. The gang and I went to talk to the security guard who was overcome by the thief. I'd already spoken to her once and wanted to follow up. But she was no longer working at the clinic and when I went to her home her mother said she'd left with a friend, a girlfriend I was told, and set off for parts unknown. Having a cynical nature about such things, it looks like someone persuaded the young lady to avoid me."

"Well, if that's the case, you should be able to figure out who that someone might be. If you can't do that, you might have to — and I know this would be tough — chalk it up to coincidence."

"More good advice," McGill said. "When we leave Washington, and you're not busy with Committed Capital, you want to go to work for me?"

"Only if I get to wear short skirts, smoke non-tobacco cigarettes and sass the boss."

McGill laughed. "I'm all in favor of the skirts and the sass."

"Okay, but now you've made me wonder. What will you and I really need when we make our getaway from the White House?"

McGill said, "Only each other … and a few creature comforts."

***

Punta del Este, Uruguay

People everywhere sneaked peeks when a new neighbor moved in nearby. It was only natural, wanting to see who you would soon be crossing paths with on a regular basis. Part of the evaluation of the new people came from judging their possessions. Did they have nice cars and good furniture?

Were there children you might have to deal with? If so, how many? Were they mindful and well mannered or raucous little dervishes?

Did the new arrivals have pets? Large or small? What was their number? Might they howl in the night or foul your lawn?

In terms of the adults, was there one or were there two? If there was a couple, were they straight or gay? Did they converse politely with each other or was there a pre-existing conflict about to open a new front on the other side of your backyard fence?

Were the newcomers respectful of the privacy of others or were they natural snoops?

That last concern was the most important to Philip Brock. He was certain the FBI was on his trail by now. The feebs had to suspect he'd fled the country, too. Turning to Interpol for assistance would be automatic.

The thing about allied law enforcement was that most countries took an interest in other nations' fugitives only if they caused trouble within their own borders. That was true in ordinary cases anyway. But Brock was wanted for conspiring to kill the president of the United States. Both the crime and the country pursuing him carried a lot of weight.

Brock had to be very careful or he'd find himself extradited in a Uruguayan minute.

So he watched the arrival of the new neighbors' possessions at the larger home directly across the street from the vantage point of a darkened window on the second floor of his new home. As far as Brock had been able to tell, only two people had seen him arrive on moving day. They'd been a thirty-ish nanny and a pre-verbal child in a stroller.

Brock had politely said, "*Buenos dias.*"

The nanny had made his day by smiling and replying, "*¿Usted es canadiense, señor?*"

Asking him if he was Canadian.

Speaking English, Brock said he was, and introduced himself as Bruce Mallory.

Replying in English, the nanny told him she'd lived in Ottawa for a year.

She thought she'd recognized his accent.

He said he'd lived in the Canadian capital as a young child but had moved to Vancouver and often spent time in Toronto. He said his accent was a blend of many things. Even American as he'd often done business in that country.

In truth, he didn't have a clue what an Ottawa accent sounded like.

So he'd fudged things as best he could.

The nanny smiled and seemed to buy it.

The people moving in across the street didn't have occasion to chat with any passerby. Then again most movers did their work in daylight hours. Right now the sun was low on the western horizon and it would soon be dark. Brock hadn't been able to judge the furnishings going into the house because it was all covered by protective blanketing.

The housing development, though, was as high-priced as things got in Uruguay. Outside of custom homes on estate acreage. Buying one of those places would have been within reach for Brock, but he would have had to purchase political protection to go along with it, if he made himself so easy to find, and Uruguay wasn't big on taking bribes.

The movers finished their labors, departed and two minutes later a Mercedes S-Class Sedan pulled into the driveway. Brock lifted a pair of Steiner 10X42 Merlin binoculars off his lap and brought them to his eyes. The magnification and light-gathering properties of the lenses might have allowed him to count the freckles on his new neighbors' faces. Only they didn't have any.

The woman was Asian. Her complexion was flawless, and far more relaxed than the last time he'd seen her, about to lift off from the helipad of the yacht named *Wastrel*. She was no longer pregnant. She carried an infant in her arms The man escorting her to the front door of their new home was … well, well, well.

Damn small world, wasn't it?

Tyler Busby had just moved in across the street.

There was no longer any question that Brock would have to act quickly. It wouldn't be long before Busby made a point of finding out who all *his* new neighbors were. In fact … both he and Busby should have learned who'd be living nearby *before* they'd purchased their new dwellings.

Brock chastised himself for being so negligent. But had Busby made the same mistake? He might have. If he'd actually come to care so much for the woman and the child with him, Busby might be off his game. But Brock couldn't count on that to continue for long.

He'd have to get Busby before Busby got him.

The only question was how to do it.

The preliminary step, of course, was to gather information. He drew the curtains and booted up his computer. He had placed Google Alerts on a raft of names back in the good old U.S. of A. Busby was foremost on that list, but the first hit to come up was James J. McGill.

Brock drummed his fingers on his desktop for a good thirty seconds before clicking on the first link to McGill. He wanted to hope something bad had happened to the man. The blurb accompanying the link said "L.A. cops surround president's husband."

Why would they do that, Brock asked himself.

It wasn't like they could ever arrest the guy. His Secret Service people would never allow that. Besides, except for defending himself spectacularly well, McGill had no record of ever getting tough with anybody. So what was the deal here?

He looked at other links under the same heading. They were

as vague as the first.

It was with a sense of foreboding that Brock gave in to his curiosity and clicked on the first link. He immediately regretted it, thinking he might just have become a phishing victim. Some smart operator back in DC had figured out he'd be watching for big news from home and had sucked him in with a come-on he'd be unable to resist.

Now, the NSA or some other government spook shop could be tapping every last byte of data on his hard drive, including the location of his Wi-Fi connection. His neck muscles started to knot with tension as listened for the sound of approaching sirens. They'd be local cops, of course, but he could see being bundled onto a plane in handcuffs and flying straight to —

Maybe they wouldn't bring him back to the U.S.

Congress, including him, had forced Patti Grant to keep Guantanamo open.

His next stop might be Cuba. He got up and started to pack a traveling bag. He had a loaded Glock 27 stashed in his Land Rover. Things got really hairy, suicide by cop might be preferable to disappearing into a government black site. No telling what they'd do to him there, given the shit he'd tried to perpetrate. That and the two guys he'd killed.

He went down to his ride, dug out the Glock and sat behind the wheel.

He thought if he shot it out right where he was, the cops might find Busby had just moved in across the street. If he had to go, he might as well take that bastard with him. Only the cops never came.

After a two-hour wait, Brock went back inside, taking his gun with him just in case. He pulled up the video he'd thought might be a trap. What he saw boggled his mind. The L.A. cops, lots of them, had wanted to bust McGill. Well, him or somebody who was in that Chevy Suburban with him. McGill got out of the SUV like he was on his way to a Sunday picnic or something, started talking to some big shot cop like you could reason with those guys and …

The picture switched from McGill to the sky.

Two army attack helicopters zoomed in and looked like they were going to *eat* the police chopper that was hanging in the sky.

Back to McGill and the top cop, who maybe was feeling more susceptible to reason now.

Then another cop in a different uniform arrived and pretty soon everybody was shaking hands. The L.A. cops dispersed. McGill went on his way: no muss, no fuss. Well, yeah. You can whistle up attack aircraft in nothing flat, who was going to give you a hard time?

Thinking that sooner or later McGill was going to come after him for trying to kill his wife, Brock started to tremble. McGill wasn't going to let him go with a handshake: no harm, no foul. He was going to take Brock's head off. Maybe not literally, but probably close.

If Brock had known just what McGill was capable of, and whose wife he was threatening, he'd have forgotten all about becoming an anarchist and going into politics. He'd have stayed in investment banking, made his pile of money and made do with that.

Now, Jesus, now, he'd have to … make an offering of Busby and …

He couldn't quite say even to himself that he'd surrender. If he did that, he'd still have to answer for Bahir Ben Kalil's death and Howard Hurlbert's, too, at a minimum. He'd probably get the death penalty. That was the price of killing a U.S. Senator.

So maybe he *would* have to do himself in.

But he'd sacrifice Busby first and see if that might make *any* difference in what punishment would be doled out to him.

He thought he knew how he might sic the feds on Busby.

His computer, apparently, hadn't been phished, but maybe he could drop some bait in Busby's digital pond. That or use some innocuous human intermediary.

Southern California

The domestic audience for the *McGill vs. LAPD* video was even larger than the international viewership, at least for the first 24 hours. Two of the more interested observers sat in hotel rooms separated by 90 miles. At the Santa Barbara Biltmore, Edmond Whelan sipped a Macallan 25, neat. At the L.A. Airport Marriott, Eugene Beck partook of a Smog City Little Bo Pilsner.

Each man offered to himself, aloud, a contradictory sentiment about what he'd just seen.

Whelan said, "That sonofabitch has got to go. Killing him would cut the heart out of the Grant administration."

Beck said, "That SOB will be almost impossible to kill. I could get my ass shot off just trying."

Seeing McGill defuse a potentially violent situation with a mob of cops scared Whelan.

Watching the same thing intrigued Beck.

He wondered if he'd have had the nerve to do what McGill had done. Get out of his car with just the one dude. The other guy had to be Secret Service. Still, if things had gotten to the point of a shooting war, McGill and the agent would've been cut to pieces.

Of course, it would have taken an overload of testosterone and a complete absence of brain cells to open up on the president's husband in broad daylight with the whole world watching. Still, that didn't mean there wasn't at least one gomer among all those cops who qualified on both counts. Things *could* have gone wrong. About as wrong as wrong ever got.

McGill had to know that. Didn't matter to him, though. He still made his play.

Guy had to have *massive* gonads.

Pretty good luck, too, the way those army attack birds showed up so fast.

All that was what intrigued Beck.

And scared Whelan.

He would have been even more frightened had he known

what the man he'd coerced to kill McGill was thinking. Namely that Beck would solve his problem by taking out the guy who was trying to play him for a sap.

The irony was, Beck, after watching the video, had become so fascinated by McGill that he was already thinking of how he *might* do him in. Just as an intellectual exercise. Right?

The answer to that question was: Most likely.

38,000 feet over Prince Edward Island

Captain Welborn Yates sat in the right hand seat of the Bombardier Global 5000 as it cruised through the night sky over the Maritime Provinces of Canada. He, his wife, their twin girls, his parents and a gentleman introduced only as Smythe, who shook everyone's hand and then retired to a private cabin, were the only passengers aboard. The pilot and first officer had brought the aircraft across the Atlantic from London, but once the New World was on the radar an invitation was extended to the guest from the USAF.

"Captain Yates," the pilot said, "would you like to sit in the right-hand seat to make sure we don't go astray over North America? We wouldn't want to cause a bother to American or Canadian air defenses."

Welborn snapped off a salute and replied, "At your service, sir."

He'd been hoping all along that they'd let him in the cockpit, if only for a moment, but didn't want to be pushy enough to ask. He thought the flight crew was showing their appreciation for his good manners. Then the pilot, Group Captain Rowan Davies, RAF (retired), shared with Welborn the fact that the crew had been informed by Welborn's father, the former personal secretary to Her Majesty, how his son's career as a fighter pilot had ended.

"Terrible thing that automobile crash taking the lives of your friends and brother pilots," Davies said. "That and ending your own military flying career."

"Yes, it was," Welborn said.

“Smashing how you settled accounts with the blighter responsible.”

Remembering how auto thief Linley Boland met his end, his small boat being rammed by a much larger vessel, Welborn replied, “That’s the word for it, all right.”

Before that discussion could go any further, Welborn saw Davies straighten in his seat. If the pilot had been standing, he would have come to attention. He said, “Yes, ma’am. Immediately.”

He gestured to Welborn to put on his headset. As Welborn did so, having seen Davies’ change in demeanor, Welborn thought the queen must have called for some unguessable reason. His guess had the right degree of prominence, but the wrong side of the ocean.

Davies whispered to Welborn as his headset was going on. “Your president.”

“Madam President, this is Captain Yates. How may I be of help?”

“Please don’t argue with me, Welborn. That would be a good start.”

“Yes, ma’am. Whatever you say.”

“I’ve reviewed your request for promotion, and taken into account your reason for wanting it. Carina Linberg is one smart lady. I’m sorry she’s no longer working for the Air Force.”

“Yes, ma’am. That is unfortunate.”

“As your request was written, however, I’m going to deny it.”

Welborn winced. He’d been all but sure he’d soon be a major. Playing it safe, though, he hadn’t said anything to Kira about it. Now, he was going to have find some other way to —”

The president continued, “I think you undervalue yourself to me and my administration. You’ve probably heard that Vice President Morrissey has announced her candidacy to be my successor.”

“Yes, ma’am.”

“My hope is you’ll stay on if she asks you to serve in a capacity similar to what you do for me.”

"I'd be honored, ma'am."

"Yes, but would you take it, if offered?"

"I'd have to talk with the vice president first."

"Of course."

"I'd also have to speak with Kira."

"Well, as the person who introduced the two of you to each other, I think that's fair. In any event, I don't think the rank of major is sufficient for your position. I've promoted you to colonel, and as you've already promised not to argue, I trust you'll accept the promotion."

Welborn tried to keep his head from spinning. "Yes, ma'am. I'll do my best to honor your faith in me."

"You must make your parents very proud, Colonel Yates."

"I try my hardest with them, too, ma'am."

"Good. Now, see if you can impress Carina Linberg as well."

"Yes, ma'am."

Group Captain Davies, held a thumb up in front of a questioning facial expression.

He'd been too much of a gentleman to listen in to the president's half of the conversation.

Welborn returned the gesture.

Then he told Davies, "Let's see if we can put a call in to South Florida."

CHAPTER 8

Thursday, March 26, 2015 — Los Angeles, California

McGill's phone rang at six a.m. The ring tone was "A Beautiful Morning," by The Young Rascals. The tune had been a hit in 1967, and the times being what they were, his mother's obstetrician had it playing in the delivery room when he was born. He'd felt a special attachment to it ever since.

He didn't even mind hearing it early that day, as he was already out of bed and tying the laces of his running shoes. He, John Tall Wolf and Elspeth Kendry were going for a run before they got down to business. Sweetie begged off, choosing to coordinate family matters with Putnam back in Washington. After the run, McGill planned to have another chat with Mira Kersten and see if his instincts about her being pregnant were on the mark.

Maybe ferret out some other reason for her requesting his help.

He thought Patti might be calling him — from somewhere other than her bath — to share news of great importance. Or just to say hello. Which was also no small thing.

Only it wasn't the president of the United States calling. It was Mindy Crozier.

So said the ID screen on his phone.

"Hello, Mr. McGill. Sorry for calling so early. Did I wake you?"

"No problem. I'm already up. Just about to go out for a run."

"That's cool."

"Where are you, Mindy?"

"Heading south on PCH." Pacific Coast Highway. "Coming back from Santa Barbara. A friend and I were on our way to San Francisco when my mom texted. She said you came by our house asking for me. You almost made Mom swoon, being who you are."

"I try to be careful about that," McGill told her.

Mindy laughed. "Ha, yeah, that's cool, too. Anyway, I thought I better come back and talk to you."

"You don't have to postpone your trip. We can talk right now."

"No, that's okay, we're almost to Malibu already, and I'd rather talk in person. Where are you going to run?"

McGill had thought to run through residential areas of Beverly Hills, feeling it should be pretty quiet that early in the morning. Now, he changed his mind. "Palisades Park, Santa Monica."

"Great. That's right on our way."

"We'll be somewhere between San Vicente and the pier. Look for two heart-throb guys and a woman with an automatic weapon."

"Okay, that shouldn't be too hard to find. Probably hook up within an hour."

Going down to the hotel lobby, McGill met with Tall Wolf and Elspeth.

SAC Kendry was doing penance, getting up early, for her over-zealousness with the LAPD yesterday. She was letting Deke sleep in while she took bullet-catching duty.

Tall Wolf was fine with the change in the running plans.

Elspeth didn't like that McGill had told anyone where they'd be running.

McGill told her, "Elspeth, you and John are armed. We faced down a hundred cops yesterday. I think we'll be all right."

Elspeth asked if she should arrange for another attack helicopter escort.

***

Moonlite Diner — Fort Lauderdale, Florida

Carina Linberg thought she was getting too thin. She'd never enjoyed cooking, and the galley on *Irish Grace,* while adequate, didn't encourage her to prepare more than the most basic of meals: grilled beef, chicken or fish. Salads were limited to two or three veggies. Sometimes just shredded lettuce with bottled Italian dressing. Even her desserts were prosaic. Supermarket pastries and Dove chocolates.

Actually, the chocolates were quite good.

Still, she was thinking of making some changes. As she'd told Welborn Yates, though, there was no way she would sell her boat. If she ever needed to get out of Dodge, metaphorically speaking, you couldn't beat a seaworthy, well-provisioned sailboat. Small yacht, if you wanted to be generous about the description. You just motored quietly out of your marina when no one was looking, set sail for any point of the compass and you were gone.

With the vastness of the world's oceans and the profusion of maritime traffic, it would be easy to hide. She wondered what it said about her, though, that she thought she might be on the run from the law someday. She had no criminal record, no intent of acquiring one. Still, at the back of her mind she thought it was a good idea to have a quick getaway handy.

The waitress brought her breakfast: two eggs, bacon, hash browns and a chocolate milk shake. That ought to pack on a few thousand calories. Of course, what she should do was eat *smarter* and get back to exercising more regularly, too. She'd once been able to do a set of ten full-extension chin-ups. Forty pushups. She hoped she could still do a small fraction of both.

She blamed both her discontentment and her itch for self-improvement on Welborn.

Colonel Welborn Yates.

The handsome, faultlessly polite young bastard had gone ahead and gotten his double-jump promotion. There was only one way in the world that had happened. The president had come through for him. More than he'd even wanted. The commander in chief must have decided a major wasn't good enough for her pet Air Force officer; so she'd made him a colonel.

Hell, maybe Patti Grant, another older woman, had the hots for him, too.

Nah, she had her own stud fantasy figure. McGill was closer to Carina's age than Welborn was, but thinking of him didn't light her up the same way. Maybe she was just a dirty old —

"Colonel Linberg, ma'am. Captain Tinker reporting for duty."

Her morning breakfast date had just arrived, and honored her with a brief salute.

Charlie Tinker had been nicknamed The Model Marine by more than a few of the women at the Pentagon, military and civilian. He might have been Welborn's dark-haired older brother. Fashion magazine handsome with a small scar on his chin from a shrapnel nick, he'd set many a lady's hear aflutter.

Only he'd limited his dalliances with females who worked outside of the federal government in general and the Department of Defense in particular. He and Carina had a friendly but completely professional relationship when they'd both been in uniform. She'd still been in the Air Force when Charlie left the Marines. The whispers were he'd gone to work for the CIA.

Carina had found that rumor plausible, but knew better than to try to verify it.

By the time she had left the service and had gone to work for WorldWide News, she'd heard that Charlie had entered civilian life and established himself as a freelance photographer specializing in war zone images with a sideline in natural disasters. She'd gotten his email address and complimented him on his work. Said they should get together for a drink sometime.

They did just that, and on their second drink Charlie revealed he was gay. Dating women was just a cover for his military days. Now that being a gay Marine was acceptable …

He would be coming out publicly the next day.

Another possible romance for Carina shot to hell, but they

remained good friends.

Charlie lived down in South Beach and was happy to accept the breakfast invitation when Carina called. He kissed her cheek and took a seat in the booth opposite her. Then he looked her over and gave his right hand a small side-to-side waggle.

"What?" Carina asked. "I look that bad?"

"You were born too gorgeous to ever look bad, but you're not happy. You're letting yourself go a little."

Carina took a long slurp of her milkshake. "I'm sure you could fix me right up, only you *weren't* born that way."

Charlie grinned. "I have straight friends, if you'd like an introduction or two."

"I'll let you know."

The waitress came and took Charlie's order. She gave him her best smile and even managed to sneak in a light touch of his arm. Never knowing both flirtations were wasted efforts.

"Men," Carina said when the waitress had departed, "even the gay ones."

"Now, now. Right after we eat, I'll sneak you into Homestead." The U.S. Air Force base in South Florida. "We'll steal a B-2, and you can drop bombs on anybody you please."

Carina laughed. "That'd cheer me right up.

"How about you let me share your breakfast and then you can share mine?"

"That way your new little friend will know you're spoken for?"

"Yeah, and we can talk about why you wanted to see me without my going hungry."

Carina pushed her plate to the middle of the table. Charlie took a piece of bacon.

"I'll understand if you can't help me, but what I'd like to know is anything you might know about our government's spooks working as assassins."

Charlie's eyes narrowed. "You might have to buy me *dinner* for that."

"Or we could discuss the subject hypothetically, if you'd feel more comfortable."

"What's going on here, Carina?"

Charlie took a look around the diner, as if someone might be closing in on him.

Only the waitress was, back with his order in a flash. She moved Carina's plate back to her side of the table, but got the message it was meant to send. Not a quitter, though, she still beamed at Charlie.

As soon as she left, Carina said, "A friend who's still in uniform asked for my help. If I give you a little bit of the situation, can I trust you to keep it to yourself?"

"I'm gay, but I'm not a gossip," Charlie said.

"Good to know. A certain person highly placed in the government is being threatened with death. This is someone who has certainly been threatened before, but this one is being regarded more gravely than most. The word is, it could be somebody connected with our own intelligence community who might actually make an attempt."

"JFK and the CIA all over again?" Charlie asked.

Carina spread her hands. "I'm just an intermediary, but the person who contacted me about this isn't a conspiracy nut."

She took a piece of bacon from Charlie's plate.

He said, "The only way I could see something like this happening is if somebody from the fringe is being used."

"Someone who's *not* a serious threat?" Carina asked.

"Didn't say that. Look, did you ever wonder what happens to all the guys who try to join special forces units but don't make it?"

"They go back to their old outfits, do their old jobs?"

"Some do, but a lot separate from the services altogether."

"Disappointment will do that," she said, knowing military misfortune all too well.

"Yeah, well, some big thinker at the Pentagon thought it was a waste of manpower, at least when it came to the guys who missed out making special forces by a whisker. All that training and a lot of skills and talents walking out the door, it seemed unproductive."

"When you say a whisker, how close are we talking?" Carina said.

"Close enough to make a man bitter. I heard a story about this one guy. He did *everything* right, aced the training, passed all the tests, qualified down to the smallest detail."

"But?"

"But he whistled while he worked. At least when he wasn't supposed to keep quiet. Other guys would be grunting and wheezing from busting a gut; this dude would be whistling a merry tune. They thought he was a mite unbalanced, but not in a militarily useful way. So they washed him out."

"Did he take it hard?" Carina asked.

"That's the thing. The powers that be saw to it that someone met him as soon as he cleared the post gate. Offered him an interesting job at a salary the chairman of the joint chiefs doesn't get."

"Who makes that kind of offer?" Within a heartbeat, Carina answered her own question. "A private security firm with a very fat government contract?"

Charlie didn't say a word, barely nodded.

From her own intelligence background, Carina was able to draw other conclusions. "This whistling guy was far from the only one to get that kind of job offer. If the special forces people are the super-elite, the guys who just missed are the near super-elite. Damn, the guy who thought up this program was earning his salary. You get high quality personnel and if one of them screws up you've got political deniability and probably no grieving widow to go on TV."

"See that," Charlie said. "Not only are you still beautiful, you're as smart as ever."

"Yeah, thanks. But I haven't figured it all out yet, have I?"

"Take another sip of your milkshake. Maybe something will come to you."

Carina did, and the rush of cold sugar and chocolate did stimulate her.

She smiled and told Charlie. "You didn't just pull this whistler guy out of your hat for no reason. If his only flaw was an overdeveloped love of music, he must have been about the best of the guys who didn't make the cut. So what was his name?"

"Don't think I ever heard it," Charlie said, "but I do recall he was one of your kind of people."

Retired Colonel Carina Linberg made the connection. "Air Force."

Palisades Park — Santa Monica, California

Directly opposite the bench where McGill, Mindy Crozier and John Tall Wolf sat was a sign that said visitors to the park used it at their own risk: The bluffs were subject to collapse. The drop-off to Pacific Coast Highway was steep, measuring close to a hundred feet. Portions of the park that city officials thought were in imminent danger of crumbling were blocked off by metal fencing.

SAC Elspeth Kendry saw the warning sign and immediately wanted McGill to do his run somewhere else. Mother Nature, she'd told McGill, wouldn't back down from committing a hostile act just because you pointed an Uzi at her. You couldn't intimidate the old girl or even reason with her.

McGill laughed and replied, "Elspeth, there probably isn't a square foot of this state where a fissure couldn't open directly beneath you."

"Good point," she replied. "Maybe you should get out while you can."

"Says the woman who grew up in war-torn Beirut," McGill replied.

"Really?" Mindy asked.

"And shot it out with desperate characters elsewhere in the Middle East."

"Really?" Tall Wolf asked.

Elspeth gave McGill a dirty look worthy of Celsus Crogher, but made no further objections. She didn't want McGill to give away her entire résumé. She took up a position behind the bench to protect his back, while turning hers on him.

If the bluff in front of him gave way, too freaking bad.

Maybe *she'd* have time to run for it.

McGill, Tall Wolf and Mindy, meanwhile, took their chances and enjoyed the ocean view.

"So you think I'm the one?" Mindy asked McGill.

"Which one?" he said.

"Whoever it was that slipped the door code to the thief. So he could get in, right?"

Tall Wolf turned his head in her direction when he asked, "What makes you think somebody did that?"

"Somebody had to do it. He didn't *guess* the combination."

"Was that something you learned about in school, how inside jobs get done?" McGill asked, getting Mindy to look back at him.

He hadn't planned to triangulate the questioning with Tall Wolf, but he could see the advantage of playing things that way. It didn't always have to be good cop-bad cop. You could have both interrogators act friendly. As long as it wasn't obvious you were acting or you weren't dealing with a sociopath, building a sense of camaraderie could open people up even better than intimidation.

Mindy said, "There was some classroom discussion about it, but we learned a lot more about how bad guys really work when we went out for drinks with the visiting cops some of our profs brought in as guest speakers."

"Sure," Tall Wolf said. "People can speak more freely in informal settings."

Mindy laughed. "You mean like right here." She looked back at McGill. "Or at my mom's house, where you wanted to talk to me yesterday."

"Yes" he said, "either here or there is good,"

"Right. But in either case, even if you think it was me, it wasn't."

McGill said, "I didn't think that. Did you, John?"

She looked back at Tall Wolf.

He held a thumb and an index finger a half-inch apart. "Maybe just a little. But I don't have any kids and Mr. McGill has two daughters."

"You guys are such BS-ers," she told Tall Wolf with a grin. "But I kind of like it that you think I'm maybe just a little bit of a bad girl."

McGill said, "It's our imperfections that make us interesting, but I think you're way too smart to blow up your whole life by helping someone steal embryos."

"Right," Mindy said. She turned to see if Tall Wolf agreed.

He nodded.

Satisfied on that point, she asked McGill, "You know who I think did it?"

"Who?"

"Dr. Hansen, that's who."

"The woman who owns the clinic," McGill said.

He and Tall Wolf leaned forward to look at each other.

Mindy asked them, "You know why I was terminated."

"I didn't know that you were," McGill said.

"Yeah, I was. Because I snooped where I shouldn't have."

"Where?" Tall Wolf asked.

"Well, one of the things that got drilled into us both in the classroom and afterward was if there's trouble between a married couple, you always look at the spouse first."

Both McGill and Tall Wolf nodded.

"So I checked the clinic's records and found out most of the embryos taken from Ms. Gersten were created with a man named Edmond Whelan. He was Gersten's husband at the time the embryos were made, but the records showed they got divorced, and the embryos were flagged as requiring a court order to release them."

McGill, who came by his paternity the old-fashioned way, asked, "Does that order apply equally to Ms. Gersten and Mr. Whelan?"

"It does for the ones they created together. There are no holds for Ms. Gersten on the embryos she made with other partners. Not that the records showed."

"Okay," McGill said, "go on."

"So, looking at the husband first, I thought he might be the one responsible for the theft, but how would he know the door code? What I did was look at the video file of the interview he and Ms. Gersten did with Dr. Hansen when they first came to the clinic."

"I can understand talking with the doctor about the process," Tall Wolf said, "but why is there a need to make a record of the occasion?"

"Self-interest," Mindy said. "The doctor explains the risks. An individual embryo might not survive being frozen and thawed. Also, there's the possibility of a catastrophic power failure. You know, like after an earthquake. All the embryos in the whole place might be ruined if something bad happened and the power went out. The doctor wants people to know there are risks. With the recordings, they can't say they weren't told."

McGill said, "That's sensible."

"Right. Well, video can show other things, too. Like the looks people exchange, whether they're positive or negative. The looks Mr. Whelan and Dr. Hansen exchanged … well, I was surprised Ms. Kersten didn't notice and object."

McGill gave a dry laugh. "The guy was coming on to Dr. Hansen while he and his wife were planning their future family?"

"He didn't *say* anything wrong," Mindy said, "but when a guy looks at a woman's boobs more than her eyes, I get suspicious about what he's thinking."

"Did the video show anything more than impolite staring?" Tall Wolf asked.

"Might have. I don't know because that's when Dr. Hansen came in and asked what I was doing. When I told her, she fired me. But I did see something else."

"What?" McGill asked her.

"A week or so before the robbery, I was out with a guy who was trying to impress me. He took me to dinner at the kind of restaurant young people who aren't rich don't dine at too often. I saw Dr. Hansen there with a man. She's not married so I didn't think anything of it. I'm pretty sure she never even saw me. But you know who that man was?"

McGill and Tall Wolf answered together, "Edmond Whelan."

"Right. The guy who liked to look at her boobs."

The White House — Washington, DC

Every political operator in the nation's capital knew that if you had bad news that had to come out and you wanted it to do the least political damage, you engaged in what was called the Friday Night News Dump. That was, you put the word out as late as possible on the last working day of the week. You made sure it was released too late to be on the national news that night, and probably too late to be included in the Sunday morning political week-in-review shows.

If you leaked a juicy story on a Thursday morning, though, it would have two nights on the national news and probably be the headline story on the Sunday morning shows.

White House Chief of Staff Galia Mindel knew all that almost from the time she took her first step. She had her office TV tuned to WWN. Didi DiMarco came on with a "special bulletin." The graphic below her face screamed: BREAKING NEWS.

Galia smiled to herself.

Looking serious and straight into the camera, Didi said, "We have news this morning that an arrest warrant for Senator Randall Pennyman, the Democratic junior senator from Georgia, has been issued by a federal court in Atlanta. The senator has been charged with several counts of fraud. Currently, the number of counts is fourteen, but a Department of Justice source says that number is likely to go higher.

"Specifically, the senator and several other people, including both members of the clergy and lay people, are accused of having bilked the congregants of churches throughout the country out of many millions of dollars by setting up fake charities that were supposedly intended to help the victims of natural disasters in the United States and abroad.

"Federal law demands that charities with tax-exempt status

must support educational, religious or charitable activities, and must specify that no part of their assets shall benefit any of their directors, officers or agents. The purported charities with which Senator Pennyman and the other unnamed individuals are involved have been converting more than 90% of the donations they received to personal use.

"Initial inquiries have shown that Senator Pennyman has offshore bank accounts with assets totaling over $10 million dollars. Authorities suspect there are still more accounts belonging to the senator which have yet to be discovered. A source told this reporter, 'We think Pennyman has enough cash stashed away that he couldn't explain it honestly even if he had a winning lotto ticket.'

"Police and federal officers in Washington, DC and the senator's hometown of Savannah, Georgia have reported that they went to the senator's homes and did not find him in either city. Calls to his cell phone have gone unanswered, and authorities say it must either be turned off or was disabled because they are unable to locate it. The public is being asked to call 911 if they see the senator but not to approach him personally.

"The same source whose comment I shared a moment ago also said, "Senator Pennyman has no criminal record, but a man in his position cannot be counted on to act rationally."

Galia clicked off the television and smiled.

Her spies had told her Pennyman had started his scam while he was still in college. He thought he'd never get caught. Even if there were suspicions, he was sure no one would be able to prove his misdeeds. Until he made the mistake of challenging Galia two days ago, saw the look in her eyes and decided it was time to run.

The SOB should have taken it as a sign and folded his con-game when Galia had destroyed his opponent for his Senate seat. What had Pennyman thought? That *he* was too smart not to get caught. Hell, *nobody* was that smart, including her.

That was why she had her letter of resignation already written and signed.

All it needed now was to be dated.

The Speaker's Office — United States Capitol

Speaker of the House Peter Profitt clicked off the TV in his office in the West Front of the Capitol. Sitting with him was House Whip Carter Coleman. Each man bided his thoughts in silence for a moment and then Coleman looked at his boss with a questioning look.

Profitt sighed and shook his head. "Taking down Randall Pennyman was more than a shot across our bow, you realize that, don't you, Carter?"

The man who counted conservative votes in the House gave a reluctant nod. "Yeah, I guess I do. It might look like the Democrats just lost one of their senators, but we lost a vote for convicting Patti Grant."

"Has to be Galia Mindel's doing," Profitt said. "That woman knows more of Washington's dirty secrets than J. Edgar Hoover ever did."

A chill ran through Coleman, and Profitt knew just what he was thinking.

"You're right, Carter. We better worry about what other sins she knows."

The Whip said, "And when she's going to use them. She didn't pick up on this scandal of Pennyman's yesterday. She had to know about it for some time. She had to be patient about digging out all the details she could, and then she *saved* it for just the right time. When it would do the president the most good."

The Speaker said, "Do you think ..."

"What?"

"Well, you know how we've been scheming and working to make sure we can control all the levers of power around here on a more or less permanent basis."

"Yeah, well, all that started to slip when we lost two seats on the Supreme Court one night at the same dinner table."

"That was unfortunate, the loss of the judicial branch's pinnacle — as well as two good men, of course."

"Yeah, them, too."

The Speaker said, "What I was thinking, though, is while we've been working on a plan to take over the federal government, maybe the other side has a plan to wreck it if we do. Because I would bet my children's inheritance it won't be long before the White House chief of staff engineers the destruction of one of *our* senators."

"In addition to those thieving fools on the Senate Armed Services Committee, you mean."

"Yes, in addition to them. But if Ms. Mindel singles out another senator, one of ours, with news of some horrendous scandal, who do you think would dare vote for the president's conviction?"

Coleman produced a joyless laugh. "Hell, she might be acquitted by acclamation."

"Or damn near," Profitt said, "and how will that make all of us fine ladies and gentlemen in the House look, after we voted to impeach the president?"

"Christ, we'll be peddling magazine subscriptions door to door."

The Speaker laughed. "I believe that profession has fallen prey to spam emails. I'd like to think we could beg for charity from our places of worship, only Pennyman's scam might have emptied all the collection baskets."

"We've got to do something," the Whip said. "Is there anything we can do to speed up giving Patricia Grant her good name back, without making it look too good?"

Profitt shook his head. "The Senate, at the very least, has to go through the motions. Put on some kind of show before they vote. But we have to be ready for the immediate aftermath. Galia Mindel and Jean Morrissey might slaughter us if we convict the president, but a lot of our voters might do the same if we don't."

"Damn, I never thought things would come to this, at least for us. But, Peter, I just can't see looking to Ed Whelan for advice on this situation."

"Neither can I," the Speaker said. "He's done well for us over the years, but I'm afraid that boy has lost his fastball."

"That's a real problem," the Whip replied, going along with the baseball metaphor, "because we don't have any young stud to call in from the bullpen either."

"Then maybe we ought to reach out to a cagey old-timer. Who was Ed Whelan's mentor?"

"Thomas Winston Rangel at The Maris Foundation. But I'm sure he's retired by now."

"Just so long as he isn't dead," the Speaker said. "Give old T.W. a call and we'll see if he has something left in his bag of tricks he never shared with Whelan."

Pacific Palisades, California

Dr. Danika Hansen pled the press of business when McGill, Tall Wolf, SAC Elspeth Kendry and Detectives Zapata and MacDuff showed up en masse and unannounced at her clinic. That didn't keep her voice from quavering and tics in both eyes from looking like they were sending out a distress call by semaphore.

"Even if I were to make time for you," she told the impromptu gathering of law enforcement types and one P.I., "I'm not sure what I could tell you."

"If you tell us anything at all," Tall Wolf said, "please understand that SAC Kendry and I are federal officers. Lying to us could land you in a federal prison for five years. Lying to the detectives from LAPD might result in an obstruction of justice charge. I don't know what penalty California provides for that —"

"You can get up to five years from us, too," Zapata said.

The blood drained from Danika Hansen's face.

Tall Wolf said, "You see: Honesty and cooperation are your best bets."

McGill remained silent, watching the others work. Over Elspeth's objection and Tall Wolf's abstention, he'd decided to take one more crack at making peace with the local cops. He called and told them of Mindy Crozier's suspicion that the clinic owner was the person who'd provided the clinic's entry code to the embryo thief, and the reason for thinking what she did. Despite any antipathy they felt for McGill, they liked Mindy's story and the reasoning that flowed from it. They showed up to join the confrontation with Dr. Hansen.

Watching the others work, McGill could see a possible glimpse of his future.

Managing a growing private investigations firm might be fun.

If he ever got restless doing that, he could always work a case himself.

Danika Hansen looked almost as concerned about the spectacle her employees were witnessing as she was about the people with badges and guns. Word of what was happening at her business was bound to get out. The people who worked for her were bound to talk with family and friends; they might even go to the newspapers and TV stations.

Someone might already be surreptitiously taking a cell phone video. Post it on the Internet minutes from now. Dr. Hansen began to sway. Tall Wolf steadied her with a gentle hand.

"Why don't we go into my office?" she said.

McGill and the others let her lead the way. The doctor took a seat behind her desk and surveyed the row of serious faces looking back at her. She saw there would be no point in trying to mislead them, especially not when she might go to prison for that alone. There wouldn't even be any point in trying to stall them.

But Danika Hansen thought there still might be room to negotiate.

Looking at McGill, she said, "I won't lie to anyone, and I'll do my best not to delay matters, but I believe in either a federal or state case, I still have the right to counsel. Am I correct?"

McGill let the LAPD answer first. MacDuff said, "Yeah, you do, but it wouldn't look good if you say your lawyer's in China or somewhere and we have to wait until he gets back."

"He's in Beverly Hills."

She looked back to McGill, who deferred to Tall Wolf.

"It's everyone's right to have legal representation," he said.

The BIA co-director got the name, address and phone number of Danika Hansen's lawyer.

Tall Wolf continued, telling the doctor, "It would be only polite to let LAPD have the first interview with you and your lawyer. I would suppose the Department of Justice will want to decide whether any kidnapping charges would apply in this case."

Dr. Hansen's eyes started to fill with tears and her chin trembled.

"I'm not saying they will," Tall Wolf continued. "At least, it's not a sure thing, but I'd suggest that cooperating with the detectives might have a positive effect on further proceedings."

Zapata and MacDuff kept straight faces, but their bodies rocked with silent laughter.

McGill looked at the two L.A. dicks and asked, "Would you gentlemen like to take things from here?"

"Yeah, sure, we got it," Zapata said.

Turning his back to Dr. Hansen, McGill whispered to the local cops.

"I don't know if we're even here, but are we close to good?"

The two detectives nodded.

"All I'd like to know now is if the guy she gives up is named Edmond Whelan."

"Yeah, okay," MacDuff agreed.

"If there's anything else you think is important and you're feeling generous ..."

The two of them grinned like hyenas. Zapata said, "Oh, yeah, sure. MacDuff and me, we're known far and wide for being big hearted."

"I've always suspected as much," McGill said.

Montevideo, Uruguay

A small debate took place late Thursday afternoon in an office of the domestic security division of the National Police.

"He is American, no question," Lieutenant Silvina Reyes said.

"There are many American accents, are there not?" Captain Antonio Calvo asked.

"Yes, of course. It is an *enormous* country."

"So you can't say you know all of them."

"No. Certainly not."

"Might not some American accents overlap with Canadian ones?"

"I would not be surprised if that is technically so."

"Then, Lieutenant, how can you be so certain this man is American?"

"It is more than a matter of pronunciation. It has to do with … attitude."

"What kind of attitude?"

"It's a sense of … ownership," Lieutenant Reyes said.

"The man did just buy a home," Captain Calvo replied. "Paid cash as we've learned."

"It's more than that. You need to live there to understand. An American is told from his first day in his mother's arms that he has rights."

Calvo nodded. "Any advanced country with a democratic government confers rights on its citizens."

"Yes, but that is where the differences begin. Americans think *they* are the source of all their rights, and that is what their Constitution says in so many words. The government's role is merely to articulate those rights and to defend them."

Captain Calvo said, "That is a fairy tale."

"Not to them. That is their true faith. They hold it to be true even when they are in someone else's country. They think all their liberties and even their laws travel with them. That is what I meant by ownership."

"I would call this more of a sense of privilege, not unlike what royalty expects," Calvo said.

Lieutenant Reyes smiled and saluted the captain.

"*Exactamente. Bueno.* Now, certain Canadians, the rich and powerful among them, might exhibit this sense of privilege, but it is far more common among Americans."

Lieutenant Silvina Reyes had lived in the United States for ten years. Her father had been a Uruguayan trade official at the United Nations during her high school years. She attended college at Washington University in St. Louis. She got her master's degree in political science at the University of Texas in Austin, where as luck would have it she fell in love with a young fellow from her homeland.

Martin Reyes' family had a military tradition and he'd had ROTC training in the U.S. So it was only natural for him to enter the army's officer corps upon returning home. Silvina thought to do the same — she acquired a bit of an American sense of entitlement herself — but decided wisely that direct competition with her new husband would not be good for their marriage.

So she'd signed up with the National Police, and was assigned to domestic security.

After the 9/11 tragedies in the United States, the Uruguayans decided they should keep a closer watch on foreigners who settled in their country, even the rich ones. With Silvina's intelligence, fluent English, advanced education and exposure to the wider world, she was considered a catch for the National Police.

She didn't even mind playing the role of a nanny when investigating new arrivals in gilded precincts like Punta del Este. Calvo trusted her so much he let his young son, Santiago, play the role of the child for whom Silvina cared.

"Very well," Captain Calvo said, "we have an American in Punta del Este pretending to be a Canadian. We could arrest him immediately and find out what he's up to. Do you think that's what we should do?"

"Where would the fun be in that?" Lieutenant Reyes asked.

"Fun?"

Captain Calvo was a desk man, didn't understand the thrill of working the street. Even in a privileged place like Punta Del Este there was an emotional charge in outwitting the opposition. Perhaps if the captain had a better understanding he would have conscripted someone else's child to work with Silvina.

"Very well," she said. "Where would the *advantage* be in that? If this fellow calling himself Bruce Mallory is here to cause us trouble, we should be watching to see who his associates are. If he is here hiding from trouble he's caused elsewhere, we should learn who might thank us for sending him home."

"But you've already told me he is American," Calvo said.

"He is, by birth and I would say upbringing. But as hard as it is for some people to imagine, Americans do emigrate to other countries. Sometimes for tax reasons or cultural preferences. Other times, though, they obtain foreign citizenship before their crimes at home can be discovered, making themselves much harder to retrieve and stand trial."

Antonio Calvo sighed. He knew without a doubt that Silvina Reyes was much smarter than he was. It was all but certain he would end up working for her someday. Better to get on her good side now.

"Very well. Continue your investigation, Lieutenant."

"Thank you, Captain."

She was about to leave when Calvo held up a file.

Lieutenant Reyes stopped and asked, "What is that?"

"Another new arrival in Punta del Este, in the house directly across the street from your American. This one and his family claim to be arrivals from Hong Kong, residents of the former British colony who grew weary of living under Chinese rule."

"Interesting," the lieutenant said.

"Possibly," the captain allowed. "Maybe your American's associates are gathering already. For what purpose, who can say? I leave it to you to find out."

Silvina Reyes gave her superior a second, more formal salute. "That is just what I will do."

Punta del Este, Uruguay

Tyler Busby looked around his new home, one which 99.9%

of humanity would have been overjoyed to call their own, and apologized to Ah-lam.

"I'm sorry about not being able to do better, but I hadn't anticipated how difficult and prolonged childbirth could be. I had little time to arrange a place to stay."

Ah-lam had been born on a junk in Aberdeen Harbor, Hong Kong. Her family of ten lived, worked, ate and slept in a space that made a sardine tin look spacious. Human waste was dumped directly into the water. Her climb in social standing and creature comfort had been nothing less than astronomical, but she'd never forgotten her origins.

"It will do for now," she told her husband.

The captain of *Wastrel* had married them. He was a licensed master mariner, but had admitted to both parties that neither his nautical training nor his experience had included the task of uniting a couple in holy wedlock.

To which, Busby had replied, "In Florida, they'll let a notary public marry people. You'll do."

He and Ah-lam downloaded a mutually agreeable script for the ceremony from the Internet. The captain spoke the celebrant's part without stumbling on a single word, and that was that. They were married.

That first night in Punta del Este, though, Busby thought maybe certain spousal obligations should have been made more clear from the start, after Ah-lam told him, "No sex."

"You mean tonight?"

"I mean until we are ready for me to bear a second son."

To show her husband she hadn't forgotten his needs, she grabbed his crotch in a friendly way and told him, "I have already sent for your favorite ladies. They will stay in Buenos Aires, and you may call on them as you wish. For the sake of not arousing suspicion, though, I have told them to dress modestly, and I suggest you allow yourself no more than two at a time."

Busby blinked, grinned, frowned and shrugged in rapid succession.

He was amazed by Ah-lam's sense of organization, pleased by the idea of revisiting former favorites, displeased that she was taking an unnecessary chance when she could have simply pleasured him personally and philosophical that they were both making the best of their circumstances.

"All right, I can live with that," he said. "When do you think you might like to have another child?"

She told him, "I will let you know."

CHAPTER 9

Muscle Beach — Venice, California

Eugene Beck had heard of the place from some of the guys he'd trained with before his last-minute washout from special forces. They'd told him Muscle Beach was a hoot — and it was pretty close to the airport hotel where he was staying. So he decided to go over and take a look.

For purposes of misleading anyone who might take notice of him, he'd applied a bronzing cream to all exposed areas of skin, gelled and combed his hair up into a field of spikes and put on wraparound sunglasses. Under the shades, in case he decided to remove them, he wore vivid blue contact lenses.

He considered applying a fake goatee, but he thought he might get sweaty, and didn't want the faux whiskers to slip. If he made himself look foolish, people would be *more* likely to remember him. Sometimes subtle changes were better.

The guys who'd told him about Muscle Beach said there were some truly eye-popping specimens there, both male and female, but said they were just protein and steroid sculptors. All their massive, chiseled musculature wouldn't get them through the first day of special forces torture. Beck knew that was a tribal point of view.

My warriors are better than yours.

Maybe, maybe not.

Beck knew for a fact that he was tougher, stronger and more resilient than all but one or two of the guys he'd trained with, and he still got washed out. Because some dicks somewhere in the process thought his whistling meant he was … what? Not a perfect fit for what they wanted? A little chickenshit reason for disqualification like that could have made a man angry. Probably would have if he hadn't gotten his own pretty cool job not two minutes after he left the training base.

Only now that had turned south on him, too.

He'd checked and Nicholas Wicklow, the DIA guy who had recruited him to be an off-the-books assassin, had himself an automobile accident. Lost control of his vehicle, missed a bridge he was approaching and went into a river in Virginia. He was still belted into his seat when his body was recovered.

It was said he'd been drinking earlier that night.

An unnamed friend told the newspaper carrying the story that Wicklow was distraught over an unexpected demand for a divorce from his wife of many years.

Yeah, sure, Beck thought.

Just as he'd suspected, with Wicklow gone, his last tie to working for the government had vanished. If he went after James J. McGill now, and especially if he got the man, he'd be described as a disaffected, mentally ill special forces washout. Who knew why he'd decided to take out his irrational anger and imaginary grievances against the president's husband?

Yeah, well, fuck that plan, too.

Not only had he aced the physical challenges of his special forces training, he was one of the smartest guys in class, too. He'd excelled in both tactics and strategy. When he'd stolen the embryos from the clinic in Pacific Palisades, they'd been identified only by the code number he'd been given. He'd been told he didn't need to know whose goodies he was taking.

Yeah, well, like they say: *Information is power.*

While that cute little security chick was still lights out from being tased, he sat down at a handy computer and booted it up. Didn't take five minutes to learn whose embryos he'd grabbed: Ms. Mira Kersten. Her and a number of guys. Most of the Daddy roles were played by some dude named Edmond Whelan.

A quick check on him turned up the fact that he and Ms. Mira used to be husband and wife, and Whelan was some kind of high level flunky for a big shot Congress-dick in Washington. Seemed somebody like Whelan would be a natural for wanting to play a dirty trick on an ex-wife.

But there were some other guys who'd splashed their sperm for Ms. Mira. One, to Beck's surprise, was an actor whose work he admired. That was the embryo Beck had taken for himself. Beck had had the mumps as a kid and the illness had left him sterile. So he wasn't going to have any kids of his own. Still, raising a kid sired by a cool movie star wasn't a bad consolation prize.

Besides learning the identities of the embryos' mom and dads, Beck also gleaned Ms. Mira's home address and her phone numbers. He intended to visit with her and ask her opinion of whom she thought wanted to do her so wrong. His money was on Whelan, but he wanted to be sure. In return, he'd tell her where she could find her stash of chilled children.

Beck was sure that whoever had put him up to the theft was also the geek who wanted him to kill James J. McGill. Beck was going to have a little talk with that guy. Impress on him the error of his ways. Maybe even whistle while he worked.

Meanwhile, as long as he was right there at Muscle Beach, he'd get a little exercise.

The place had a fenced-in area with various kinds of workout stations like you'd find in a gym. Those were all in use, and most of them had guys waiting in line. A fair number of gawkers watched the guys working out and even the specimens just shooting the breeze with one another.

Beck didn't feel like waiting or being scoped. And, really, until you saw him in action, his physique looked fairly normal. Sure, he was lean and toned, and when he got his pulse rate up a lot of definition jumped into view, but strolling along in a loose T-shirt and knee-length shorts, he just looked like a guy who ate right and didn't spend all day sitting on his backside.

A construction worker young enough to be out looking for a cutie, maybe.

Right out on the sand, Beck saw a couple of installations for doing pull-ups and dips. The pull-up bar had a guy using it, but the parallel dip bars were open. A small but growing crowd of onlookers was counting aloud the number of repetitions the dude on the chin-up bar was doing. "Fifteen … sixteen … seventeen …"

Guy was as regular as a metronome and with his shirt off, he was impressing a lot of the girls. His arm muscles might've been steel springs, as easy as he made his reps look. He caught sight of Beck and, give him credit, knew the new arrival was something different.

Beck gave the dude a small nod and set about doing some dips.

"Eighteen … nineteen …" the chin-up counters voiced.

Only not all of them were watching the first guy now; some of them had turned to look at Beck. He was making his reps look even easier that the other guy. Beck seemed to *float* up and down. No effort at all. A few people started to count for him.

The dissonance between the two counts started throwing off the chin-up guy's rep counters. That broke the dude's concentration. He got pissed-off and stopped his sequence at either twenty-five or twenty-six, depending on whose total he found accurate.

By now, more people were watching Beck.

His count was up to twenty and rising.

The chin-up guy elbowed his way to the front of the onlookers and said with contempt, "Dips. Any limp dick can do a ton of dips."

Hearing that, several people took a step back. Nobody wanted to take a punch or a kick meant for someone else. Beck reacted nonviolently, but still in a way that sent a clear message. He levered himself from a dip position to a handstand on the parallel bars.

Made it look easy.

Then he started doing vertical push-ups. "One … two …

three," the crowd counted.

When he got to a dozen, he hand-walked to the far end of the bars. He dismounted smoothly and turned to face the onlookers. They gave him a round of applause and he returned their gesture of appreciation with a bow.

The guy who'd been doing the chin-ups had left.

Beck was glad to see that. Showed some people still had common sense.

He gave a wave of farewell to the crowd.

He'd go back to his hotel, take a shower, get a bite to eat and go visit Ms. Mira.

Washington, DC

Repressing a sigh, White House Chief of Staff Galia Mindel put in a call to the only other woman in Patricia Grant's professional life who had meant as much to the president as she did: Dorie McBride, the legendary Hollywood talent agent who had spotted a young Patti Darden and moved her from modeling to movies.

Dorie's approach had been simple. "Honey, you're much too smart to limit yourself to pouting for still photographs. And you didn't go to Yale to major in runway strutting. Come to Los Angeles and let people hear what you have to say."

In films, Dorie meant. Patti Darden starred in three of them. The reviews of her performances started with mild praise and grew progressively stronger. So did the box office for each of her movies. She was on the verge of becoming bankable when she met Andrew Hudson Grant, billionaire philanthropist, and he wooed her, married her and took her home to Winnetka, Illinois.

Never one to sit idle, Patti had involved herself with a number of good works.

She'd helped Jimmy Carter promote Habitat for Humanity and even rolled up her sleeves to work on the construction of a handful of houses with the former president. A picture of her and Carter driving nails next to each other was published in People Magazine. That was when Galia took an interest.

She met Patti at a lunch hosted by Dick Bergen, now the Senate minority leader, then a downstate Illinois Democratic congressman. Galia's approach had been as direct as Dorie McBride's.

She told Patti, "You don't need to limit yourself to helping people one house at a time. You want to have a national impact? I can get you elected to Congress."

Patti was intrigued. She spoke with Andy. A string of doctors had recently told them the depressing news that both of them were infertile. They would conceive and bear no children of their own. Adoption remained an open question, but both of them agreed it would be helpful for Patti to have a new career of her own.

Neither of them had thought of Patti going back to Hollywood.

But Dorie McBride had, and was counting on it.

Until Patti announced her candidacy for a House seat and then won it.

Dorie blamed Galia for spoiling all her plans. They'd met a number of times over the years, including at two inaugural balls. The political equivalent of after-parties for the Academy Award presentations. Even without an unkind word or even a smirk from Galia, Dorie felt that Galia was flaunting her triumphs.

Not that Dorie let the president see her hard feelings.

Well, maybe a little.

Answering Galia's call that day, Dorie said, "You want something, don't you? You've got some nerve."

Galia said, "Neither of us got where we are by being shy."

"I should hang up right now."

"You could do that or you could try to be helpful to the president."

Galia had heard that Dorie once suggested she might find a sitcom for the president after she retired from politics. Galia waited until she got home before laughing, but who knew if the Hollywood agent still harbored show biz hopes for Patti Grant? Scoring a coup like getting her most famous former client on film would certainly put Dorie back on the map in La-La Land.

"What do you mean?" Dorie asked.

"Do you still know who's sleeping with whom out there?"

"I wish I was still having sex with someone, if that's what you mean, but, yes, I still know who's boffing whom, if they're important in the business."

Galia asked, "How about if only one of them is?"

Dorie sighed. "I'll do this only if *I* decide it's important to Patricia. Give me a name."

"Mira Kersten."

Laughter pealed from coast to coast. "She's not important but the guy she's sleeping with is. He loves her for her politics, at least for now. And yes, someone like him might be of importance to Patricia. He might contribute to her new venture capital firm."

She gave Galia a name, a big one.

"Would you know if that gentleman has impregnated Mira?"

"Jesus, no, I don't, but why would he?"

"You just said he loves her," Galia said.

"Not like that. I don't think he's capable of that kind of relationship."

"Could you find out, as definitively as possible."

"You wouldn't stoop to using Patricia for your own purposes, would you?" Dorie asked.

Of course, I would, Galia thought. Same as you, you old bag.

What she said was, "It might make a difference in the president's trial in the Senate."

"You are doing your best to protect … the woman we both love?"

"Why else would I call you?" Galia asked.

"All right then, damnit. I'll find out. Tell you as soon as I know."

Galia said to use the number of her new phone. One she'd bought from a drugstore that morning. Wearing a wide-brimmed hat and sunglasses. And would throw away after she heard back from Dorie McBride.

The White House — Washington, DC

"Can a girl get a cup of coffee in the White House Mess?" the voice on Welborn Yates' office phone asked.

"Colonel Linberg, is that you?" a surprised Welborn asked.

"It is, Colonel Yates. I'm out front with the uniformed Secret Service guys. I asked them to frisk me and let me in to see you. They said I had to call first, and declined to lay hands on my person. Someone my age can't even get a guy to cop a feel anymore."

"I'll have to decline that honor, too, but I will buy you some coffee."

"Good, because I have some news for you."

"Please put the Secret Service officer in charge on the phone."

She did and five minutes later she was escorted into the White House Mess. Welborn was already there. He had a corner table staked out with two cups of steaming liquid on the table. He stood and saluted as Carina approached even though she was wearing civilian clothing.

She returned the salute and stood there looking Welborn in the eye.

He knew what was expected of him. After a quick glance around the room, he gave her a hug. Keeping it brief and making sure his hands stayed above her waist. With a smile, she sat and added some cream and sugar to her coffee.

Welborn was having green tea, neat.

He said, "You're just teasing with this pretense of personal affection, right?"

"Were you smitten with me when we first met?"

"I was young … but yes."

"I found that endearing. When I'm lonely, my thoughts turn to you, unbidden."

Welborn did his best to keep from blushing.

"That's very flattering, but I'm married now and the father of two."

"You're also still in uniform. We wouldn't want *you* to get charged with adultery."

"That would be too ironic, among many other things," Welborn said.

"Had you met your future wife before or after you began your investigation of me?" Carina asked.

"After, just after."

"Did you ever wonder about that, the timing?"

Welborn shook his head. "Never gave it a thought."

But he was doing so just then, and a look of enlightenment dawned on him.

"Well, I'll be," he said.

"Many things, I'm sure, but probably not damned. So who do you think it was who set you up with your future wife to save you from my womanly wiles, the president or McGill?"

"Both of them," he said, "but the idea probably originated with Mr. McGill. He'd have been the one to think he shouldn't let my investigation of you be compromised by … unprofessional behavior. If I had messed up, it would have embarrassed the president, and he wouldn't have wanted that. He was protecting his wife."

"Another gentleman when I keep looking for rascals." She sipped her coffee.

"I know a few," Welborn said.

"You're the second man I've met today who's offered to set me up with someone else. Faint praise, if you ask me."

Welborn took a frank look at Carina Linberg, to the point where it made her squirm.

"Careful," she said, "I might jump over the table and assault you right here."

Welborn smiled. "There's *nothing* wrong with the way you look. No hideous wrinkles. My bet is you'll find someone who'll make you happy within a month."

Carina smiled ruefully. "Psychic now, are you?"

He shook his head. "Just a feeling."

"Okay. We'd better get down to business, now that my personal happiness is assured. I've got a name for you, Eugene Beck. He may be the guy you're looking for; in fact I'd be surprised if he isn't. That's why I flew up here."

Welborn moved his cup of tea aside, leaned forward and spoke quietly.

"You're speaking of the threat to Mr. McGill's life?"

She nodded and leaned forward, too. "I heard about this little program the DIA was running, might still be. You should use your position here at the White House to double-check what I'm going to tell you. Make sure it's valid."

She told him about Beck's time in special forces training and the reason for his peculiar, last-minute wash-out. Then she added the information about the death of his DIA recruiter and handler, Nicholas Wicklow.

"The man died in an auto accident?" Welborn repeated.

"Yeah. Convenient, huh? Now, there's no way to connect Beck to the government."

"More than that," Welborn said. "There's no way for Wicklow ever to testify about what Beck did to earn his keep as a contractor."

"My guess is he wasn't teaching people close order drills."

"No, it had to be something more sinister than that."

The fact that Wicklow had died behind the wheel, especially if the accident was arranged, hit home for Welborn. If Wicklow had any family, they deserved to know the truth.

"I'll check all this out, Colonel," he told Carina, "but I'll pass the information on to Mr. McGill right away."

She said, "I know we talked about how I might use some of this information as story material, but I'm going to pass on that. Don't want to get too deeply involved here. It's way above my pay-grade, even if I'm not in the military anymore and have more money than anybody in the government except Patricia Grant."

"I think that's a wise choice," Welborn said.

As discreetly as possible, he took one of her hands in his.

"Did I ever mention to you that my father used to be the personal secretary to the Queen of England?"

She laughed and said, "No, you didn't, and that's a tidbit I might put into a story."

"Fine, fair trade, but what I was thinking is, Dad knows any number of smart, sophisticated eligible fellows. How do you feel about Englishmen?"

Carina grinned. "I might give one a try, as long as he's a bit of a rascal."

Century City Mall — Los Angeles, California

"How far along are you?" McGill asked Mira Kersten.

The two of them stood outside a business calling itself Giggles N' Hugs, self-described as a children's restaurant and play space. He'd called her; she told him where she was. Finding her was that simple.

Standing in an arc around McGill at a distance of twenty feet or so were John Tall Wolf, Deke Ky, Elspeth Kendry and Sweetie, who'd caught up with the others. Just beyond the boundaries of the mall stood a cluster of high rises.

The buildings were neither tall enough nor sufficiently numerous to be called a skyline by the standards of Chicago or New York, but west of the Mississippi, they'd do. And the big cities of the Midwest and the East didn't have open-air shopping venues that could be enjoyed year 'round.

"Far along with what?" Mira replied.

"Your pregnancy."

Mira had told McGill she was at the kiddie place with a friend and her child.

She lightly patted her flat midsection. "Not too far, I'd say."

McGill sighed. "Do you want me to keep looking for your embryos? Do you want me to call Galia Mindel to get an answer to my question?"

Mira looked down at her shoes for an answer.

They apparently told her to play things straight.

"My answers are yes and no. Let's get something to drink."

As a further sign that she was with child, Mira led McGill to a table outside a juice bar, not one that served alcohol. Mira had The Hot Lei; McGill went with The Pipe Cleaner. L.A. being L.A., plain old apple or orange juice were too mundane to be available.

"To answer your question," Mira said, "I'm six weeks pregnant."

"Everything going okay so far? I'm guessing it is."

"Kind of you to ask. Yes, all is well. But then you have another reason for wanting to know, don't you?"

McGill nodded. "I'm curious why you didn't tell me up front."

"Who did tell you?"

"No one. Your general appearance, a certain radiance actually, registered with me, but the reason for it didn't click immediately. Then I remembered the times I saw my ex-wife looking pretty much the same way."

Mira laughed. "Really? I just thought I was looking healthy. Clean living and all that. Never paid too much attention to other women when they were pregnant. What has caught my eye is that your escort, the Secret Service people, the BIA guy and the new woman, all seem to be on high alert. The blonde, she's your partner, isn't she?"

"Yes, she is, Margaret Sweeney. The reason everyone is keyed up is my life was threatened recently. It's something we all think should be taken seriously. But the timing of the threat makes me think it has something to do with my investigation out here."

"Meaning it has to do with me, and I didn't tell you everything I might have."

"Exactly. Hiring a private investigator doesn't necessarily mean baring your soul entirely, but given the nature of your problem, the fact that you're pregnant seems relevant."

Mira took a swig of her juice. "Okay. I got knocked up the old-fashioned way. Thought I was protected against that, but as they say no contraceptive is perfect."

"You're going to have the baby?"

"I am. Flies in the face of all my elaborate planning, I know. But I admire the man who will be my child's father. I'm already monitoring both my health and the baby's closely. I'll be working and hoping for a good outcome."

"My best wishes," McGill said.

"Thank you. I'd still like my embryos back, though. So far, I'm enjoying the pregnancy experience. I can see doing it again."

McGill just looked at her.

Mira said, "If you're wondering whether the dad and I will get married, there's no plan for that. I've told him he can have as little or as much involvement with our child as he wants."

"Very liberal of you," McGill said.

Mira grinned. "Yeah, well, that's my kind of politics, isn't it?"

"Straight down the line? Some people pick and choose, depending on the issue."

"Well, I will admit I think of the money I make as *mine*. After taxes, of course. I feel pretty much the same about the property I own."

That attitude raised a question in McGill's mind, but he decided to keep it to himself for the moment. What he might do, though, was raise the subject with Galia. He left that possibility unspoken as well.

What he did say was, "Has there been any further contact from Edmond Whelan?"

That caught her off guard. "No, why would there be?"

"Well, if he doesn't get his master plan back, and still thinks you have it, it seems likely he'll try to turn up the pressure."

"Jesus, I didn't think of that. I mean, with you looking for him and the embryos, wouldn't that be foolish?"

"How would he know I'm working for you?"

She laughed. "There was that video, remember? You versus the world or at least half of the LAPD. Everybody's seen it, and Ed's pretty self-centered. He's going to think you're in town because of me, and him."

Given the nature of Washington-based egos, McGill couldn't argue.

Still, he said, "Someone like that is also probably used to getting his way. He might become, let's say, more insistent, if he's kept waiting."

Mira took another hit of her juice, looking like she wished it was something stronger.

McGill asked, "Would you like me to have Ms. Sweeney keep you company for the next few days."

"Is she good?" Mira asked. "At protecting people, I mean."

"She saved my life," McGill said. "Took a bullet that should have been mine."

Even with that endorsement, it took Mira a moment to say yes.

"Start now?" McGill asked.

She nodded her head. He gestured to Sweetie. She came over and McGill introduced the two women. An arrangement was worked out for 48 hours of protection with an option for two more days. Sweetie accompanied Mira back to her car.

McGill was sure Mira knew he'd made the offer so Sweetie could snoop on her, as well as keep her from harm. That was okay. There were precious few people Sweetie couldn't get to see the light, do the right thing despite contrary impulses of self-interest.

And if Mira suddenly *remembered* something she should have told McGill, Sweetie would be the perfect channel of communication.

What Sweetie also represented was a complication to two observers standing outside McGill's ring of protection.

Ed Whelan and Eugene Beck, looking on from different points of view, neither knowing or recognizing who the other was, had seen the chat between McGill and Mira. Each of them wanted to speak with Mira privately. Now, each of them had to get past Sweetie.

Both of them began to plan.

WWN Studio — Washington, DC

Ellie Booker had a long track record of breaking big stories and a first-look deal with WorldWide News. She had not been pleased when network CEO Hugh Collier hired Didi DiMarco. Didi was thought of mostly as an on-air talent, a pretty face who didn't trip over her own tongue.

Ellie knew better. Didi was smart and produced her own show. She hustled for the biggest and best stories she could find, and often came up with ideas no one else had even considered. Her hiring was meant to reduce any leverage Ellie might have over Hugh when it came to whom he'd depend on to deliver his networks next big scoop.

True, Ellie had only recently done an exclusive story with the president in the wake of her impeachment, but Didi quickly followed that with her own interview of Jean Morrissey, and right now the VP had more media heat than the president. Any way you looked at it, Patti Grant was a lame duck near the end of her run in the White House. Jean Morrissey might well be the next most powerful person in the world. In the meantime, it looked certain the VP intended to kick political ass.

Covering that kind of thing was always fun.

In terms of their respective stature in the media world, it was beginning to look like Ellie represented the past and Didi was the future. Maybe so, but Ellie was not going to exit quietly. She was going to do her best to —

Answer her own damn phone when it became apparent her secretary wasn't at her desk.

Hell, maybe she'd defected to Didi.

"Booker Productions," she snapped.

After a moment of silence, a heartbeat before Ellie would have slammed the phone down, a quiet, polished male voice said, "May I speak with Ms. Booker, please?"

In addition to all her other news-gathering faculties, Ellie had a keen ear. If she heard a prominent person speak more than once, the mental recording got neatly filed for instant recall. She said, "Mr. Chief Justice, is that you?"

Craig MacLaren said, "I'm afraid it is."

Taking a risk, she joked, "Is this about my unpaid parking tickets, sir?"

MacLaren laughed. "I'm afraid you'll have to take those up with the attorney general."

"Yes, sir," Ellie said with a smile. "How may I help you?"

"First, let me say I've long admired your work."

"Thank you." Ellie was honestly flattered, but whenever someone buttered her up it always made her leery about what might come next. She was not a trusting soul. Life had taught her better.

MacLaren continued, "I was wondering whether you'd think a limited series of commentaries from me might be of public interest."

"That would depend, sir. If you're thinking about speaking on biographical matters, that might be better addressed with a book. I could recommend a good collaborator or two to work with you. On the other hand, if you wish to address issues of law in a televised forum, I'd be honored to work with you."

"At WWN, you mean?"

A thought flashed through Ellie's mind. It was time to fire a shot across Hugh Collier's bow, that Aussie prick.

"We could do it at WWN or if you'd be more comfortable at PBS, I have friends there who I'm sure would be happy to work with us."

"Yes, it might be better to work with a non-profit."

"What is it you have in mind, sir?"

When the chief justice told Ellie, she had to restrain herself from jumping up and down and shrieking with joy. Making sure she had her emotions under control, she replied, "That would be very interesting, sir, and completely unprecedented. Are you sure you want to do this?"

"I've given the matter serious consideration. I feel *obligated* to do it."

"Yes, sir."

"I'm also certain there will be countervailing voices."

"You can bet on that, Mr. Chief Justice. The blowback will be considerable."

"If you think it might damage your career, Ms. Booker, I'll

understand if you wish to decline my offer."

Ellie laughed. "Don't worry about me, sir. I think one of the reasons you called me is I have something of a reputation as a street fighter."

MacLaren said, "I am counting on that."

Los Angeles, California

Calling the White House from his hotel suite, using the cell phone he'd been assured would defeat the best efforts of any hacker, foreign or domestic, McGill told Patti, "I was right, Mira Kersten is pregnant."

Not to be outdone, the president told McGill who the child's father was.

To his surprise the dad was an actor whose name he actually knew. Him and most of the rest of the English-speaking world. He even liked the guy's movies.

"I won't ask you for your sources," he told Patti, "but I have a strong hunch."

"Hunches are allowed. Keeping them to yourself is highly advisable. You're not chafing under the weight of two Secret Service agents, are you, Jim?"

"I can manage. Elspeth's okay with me; Deke's my kid brother by now. Having Sweetie along to work one last case with me, well, that's kind of bittersweet. Can you believe she's thinking of going into politics?"

"Yes, without any difficulty. Margaret lives to serve."

"And kick some backside when necessary."

"An integral part of public service."

"Anyway, I'm doing fine, working the case and not feeling threatened."

"Good. We've winnowed out the name of a man who might be the instrument of the threat against you: Eugene Beck. He's ex-military and came within a few musical notes of becoming a special forces operator."

Patti explained what she meant by that.

McGill was amazed. "They didn't take the guy because he likes to whistle? Hell, *I* do that sometimes."

"I've noticed," Patti said. "You do it when you practice your Dark Alley choreography."

McGill said, "Never heard my workouts described in dance terms before, but with my personally provided soundtrack, I guess it's apt."

"The Secret Service is looking for Mr. Beck. If he's found on the far side of the world, then we'll know it's someone else who means you harm."

Sounded better than "wants to kill you," McGill thought.

"If it is him," he said, "I'd like to know what he looks like, in advance."

"Elspeth has photos. I'll send word that you can see them."

"Thank you. It would also be a good thing to know who sicced Beck on me. The name Edmond Whelan comes to mind."

"Yes, it does. It's no coincidence that this threat occurred just after you started a new investigation. The Secret Service went to talk with Mr. Whelan, but so far they've been unable to locate him."

"Making it all the more probable he's behind it, and I'd bet Eugene Beck isn't off climbing Mount Kilimanjaro. Even so, it seems to me we have a lot of bad guys hiding out on us lately."

Patti chuckled.

"What's funny?" McGill asked.

"I probably shouldn't tell you this, but what the hell can anyone do to me? I've already been impeached. I'm about to be tried in the Senate. If they can't take a joke, fuck 'em."

It wasn't often McGill heard that vulgarity from his wife, even in private conversation, but he felt exactly the same way.

He said, "Right. Especially if you have good news. I'd love to hear it."

Patti told him about Special Agent Abra Benjamin's strategy for finding Tyler Busby.

"That's really smart," he said.

"Yes, well, we just got word through informal channels that several of Busby's favorite shady ladies are on their way to Buenos Aires. Now, if we were talking just one or two courtesans, some other dirty old man might have the same tastes, but we're talking six of them here, and two others begged off."

McGill thought about that for a moment.

"No witty observation?" Patti asked.

"Seems like a bit much is all," he said. "He could be mainlining those pick-me-up meds and not take care of a crew like that."

"How romantically put."

"Not much romance involved when you're paying for it."

"Point well made, but you have something else in mind, don't you?"

McGill said, "Having lived in the White House for some time now, I've noticed that underlings have a tendency to try to overdo when it comes to pleasing the boss."

"You think someone working for Busby ordered a full menu for him?"

"Could be. Try to cover everything he might like. That person could be the buffer between him and the women. If the intermediary spots anything that doesn't look right, word is passed to Busby and he disappears again. Or ..."

McGill took a moment to develop his thought.

Patti, knowing just what he was doing, waited patiently.

"Or someone who's just as smart as Special Agent Benjamin is using this shipment of prostitutes as a test. Waiting to see if they draw the attention of law enforcement. If they do, the getaway plan is already in place. If they don't, well, Busby gets to have his idea of a good time."

"So your suggestion would be?" Patti asked.

What McGill had to say made the president pause to think.

"I'll have to consult with the FBI on that. I'm not sure I should issue an order on something like that."

"Just an idea."

Patti said, "One more thing, Jim."

Anticipating his wife, he said, "Be careful with Beck out there?"
"Let Elspeth and Deke do the heavy lifting."

Walter Reed National Military Medical Center — Bethesda, Maryland

The nurse in Joan Renshaw's hospital room, just about to leave after recording the patient's vital signs, jumped as if somebody had yelled, "Boo!"

Returning to earth, she turned and looked at the patient.

Her eyes were open. Not just for a blink but steadily. Attempting to focus.

And Renshaw raspingly repeated the word that had startled the nurse.

"Water."

CHAPTER 9

Friday, March 27, 2015 — Washington, DC

"I'm not screwing the bastard," Special Agent Abra Benjamin said. "I don't care if the order came straight from the White House."

She sat opposite FBI Deputy Director Byron DeWitt in his office.

The Andy Warhol serigraph on the wall of Chairman Mao gazed down on them.

Before DeWitt could respond, Benjamin asked, "You're taking that portrait with you when you go, aren't you?"

"Who says I'm going?" DeWitt replied.

"It's an open secret."

"My least favorite kind."

"Everyone knows about you and Vice President Morrissey."

"What do they know?"

"That you're more than just casual friends."

DeWitt knew that Benjamin, his former lover and the mother of the child they'd given up for adoption, was trying to play him. She was seeking confirmation of what he was sure remained only speculation at that point.

He said, "Well, I hope you'll keep this to yourself but …" He maintained a straight face as Benjamin leaned forward. "But next year, at a date that remains to be determined …"

DeWitt paused as if he'd just thought better of revealing a confidence.

"What?" Benjamin asked, expecting to hear a wedding announcement.

DeWitt said, "Vice President Morrissey and I will be ..." he dragged it out for one last delicious second. "We'll be competing on 'Dancing with the Stars.'"

Benjamin sat back and grimaced. Wanted to call DeWitt a bastard. But her all-consuming sense of ambition prevented that so she returned to a variation of her original question.

"How much do you want for your Mao portrait?"

DeWitt grinned. "Hard to say. The price of Andy's work can go up faster than Apple stock on the eve of a new iPhone introduction. Last year, a dealer in Manhattan offered me an even million dollars for it."

Benjamin hadn't been expecting a figure like that.

She blinked and said, "Jesus."

"Yeah, but she said that was because it had a double cachet: the artist's, of course, and a little bit of me because of where I've had it hanging these past several years."

"Why do you have it here instead of at your home?"

"I like to see the effect it has on people."

"Me, too," Benjamin admitted.

"Also, my insurance premium here is only 10% of what it would be at my place. After all, who's going to burgle the office of the deputy director of the FBI?"

The look on Benjamin's face said she might take a run at it.

DeWitt steered her toward a more productive direction.

"No one is asking you to screw Tyler Busby, only set yourself up to make his arrest. Think of what it would do for your career. Capturing someone who had to be a big player in a presidential assassination attempt. Why, if Jean and I win that dance competition, you just might inherit this office and be able to hang your own piece of subversive art."

Benjamin had been considering that possibility, but at the

moment she picked up on the hint DeWitt had just dropped. By using the vice president's first name with such casual ease he was admitting his intimacy with her. Even if they had no wedding plans, yet, they were spending time between the sheets.

Hearing that made Benjamin's heart sink a bit. She'd gotten together with DeWitt as a career move, but she'd come to appreciate, even care for, him as a man. He'd been a considerate and generous lover. God knew he was good looking, too. There were times, fleeting though they were, that she thought she should have taken a maternity leave from her job and kept their baby. Married him and …

There was no point going too far down that road.

She'd only make herself crazy.

"Give me the briefing again," she told DeWitt, "what you got from the White House."

He nodded and said, "It came from the Oval Office, but my guess is James J. McGill was its author. He's playing off your handiwork and what it set in motion. If you'll remember, two of the six ladies requested to service Tyler Busby's carnal needs declined the opportunity. Their names are Aubine Fortier and Gila Klein."

Benjamin nodded and said, "Making what's not a great big intuitive leap here, you don't think I could fill in for a French woman —"

"Who's also a blonde."

"But you do think I might take the place of a, what, Israeli frecha?"

"I'm sorry, what?" DeWitt asked, not understanding. "A hooker?"

"Close enough. Frecha is slang borrowed from Arabic. Literally, a chick, as in poultry. Colloquially, a bimbo."

DeWitt smiled, happy to expand his linguistic horizons.

"Well. You got the nationality right," he said. "Ms. Klein is Israeli, but she was born and raised in Manhattan."

As was Benjamin. She sighed. Almost anything to get ahead, she thought.

"I hope you're thinking I should let the procurer approach me," Benjamin said.

DeWitt nodded. "That's the only way it would work. We know the hotel where the girls will be staying in Buenos Aires."

"Thanks to me," Benjamin said.

"Exactly. It's top-end. You could be visiting wealthy extended family in B.A. Stop in to the hotel bar for a drink looking like a million dollars and —"

"Wait for a pimp to sweet-talk me into peddling my body."

"Well, don't settle for just any life of vice. Try to make sure Tyler Busby is waiting on the other end."

Benjamin rolled her eyes. "I'll keep that in mind."

DeWitt said, "Hey, come on. You have to think it'd be pretty cool to have Busby invite you over for what he thinks is going to be a good time and you bust his ass."

Benjamin could imagine that scenario and smiled.

"Yeah, it would."

"You can't have my Warhol," DeWitt said, "but I'll help you find something good to hang on the wall when you take over this office."

Benjamin said, "Deal."

Great Falls, Virginia

A prominent financial magazine had recently named Great Falls as first in the nation on its list of top earning towns. The residents of a number of locales in Silicon Valley shook their heads in disbelief and laughed at the quaintness of print media. Even so, the ritzy Washington suburb did all right for itself. The housing stock ranged from gracious to gargantuan and the natural beauty of the area was nothing short of spectacular.

The town also had a reputation as the landing spot for many of the prominent figures who came to Washington to *serve* the national interest. The fact that they just happened to grow wealthy in the process was simply a sign of the genius of American democracy.

Their number included current and former U.S. senators, directors of the FBI and CIA, syndicated media figures and the owner of the local NFL franchise.

Also included among this elite was Thomas Winston Rangel, retired head of The Maris Foundation think tank, known as T.W. to those he deigned to call friends. On that morning he received at his home Speaker of the House Peter Profitt and House Whip Carter Coleman. As Rangel no longer bothered with going into town, the congressional leaders came to him.

Exactly as they would do with their top campaign donors.

Rangel's houseman, Roosevelt, showed Profitt and Coleman into the solarium, got them seated, inquired as to their needs regarding food and drink, told them the maid would bring their coffee and Mr. Rangel would join them presently.

Once they were alone, Coleman asked Profitt in a quiet voice, "Not that I'm questioning Roosevelt's qualifications to do his job, but do you think T.W. hired him for his name? You know, just to have someone with the same name as the Democrats' most famous president waiting on him hand and foot."

Profitt looked around to see if any of the nearby plantings might be hiding a camera or a microphone. Deciding everything he saw was organic not electronic, he nodded. "It's possible. After all, T.W. was the guy who first suggested that our party do its best to repeal Social Security. If that isn't a fuck you to FDR, I don't know what is."

Coleman smiled and shook his head.

"What?" Profitt asked.

"I was just thinking if Roosevelt, the president not the houseman, hadn't gotten sick and had some longevity in his family, he might *still* be president."

Profitt feigned a shudder, and then said with a laugh, "At least that would have spared us Patti Grant."

For a minute or two the speaker and his whip played a game of conjecture, guessing what other kinds of firsts the Democrats, and don't forget Cool Blue now either, might nominate as their presidential candidates. They ran through several possibilities, chuckling at each one.

Coleman said, “It might even come full circle to where running an old white guy might look innovative.”

The two of them laughed, until they heard T.W. Rangel make his approach, with a maid pushing a silver serving cart bringing up the rear. Profitt and Coleman got to their feet and extended a hand to their host. The strength of Rangel’s grip surprised both of them.

They all sat and accepted their cups of coffee from the maid. Rangel gave her a smile and a nod. She departed and he wasted no time getting down to business.

“You gentlemen are in quite the pickle, aren’t you? What with your premature impeachment of the president and the vice president threatening to gut Congress if the president is convicted. But that’s not going to happen, now is it?”

Both Profitt and Coleman shook their heads.

Continuing his use of the Socratic method, Rangle asked, “Why not?”

Coleman, the vote counter, said, “With the arrest of four of our senators, getting to the two-thirds majority needed for conviction will be impossible. We’ll never get enough Democrats to vote with us.”

“You won’t get *any* votes from the other side. Not after Senator Pennyman, Democrat of Georgia, had his crimes exposed. You know who was responsible for that, I trust. If you don’t, you’d both better resign your offices, go home and pray your own sins aren’t brought to the attention of the Department of Justice.”

Coleman looked as if he was about to protest that his soul was spotless, but Profitt laid a restraining hand on his arm.

“T.W., for the sake of discussion, let’s say that Carter and I haven’t violated any laws. I’m sure, though, we’ve both found ourselves in situations that would be embarrassing if they were made public. Who hasn’t?”

Rangel didn’t claim to exist in a state of grace. He only remained silent.

For his part, Coleman settled down, his indignation yielding to honest self-assessment.

Profitt continued, "But I understand what you're saying. It had to be Galia Mindel who exposed Pennyman. She sacrificed him to get the other Democrats to fall in line."

"Exactly. And if you really wanted to take down Patricia Grant, what should your first step have been?"

"Get rid of her chief of staff first," Coleman said.

"Yes, and then you should have gone after Jean Morrissey and for the *coup de grace* taken out James J. McGill. And by that I mean destroy his reputation, not kill the man himself. Had you laid that groundwork and then accused the president of Erna Godfrey's murder, you'd likely have succeeded in convicting her. She might even have been willing to resign. And chances are there would have been no retaliation against the thieves and fools in our party. We'd be looking at a run in power that would be unprecedented in its length."

Profitt and Coleman looked at each other, thinking the same thing about Rangel.

Where the hell were you when we needed you?

The question was unspoken but Rangel made a further point.

"Your biggest mistake was trusting Edmond Whelan. As a young man, he showed great promise. His problem was, like so many others, he never lived up to his potential. You gentlemen, though, are older and should have been wiser. You might have retained me long ago to keep an eye on Ed, make sure he didn't go off the rails. But you came to me only now, after things have been so badly botched."

A small shake of Rangel's head told both Profitt and Coleman how pathetic they were.

As career politicians, though, they were immune to shame.

Their only interest now was pulling their party's backsides out of the fire.

Profitt said, "So how much will it cost us to get you on board, T.W.?"

"Figuring in a premium for the urgency of the situation, of course," Coleman added.

Rangel told them what he wanted.

They agreed without hesitation, answering the question that had occurred to them only a moment earlier. Where had Rangel been when they needed him? Waiting for his windfall just like everyone else in town.

After Rangel had dismissed his visitors, he went to his study and wrote out his notes on the meeting, including the political strategy he'd devised for his new clients. Get the nation's most well-known general, Warren Altman, former Air Force chief of staff, to be the GOP's presidential nominee in 2016. True, Altman was not a military figure on a par with Eisenhower or even Kennedy, but he had flown combat missions.

He'd dropped bombs and killed people.

Enemies of the United States.

Let the Democrats nominate their lady hockey player and see how well her record matched up against that. Altman was also a well-known public personality. He'd been a talking head for WorldWide News and later Satellite News America for years. He'd become a polished performer. People who didn't know any better would trust him to keep them safe.

Goddamnit, you mess with Warren Altman, he'll open his bomb bay doors and unload on your sorry ass.

For a lot of voters, you couldn't do more for providing peace of mind. Better still, he'd never been a member of the public's most despised class: the career politician.

There would be other bases to cover, of course, but as a broadcaster Altman had shown an ease with reading his script and sticking to it. Beyond that, he was a tall, strong, physical presence. He'd intimidate reporters with nothing more than a forceful look. Pretty soon, they'd be asking questions that were meant to please him.

All of that, of course, had to take place after the nonsense of Patti Grant's trial in the Senate had been disposed of quickly and put well behind the party. The conservative side of the aisle would unanimously vote to convict, to please its base; the liberal members would vote to acquit to serve its own electorate, and not bring the wrath of Galia Mindel down upon them.

Soon, it would be yesterday's news, and while the president would remain in office, she would be a nonentity for the remainder of her term. By her close association with the president, Jean Morrissey would also be politically weakened. Twenty-sixteen would be a tidal wave election year for the right. The White House would be theirs again and their majorities in both houses of Congress would swell.

Maybe they would even filch the Democrats' theme song from them.

"Happy Days Are Here Again."

That final thought brought a crocodilian smile to Rangel's face. He put his pen down and left his handiwork on his desk for Roosevelt to file. He didn't worry about his servant or anyone else reading what he committed to paper. Rangel composed his thoughts in classical Greek.

The flaw in Rangel's thinking on personal security was two-fold.

Roosevelt worked for Galia Mindel as well as for Rangel.

And she knew people who were also literate in the ancient language.

Before filing the papers, Roosevelt photographed them with his phone and sent them to a false-front email address where they would be be reviewed within minutes and put to appropriate use before the end of the day. Somewhere, Galia's spy was sure, FDR was having himself a good laugh.

The Oval Office — Washington, DC

Galia Mindel had yet to hear from Roosevelt, but another

operative had reported in, causing the chief of staff to hustle down the White House hallway to the Oval Office. Stopping at the desk of the president's secretary, Edwina Byington, she asked, "Is the president in?"

"Yes, ma'am."

"Is she alone?"

"She is."

"No visitors or no phone calls until she and I are finished."

"Just as soon as the president confirms that, yes, ma'am."

Edwina was one of the few people in the White House who had never been intimidated by Galia. Sometimes that rankled; other times it was reassuring. It was good for the chief of staff to know she wasn't the only tough-minded broad protecting Patricia Grant.

"You'll get it," Galia told Edwina.

She strode into the Oval Office firmly closing the door behind her.

The president, Galia saw, was looking out at the White House grounds lost in thought. It was a not uncommon pose for chief executives nearing the end of their terms, she was sure.

"Pardon me, Madam President, I need a few minutes of your undivided time."

Patricia Grant turned and looked at Galia, asking her, "Do you know what I've just done?"

"No, ma'am," Galia said, hoping not to hear anything that might tarnish the president's legacy.

"I was thinking how much my legal fees might amount to, you know, for defending me in my Senate trial." The president laughed. "I thought I'd better not get caught short, have to make fund-raising appeals to any friends I have left."

"Yes, ma'am? I trust you'll have no worries on that point."

The president laughed deeply. "You said we need some time to ourselves? Let me pass the word to Edwina. Have a seat, Galia."

The president took her own chair behind her desk.

She told her secretary no interruptions except for her husband or step-children.

Then looking her chief of staff in the eye, she said, "If I've never told you before, Andy left me money separate from the funds that support the Grant Foundation."

"You never talked about it, ma'am, but I assumed that Mr. Grant provided for you."

The president nodded. "A blind trust, so there'd be no political damage to me. I explained that to Jim, but he said it was none of his business. Didn't want to know anything about it." She beamed. "He said he loved me for my smile not my money."

Galia nodded. "Mr. McGill's charm is legendary."

"You have come to like him, haven't you, Galia?"

"Yes, ma'am. A man saves your life, you'd be an ingrate not to think well of him."

"Jim said he didn't want to have to break in a new chief of staff."

Galia snorted.

"Anyway," the president said, "I breached the terms of the trust to see how much loot I have to my name."

"And?"

"And it turns out I'm one of the richest persons in the world. I have billions upon billions at my personal disposal. Andy's gift for brilliant investing has lived on long after him."

Galia took a moment to consider the situation. "That must be both comforting and a bit heartbreaking."

"It is both those things, but what also struck me is when I leave the presidency, I'll be faced with another enormous burden: doing the right thing with this vast amount of money. Keeping all of it just to have it would be immoral. I could simply shift it to the Grant Foundation, but I think … I think it calls for some new planning."

"You might tuck away a million or two for Abbie, Kenny and Caitie," Galia said.

"If Jim will let me, of course, but that would be just the tiniest start."

"You'll think of something, Madam President. The last time I looked, there were still more problems in the world than resources to solve them."

The president said, "You're right. Now, what problem have you brought me to solve?"

Galia squared her shoulders and said, "Joan Renshaw is awake and talking."

Patricia Grant blinked. "She's emerged from her catatonic state?"

"Yes, ma'am. From what I've been told her first request was for a drink of water. Then she asked for solid food. She seems to be regaining situational awareness and mental competency at a steady pace. The doctors can't yet say whether her recovery is temporary or permanent. In either case, though, we have to be prepared."

"For what exactly, Galia?"

"For the very real possibility that a spiteful Joan Renshaw will still have hard feelings about you. That she'll lie and say you intentionally put her in that cell with Erna Godfrey. That you implicitly intended for her to kill Erna. That a subpoena from the Senate will require her to appear at your trial where she'll lie about you to the country and the world."

The president thought maybe she'd just buy Joan off with a presidential pardon and a spare billion dollars that she'd never miss anyway, but some ideas you didn't share with anyone.

"Do what you think is necessary, Galia, but do *not* go anywhere near Joan Renshaw. That would be the worst mistake we can make. Call my lawyers. Advise them of the situation. Say I'll talk to them after they've had the time to consider this development."

Galia nodded. She was glad to see the president was thinking clearly.

The president talking with her lawyers would be privileged conversation.

All Galia had done was to inform the president of the new situation. Received instruction to stay clear of Joan Renshaw. If she had to testify at the president's trial, that fact would play to the president's favor.

In the meantime, she had to make sure her spies at Walter Reed overheard every word that came out of Joan Renshaw's mouth without giving themselves away. Before even that, though, she needed to follow up on what she was about to do before she got the news about the brewing potential crisis. Call James J. McGill.

Los Angeles, California

The Commercial Crimes Division of the LAPD had its offices on First Street. Detectives Zapata and MacDuff worked out of the Burglary Special Section. They invited McGill and company to a sit-down in their unit's conference room. The purpose of the meeting was to share information.

On the drive downtown, John Tall Wolf had asked McGill, "Do you think a spirit of cooperation is finally taking hold?"

"I've been trying my best to be agreeable," McGill said.

"I've noticed." Tall Wolf shrugged. "Maybe it's paying off."

"But you still have a reservation or two?"

Tall Wolf chuckled. "A *reservation?*"

"Speaking generally not ethnically."

"Sure. Let's just say I'll withhold judgment for the moment."

McGill said, "I'm taking a wait-and-see attitude myself."

If not gracious, Zapata, MacDuff and their commanding officer Lieutenant Emily Proctor were polite. Coffee, tea and soft drinks were offered. To avoid reinforcing a cliché, no donuts were made available.

Lieutenant Proctor, a fit strawberry blonde in her thirties, greeted McGill and his federal entourage with seeming good feelings. Said it was her pleasure to meet all of them. She got the visitors seated before she and her men sat. Then she turned things over to Zapata.

"The department wants to bring you up to speed on the interview Detective MacDuff and I conducted with Dr. Danika Hansen. To cut to the heart of the matter, once she had her lawyer present and had conferred with her, Dr. Hansen admitted that she had given the key code to her clinic to Edmond Whelan. She also said that she had dinner with him prior to his visit to her clinic."

Zapata looked at MacDuff, passing the verbal baton to him.

MacDuff said, "She denied having any intimate relations with Whelan. Said the only physical contact they had was a couple of handshakes."

McGill said, "You mind if I ask whether you and your partner believed her?"

The two detectives exchanged a look.

Zapata said, "I have my doubts, but that's just me. I'm suspicious by nature."

MacDuff added, "I don't think she'd be a good enough liar to pull off a false denial. I didn't see anything in her eyes to make me doubt her. The impression I got was she'd have liked it if he'd tried something but he didn't."

McGill nodded. Not necessarily in agreement, but as an indication the detectives should continue with their story.

"Anyway," Zapata continued, "what Dr. Hansen said was she and Whelan went to the clinic after they had dinner. The doctor admitted having one drink more than her usual and was fumbling with the keypad to open the door. Whelan asked for the code so they could get in. She told him and he opened the door."

Tall Wolf said, "If the doctor had made at least a couple of attempts to enter the code and Whelan was watching, he'd have had an approximate idea of the required numbers. Once she told him it would be easy to both hit the right keys and remember them."

"That was my thinking, too," Lieutenant Proctor said.

It looked to McGill as if both Zapata and MacDuff were hard put not to roll their eyes, but he thought Tall Wolf had made a good point, and if the lieutenant had worked that out, too, good for her.

"Yeah, so what happened next, according to the doctor," Zapata said, "was she showed Whelan the cold storage tank where his embryos were."

MacDuff said, "That's why he wanted to make the after-hours

visit in the first place. To see that his … genetic material was well cared for. He didn't want to drop in during office hours because he's some kind of big shot back in D.C. and didn't want anyone to notice."

"Never heard of the dude myself," Zapata said.

"I hadn't either," McGill said, "and I live there. But I'm told he's a very important behind-the-scenes guy."

The lieutenant nodded. "We have people like that here, too."

Zapata continued, "Anyway, the doc and Whelan saw that everything was jake, they talked a little bit and he drove her home."

"Did that brief conversation include any mention of my client, Mira Kersten?" McGill asked.

"Yeah, it did," MacDuff said. "Whelan said he'd be filing court papers asking that Ms. Kersten not be allowed to destroy any of the embryos she and Whelan had made together."

McGill thought about that. "Were any of the embryos Ms. Kersten created with other partners stored in the same container?"

"As a matter of fact, yeah," Zapata said. "Surprised you know about her other boyfriends."

McGill said, "My client told me. She also said she's pregnant right now by traditional means."

"Did she mention the father's name?" Lieutenant Proctor asked.

"She did, but it's not my place to say."

"How about if we make a guess?" she said.

She gave McGill the name of the movie star Mira had said was the future father.

"Interesting," McGill said, adding nothing.

"So here's the situation," Lieutenant Proctor summed up. "Dr. Hansen was the one who provided the illegal means of entry to her clinic to Edmond Whelan and even showed him the target storage container. But she did so while intoxicated and was conned into coming across with the information. My guys believe that while she was foolish she had no criminal intent. The next logical steps in the investigation are to interview Mr. Whelan and one of the biggest names in the movies."

Tall Wolf said, "Only you haven't been able to find Whelan."

"Not yet," MacDuff said, "but if he's in town, we will."

"And if he's not within the city limits, you'll need outside help," McGill said.

Lieutenant Proctor nodded. "We thought with your obvious connections to the federal government and Co-director Tall Wolf's presence you might be able to help out, Mr. McGill, should that prove necessary."

"Absolutely," McGill said, "happy to help. But doesn't the movie star live in town?"

"Beverly Hills, and right now the BHPD is sensitive about us overstepping our jurisdiction," the lieutenant told McGill. "Beyond that, the gentleman in question is a notoriously private person. Just getting to talk to him could be a struggle."

"Rich people, huh?" McGill said.

"Yeah, right," MacDuff agreed.

"However," Lieutenant Proctor said, "the individual, himself, is something of a politics groupie."

McGill arched his eyebrows. "You want me to get the president to intervene?"

Proctor held up her hands. "We understand she's quite busy right now, but the thing is, our guy out here? The movie star? He's also a big fan of yours."

McGill laughed. "Strange old world, isn't it?"

Zapata added, "Getting freakier all the time."

On the way out of the building, Tall Wolf told McGill, "I've never been starstruck. If you don't mind, I'll beg off on Beverly Hills and check out how Jeremy Macklin, the scandal website reporter, is doing on my cousin's reservation."

"That's fine," McGill agreed. "We'll get back together later."

Beverly Hills, California

All it took was a few calls and five minutes alone in the back of his L.A. ride. Easy as that, McGill got the movie star's phone number from Dorie McBride, Patti's former agent. He got Dorie's number from Edwina Byington, the president's personal secretary. Didn't even have to bother his wife with a request.

He did ask Edwina, "How's our girl doing?"

"The president, sir? She's bearing up admirably."

"Come on, Edwina. After all this time, you must think of the president in personal terms, too."

"I do, sir. I love her like a daughter, but I'd never be less than correct at work."

"Edwina, remind me when I get back to Washington to take you out for a beer."

"If you really want to get me talking, sir, make that a shot and a beer."

McGill laughed. "You're on."

The reclusive movie icon answered his own phone, at least when he liked the name that came up on his caller ID.

"Jim McGill?" he asked.

"Yeah, I make my own calls. Keeps me grounded. That's especially important when you live in Washington."

"Here, too."

"Would you mind if I drop by and asked you a few questions? I'll keep it short."

"I hope you won't. I have some questions I'd like to ask you, as well. I'll start right now, if you don't mind. Have you ever thought about playing a part on camera?"

For a moment, McGill was dumbfounded.

Then he laughed.

The star said, "Should I take that as a no?"

"I doubt if I could play myself, much less anybody else."

"You might be surprised."

"I'd be *astounded*."

"How about this? I'll answer your questions for as long a time as you'll listen to what I have in mind."

"Listen without making a commitment?" McGill said.

"Yes."

"Okay, that's fair."

"Good. One more thing. Did anyone ever tell you that you look like Rory Calhoun?"

Now, the guy had piqued McGill's interest.

Pacific Palisades, California

The first thing Sweetie had done after accompanying Mira Kersten home was to check out her house's security system. With a smug note in her voice, Mira had asked, "Great, right? Can't do better."

"Only one thing missing," Sweetie told her.

"I won't own a gun," Mira said.

Sweetie smiled. "I won't ask you to; I have my own."

"What then?"

"Do you have any allergies?"

"Only to retrograde politics," Mira said.

"Good. Let me make a quick call. You know the name of the nearest Catholic church."

Mira was a Methodist when she bothered to attend services at all, but as a political animal she knew where religious voters gathered and gave Sweetie the name she needed. Sweetie made a call and within an hour had what she wanted: the loan of a small friendly dog with an outsized fearsome bark. She struck a deal with the owner to rent him by the day.

The beast's name was Dudley, and Sweetie had him eating out of her hand in short order.

Mira didn't mind having the dog in her house. "He's kind of cute for a mutt, but I don't see him being much help in a fight."

"I don't want any help with that. If someone tries to break in, it's his eyes, ears and voice I'll be counting on. I want both of you to hide and you to call the cops, if you hear me yell."

"So you don't trust my high-tech system."

Sweetie said, "Up to a point, it's fine, but my general impression is pretty much anything that's electronic can be hacked. Unless you've got the dog whisperer after you, Dudley should raise Cain if somebody tries to break in."

"Okay, let's just hope he doesn't pee in the house to mark new territory or something," Mira said. "In my experience, males of any species are pretty much like that."

Sweetie took Dudley out before bedtime and had a long, instructive talk with him.

Both women and the canine passed a peaceful night.

All of Mira's furnishings remained unblemished.

The only thing that was out of place was the guy sitting in an armchair in Mira's living room. He had Dudley curled up on his lap looking blissful as the guy stroked the dog's head with a gentle touch. Mira, on her way to retrieve the morning paper from the front doorstep, saw the intruder. She jerked to a stop and her throat constricted to the point that she had to struggle for a breath.

Not that the guy looked particularly threatening. He wore a Dodgers' cap, had bright green eyes, a surfer's tan, a graying goatee and the lean, strong build of a track-and-field athlete. He was dressed for running, too. A t-shirt from UCLA, Nike shorts and shoes. He smiled at Mira, which did nothing to put her at ease.

She hadn't even been born when the Manson family had killed Sharon Tate and those other poor people, but the horror of that bloody home invasion had echoed through the decades. The idea that the wealthy and famous were as susceptible to being killed under their own roofs as anyone else had become a cautionary tale to the people of means in Southern California. In large part, those murders had given rise to the private security industry in the state and around the country.

"Nice dog," the guy said.

The guy was sitting still, except for a foot he kept tapping.

It seemed to be keeping time with an inaudible beat.

Mira was still trying to find her voice when Sweetie said from behind her, "Then you should let him go so you don't bleed all over him."

The guy saw Sweetie pointing her Beretta 92 FS at him. He took a moment to assess his degree of jeopardy before saying, "I believe you just might shoot me."

He took his hands off Dudley, but the dog remained on his lap. Until the intruder gave him a slight nudge and said, "Be good." The dog jumped to the floor and the guy got to his feet, not rushing things, keeping the threat level low.

Even so, Mira had the sense to scurry behind Sweetie.

"Call 911," Sweetie said.

The guy put both his hands up, not high, just trying to placate the woman holding the gun on him. "I've seen your picture," he told Sweetie. "You work with James J. McGill, don't you?"

Sweetie didn't respond.

Mira did. "Who are you? What do you want?"

"I'm the guy who stole your embryos, not that I'd repeat that for the record. What I want is to offer you a trade: You tell me the name of the person you think was most likely to have hired me to do the theft and I'll tell you where you can find your embryos."

"Don't do it," Sweetie told Mira. "Jim will find them for you."

The guy smiled and looked at Mira. "You know, I believe she might be right. That McGill fella, he's got some track record from what I've read. Thing is, I don't think he'll be able to find the embryos *in time.* I started a clock running before I came here. After a certain point, those little sweethearts come out of cold storage, and we all know how perishable they are."

"Edmond Whelan," Mira said. "Do you know who he is?"

"Can't say I do."

Mira told him.

The guy sighed. "Somebody working for the federal government. I should've known."

"Where are my embryos?" Mira asked.

The guy gave her the name of a facility in Anaheim. "Not far from the happiest place on earth. Or is that Disney World in Florida? I always get them confused."

The guy gave Mira a casual salute and turned to leave.

Sweetie said, "Stop. You entered this house illegally. That's a crime."

"And you're making a citizen's arrest?"

"Yes."

The guy frowned, looked as if he was trying to remember something. "Your name's Margaret Sweeney, isn't it? I think that's the name I saw with your picture."

Sweetie didn't respond, just held her gun steady.

"I admire what I read about you." He looked at Mira. "Do you know that this woman jumped in front of Mr. McGill and took a bullet meant for him. I believe someone like that might possibly shoot me if I tried to leave without her permission. What I'd like to know from you, Ms. Kersten is this: Do you want to press charges against me or would you rather resolve my little trespass quietly? I promise you, your embryos will be right where I said they are."

In a by-the-way manner, he added the code number for the storage unit she'd want.

Mira nodded and said, "I won't press charges. Let him go, Ms. Sweeney."

"You're making a mistake," Sweetie said.

"It's my house and my choice."

Looking at Sweetie, the guy said, "Are we good?"

"Not even close."

"But you're not going to shoot me."

"Not so long as you leave and keep going."

"I'll take that deal. Sorry for any distress I caused."

He turned to go and Dudley hurried forward to leave with him.

The guy crouched down, stroked the dog again, and said something to him in a voice too soft for Sweetie and Mira to hear. The dog offered a small whine of disappointment but turned and trudged back to Sweetie. The guy almost danced to Mira's front door and left with a wave over a shoulder, never looking back.

Averse to using profanity, Sweetie nonetheless said, "Cocky SOB."

She gathered her things and took Dudley back to his owner.
Leaving Mira Kersten alone to provide for her own safety.

Beverly Hills, California

The movie star's house wasn't quite as big as the White House, but then it wasn't the nerve center of what used to be called The Free World. It did seem to have many of the same amenities, including butlers and security guys armed with automatic weapons. They even had the nerve to ask Deke and Elspeth to surrender their weapons at the gate.

Elspeth said, "Better men than you have tried."

Deke looked like he fell in love with his boss in that very moment.

McGill prevented the outbreak of hostilities. He told the security honcho. "Talk to the homeowner. Tell him we'll have to call off our meeting if your people can't trust the Secret Service. We'll wait right here."

The decision was swift in coming. Hollywood stepped aside. Washington prevailed. The valet in the house's driveway was much more understanding when Leo said only he drove the vehicle and it would have to stay parked out in front.

"In case the boss needs to make a quick getaway," Leo explained.

"Of course," the valet said.

Their host met them at the door, greeted McGill with a handshake and asked Elspeth whether she'd prefer that the meeting take place indoors.

"Definitely. With the drapes closed." She looked at McGill. "If that's all right with you."

McGill asked his host. "You have a wine cellar?"

The star nodded.

"Maybe we could each have a glass of something with a low alcohol content."

"I'll ring the sommelier. Would you care for a snack?"

"A little fruit and a piece of dark chocolate maybe."

"Done."

McGill smiled inwardly. In the old days, he'd have asked for a cup of coffee and a brownie. Walking through the house on the way to the cellar made him think of the future not the past. The scale of the rooms and the quality of the furnishings would have wowed him, had he not spent the past six-plus years in the country's most famous residence. The tone of the star's home was decidedly masculine but understated. Everything from the lighting fixtures to the hand-woven rugs exhibited not just craftsmanship but a subtle artistry.

Just passing through was an exercise in visual indulgence.

McGill wondered if living there would be enough to overwhelm his senses.

For the first time, he was also forced to think of what kind of place he and Patti would soon call home. His house in Evanston had seemed fine when he'd been a bachelor father police chief, helping to raise his three children. It was homey, safe and the roof didn't leak.

Now, it struck him as humble, to be kind about it, suitable for someone … who hadn't changed more than he ever would have imagined possible. Good God, was he becoming a … no, he wasn't a snob. But he also wasn't the man he used to be.

Patti still owned the lakefront mansion in Winnetka where she had lived with Andy Grant. Only Andy had been blown to bits there. And later McGill had thrown Damon Todd out a window there, just before that particular madman could detonate another explosive device. McGill didn't think either he or Patti would consider it a peaceful place to revisit.

So where would they go?

Before he could begin to grope for an answer, he saw he'd entered a cellar that looked like it belonged to a chateau in France — and perhaps it had been imported board by board, barrel by barrel. A table for two had been set up. An open bottle of wine, a basket of fruit, a tray of chocolates, two glasses, and plates and silverware had been placed on a tablecloth as radiantly white as a newborn's soul.

The movie star gestured to McGill to take the seat of his choice.

Before he sat, the star said, "I'd be pleased to offer your special agents something non-alcoholic to drink if they'd like."

Elspeth answered for herself and Deke. "Thank you, but no. I'll need to stand watch where I can see Mr. McGill. Special Agent Ky, I think, will need to wait upstairs. I'm not getting any cell signal down here. We have to stay in touch with the outside world. You have any signal, Special Agent?"

Deke shook his head.

"See what you can get at the top of the stairs. Stay as close as you can."

Deke nodded and left.

She hadn't seen any sign the star had a weapon on him. Said a silent prayer all would be well and stepped back as far as she could while keeping Holmes in sight.

Left to themselves, the star sat opposite McGill and told him, "Before we get down to business, I just want to say I'd appreciate it if you'd tell the president I've always supported her and think what's going on in Washington now is politics at its absolute worst."

McGill didn't see anything but sincerity in the man's face, but then he was an accomplished actor. Giving him the benefit of the doubt, though, he nodded and said thank you.

The star also gave McGill a conversational opening. "Is your visit today about Mira Kersten and me?"

"It is, but why would you think that?"

"Well, I assume you're in town on business not pleasure or you'd be back in DC standing at the president's side. Since you're here and you want to speak with me, I had to ask myself why that would be. The only unusual thing happening in my life is that I'm going to become a father for the first time."

The star had a reputation for being intelligent, shrewd enough to negotiate some of the most favorable contracts an onscreen talent in Hollywood had ever known. That was how he paid for a home like this one, and he had another that was supposed to be even grander in Italy. McGill did his homework, too.

"You're right," he said, "it is about Ms. Kersten. She hired me to locate some missing property — if she hasn't already told you."

The icon took a moment to think about that.

"You mean our embryo?" he asked. "That's the only possession we hold in common. Well, that and the child she's carrying."

McGill said, "One child in the process of gestation, another possibly awaiting the same development. Seems like quite a significant connection."

The host poured wine for each of them and took a sip from his glass.

"So the embryo is missing." He sipped his wine and watched as McGill nodded. Having gotten the answer to his question, he said, "Damn."

"I'd feel the same way," McGill replied. "It's not nearly as bad as a kidnapping, but it's a first step toward feeling that way."

"Yes, it is. I'm surprised Mira didn't tell me."

"I was hired to get all her embryos back."

The star looked at McGill with a new degree of interest.

"*All* of them? There are others?"

McGill nodded, and his host's attitude shifted to the philosophical.

It wasn't like Mira was the only woman in his life.

"Do you think you'll get them back?" he asked McGill.

"I think there's a chance, maybe even a good chance. The thief has asked for ransom so it's even money he's preserved the embryos. Ms. Kersten says she doesn't have the compensation that's being demanded but I think she might have an idea of who does."

"Why do you think that?"

"It's a political thing, what the thief wants, a document. She'd have a better idea than I would as to who might be holding the ransom item. What I need to know is how motivated Ms. Kersten might be to see that a deal is worked out. I'd think she would want to see the embryo the two of you made returned, but if she's already pregnant by you that motivation might not be quite so strong."

The star emptied his glass and poured more wine for himself.

McGill took the first sip from his glass.

"Mira and I are friends," the star said. "We share the same politics, we enjoy talking with one another, making plans to help the world, as we see things. Sometimes our ideas are practical, other times they're fanciful. Occasionally, they're hilarious. We make each other laugh."

"But you don't think of making your relationship formal?" McGill asked.

"You mean getting married? No. Neither of us even brought up the subject."

McGill declined to comment.

The star offered him a famous smile. "I know you've been married twice, and you do look like Rory Calhoun, so I'm sure you've had other opportunities to form, shall we say, lasting relationships. But you probably haven't had the weight on you of knowing there are millions of women in the world who think they'd like to spend their lives with you simply because of what they've seen on movie screens."

"No," McGill said. "Sounds scary."

"It is. Definitely makes you cautious. One of the things I like about Mira is she never pushed herself at me. We met at a political fundraiser, ate dinner at the same table, had a great conversation and said good night with a simple handshake."

"Must've been a relief for you," McGill said.

"A breath of fresh air. Our mutual political interests led our paths to cross again on a number of occasions, and one night I invited her back here. The moment I did, I began to regret it, thinking my motives might be misinterpreted. Mira behaved like a perfect lady."

"Didn't assault you?" McGill asked with a grin.

The star laughed. "To tell you the truth, I was a bit insulted. Wondered if I was losing my looks and would be reduced to playing character roles in the future. Anyway, I was the one who brought up the idea of what a child with the two of us as parents would be like."

"But you didn't think of just doing things the usual way," McGill said.

"Not just then. I think it was a perverse effect of being exposed to so many stunning women in the course of my work. I just didn't feel stimulated that way with Mira at the time. I mean, she's quite a nice looking woman, but … Well, how do you view other women after being married to Patricia Grant?"

McGill blinked. He'd never really thought of things that way.

"You mean there are other women?" he asked.

"Exactly. I've read you get along famously with your ex-wife, but whatever feelings you may still hold for her, I imagine they're not the same as the ones you have for the president."

McGill said, "No, they're not."

"Well, that's how I felt about Mira. Only I could see having a child with her. She's a wonderful person."

"But you did impregnate her the old-fashioned way."

"Yes, I did. That was … timing, I guess. It was unplanned, but everything just felt right that particular night."

McGill took another sip of wine. His next few questions were not going to be easy to ask. His host anticipated him, relieving him of the burden.

"If you're wondering whether Mira wants any child support, she hasn't. She's never asked for or even hinted at requiring any kind of material offering. That's been quite pleasant, too. When she told me she was pregnant, she said I could play any role I wanted in the child's life: starring, bit part or none at all."

"She told me the same thing. Have you made up your mind?"

"I've thought of little else recently but, no, I haven't decided. May I ask how you felt when your wife told you that she was pregnant?"

McGill smiled. "The first time? I swept her up into my arms and …" He paused to remember. "That was probably the most memorable kiss of my marriage to Carolyn."

His host frowned and sighed. "I kissed Mira's cheek. I should have done better."

McGill didn't comment on that. Instead, he asked, "Has Mira's pregnancy had any effect on how you feel about the embryo the two of you created?"

"What do you mean?"

"Is it more or less valuable to you with one child already on the way?"

"You know, I actually did think about that. I thought if the first kid turns out great, it would be foolish not to do another."

Just like a movie sequel, McGill thought, but didn't say so.

"You have three children," the star said, "what's your experience been?"

"Each one is more challenging, but you also have more experience to see you through. For me, maybe I've been lucky, but each of my children has further enriched my life."

"I can see that," the star said with a nod. "I can definitely see that."

McGill decided *he* had seen and heard all he needed. Mira Kersten had conducted as subtle a seduction as he'd ever known. She'd landed one of the biggest names in show business and the guy still didn't have a clue that he'd been hooked. She hadn't asked for a dime, but McGill would bet she'd be compensated to the tune of millions. For the kids' needs, of course, but also for being the mother of the star's children.

He and Mira might never marry. Neither of them might ever want that. But they'd always be the best of friends. Oh, well, McGill thought. Who was he to judge? He and Carolyn thought they'd always be together, and that didn't happen. They both found new mates to whom they were better suited.

They'd both taken good care of their children.

And they were still very good friends.

For the star's part of their bargain, he wanted McGill to consider being the set-up man for a cop show the star was considering doing on a premium cable TV channel. McGill would appear at the beginning of each episode and explain how a particular crime normally occurred and synopsize how the investigation might go. Then at the end he would summarize how things could fool even the savviest of detectives.

"So, really, you wouldn't have to do any acting," the star told McGill. "You'd just have to be yourself and narrate some fact-based exposition. I've seen you speak on television and I'm sure you're more than up to the job. Do you have any plans for when you and the president leave the White House?"

"I'm thinking of expanding my private investigations business," McGill admitted. "Might even open an office out here."

The star beamed, "That'd be perfect. You could do each job without neglecting the other."

In the fashion of show biz, McGill's host wanted to discuss monetary terms, but McGill held up a hand. "Before we get into any of that, I think I'd like to look at a script or two and see what the writing is like. Might help to know who you have in mind for the cast, too."

The star laughed in good humor and gave McGill a three-clap round of applause.

"You're sounding like a producer already. You'll probably be talking about an equity position next."

Before they could talk about anything else, Deke reappeared.

He had Sweetie with him.

One look told McGill something big had happened.

Santa Monica, California

John Tall Wolf did what would be unimaginable for most Angelenos: He took public transit from downtown L.A. to Santa Monica. He made the trip on the Rapid 10 Express Big Blue Bus. A light rail line linking the two points was due to open next year, but just then the bus was the way to go if you didn't want to drive. Not driving was an aberrant idea for most Southern Californians. With the ever growing crush of traffic and the expansion of public transit, though, attitudes were beginning to shift.

For two dollars, Tall Wolf thought it was a bargain to let someone else fight traffic.

The view from the bus window also gave him a better vantage point to survey his surroundings. He'd been to Los Angeles before on business, but he'd never really gotten a feel for the place. Riding the bus, looking things over, he came to a new understanding.

Los Angeles, he decided, was the victim of its own natural beauty. The landscape was gorgeous: mountains, hills, and a desert turned verdant by imported water. The air was warm, soft and dry. The smog could be problematic, but on that particular day a steady breeze was pushing exhaust emissions elsewhere.

The main drawback was too many people wanted to take advantage of what looked like, at first, easy living. Overcrowding brought its own hardships. Competition for homes and apartments pushed housing costs to surreal levels. Providing public services to the largest state population in the country demanded high taxes. At the most fundamental level, the city, like the rest of California, was running short of water.

There were work-arounds for a lot of problems.

Insufficient water, though, was one that seemed insurmountable.

Tall Wolf got off the bus at 2nd Street and stopped for an ice cream cone at a shop on Ocean Avenue. He took his treat across the street to Palisades Park and sat on a bench looking out at the Pacific. Maybe, he thought, desalination was the answer to the water shortage. He didn't know enough about the technological challenges of that to say for sure.

If purifying sea water did prove to be the solution, he could see the state becoming even more crowded and expensive. Ultimately, the advantages of living in a desirable place would cross lines with the frustrations brought on by congestion and the population would recede. That or the long overdue arrival of The Big One, the monster earthquake that had been predicted for decades, would kill thousands, send even more packing and scare off an unguessable number of people from ever coming.

In the meantime, Tall Wolf had to concede, the place did have its appeal.

He took out his phone and called Jeremy Macklin, the online publisher of *The Scandal Sheet*, who was currently hiding out on the Northern Apache reservation in New Mexico.

"Let me call you right back," Macklin said. He did so in a matter of seconds. "I'm using a burner phone now." One that couldn't be traced to him. He gave Tall Wolf its number.

"Everything okay?" Tall Wolf asked.

"Yeah, no storm troopers kicking down my door, and the cabin I'm using is surprisingly comfortable. Looking at the bigger picture, I'm impressed by the resources available to the community at large out here. L.A. should do so well."

Tall Wolf told him, "The rez has some signed contracts in place with Big Energy to tap their natural gas resources. Some friends and I made sure that they got a good deal and the environmental impact will be kept to a minimum."

"What're you saying," Macklin asked, "the bad guys didn't come out on top? I'm out of business if that shit keeps up."

Tall Wolf laughed. "Maybe you can find a teaching job out there."

"You joke, but let me tell you, I've already found two kids working on the school paper who are natural writers, a boy and a girl. I'm having a hell of time trying to encourage their talents, though, when I know there are fewer people reading newspapers every day."

"Just go easy on the cynicism and let them fight their own battles."

"Yeah, I suppose. But being the skeptic I am, my guess is you didn't call just to say hello. So what do you want?"

"You still keeping in touch with your sources here in L.A.?"

"Yeah, your cousin Arnoldo has been investing in communications. There's good cell service here, satellite TV and computer connectivity, too. Let me guess, you're looking for anything that might have Mira Kersten's name attached."

"You must've been a pretty good reporter," Tall Wolf said.

"Still am. Okay, I suppose I owe you something for finding me a place to hide. Here's something I just learned. Might not seem like much to most people, but in L.A. terms it is. Ms. Kersten has left her old talent agency, a respectable but middle-tier place, for one the biggest, hottest shops in the country."

Macklin provided a company name that even Tall Wolf recognized.

The BIA Co-director drew the proper inference. "Something big is in the wind for the lady?"

"You got it. Thing is, there's no apparent reason for why Mira Kersten was taken on as a client. That means it's a case of know-who. Somebody with a lot of juice is behind her good fortune. I believe we discussed that possibility back in Santa Monica."

Tall Wolf chose not to rub it in by telling Macklin he was looking at the ocean right now.

"We did. You also mentioned Ms. Kersten was about to lose her local TV job. So it would seem she's enjoying quite a remarkable turn of fortune."

Macklin laughed. "Yeah, ain't life grand? She must have a pure heart. That or her secret admirer is your basic show-biz titan."

"Could be a merit-based decision."

"You believe that, I've got an Indian reservation to sell you."

"Some of them are quite valuable," Tall Wolf said, "the ones with natural resources."

"Good point. There's one other thing I found out."

"Yes?"

"I looked into Mira Kersten's past to see if someone there might be the source of her good fortune."

"I was thinking of doing the same," Tall Wolf said.

"You probably should. Every leap year or so, I miss a relevant tidbit. But what I found out was she was married to some guy named Edmond Whelan. Never heard of him and for a good reason. He keeps a real low profile, but I know some people who work the Capitol Hill beat and they told me he's a real power behind the throne in the House of Representatives hierarchy."

Tall Wolf kept his own knowledge of Whelan to himself.

"And how does that relate to Ms. Kersten?"

"I don't know for sure, but I found it very interesting that Whelan recently got his own heavyweight agent."

"He did?"

Macklin said, "Yeah, the literary kind. Edmond Whelan is going to publish a book."

Los Angeles, California

Leo Levy was driving McGill, Sweetie, Elspeth and Deke to the Santa Monica airport. McGill had been tempted to ask for a police escort, but he'd been told the executive jet that would take everyone back to Washington wouldn't be ready to fly for an hour. Upon hearing how much time he had to work with, Leo told McGill , "No problem, Boss. I'll make it with time to spare."

The call McGill had run upstairs to take at the star's mansion had come directly from the president herself. Sweetie, Elspeth and Deke had given him the room to speak privately. Before McGill had been handed Deke's phone, the special agent had the presence of mind to tell him, "It's not any of your kids, but it does sound important."

McGill's heart continued to race from more than physical exertion despite the reassurance.

He took his wife's call by asking, "What's wrong?"

Hearing the tension in his voice, Patti said, "Calm down, Jim, please. I'm calling you so you don't hear this news from anyone else."

Catching his breath and doing his best to sound calm, McGill repeated himself, "What's wrong?"

"I was just informed by a call from the Senate majority leader's office that my trial will be moved forward to this coming Monday. The official reason of that august body is that it has too many important responsibilities to address to let the little matter of booting me from office linger."

McGill responded with a humorless laugh.

Having a tooth drilled was a fleeting experience compared to watching the Senate work.

In normal times anyway. So McGill asked, "What's the rush?"

Across the breadth of the continent, he heard the woman he loved sigh. "The political forecast from people who should know …" Galia and her spies, McGill understood. "… is that my trial should have been a relatively brief affair, given how certain everyone was as to how the vote would go." Meaning Galia had intimidated any weak-kneed Democrat who might otherwise have voted to convict the president. "However, there's been a new development. Joan Renshaw has regained full consciousness and is talking to a staffer working for the House committee that will act as the prosecution."

"And she's saying what, exactly?" McGill asked.

"We don't know for sure, but the assumption has to be that I put her into a cell with Erna Godfrey for the express purpose of killing Erna. Also that I'd pardon her for her crime."

McGill didn't bother wasting the time to say that was bullshit.

What he did say was, "It wouldn't surprise me if the woman remained awake and coherent just long enough to testify. After that, oh my, there could be a fatal relapse."

His conjecture was greeted with a long moment of silence.

"You don't really think —" the president began.

"I do," McGill said.

He knew that news of Joan Renshaw's awakening must have come from Galia's spies at Walter Reed. It also wasn't hard to imagine that a lie from Erna Godfrey's killer saying that she'd committed her crime at the president's behest might give any wavering Democrats the cover and the nerve they'd need to vote to convict. Hell, if Renshaw's testimony came across as plausible, it might be grounds for a landslide vote against the president.

"Where I'd start," McGill said, "I'd put the word in Ms. Renshaw's ear what her fate might be. Let her know there are people out there who won't want to give her any chance to recant her lie. See if she still feels like telling it."

"Hold on a second, Jim."

He overheard a muffled conversation, the tone not the words. Still, he got the impression his advice would be acted upon. Someone in Galia's shadow army would pass the word to Joan Renshaw. Let her start to sweat, know her future would be far the worse for any further misdeed.

Serve her right if her brain short-circuited again.

When Patti came back on the phone, she said, "I was going to ask you if you wanted to come back to Washington and sit beside me in the Senate. Now, I think I'd like you to be there. Please be with me, Jim."

"You couldn't keep me away," he said.

McGill sat in the back of the armored SUV with Sweetie on the way to the airport. The privacy screen was up and both Elspeth and Deke had squeezed in up front with Leo. McGill listened to his old friend tell him of her confrontation with the intruder at Mira Kersten's house.

Sweetie concluded, "You were hired to get the embryos back. Looks like that's been accomplished now, even if it wasn't the way we expected."

"You think this guy was telling Mira the truth?"

"I got that impression, yeah."

McGill trusted Sweetie's judgment. With her years of experience as a cop, she knew when people were lying and when they weren't. Polygraph machines weren't as accurate.

"And the dog you brought in was sitting on the guy's lap?"

"That was probably the thing that scared me the most. Where do you get training like that? Just the scent of a stranger on the other side of the door should have set Dudley off. But somehow the guy kept him quiet while beating the security system and opening the lock on the door."

McGill shook his head. "Something like that, he'd have to be trained by an intelligence agency of some sort, civilian or military."

"Yeah, unless he just flew in from the planet Krypton with a box of Milk Bones."

McGill grinned. "Maybe we could reason with that guy."

"Oh, this guy was perfectly reasonable. Slick as the road to hell, too. He committed a crime, got what he wanted and walked away with the victim's consent."

McGill said, "That is pretty impressive. What's he look like?"

Sweetie took out her iPad and lit it up. She said, "Putnam got me this thing. He knows I'm technology averse, but he showed me some of the benefits. One of them is an app that makes the old IdentiKit package look silly." Sweetie brought up an image of the man she faced off with at Mira's house. "That's not quite photographic quality, but it's very close to the way his face looks."

McGill said, "If his eyes are that green, he had to be wearing colored contact lenses. Was his skin that shade of brown? Are the wrinkles around his eyes real or cosmetic."

"All good points," Sweetie said. The program actually suggests a variety of skin tones based on the shape, size and placement of the facial features. Does the same thing with eye colors. I dialed back the eye wrinkles myself by 50% and this is what we have."

The new face McGill saw belonged to a white man in his mid-to-late thirties.

He looked at it until the likeness was well established in his memory.

"How big is he?" McGill asked.

"Just a tad smaller than you. Maybe six-one, one-eighty or a few pounds under."

"Anything else worth knowing?"

Sweetie said, "He tapped his right foot the whole time he was sitting with the dog on his lap and talking with Mira and me. Didn't seem like a nervous tic. More like he was listening to music only he could hear. And when he got up to go he almost glided. The guy has seriously good muscle tone and balance. He's probably real quick when he needs to be."

"Good to know. Do you have any idea what kind of imaginary

music he was hearing?"

"His foot was beating like this," Sweetie said.

She tapped the seat with her hand.

"Four-four time," McGill said.

"You know more about music than me."

McGill fell silent for a couple minutes. Sweetie waited for him.

He said, "The threat against my life was probably made by someone who also threatened a man with covert rendition. That sounds like someone who might have an intelligence agency connection, too. You think the guy you saw might be the same one who's coming after me?"

"Why would that guy, the one threatening you, want Edmond Whelan's name? Wouldn't he already know it if there's a connection?"

McGill threw his hands up. "Don't know. Spy stuff is beyond a simple cop like me."

Sweetie laughed. "Yeah, right. Name me another simple cop who wound up married to the president."

McGill couldn't. He and the others just got on the plane and took off for Washington. Right after takeoff, he called their L.A. hotel and left a message for John Tall Wolf, letting the BIA man know about their abrupt departure.

Pacific Palisades, California

Mira Kersten hated to admit it, but she felt anxious returning home after making a trip down to Anaheim to verify the intruder's claim that her embryos were, in fact, being stored there. They were. That was a big relief, but she didn't want to leave them anywhere a thief had put them. The SOB might have a way to take them back. She also didn't want to send them back to the facility from which they'd been stolen in the first place.

After a quick online search, she settled on a fertility clinic in Brentwood. The director there assured Mira their security was the best. It wasn't far from her home either. They sent a special vehicle with cold-storage capacity to fetch the embryos. Mira trailed it all the way to make sure nothing went wrong. She wrote a check to the new clinic for the next twelve months.

With all that out of the way, she went out to dinner, eating alone.

It wouldn't be long now before she moved to New York and her new job. She had mixed feelings about that. She'd grown up in Connecticut, had made frequent visits to Manhattan and Boston as a child and teenager. By the time she went to college at Brown University, those places were old hat for her.

Still, New York was where the big TV news jobs were, and WorldWide News had promised her a plum slot. Way better money than she'd ever made before. Only it wouldn't come close, she felt sure, to the money that would flow her way after bearing two children for Hollywood's hottest male actor. Sitting back, hiring a really good nanny, and enjoying the more relaxed California lifestyle would be more to her liking.

She paused to wonder if that was her flood of pregnancy hormones talking.

Did she really want to give up being a go-getter for a life of indolent affluence?

Right then, yeah, she pretty much did. At least for the moment. If things changed later, she'd do a turn-around. It was only after leaving the restaurant, on the drive to the Palisades, that she remembered her home had been violated. Even with an armed bodyguard and a dog on hand.

Now, she had neither of those safeguards, and for all she knew the guy had returned because he'd thought of something else he wanted to know. Or steal. Or maybe just kill her to make sure she could never testify against him.

Within minutes, Mira was scaring herself silly.

Problem was, things might get complicated if she called the police to check out her house before she entered it. She'd have to explain why she was fearful and needed protection. The police wouldn't like it that she'd let a home invader go without even reporting it to them. Or tell them she'd recovered her embryos.

The uniformed cops might even check *her* out and wind up bringing those two prick detectives in to question her. She didn't need that shit. Gritting her teeth, she pulled into her driveway, popped the trunk and took out the lug wrench. Just gripping the thing made her think its only value was symbolic. If she tried to bash the guy who'd broken in that morning, had he returned, he'd probably take it away and turn her into tapioca with it.

Still, she couldn't leave the wrench in the car.

As a tool for self-delusion, if nothing else, it had value.

She crept up the curved, landscaped path to her front door. It was only when she came to within a few feet of the threshold that she saw a note taped to the front door. That was enough to paralyze her. She wanted to turn and run, hope she could make it back to her car before anyone grabbed her. Petrified as she was, though, she took the opportunity to read the message.

Honey, I'm home. Your first love, Ed.

The heart that was already hammering in Mira's chest took it up another notch, now stoked by anger. Her sonofabitch ex-husband, Edmond Whelan, had broken into her home, too? After he'd had her embryos stolen? The nerve of the bastard.

Mira's grip on the lug wrench tightened.

She was sure now that she'd be the one to use it; she'd turn Ed's skull into pulp.

The front door was unlocked. She threw it open and stormed inside. Stopping dead in her tracks when she saw a man who appeared to be a total stranger. Some geek with a shaved skull and a struggling attempt at a goatee.

Then he said, "Surprise, I've come to give you your embryos back."

That was Ed's voice, all right, and when she looked closer she recognized his eyes, too.

"What the hell happened to you?" she asked. "Where's your hair?"

Whelan frowned and looked as if his umbrage might be expressed physically.

Until Mira slapped the lug wrench on an open palm and shook her head.

"Unh-uh, pal," she said. "Anyone kicks ass around here, it's gonna be me."

She took a step forward and it thrilled her to see her ex-husband retreat two steps.

"Hey, come on, Mira," Whelan said. "I've come to make peace between us. Really. I'm going to tell you where the embryos are … and sign a release, too, so you can use any of them any time you want."

"Except for the one you destroyed and photographed trying to intimidate me, right?"

Mira started forward again. Whelan backed right into an armchair and plopped down onto it. Before he could regain his balance, Mira gave him a nice little rap on a shin bone.

"Ow, shit! That hurt, Mira!"

"Damn right it did, just what you deserved, ruining that embryo. Ending a potential life."

She saw he was about to make a wisecrack. Something along the lines of conservatives being the ones who were pro-life. When they weren't advocating for capital punishment. Or shilling for the right to own assault rifles. Only he'd thought better of saying any of that.

She honestly had him scared.

"I ought to ring this wrench right off your head," she said, "only it looks like you've already done enough damage there. Christ, did you lose all your hair at once or what?"

In a sullen voice, Whelan said, "I *shaved* my head … I only had a bald spot."

"And what, you never thought of a transplant or a weave? You've always been pretty much of an asshole, Ed, but at least you were good looking."

Mira sighed. Her anger was dissipating fast. All she felt was regret that she'd spent so much time with Edmond Whelan because, honestly, he had been something to look at. Made her damn schoolgirl heart race. She felt like tossing the damn lug wrench aside, but didn't.

Doing that might turn out to be a mistake.

"I could still do that, you know," Whelan said.

"What?"

"Let my hair grow back in, do something to cover the spot."

"I don't care, Ed. With any luck, I'll never see you again."

"I didn't destroy the embryo, Mira. That was a stock photo. I did a cut and paste."

She looked at him closely and saw the lie immediately.

"Okay, I did dispose of it, but I am sorry," he said. Whelan drew himself up, sat in an erect posture. "What the hell did you expect me to do after you stole my work?"

Mira only shook her head. "You mean your brilliant scheme for wing-nuts *uber alles*? You know, there was a time when that actually worried me. I did think I'd have to do something about it. Only I started to see how often your predictions were wrong and your plans backfired. The only purpose for revealing your masterwork now, Ed? That would be to work up a comedy act."

Anger flared in Whelan's eyes, and Mira saw it.

"Go ahead," she said. "Try something. We stepped away from each other far too peacefully. There should have been some bloodshed, but —" A thought struck Mira, taking her in a completely different direction. "I take it back. Beating on you physically would be a poor substitute for the idea I just had."

Knowing better than to overlook his ex-wife's intelligence, Whelan said, "What's that?"

"I'm going to tell you who really stole your precious unpublished doctoral dissertation."

"Who?"

She gave him the name, and the truth of her revelation made him wince more deeply than the rap on his leg with the lug wrench. Whelan got to his feet without any hint of intending to harm Mira. It was simply the prelude to his exit.

"I should have seen that," he said.

"It's easier to suspect enemies than friends."

He nodded and gave her the name of the clinic in Anaheim from which she'd already retrieved the embryos. He'd come across with the information he'd promised. Mira thought Whelan's honesty deserved some measure of recompense.

She told him about the intruder who'd visited her that morning.

"The guy wanted to know who hired him to steal the embryos. Seems like he should have figured out it was you, the ex-husband. Who knows? Maybe he did and just wanted me to confirm it. If so, that's what I did."

Edmond Whelan seemed to shrink before Mira's eyes.

"What?" she asked. "You paid the guy for his work, didn't you?"

Whelan didn't say a word.

"Hell, Ed, if you didn't, you better get him his money fast. This wasn't some guy you want to jerk around."

As in try to coerce him into killing James J. McGill, Whelan thought.

He realized that now it would be so much easier for Beck to kill him than McGill.

The echo of the whip ran from his ex-wife's house.

Buenos Aires, Argentina

Special Agent Abra Benjamin signed the registration form of the five-star hotel on the Avenida Alvear and had the bellman take her luggage to her suite. She headed directly to the lobby bar, taking a table with a street view and putting in an order for a Chivas Regal. After completing the 5,290-mile, 11-hour flight from New York, sleeping only intermittently, studying her new identity and getting up from her seat every hour to walk the length of the executive jet's cabin so she didn't develop a deep vein thrombosis, she was tired, wired and more than a bit cranky.

Normally, she was the most moderate of drinkers. It was always a matter of professional advantage to let everyone else get more soused than you did. Even so, you couldn't forgo at least a little booze or you'd be looked at like you were a prig or some other figure of suspicion. Like most things in an ambitious woman's life, deciding how much to drink was a balancing act.

But, damn, didn't that glass of fine Scotch go down like something that would get you evicted from Eden. It warmed her from head to toe, loosened knotted muscles and made her feel two-thirds human again. One more might put her over the top and let her sleep like Mom was singing a lullaby.

She was just about to order a second drink when the waiter and someone else anticipated her. "The gentleman at the bar sends his regards, *Señora,*" the waiter said, presenting her with a second Chivas.

There was no confusing whom the waiter meant. At that late hour, shortly before closing, there was only one guy at the bar, whether he was a gentleman or not. He looked old enough, just barely, to fit the description and he was wearing a well-tailored suit. His hair was a bit oily, but who knew if that was the style south of the equator?

Abra told the waiter, "Thank you. Would you also do me a favor?"

"Certainly, *Señora.*"

"Tell the gentleman I said he should match your tip to the price of this drink."

The waiter arched an eyebrow. "At one hundred percent?"

"More if he's feeling generous."

The waiter couldn't quite hide his smile. *"Sí, Señora."*

Abra watched as the waiter delivered his message. The guy who'd bought Abra her drink looked across the room at her. She raised her glass in a salute. The big spender took out his wallet and gave the waiter a currency note that earned him a bow.

Then he took it as assumed that he was free to join Abra.

The closer he got, the more she liked his looks. He was a very handsome fellow. Might have been a telenovela actor for all she knew. Maybe she should let him know the wet-head was dead, even in Argentina.

Of course, an old American TV commercial slogan might be regarded as offensive in another culture. Abra decided not to get too cute with the guy. She'd just play the part that was written for her. She was a well-off, headstrong woman from New York visiting distant relatives while waiting for —

The guy to surprise her by taking her hand and kissing it.

Abra laughed. It was either that or get to her feet and clock him.

"I have made a mistake?" the guy asked without looking at all embarrassed. "You are not European?"

"If I were, would you be speaking English? I don't look like a Brit, do I?"

For just a moment, he looked to Abra like he realized he had made a mistake and she'd spotted him for a bullshitter. If he was the guy she was looking for, she didn't want to scare him away. She gave him a wink and said, "Hey, I'm just joking. The last man who kissed my hand was my grandfather, that's all. It caught me off guard, but thanks for the drink."

His confidence restored, the guy asked, "May I join you?"

"Only if you'll drink with me. Understanding this is my last one for the night."

While he was still on his feet, the guy gestured to the waiter, who was monitoring developments closely.

"Lo mismo para mi." he said. The same for me. He took his seat.

His drink came quickly and he raised his glass to Abra. *"Salud."*

"L'chaim," Abra replied.

The guy smiled. They both sipped their Scotch, and the guy asked Abra, "You are Jewish?"

"I am," she said, fighting off a yawn. "Is that a good or bad thing for you?"

"I am open minded on the subject of religion. I was raised Catholic, but I do not go to church very often any more."

"No? You don't want to go to heaven?"

"Yes, of course. Every day I train myself for a life of eternal bliss."

Abra laughed and took another sip of her drink. "That's pretty good."

The guy gave her a charming smile and changed the subject.

"May I ask what brings such a beautiful woman to my beautiful country?"

Abra, sticking to her script, said, "I'm following my lawyer's advice."

"He said to visit *America del Sur* and be sure to start in Buenos Aires?"

Abra smiled broadly, as her stage directions said she should. "He told me to visit my most distant relatives and he'd get me the biggest divorce settlement any woman could want."

"Bravo. This is a gentleman who clearly has your interests at heart."

"His, too. He gets a cut of every dollar he squeezes out of that bastard I was stupid enough to marry." Abra took a hit off her drink, an improvisation. "That's the last time I ever let my mother tell me that a man is a great catch."

Her new friend beamed in delight. "You followed your mother's advice about choosing a husband?"

"I said I was stupid, right?" Abra started to slur her words, just a little.

"No, no. That I can not believe." He shrugged. "It was only your mother who misjudged."

"Yeah, well. She was right about him being rich, and I'm going to skin him good. So that part will work out all right."

"Other matters were not so … fulfilling?"

"Hey, let's not get too cozy here. I mean you bought me just the one drink."

"Only because you set that limit."

Abra squinted as if her vision had started to blur. "You know what, I'm not really stupid. I know when I'm tired and I've had enough to drink. It's been fun, but I'm going up to my suite now, alone. Thanks for the drink."

As if he were the perfect gentleman, the guy got up and helped Abra to rise. He placed a hand lightly on a forearm, nothing more. But still got a sampling of the merchandise. Nice firm muscle tone. Standing back at an appropriate distance, he asked, "May I have the pleasure of knowing your name?"

"Wendy Wasserman. That's my married name. If we see each other again after my divorce is final, I'll let you know if I change it."

He nodded and smiled. "I am here quite often."

"Yeah? What's your name?"

"Guillermito Medianoche."

Abra frowned, as if trying to concentrate. "I took some Spanish in school." A true statement. "So your name is … Billy Midnight?"

With a small bow, he said, "At your service, *Señora*."

"You're not the devil, are you?"

Giving Abra a grin, he said, "Only on certain occasions. And you, by any chance, have you ever visited Israel?"

"Sure, several times," Only once, in fact. "I have a cousin who lives there, married a local boy. Now, they have kids. A home in Tel Aviv and a house on the beach."

"Why did you not hide out there?"

"My bastard, soon to be ex-husband, has family there, too."

Her script had anticipated that question.

Billy nodded, executed a small bow and said, "It has been a pleasure to spend this time with you,Wasserman. I hope we will have another chance to talk. *Buenas noches*."

He turned and sauntered out of the bar.

Abra wanted to question the waiter about Billy Midnight, but decided that would be out of character for Wendy Wasserman. She only nodded at the waiter and gave him a small smile. Let him know she thought of him as a person not a menial.

Stepping very carefully, which due to fatigue and the two drinks was a necessity, Abra made her way to the bank of elevators and up to her suite. She kicked off her shoes and slipped out of her dress, fell on the bed and bounced back up to pee.

Returning to bed, her head spun as it hit the pillows …

Even so, she was sure Billy Midnight was the pimp she was hoping to meet …

If he knew American accents, he'd know she was from New York, and had connections to Israel, too …

A perfect substitute for the hooker who'd begged off banging Tyler Busby …

Still, she'd have to make Billy work to lead her into a life of depravity …

With that happy thought in mind, Abra fell asleep.

CHAPTER 10

Saturday, March 28, 2015, The White House — Washington, DC

Upon arriving home, McGill had asked Patti if they could skip any talk of business, hers or his, until the morning.

"Gladly," the president said. "Until the sun rises, I'm just some dame you picked up and took to a fancy hotel guarded by Marines and guys with machine guns."

"So you're saying the neighborhood's not so good?"

"It's rotten with politicians, but we won't talk about them either."

They didn't. Beyond endearments and occasional banter about their kids, they didn't talk at all. Other forms of communication more than sufficed. When the new day did break, however, it was time to get back to the real world.

Patti told McGill just how much money she had to her name.

"Yikes," he said.

Then McGill told Patti of his opportunity to be on a TV show.

"Double yikes," she said.

"Yeah, but who knows if the writing will be any good?" he said.

"You're smart to wait and see about that. Most actors will take almost any role because they need to work. You, lucky man that you are, have a rich wife."

"And two pensions and a small business above an accounting

firm."

Patti took McGill's hand. "I've heard rumors that your business might be growing, beyond the European office in Paris. Is that true?"

"I'm considering opening another office in L.A." McGill looked thoughtful for a moment. "If I do that, I don't see how I could neglect to do the same back home in Chicago."

"Sounds like you might be very busy."

"Could be," he said, "but if you like, you could buy a small tropical island for just the two of us, and I could spend my days collecting sea shells and rubbing sun screen all over you."

Patti said, "That does sound appealing, but I have this new venture capital firm to get off the ground."

"That's right, you do, and I think it's a terrific idea. I know, maybe your appointments secretary could get together with my appointments secretary and work out a schedule of when we might see each other."

"How romantic. The idea almost makes me swoon."

McGill laughed, got out of bed and extended a hand to Patti.

"As long as we're both here right now, we might as well shower together. I'll wash your back, you wash mine. No need for scheduling at all."

She took his hand, stood and wrapped her arms around his waist.

"Promise me, Jim, we'll never bring our appointments secretaries into the shower with us."

"Certainly not," McGill said. "Water conservation goes only so far."

After the president had gone down to the Oval Office, McGill made a quick trip to his White House Hideaway. He looked around at the huge leather sofa, the fireplace and the artwork on the walls he'd bought with Patti. He murmured to himself, "Damn, this is the one room in the place I'm going to miss."

Oh, well, he thought, with Patti's money, he could ask for a copy of the Hideaway as a birthday gift. He plopped down on the sofa and called Los Angeles. It was just after six a.m. on the Left Coast. He hoped the person on the other end wasn't still in bed or in—

"Goddamnit, I told you not to call!"

A bad mood.

"You did?" McGill asked. "I don't remember that."

"Terry?"

"Jim McGill. Sorry about the early hour."

"*James J.* McGill?"

"Yes, but don't let that spare me any righteous anger."

Lieutenant Emily Proctor of the LAPD laughed. "Oh, sure, and while I'm at it, let me give the president an earful, too."

McGill said, "Please don't do that. She has too many troubles as it is."

"Yeah, I've heard. Probably shouldn't have said that. Hey, tell her I'm rooting for her."

"I will. Every bit of good will helps shore up her morale."

"So what can I do for you, sir?"

"I had to leave town in a hurry and —"

"You're not in L.A.?"

"I'm back in Washington, but I thought your detectives, Zapata and MacDuff should know that Mira Kersten got her embryos back. At least, I assume she did."

"How'd that happen?"

He told her about the guy who stole them dropping in uninvited at Mira Kersten's house.

"So your partner, Ms. Sweeney, had a gun on a home invader and Ms. Kersten said to let him go."

"In a nutshell, yes. I can send you a computer-generated likeness of him, if you like."

"I would, yeah. I get the feeling that Ms. Kersten has a secret or two to hide."

"You're probably too young, but John Lennon had something to say about that."

Emily chuckled and said, "I know what you mean. My dad used that line on me when I was growing up. 'Everybody's got something to hide except me and my monkey.'"

"Was your father a cop, too?" McGill asked.

"Worse, a lawyer and city councilman."

"So you know politics isn't a pretty business, to put it mildly. This whole situation, stealing the embryos, was mostly political, I think, with a little crime thrown in for spice. Though I'm sure Ms. Crozier could have done without getting tased."

"Yeah. Let's not forget that. I still want to catch this guy."

"I'd like to get my hands on him, too. Anyway, I just wanted to give your department a heads-up. Zapata and MacDuff might do a last interview with Ms. Kersten, but I don't know if they'll want to go much farther than that."

"They'll go as far as I tell them to," Lieutenant Proctor said.

"Sure. Anyway, I hope my information helps the LAPD."

"Your assistance is much appreciated, sir."

McGill said goodbye, having the feeling that if he did open a shop in Los Angeles it would be a good thing to have Emily Proctor as a friend. He had a feeling the young woman was going places. High places.

He called Sweetie and asked her to forward a copy of the thief's likeness to L.A.

McGill was just finishing breakfast in the Residence dining room when his phone rang. The ID screen told him Ellie Booker was calling. She was the only member of the media his phone didn't automatically divert to voice mail.

He answered by saying, "I hope there's some small chance you have good news, Ellie."

"What I have is *important* news. I'm going to interview Chief Justice Craig MacLaren in fifteen minutes. You and the president will want to be watching."

McGill's mind took a beat to think about that. He wondered for a moment if he'd missed a day somewhere and had woken up on Sunday not Saturday. No, he hadn't slept that long; it was Saturday. Normally, that was the quietest day of the week. The political news and analysis yakfests weren't due for another 24 hours.

Meaning that something big, a story that wouldn't wait, was about to break.

"What's happening, Ellie?" McGill asked.

"I can't say a word before we go on. Just be sure you and the president are watching."

"On WWN?

"No, PBS. We'll also be streaming on WETA's website."

The Washington affiliate of the Public Broadcasting System.

"Come on, Ellie, give me a hint."

"Can't. Gotta go. Watch."

With that, she was gone.

McGill picked up a house phone and called the Oval Office. He got the president's personal secretary, Edwina Byington. He said, "Edwina, unless the president is busy acting as commander in chief to stave off an invasion of the United States, I'll need to see her in the Oval Office in the next ten minutes. Better get Chief of Staff Mindel in on this, too, if she's in the building."

Unflappable as always, Edwina replied, "Yes, sir. Will you need coffee, tea and a bite to eat as well?"

Chevy Chase, Maryland

Senate Majority Leader Oren Worth, Republican of Utah, opened the door of his suburban Washington home and admitted Associate Supreme Court Justice Daniel Crockett. Worth's house was one of the few in the immediate surroundings that did not have household staff. Not because Worth lacked the wherewithal — his fortune was measured in the billions — but owing to his sense of self-reliance and efficiency.

Worth believed you did for yourself whenever possible. The shortest distance between two points was never a line that ran through any sort of unnecessary staffing. Much less a bureaucracy.

Many of the people in the GOP and in True South regarded him as something of an eccentric. More than a few on the ideological right doubted his commitment to several of their most cherished causes.

Neither of those concerns had slowed his nearly instantaneous rise in his party's hierarchy. Worth was by far the richest man in Congress. Educated as an engineer at the Colorado School of Mines, he'd made his first bundle in the decidedly unglamorous but essential field of copper mining. He'd also gone on to Stanford's Graduate School of Business. The joke, though, was that somewhere along the line Worth must have studied at the King Midas School of Alchemy because everything he touched turned to gold.

Worth also scared the hell out of a lot of people in Washington. They feared that he might be the harbinger of a new breed in national politics: the hands-on billionaire. Someone who was not content to throw his money at professional candidates and have them do his bidding. But someone who had the smarts, drive and most of all money to get in the game himself and exert direct control. Caesars in the making.

"Good morning, Mr. Justice Crockett," he said, extending a hand in welcome to his guest. "We'll be meeting in my home office, if that's all right with you."

Crockett shook hands and smiled. "That's just fine, Mr. Majority Leader."

Worth led Crockett into a room with a gleaming oval cherrywood table at which sat Speaker of the House Peter Profitt and House Whip Carter Coleman. Both men stood and shook Crockett's hand. He and Worth sat opposite the two leaders of the House. The seat at the head of the table remained empty.

Worth's explanation for that was it would be for the next Republican or True South president. The implication was clear. He, more likely than anyone else, would fill it eventually. The host offered a choice of drinks to his guests: spring water or *sparkling* spring water.

Lemon slices were available for those preferring a bit of zest.

Crockett accepted his libation with good grace, and then he

got right into his reason for asking to speak with the others. "In a few minutes, Chief Justice MacLaren is going to speak to Ellie Booker on PBS and its website. He called me and the other justices this morning to inform us of what he's going to say. When I asked if I might share the news with interested parties, such as yourselves, he said to feel free."

Worth nodded, wearing a thin smile. "Such a small lead time won't give us any chance to issue a pre-emptive response. So he's not losing a bit of advantage. Assuming, Mr. Justice, that you've heard the news only recently and brought it to us as quickly as you could."

Crockett nodded. "I did take the time to shower, shave and relieve myself."

The others gave polite chuckles and Worth said, "Well, I don't think we can fault you there."

"All right then, here's what the Chief is going to say," Crockett told them.

As he laid out MacLaren's plan, watching the apprehension grow in the faces of Profitt and Coleman but not Worth, he thought of his own reasons for bringing the news to these men in person. The first, of course, was that he wanted Craig MacLaren's job should fate or personal choice remove him from his preeminent seat on the court: Crockett wanted to be chief justice.

He also wanted to help shape the court when other associate justices retired or passed on. He wanted to be the one the next president turned to first when seeking advice on nominees. If he could swing both ends of his calculations, he might wind up being the most powerful and important man in Washington for a very long time.

He'd briefly thought of running for president himself, but he came to realize he'd never pass muster with the True South voters. Despite his Tennessee roots, he'd likely be called a SINO, Southerner in Name Only. Besides that, handicapping the opposition, he didn't think he'd be able to beat Oren Worth.

The man's personal fortune, used as a source of campaign

funds, would be an insurmountable advantage for Worth. Beyond that, Crockett thought that Worth wanted the job more than he did. In Worth's mind, his senate seat and majority leader position were just stepping stones to the Oval Office. Truth be told, Crockett preferred the Supreme Court. The appointment was for life, eliminating the need to ever grub for votes again, and nobody in either the executive or legislative branches could reverse a high court decision.

They could only propose and pass laws that *conformed* to the justices' decisions.

There was a real sense of personal satisfaction in that.

Of course, even a chief justice could be impeached, but the chances of that were …

Well, let the leaders of Congress in the room see just how hard it was going to be for them to impeach a president they all despised.

Hearing the last of what Crockett had to tell them, Worth clicked on the television in the room to hear it again from the chief justice himself.

Burbank, California

Eugene Beck switched hotels after talking with Mira Kersten. He didn't necessarily think anyone was closing in on him. It was simply good tradecraft. A moving target was harder to hit than a stationary one. Harder to spot in the first place. He took a room at the Marriott near Bob Hope Airport in the San Fernando Valley after contriving a different appearance than the one he'd showed to Ms. Kersten.

He had no trouble believing her assertion that Edmond Whelan was the man who hired him to steal the embryos. Hell, Whelan's name was in the clinic's records. Just a little bit of plowing through public records revealed the man was Mira Kersten's ex-husband. Bad blood between former spouses was as common as butter on popcorn.

Whelan wanting to retrieve his genetic building blocks was

also easy to understand.

Beck confirmed what Mira Kersten had told him about Whelan's occupation. He found a biographical profile in the *New York Times.* The guy was chief of staff to House Whip Carter Coleman. More than that, Whelan was identified as a former protégé of Thomas Winston Rangel, a deep thinker, at a policy palace called The Maris Institute.

The picture of Whelan accompanying the *Times* story made him look a bit like a grown-up version of Opie Taylor from *The Andy Griffith Show.* Mostly it was the eyes that were different. They were a lot more wised up. Beck didn't have any doubt this prick could want someone dead, if it would serve his purpose.

Using a data base in the international security firm that had been his nominal employer when he went globetrotting to kill America's enemies, Beck found Whelan's unlisted home address and phone number. He also located Whelan's work schedule in Representative Coleman's office. That information was supposed to be off-limits to private-sector firms and individuals, but the Chinese and the Russians weren't the only people who hacked the U.S. government.

What ticked Beck off was discovering that Whelan was out of the office.

A note on the guy's calendar said he was taking *personal time.*

Wasn't that too damn precious for words?

Your taxpayer dollars at rest. Shit.

Beck was sitting in front of his laptop trying to figure out how to find the bastard when a Google Alert popped up on the screen. Subject: James J. McGill. The president's husband remained a subject of interest for Beck. He really didn't have any intention of killing the man; he just couldn't stop thinking about him.

The guy was something of a modern marvel, if you looked at his years in Washington. He'd kicked a senator's ass on a basketball court. Basically told a Congressional committee to go fuck itself and got away with it. Pounded a half-ass militia leader into pudding in front of his troops just outside the U.S. Capitol.

The man was all sorts of a badass, and lucky enough to marry the president, too.

Getting the upper hand on someone like him, one on one, might be a real challenge. The kind of thing to engage the imagination of someone with Beck's training and temperament. Would he be able to humble McGill man to man?

Beck's first thought was, of course, he could.

McGill had to be ten years older than him, at least. Must be pushing fifty if not older. No matter how hard you trained or what natural ability you started with, time slowed everyone down. Hell, Beck thought he had to be fractionally slower than he was a few years ago. Going up against McGill would be a good test to see just how much he'd lost.

The question was, how could he set things up so the man's Secret Service agents didn't just gun him down before McGill had to handle his own self-preservation.

The Google Alert told him that McGill would be accompanying the president when she appeared for her trial in the Senate on Monday. That being the case, Beck figured McGill must have left L.A. and be on his way back to Washington, if he wasn't there already. Beck thought that was cool, a man standing by his woman that way.

He'd bet McGill would be staring daggers at those prick senators looking to do Patricia Grant in politically. *You mess with my wife, you're going to be some sorry SOBs.* He could see McGill's eyes telling them that without ever saying a word.

The irony here was the more Beck felt admiration for McGill, the more he wanted to test himself against him. He also thought a political animal like Whelan would have to hustle his ass back to DC to see the possible fall of a president. That being the case, the two guys he wanted to meet being in the capital, there was only one thing left for him to do.

He booked himself a nonstop flight from Bob Hope to New York City on Jet Blue. There were no direct flights from Burbank to Washington. But DC was just a hop from the Big Apple.

The White House — Washington, DC

Patti and Galia were already waiting in the Oval Office with an iBook set up on a coffee table in front of a silk sofa. McGill entered and took a seat to his wife's right; the chief of staff sat to the president's left.

A moment before the interview began to stream, Patti told McGill, "I passed the word along to Jean Morrissey. I'll want her in on the discussion once we hear what the chief justice has to say."

"Makes sense," McGill agreed.

"Have you heard that Jean's been seeing Byron DeWitt socially?"

McGill shook his head. He asked, "Did that start before or after she announced her candidacy to become president?"

Patricia Grant didn't know.

Galia said, "Before."

McGill nodded. "Maybe there is a hint of genuine feeling then."

Before that discussion could go any farther, Ellie Booker appeared on the screen, "Good morning. I'm Ellie Booker. I'm here at the Washington home of Craig MacLaren, the chief justice of the United States."

The picture widened to include MacLaren sitting in an armchair opposite Ellie.

"Good morning, sir."

The chief nodded. "Good morning, Ellie."

"You informed me recently that you have something you'd like to share with the American people regarding President Grant's upcoming trial in the United States Senate. Well, sir, we're now sitting before a camera that will broadcast what you have to say to the entire country and stream your words on the Internet to the whole world. Please let everyone know what's on your mind."

McGill took Patti's hand, offering both comfort and strength.

The chief justice paused to take a breath and then began. "As you know, Ellie, I will be presiding over the president's trial which will start just two days from now. There's no matter short of a declaration of war that's more important for our legislative branch to consider than the impeachment, trial and possible removal from office of our country's chief executive.

"Everyone involved should take their responsibilities with the utmost seriousness. That includes the members of the House and the Senate ... and me. The roles and responsibilities of our legislators are clearly defined. They examine any charges alleged against the president, decide whether the alleged offenses rise to the level of the high crimes and misdemeanors as contemplated by the Constitution and then vote whether to impeach and convict or not.

"The House of Representatives has already decided to impeach, and now a number of its members will act as the prosecution team in the trial to be held in the Senate. That's where I come in. I am to *preside* at the trial. The problem with that is the Constitution provides no clear guidelines as to what judicial authority I have in the proceedings.

"For example, at the impeachment trial of President Andrew Johnson, a Democrat, in 1868, Chief Justice Salmon Chase claimed the authority to decide procedural questions. The Senate's Republican majority overruled him twice, rendering his power over the proceedings nil. In the 20th century, during the Senate trial of William Clinton, a Democrat, Chief Justice William Rehnquist, a Republican, also decided he could rule on procedural questions. The Republican majority in the Senate neither objected to his position nor overruled him.

"So what I'm looking at here are two conflicting precedents that have one thing in common: partisan preference. Senators will show deference to a chief justice of their own party but not to a chief justice of another party. Now, party loyalty is all well and good when it comes to wrangling over and compromising on the details of writing legislation, but there's no place for partisan politics when it comes to deciding the fate of a president, a person voted into office by Americans living from border to border and coast to coast.

"Given our current political realities, I have no doubt that if

I were to claim authority to rule on procedural matters during the upcoming Senate trial of President Patricia Grant, my fate would be that of Chief Justice Chase not Chief Justice Rehnquist. I supposed I could resign my position as the presiding officer at the trial or even my seat on the Supreme Court in protest, but doing that would not further the interests of justice, as I see it.

"All that being said, I'm here today to say that I've chosen to assume other roles vital to our democracy during the president's trial. I will become an expert witness and a reporter on the proceedings. I will inform all of our fellow citizens whether the behavior of the Senate and the prosecution team from the House conforms with the norms of justice seen in any other American courtroom. If the rights of the accused are observed, I will praise all involved; if the proceedings veer in the direction of political animus seeking political advantage, I will condemn this behavior and articulate it in fine detail.

"Either way, I will make my findings clear to every American and all other interested parties around the world, and I will do so each day of the trial."

Ellie let a long moment of silence pass.

Then she said, "So, basically, sir, you are putting Congress on notice. Telling them they'd better play things straight."

"Yes," MacLaren said, "I suppose I am."

Buenos Aires, Argentina

FBI Special Agent Abra Benjamin took a phone call from Deputy Director Byron DeWitt in her hotel suite. He said, "Didn't wake you up, did I?"

"What, you thought I was up partying on my first night here?"

"Jet lag or travel fatigue was what I had in mind," he said, "and as I remember, you're not really a morning person."

True enough, Abra thought, she could be bitchy in the morning, and Byron knew as much from waking up in the same bed on several occasions. But it was more than a matter of her circadian rhythm bothering Abra just then. Hearing from Byron while she was still lounging in bed made her realize she wasn't going to have the pleasure of his company between the sheets ever again.

He was going to marry that damn Jean Morrissey; she just knew it.

Byron was going to become the next James J. McGill. God! For a woman driven by ambition, it was galling to see a former boyfriend skyrocket to the top of the heap. Even so, she wouldn't help her own cause by being surly with him. He'd always behaved decently to her, even after they'd ended their sexual relationship.

So doing her best to stay on his good side could only help.

But she'd be damned if she would ever vote for Jean Morrissey.

"Are you still there, Special Agent?" DeWitt asked.

"Yes, I'm here, Mr. Deputy Director, and I'm sorry that I'm behaving badly. I'm not jet-lagged; there's only a one-hour difference between Washington and B.A. I'm also not tired, because I slept well. I'm just a terror in the morning most days, as you rightly remembered."

"I try to recall only the good things," DeWitt said.

The fact that he was still being a nice guy only made Abra more angry that he was going to marry someone else. Still, her yearning to rise high in the world muted any impolitic response.

"A wise choice, sir, I'm sure. How may I be of service?"

DeWitt asked whether she was well situated and had started to look for Tyler Busby.

"I'm pretty sure I got hit on by the pimp servicing Busby's needs last night, assuming the Bureau sent me to the right hotel. The one with the other flawed ladies."

She gave DeWitt the details of her encounter with Billy Midnight.

"That's great," he said. "So what's your next step?"

The question was no sooner asked than there was a knock at the door to the suite. It was neither loud nor insistent but it was clearly audible with the door to the bedroom open. Even DeWitt could hear it.

"Room service?" he asked.

"Didn't order any. I left a do-not-disturb message with the front desk."

"Call hotel security," DeWitt said.

"Maybe I'll just shoot through the door," Abra replied.

"You don't have a gun … I hope."

"I still know how to take care of myself."

The knock at the door sounded again, a bit louder and more imperative now.

"I've got to go, Byron."

"Be careful, Abra."

It comforted her that they'd reverted to first names in a moment of possible danger.

There was still some measure of personal concern between them.

She hung up and threw on a robe. Walking to the door, she said, "Coming. Who's there, please?"

A voice responded, "It's me, Billy. From last night."

Sonofabitch, Abra thought, maybe she would be the agent to take down Tyler Busby.

Wouldn't that look good on her résumé?

"How do you know the number of my suite? Did you follow me?"

He hadn't; she'd been careful about that. Still, it didn't hurt to mislead him about her watchfulness.

"No, of course not. I would never do such a thing. I … simply have friends in this hotel. Business contacts you might say. May I please come in? I have what might be an interesting proposition for you to consider."

Abra thought quickly. Let him in or put him off. She went with letting him in; she'd watched the way he moved last night. The guy was no athlete. She was and she'd had training both at Quantico and, well, Israel.

She opened the door and told Billy, "Breakfast is on you. I don't like anyone snooping on me."

Billy smiled, stepped inside and took a peek at her cleavage.

Abra noticed that, but neither pulled her robe more tightly closed nor chastised him. She only turned her back on him and took a seat at the suite's dining table. She crossed her legs and waited for Billy to join her, more sure than ever that he worked in the sex trade. Having subverted at least one well-placed staffer at a five-star hotel to get her suite number, there was also a chance he dealt with clients of Busby's stature.

Billy stopped at the nearby wet bar and picked up a house phone.

"What would you like to eat?"

"Coffee with cream, half a grapefruit, uncooked oatmeal with brown sugar and a split of good champagne."

The first three items were her typical breakfast, the bubbly was a bit of improv. Abra decided it wouldn't be a bad idea to let Billy think maybe she had a little drinking problem.

He ordered for her in Spanish. She listened closely and didn't hear anything but what she requested. Still, the fix could have been put in ahead of time. He might have offered to buy breakfast if she hadn't demanded it. Slip a mickey into the coffee, and she'd be at his mercy.

If he even knew what mercy meant.

She decided not to touch any of the breakfast, while he was in the suite or afterward.

It would be tragically funny, having told Byron that she could take care of herself, if she wound up dead. "So what do you want, Billy? What's this interesting proposition of yours?"

Nice choice of a word, she thought. Proposition.

He sat across the table from her and smiled. "I was thinking about what you said last night: that at least your marriage had succeeded in terms of the money you would take from it. A very practical attitude on your part."

"Gee, thanks," Abra said, her tone flat.

Billy read the subtext and dropped the rest of the canned corn he'd prepared for her.

"Very well, I will come to the point. I have heard from many

American women that divorces in your country can take quite a long time to come to resolution. Years, possibly."

Abra produced a harsh laugh. "Until hell freezes over, according to that schmuck I married."

"Yes, well, that is what I mean. Perhaps you have the means to wait him out in a place such as this." He gestured to the lavishly furnished suite. "Or perhaps you do not."

"Okay," Abra said, "here's where we get to the good part, right? You're going to tell me about all the money I can make until my divorce settlement comes through and what I have to do to get it." She held up a hand as Billy began to speak. "No, don't tell me. I bet I can guess. What we're talking about here is sex. Good old S-E-X."

Billy nodded.

"Well, thanks for being honest," Abra said." Try to keep telling the truth. Is this the plain old man-and-woman hokey-pokey activity we're talking about here? Or is it a crowd-and-freak scene?"

"Most likely it is one-to-one, heterosexual, within conventional practices. Possibly, there might be a second woman."

"But just the one guy?"

"Yes."

Abra leaned forward. "And he can pay well enough to interest someone like me?"

Billy mentioned the fee available for a week of Abra's time.

She smiled, honestly impressed. "Wow. He must be one rich SOB. You're sure there's no bondage and whips involved here?"

"No, nothing like that."

She sat back, stared at Billy, her arms folded across her chest.

"I bet this horny bastard likes his privacy, doesn't he?"

"Being discreet is part of the job, yes."

"Okay, tell me where I'd have to go. Is he right here in the hotel?"

Billy shook his head. "No, not here, but not far. I can take you with no problem."

"Unh-uh," Abra said, shaking her head. "Mama told me never to get into a car with a strange man. I might wind up in the Middle

East getting poked by some old shit who thinks he's a sultan. You tell me where to go and I find my way there at the appointed time or you can take a walk right now."

Billy glared at Abra and she knew just what kind of misogynistic crap was surging through his mind. He wanted to *force* her to be obedient and, more than that, he wanted to *bang* her before his client ever got the chance. She told him as much.

"You want to sample the goodies, don't you?"

Billy got to his feet, the first move toward coming around the table.

Maybe even over it.

Abra pointed at his chair and said in a commanding voice. "Sit down. I'm going to tell you something." She stared at him, never blinking, until he complied. "I told you about my cousin and her husband in Israel. Well, her husband is IDF special forces. The six months I stayed with them, I got training in marksmanship and close quarters combat every single day. Just like my cousin did. Her husband is a big believer in women knowing how to protect themselves. You come at me, I'm going to put you in a wrist-lock or an arm-bar and run you right through that window over there in the living room, and we're on the seventeenth floor, aren't we? It'd be a shame if you landed on someone walking by the hotel, but I'm willing to take that chance."

Abra had delivered her spiel in a cold monotone. Every word rang true, because it was all true. Billy got up again and went to the door to the hallway. Abra stopped him there.

"Hey, I am interested in that money on my terms. If you get over your pout, let me know. Just call. There's no need to come back."

Billy left and Abra locked and bolted the door after him.

She called room service and canceled the order.

Then she called Byron back. Even if Billy didn't give in to her demands, the deputy director could have other FBI agents trail Billy, find out where he lived, wiretap him. Hell, kidnap the prick if it came to that. They'd find out where the other hookers were being taken to haul Busby's ashes. Then they'd grab the big prize and fly him back to the U.S.

That wouldn't be as much fun as slapping handcuffs on him personally, but it would deserve a big promotion. What more could a girl want?

The White House — Washington, DC

The president closed the lid of the iBook and she and McGill turned their heads to look at Galia, an unspoken question in their eyes.

"What?" the chief of staff asked. "You think I have the kind of pull with the chief justice of the United States to get him to do what he just said?"

McGill replied, "There's no doubt in my mind you'd do whatever was necessary. The only question is whether you have the leverage."

The president remained silent.

"I don't," Galia said. "Craig MacLaren is someone I've never wanted to manipulate, and I doubt I could have found a handle on him if I had.

McGill persisted. "So you had *nothing* to do with MacLaren's bold move?"

The chief of staff shook her head.

"How do you think his move will play with the other side?" the president asked. "How will our adversaries in the House and Senate respond?"

A smile lit Galia's face. "They'll huff and puff and maybe even pass gas in public, but there's not a damn thing they can do. The job of presiding over the impeachment trial of a president is articulated in the Constitution. If they try to force MacLaren out simply because he says he's going to use his First Amendment rights to analyze the proceedings, they'll be roasted alive by public opinion. Besides, even if they succeeded, Jean Morrissey would be the next in line to preside, and that would be something to see. If they tried to get rid of her, too, well, it might be time for a new revolution."

McGill looked at his wife. "Thank God, we've got the commander-in-chief on our side."

Patti Grant held up a hand. "Let's not get too melodramatic. There's not going to be any coup d'état in the United States. My view is Craig MacLaren just streamlined things for my legal team and me. Whatever questions the prosecution has will be factually oriented. Did I have any prior agreement with Joan Renshaw to kill Erna Godfrey, and if so is there any proof of the conspiracy? Political posturing and theorizing will have to take place outside the Senate."

McGill nodded. "I think that's right. Inside the Capitol, things are going to move at a snappy pace. The votes on the GOP-True South side are fixed. The only question is, can we hold enough Democratic votes to avoid the two-thirds requirement to convict?"

Patti and McGill looked at each other.

Then both of them turned their eyes to Galia.

Walter Reed National Military Medical Center — Bethesda, Maryland

Joan Renshaw woke up in her hospital room. It took a long moment to orient herself. She felt so damn weak that separating her eyelids had taken a conscious effort. Still, that simple task was easier this time than the previous one. The next chore was getting her eyes to focus. Blinking helped in the way windshield wipers cleared a driver's view of the road.

Christ, she wondered if she'd ever be healthy again.

She also asked herself whether the investigator from the House prosecution committee would come back for another statement. Basically, all she'd done last time was answer one question in the affirmative.

The woman in her off-the-rack business suit had identified herself as Janine Bosworth and asked: "Did the president, Patricia Grant, arrange for you to be put in a prison cell with Erna Godfrey for the purpose of having you kill Mrs. Godfrey?"

Thinking about that now, Joan realized it was what lawyers called a leading question. The point was to paint a bull's-eye on the person whose life you wished to ruin. That had worked just fine for Joan. She hated Patti Grant.

She'd croaked out, "Yes."

One syllable was the extent of her testimony.

That was good enough for Janine Bosworth. She said, "I may or may not be back with other questions. Or someone else might come and talk with you."

A real bleeding heart that Janine. Hadn't asked Joan if she was feeling better, what her outlook was, hadn't even said goodbye. More important than any lack of social graces, the bitch hadn't talked about offering any consideration in return for Joan's testimony when it came time to testify under oath. Leniency at the least, a walk in the best case.

Joan knew that freedom in the short term would be a real reach. She had conspired to kill the president of the United States, and she'd actually choked a woman to death. But she planned to swear to God and on her mother's grave that she could not remember doing either of those things. That way maybe she could get out of prison in, say, five years. After Patti Grant had been out of office a good long time and nobody much gave a damn about her anymore.

Of course, it would be tricky trying to convince people she was sincere in saying she couldn't remember her own guilt in two crimes while being crystal clear on the president arranging the death of that awful bible-thumper Erna Godfrey. God but she still hated that woman, would strangle her again, only more slowly, if she got a second chance.

Of course, she'd have to mask her enmity for that damn Godfrey woman if she was called to testify against Patti Grant. She'd have to make it clear she'd choked her out only because the president had promised to offer her a pardon. Hah, wasn't that a laugh?

Doing so much heavy thinking was wearying Joan.

Only she was scared spitless about going back to sleep. How could she know she would wake up after four, six or eight hours? Maybe she'd never regain consciousness again. Of course, if she was sentenced to life in prison, maybe that wouldn't be a bad way to go.

In the end, though, it wasn't her choice whether she would lapse into sleep. She was so damn tired it was inevitable. Just as she was about drift off, Joan noticed something that struck her as more than a bit strange. Someone had left a vase of flowers on the tray next her bed, and there was a card with the bouquet.

"No way, no damn way," Joan muttered.

She wasn't at The Betty Ford Center drying out. She had to be in a prison ward. Who the hell got flowers in prison?

Straining hard, she reached out and plucked the card from the flowers. Opening the envelope and positioning the card so the light hit it straight on was yet another chore. Lastly, she had to interpret the cursive handwriting.

After she managed all that, she saw: *The truth may or may not set you free, but a lie will guarantee you a very bad time.*

Understanding the nature of the threat that had been delivered to her — lie about the president at your own peril — Joan reached another milestone of recovery. She screamed at the top of her lungs.

Punta del Este, Uruguay

"What's the little guy's name?"

Lieutenant Silvina Reyes of the Uruguayan National Police looked up from changing the diaper on Santiago Calvo, the infant son of her superior Captain Antonio Calvo.

"Momentito," she replied to the American who was pretending to be a Canadian and calling himself Bruce Mallory. Her mind whirled with the question of why the man had approached her. His motive did not seem to be lechery, at least not so far.

She finished cleaning Santiago's bottom, fastening a fresh diaper on him and putting the soiled one in a carry bag.

"*¿Cómo está, Señor?*" Silvina asked.

"*Bueno, y usted?*" Good, and you?

"*Bueno tambien.*" Good also.

To Silvina's ear, the American's confident tone told her he spoke more than a little Spanish, possibly might be fluent, but she couldn't place his accent. It wasn't from New York, St. Louis, Austin or any other place she'd visited in the U.S. Still, she would know better than to speak her native language and think he wouldn't understand her.

She said in English, "The *niño,* he is called Santiago."

"Named in honor of Saint James, is he?"

That tidbit of knowledge surprised Silvina, and she let the emotion show on her face.

"Names and their meaning are a hobby of mine," the man said.

No doubt because you use more than the one your mother gave you, she thought.

Still, she played the innocent.

"Do you and your wife need a nanny, *Señor?* I have a friend who —"

He waved his hand. "Thank you but no. I am not married and I have no children. What I'd like to know is if perhaps you know a policeman."

"*Señor?*"

"I saw a new neighbor move in across the street from me. I believe he's someone I've seen before, in the United States."

"*¿Sí?*"

"If I'm not mistaken, he is a very famous man."

"From the cinema?"

The man calling himself Mallory shook his head. "No, this man is famous for the crime he tried to commit."

Silvina tried her best to make her body shrivel in fear. Even so, she tilted her head forward attentively and said, "*¿Qué?*" What?

"He tried to kill the president of the United States."

Silvina covered her mouth and let her eyes go wide in horror.

Thinking to herself *mierda santa* — holy shit — is this guy for real?

"Who is this man?" she asked trying her best to make her voice tremulous.

"I don't know what he's calling himself here, but his real name is Tyler Busby."

"Why do you tell me this, *Señor?*"

"Well, I can't say for sure, but my guess is the American government has put a bounty on his head, a reward, yes?"

Silvina played dumb, pretending not to understand.

"Una recompensa. ¿Comprende?"

Silvina's impression that Bruce Mallory spoke more than a little Spanish was just confirmed.

"Why don't you take this money for yourself?" she asked.

He looked all around before telling her, "I'm hiding out."

That admission genuinely caught Silvina off guard. She pulled Santiago's pram back a step, ready to shove the child out of harm's way if she had to defend herself. But Mallory only held up his hands to reassure her.

"I have two brothers. Each of them is trying to take over our father's company in Vancouver. I'm the one who can cast the deciding vote, but I don't want to do that. I want my brothers to settle things between themselves. Do you see?"

Silvina felt sure Mallory was lying, but she had to admire the plausibility of his story.

So she nodded.

He went on, "If you have family or a friend in the police, you could arrest this man and claim the reward. You'd all be heroes."

"Busby?" she said to be sure. *"¿Dónde está?"* Where is he?

"Tyler Busby. He lives with his wife and their baby in the big house on the right hand corner of the next block. You see it?"

Silvina looked and nodded.

"Do you know any police officers?" Mallory asked.

"Oh, yes. The husband of my sister."

"Is he is up to handling something like this?"

Silvina made a show of thinking before shaking her head. "I do not think so, but *his* brother is. He is …" She searched for the word. Then she smiled, "The detective, yes?"

She wanted to see how Mallory reacted to that and was pleased by the result.

Apprehension flashed in his eyes. The involvement of an investigator was more than he'd counted on. Still, he tried to cover his discomfort with a smile.

"That's great. So he'll do it?"

"Oh, yes, I am sure."

"Great. Well, don't waste any time, and please don't mention me to anyone."

Silvina smiled innocently. "As you prefer, *Señor.*"

Los Angeles, California

Upon returning to his hotel the prior evening, John Tall Wolf had been presented with a message from Jim McGill. The note was prompted by events on the far coast. It made Tall Wolf wonder what was going on. He was almost tempted to call Marlene Flower Moon to see what she might know. Almost.

McGill said: *Had to hurry back to Washington. Client has located missing property. Sorry to leave you behind. Fly to destination of your choice first class; McGill Investigations will reimburse. If you want to remain in L.A. a day or two, please use my suite on my tab. JMcG.*

Tall Wolf had to admire the man's style. He'd accepted McGill's invitation and moved into his suite, intending to stay just the one night. He didn't want to spoil himself. Not that he was so worried about debasing his character that he declined to have room service send up a hearty breakfast.

Despite the plush surroundings and creature comforts, though, he felt less than satisfied with the outcome of the case. Having the bad guy tell you where he'd stashed the stolen goods preempted the satisfaction of finding them yourself. Also, you couldn't count on that happening more than once in a lifetime. So it was best to work things out on your own.

He decided to go see Mira Kersten and get her take on things.

After all, the bad guy was still out there awaiting capture. You didn't get to commit a crime and then say, "Oops, sorry. All better now." Far preferable, the thief should reflect on his moral shortcomings while doing a substantial stretch of prison time.

Tall Wolf hoped he wouldn't have to explain his reasoning to Mira.

Some people, after an unpleasant experience, just didn't want to be bothered any further.

Mira Kersten, it turned out, wasn't one of them. She opened the door to her home with anger burning brightly in her eyes. She asked Tall Wolf immediately, "You know what that sonofabitch did?"

"You have any particular SOB in mind?" Tall Wolf inquired.

The response brought Mira up short. Made her stop and think. She walked away from Tall Wolf but left the door open. He took that as an invitation to come on in. He followed her into the living room. She plopped down on the sofa, still lost in thought.

When she looked up and realized Tall Wolf was still with her, she said, "It could be either of them, I suppose, that freaking thief or my bastard ex, Ed Whelan."

"If you're speaking of your embryos," Tall Wolf said, "I thought they were returned. Or at least you know where they are."

"I know where they are, all right, *except* for the one I want the most."

"The embryos are still on ice and you already have a favorite future child?" Tall Wolf asked.

Mira looked at him as if she were about to snap out a rebuke, but she took a moment to consider the question and had the honesty to bob her head. "Sounds harsh, doesn't it?"

"Leaves room for criticism," Tall Wolf said. "Might even be the topic of some future nursery rhyme. Something dark and full of snark."

She laughed. "Yeah, well, unless Shel Silverstein comes back from the dead, I won't worry about that."

Tall Wolf grinned and took a seat without asking first.

"How'd you find out an embryo was missing?" he asked.

"The new place where I'm keeping them is meticulous. I told them how many I thought I was entrusting to them. They did a count, called me and said I was off by one."

Tall Wolf only nodded.

"You're not going to ask me who the father is?" she said.

"My guess: the same fellow whose seed you're bearing right now."

"Yeah, I guess that's pretty logical."

Tall Wolf let a second moment of silence go by.

Mira read between the unspoken lines; she was no dumb bunny.

She told Tall Wolf, "You not only know who the father of my preferred child is, you know the hunt is still on. I want you to find that particular embryo. You and Mr. McGill. His friend, Ms. Sweeney, too. All the king's horses and all the king's men, if that's what it takes. Well, damnit, now you've got me talking in nursery rhymes."

"They're infectious," Tall Wolf said, "but Mr. McGill is likely to be busy in the coming days. I can't speak for Ms. Sweeney but —"

"But we didn't part on the best of terms whether she has the time or not. She wanted me to call the cops while she had a gun on the thief. I said no."

The grimace on Mira's face told Tall Wolf there was no need for her guest to criticize the decision. "What about you?" she asked. "Will you find the embryo for me?"

"I'm an employee of the federal government. Somewhat highly placed, too. My presence is an unofficial favor to Mr. McGill."

"Well, hell."

Never much of a weeper, Mira nonetheless looked as if she might cry.

"Lucky for you," Tall Wolf added, "I don't like to leave jobs unfinished."

"You'll keep going?"

"I want to find the original thief. If your ex-husband has a hand in the matter, too, he should be easier to locate. Can you describe the thief for me?"

"I can do better than that." Mira took out her phone and pulled up a photo. "That's a picture of a composite Ms. Sweeney made with her iPad. It's a very good likeness."

Tall Wolf gave her the number of his phone and she emailed the photo to him.

"Now, I want to ask you a question," Tall Wolf said.

"What?"

"Do you know if your ex-husband is writing a book?"

"Ed? He's all about secrecy, not ..." A newly arrived thought silenced her.

"But?" Tall Wolf asked.

"He's shaved his head, and I saw him drive off in some fancy new sports car."

Tall Wolf raised an eyebrow. "Your ex came to see you?"

She nodded. "He still thought I had his masterpiece. He gave me the name of the same clinic the thief did. The place where I found my embryos. Ed was pleading that he'd only wanted a swap all along. I told him I really didn't take the damn thing."

Tall Wolf sat back, crossed his left ankle over his right knee and smiled.

"What?" Mira asked. "You've got something?"

Tall Wolf nodded. "Maybe you've just been away from Washington too long or you'd probably see it, too."

Given that hint, Mira made the leap. "Ed's going to publish his thesis commercially? That's crazy. He's been wrong as often as he's been right. His schemes have backfired as many times as they've succeeded. He'd look foolish."

Tall Wolf said, "Publishing houses still employ editors, don't they?"

Mira nodded and then smiled. "Some of them do, I think, but knowing Ed and assuming you're right, editing wouldn't even be necessary. He'd cut out all the embarrassing miscalculations and failed schemes before he ever submitted the manuscript."

"There you go," Tall Wolf said. "He's packaging himself for success."

She thought about that and nodded. "I can see it. The audience for his book, movement conservatives, will lap it up like free booze. It would sell like sheet music to a church choir. He'd make a bundle. On top of that, it'd be a gigantic ego stroke for Ed. He'd probably be able to get the funding to set up his own think tank and have a solid-gold sinecure for the rest of his life."

"Explaining why he had to come at you so hard when he thought you stole his original manuscript. It would reveal all his warts," Tall Wolf said.

Mira nodded. "I told him who I think really took the damn thing."

"Who's that?"

She told him. "That's another guy who'd be really embarrassed if the first edition of Ed Whelan's big book of political bullshit ever gained wide attention." She told Tall Wolf why it would ruin that SOB's reputation.

He agreed with Mira's thinking.

"There's one more thing you should know," she said.

"What's that?"

"I told Ed that the thief was looking for him, and he was so scared he almost wet himself. I thought Ed might have stiffed the guy on his fee for grabbing the embryos. He was always a cheap bastard. But thinking about it a bit more, it could be something other than an overdue bill that has him in a sweat."

"You have any idea what that might be?"

Mira shook her head. "Not specifically, but it has to be one of three things, doesn't it? Ed is in fear he might lose his job, his reputation or his precious pink heinie."

"Mortal jeopardy?" Tall Wolf asked.

"Ed was pretty damn scared. I wouldn't rule it out."

Tall Wolf got to his feet. "Okay, thanks.

Mira said, "So, if you catch the thief …"

"If he has the embryo and it's viable, I'll see that it's safely returned."

"Thank you." She took a beat before asking, "You think in my own way I'm just as terrible as Ed, don't you?"

He shrugged. "I try not to judge. When I can help it."

"What would you do? You know, if you had, say, two embryos available to you that came from different women. Wouldn't there be something that would make you choose one over the other?"

Tall Wolf said, "I'm all for advances in medical science, but I'd try to use it only to simplify my life not complicate it."

John Tall Wolf went back to his hotel, got his bag and checked out. He was about to leave for LAX and catch a commercial flight to Washington when he had another idea. He called Jeremy Macklin on the Northern Apache reservation in New Mexico. Before he could do more than say hello Macklin jumped all over him.

"You know what your cousin wants me to do?" the online scandal sheet reporter asked.

"Become the dean of the school of communications at his new university?"

A long pause ensued before Macklin said, "Is this some kind of conspiracy the two of you have cooked up?"

"It is," Tall Wolf admitted. "We're plotting to make life better for as many underserved kids as we can. Sometimes innocent people like you just get roped in by circumstance."

"Is this for real? Arnoldo Black Knife is going to pour a ton of energy-income money into starting a big-time university on an Indian reservation in New Mexico?"

"I mentioned to him that was what John D. Rockefeller did with the University of Chicago. Things are only at the discussion stage right now, but the fact that he's mentioned it to you and apparently asked if you'd like to play a role —"

"Exactly the one you mentioned."

"Sounds appropriate to me," Tall Wolf said. "Arnoldo must be moving forward."

"We didn't get around to talking about his schedule, but would the school be just for Native American kids?"

"Maybe at first, but it will probably evolve into something like Berea College in Kentucky. You know, a diverse student body with no tuition for anyone who's admitted. Given that family income falls beneath a certain ceiling."

After a shorter pause, Macklin said, "You know, that sounds pretty damn cool."

"Yeah, I think so, too, and if you worked on a school-year schedule, that'd leave you a fair amount of free time every summer to get back to the beach in Santa Monica."

"Ha! That sounds great."

They left plans for a brighter future right there. Tall Wolf asked if Macklin knew of any show biz moguls who might be heading back east that day in a company plane and wouldn't mind a humble public servant bumming a ride. Macklin took a moment to check his sources, make some calls and then offered Tall Wolf a choice of three flights.

He took the one heading directly to DC. First class commercial air travel was all well and good, but for endless leg-room you couldn't beat an executive jet. All Tall Wolf had to do to earn his cushy ride was tell the producer who owned the aircraft a little bit about the investigations he did for the BIA, and listen to the guy suggest that maybe he could develop a pay-cable TV series based on Tall Wolf's exploits.

By the time they landed in Washington, Tall Wolf had to be honest with himself.

Maybe he was getting a little spoiled.

Great Falls, Virginia

Everyone was spoiled at Bright Wing Country Club where House Speaker Peter Profitt and House Whip Carter Coleman met with T.W. Rangel. As a place where three wealthy old white guys could blend in with the early-bird dinner crowd, though, it couldn't be beat. Still, just about all the members recognized Profitt and Coleman. They were on the golf course there more often than they were on the floor of the House. They were well known as being among the players most likely to take a mulligan.

Far fewer knew Rangel. He didn't play golf and consciously avoided media exposure. But in demeanor and dress he might have been the chairman of the membership committee. The three men convened in a private dining room. They all had the filet mignon, well done. At Rangel's insistence, they abstained from alcohol until their business was concluded.

Rangel had also been the one to suggest using the country club. "What with the upcoming trial of the president in the Senate, certain media outlets might have assigned stringers to follow your movements," he told the congressmen, "and report on anything curious you do."

The two politicians said they were outraged by the very thought that they might be tailed like members of organized crime.

"Remember what Mark Twain had to say about that," Rangel told them. "'There is no distinctly native American criminal class except Congress.'" He added, "Also recall with whom we are dealing."

"Galia Mindel," they said in unison.

"Exactly. If you don't think she has minions among the media, you should retire now."

Profitt said, "She's exactly why we're here, T.W. Someone got to Joan Renshaw at Walter Reed."

"What do you mean?" Rangel asked.

Coleman told him about the flowers and card delivered to Renshaw's room.

Rangel understood that the speaker or his whip must have come by their information from a paid insider on staff at the hospital. He didn't ask for confirmation on that point. It would have been both rude and a rookie mistake. He wouldn't want to admit to — or lie to — a federal prosecutor that he knew Profitt and

Coleman had suborned someone at Walter Reed.

Still, he was curious about one thing: "What did the card say?"

Coleman told him verbatim. "The truth may or may not set you free, but a lie will guarantee you a very bad time."

Rangel took a moment to think. "Plainly but artfully said. No beneficial promise is made, and if punishment should occur it would be the result of Ms. Renshaw's own moral failure, not the work of some outside party. I'm not a lawyer, but I can imagine that's how one might defend the author of that note. I don't suppose the floral delivery person was caught."

"No," Profitt said.

"And now you gentlemen are worried that Ms. Renshaw might withdraw her statement implicating the president as being responsible for Erna Godfrey's death."

The speaker nodded. "That's not all." He turned to the whip. "Why don't you deliver this bit of bad news, Carter, in case Mr. Rangel didn't have his TV on this morning."

Rangel summoned a small, dusty laugh. Watch television on a Saturday morning? Him? That was the funniest thing he'd heard in years.

Coleman told him about Chief Justice MacLaren's announcement that he would comment on the way the trial of the president by the Senate would compare to the norms of a typical federal courtroom.

The whip added, "If we do one little thing that looks partisan, that California bleeding heart is going to come down on us like a high plains hailstorm. Majority Leader Worth and the speaker and I have been trying to think how we can stop MacLaren from criticizing us but the best we can come up with is to accuse *him* of playing favorites, if he speaks up."

Rangel shook his head. "That will only reinforce the partisan divide between the right and the left. The muddled middle will go with whomever they respect more, the chief justice of the United States or Congress."

Profitt said, "Yeah, well, we can guess what the betting line on that one would be. Voters in the middle of the political spectrum hate the high court maybe half the time, but they hate us *all* the time. So what do we do, T.W.?"

"You call Ms. Renshaw to testify. If she repeats her statement that the president used her to kill Erna Godfrey, that's your best case. You vote to convict. If Ms. Renshaw comes before the Senate and denies that she ever made such a statement, you bring in your investigator to testify, the woman who took Ms. Renshaw's statement affirming that the president is guilty as charged. Please tell me your agent recorded Ms. Renshaw's accusation."

The two congressmen nodded.

"She did," Profitt said.

"Thank God for small favors. Try not to lose the recording before it might need to be used. Even with it in hand, though, the other side will say it merely documents a lie."

Coleman said, "It might be helpful in getting the Democratic votes we need to convict, if Renshaw doesn't change her original story."

Rangel sighed. "Gentlemen, the lesson of this exercise is that impeachment really should be left for serious offenses that are plain to everyone. The least taint of political punishment makes the process counterproductive. What the two of you and Majority Leader Worth want right now is to have the briefest trial and the swiftest vote possible. Let each side vote its interests. The required two-thirds majority necessary for conviction will not be reached. Please believe me that Galia Mindel is saving her biggest guns against wavering Democrats until the last moment. Then she'll make plain that ending Patti Grant's career will also be committing political suicide, and tell me, please, how often does that happen?"

"So we just eat a big plate of humble pie and like it, is that what you're saying?" Profitt asked. "We live through one last year with Patricia Grant as president?"

"Mr. Speaker, with whom would you prefer to deal? A wounded, dishonored Patricia Grant who has no choice but to leave the White House at the end of her term or a fire-breathing

Jean Morrissey with two possible terms in office ahead of her and an enraged Democratic Party that will vow to stop at nothing to defeat our nominee next year?"

The speaker sighed and conceded, "You're right, T.W."

"It's still a damn bitter pill to swallow," Coleman said.

Rangel offered them a measure of consolation. "Here's what you do leading up to the presidential election next year: You do everything possible to bring Galia Mindel down. If you can do that, you'll really scare the Democrats. Succeed at that and their top political people will be afraid to sign on with Vice President Morrissey. They'll think if you can get Galia, you can get them, too."

"I like it," the speaker said. "If we can get Galia Mindel, that'll take a lot of the gloss off Patti Grant's record, too."

"Yes, it will. I think there's one more thing you should work on: Put Chief justice MacLaren under the microscope. See if you can find the least indiscretion. Something we might be able to embroider upon. Having the top seat on the Supreme Court come open would be as nice a gift as a new president from our side could want."

Washington, DC

John Tall Wolf's VIP treatment continued when he arrived at Reagan National Airport in DC. James J. McGill's own car and driver, Leo Levy, were waiting to take him to the White House. Also present was Colonel Welborn Yates, USAF. He told Tall Wolf he was from that armed service's Office of Special Investigations but he was detailed to attend to the president's personal needs and worked at 1600 Pennsylvania Avenue.

Hearing all that, Tall Wolf gave a soft whistle and asked, "How'd you gentlemen know where to find me?"

Welborn said, "We spoke to your Co-director at the BIA's Office of Justice Services."

"Marlene Flower Moon," Tall Wolf responded.

"Yes. She said to look for you at the best hotel in town, wherever you were working or, if you were traveling, in an executive aircraft. The word she gave us was you're an exceptional investigator but you do enjoy your creature comforts."

Coyote knew him all too well, Tall Wolf thought.

"We called the hotel where you were staying with Mr. McGill," Welborn continued. "When they told us you had checked out, we checked both commercial and general aviation flights leaving Los Angeles."

Tall Wolf nodded. "Sounds like you're a fair hand at investigations yourself, Colonel."

"Thank you. I've had the advantage of top flight training, both institutional and informal."

The BIA man read between the lines. Colonel Yates had been tutored by McGill.

They reached a gleaming, armored Chevrolet sedan waiting at the curb outside the terminal. A pair of airport cops stood watch over the vehicle to make sure it wasn't towed or stolen. Leo Levy shook hands with the cops and thanked them for their help.

Then the three men were on their way.

"Why are we going to the White House?" Tall Wolf asked.

"The president would like a word with you. Mr. McGill would also like to see you."

Tall Wolf raised his eyebrows.

"The president?" His tone implicitly asked what that was all about.

"I'm sure she'll tell you" Welborn said. "Meanwhile, I've been asked to brief you about Eugene Beck."

"Who's he?" Tall Wolf asked.

Leo piped up. "That fella we were all looking for out in L.A."

"The embryo thief?"

"Yes," Welborn said. "I've heard he's told Mr. McGill's client where she can find her personal property."

Tall Wolf said, "Up to a point. I spoke with Ms. Kersten this morning. She shed some light upon the case, including the fact that one embryo is still missing. She asked me to keep looking for it. I explained that I don't take private clients, but I also don't like to leave a job unfinished. I'm not going to be told to back off, am I?"

"I don't think so." Welborn frowned. "I don't see why the thief would hold back on just one embryo. Is it to hold as a bargaining chip if he's caught?"

Tall Wolf said, "*When* he's caught, if I'm allowed to continue the investigation."

Leo laughed. "You always get your man, partner?"

"So far. Mostly through dogged determination."

Welborn said, "Leo and I have read your file, Mr. Co-director. You've got more going for you than just persistence."

"Well, I made good grades in school, and I've had some fine training, too."

"Okay," Welborn said, "if you're intent on nailing him, you should know Beck is one dangerous character. He came within a whisker of making Air Force special ops. He drew a paycheck from a private defense contractor after he washed out. I can't tell you what he did in that capacity, but I will say it was very dangerous work and he always succeeded, too."

Tall Wolf said, "I'll take that to mean he's faced combat or its equivalent, and since he's still alive and thieving other people likely aren't."

"As I said, I can't speak to that directly, but what I've read says Beck likes to whistle a merry tune as he goes about his work."

"That might mean all sorts of things," Tall Wolf said.

"None of them especially good," Leo added.

He pulled up at the Southwest Gate of the White House grounds and talked to the uniformed Secret Service officers. Assured them the big fellow in the back seat was one of the good guys.

Tall Wolf turned to Welborn and told him. "It's mostly about the leg room."

"What is?"

"The private planes and luxury hotels. The other amenities are great. But the leg room is a necessity."

Welborn nodded at the White House as they cleared the checkpoint.

"There's plenty of that in there."

Montevideo, Uruguay

Lieutenant Silvina Reyes and Captain Antonio Calvo peered at their respective iPads in the captain's office. They were reading about the life and times of the fugitive billionaire, Tyler Busby. They'd heard the story, of course, about the planned assassination of the American president. But that was two years ago, and it had happened far away in the giant country north of the equator. So much news was always gushing out of *los estados unidos* that they had forgotten Busby's name, if they'd taken notice of it in the first place.

Silvina read English much faster than the captain, so she'd moved on from the press accounts about Busby's doings to a gallery of Google images of the man. It was surprising to her how consistent the man's appearance remained throughout the years. Oh, he'd aged, certainly, but not nearly so fast as most other people. For a man in his 70s, he still look looked fit and full of energy. Well supplied with ego, too, she thought.

His hair remained full and only slightly streaked with strands of silver. His jawline was firm and his body was lean. His eyes were his best feature, clear and piercing blue, looking like they'd seen wonders and knew secrets others could not even imagine. Throw in his endless access to money, Silvina thought, and there would be women of all ages willing to please him.

The captain looked up from his reading. "The government in Washington wants this man very badly. They would be very pleased with little Uruguay if we handed him to them."

"You and I might reap a reward as well. Not money perhaps, but advancement. The regard of our superiors and the pride of our fellow citizens. But there is one problem, maybe two.

Captain Calvo sighed. "There are always problems. Tell me the ones you see."

"Well, we don't know for sure our informant is reliable. He might simply have made a mistake."

"Or he is right," Calvo said, "and Señor Busby is in Uruguay because he made powerful friends in our country before he arrived."

"Exactamente."

Uruguay's government had a reputation for probity, but people were people, and even the best of them could fall prey to stunning lapses of judgment. The two cops knew they'd have to be careful. They didn't want to see a potential triumph turn into a professional disaster.

Nevertheless, the captain said, "This is worth the risk, something that should be pursued. I'm going to have our people watch this fellow."

"Dressed as those who might be serving the wealthy."

Calvo rolled his eyes. "Who was it that made you a nanny?"

Silvina gave her superior a friendly salute.

"You, *mi capitán.*" She added, "We should alert all our customs people that this gentleman might decide to leave the country at any moment. Busby hasn't remained free by being careless. Even if he has powerful friends, he may already have an uneasy feeling that the *policia* are taking an interest in him."

Calvo smiled. "If he is the man in Punta del Este, he just might. I'll alert customs."

"Tell them we especially need our female officers to be on alert."

"Why women?"

"Busby may have changed many things about his appearance, but I think his eyes will be the same. I think he is too vain to change their color with contact lenses. A woman would notice his beautiful blue eyes more readily than a man would. Tell them to look at the eyes."

Calvo remembered his premonition that he'd be working for Silvina Reyes one day.

"Sí," he said.

He made the call to customs and had no sooner put the phone down than it rang again.

The captain listened to the caller and said, "*Bueno,* bring him in. Yes, to me directly."

He looked at his future boss and said, "The American you said who was pretending to be a Canadian?"

"Yes?"

"The one who said he was hiding from his brothers?"

"Yes, I know who you mean."

"*He* was trying to escape. He was just picked up trying to board the ferry to Buenos Aires. He has been placed in custody and will be brought to us here directly."

Lieutenant Silvina Reyes got to her feet and executed a proper salute.

"*Bravo,* Capitán Calvo."

He'd been the one to say if the tip Silvina had received was legitimate the fellow who had provided it, this Mallory *hombre,* would try to make himself scarce. Someone who could afford to live in Punta del Este wouldn't be motivated by money. His self-interest was likely rooted elsewhere.

Perhaps Mallory's thinking might be if a big fish got caught, pursuing the little fish would be less compelling. Only Captain Calvo was not the sort to ignore minnows. They, too, could be tasty.

The two police officials were tempted to hug each other but they settled for shaking hands.

Knowing they might be on the verge of making themselves legends.

Buenos Aires, Argentina

La Avenida Alvear, on which Abra Benjamin's hotel was located, served as the main thoroughfare for Buenos Aires' Recoleta District. For shopping, dining or simply being seen, it was the place to be in Argentina's capital. It also featured the city's most famous cemetery.

Fitting, Benjamin thought, reassessing the way she'd handled things.

Her opportunity for a serious promotion might be dead and buried.

She strolled the avenue, pretending to window shop in front of designer clothing stores. She thought she would have looked good in several of the outfits she saw, but she was paying particular attention to the reflections in the glass. She didn't notice anyone either following her or even giving her a second glance. As for the clothes she might have liked to buy, they were priced way the hell out of her budget.

If there was anything that could ruin her day, it was the thought that she'd made a terrible error in judgment on her climb to the top of the FBI ladder. Not that things were a total loss so far. She felt sure Billy Midnight was the pimp catering to Tyler Busby's horniness, and she'd passed his name and description on to the FBI desk at the U.S. embassy in town.

Byron DeWitt was probably organizing a team to find and watch Billy right now.

Which meant he'd probably get most of the credit for bringing Busby down. Not that he cared about accolades anywhere near as much as she did, but Director Haskins had to be aware that Byron, his right-hand man, had one foot out the door already, and he'd want to do whatever he could to persuade Byron to stay on. Making a national hero of him might just turn the trick.

Thinking of tricks, Abra knew she'd be in a much better position to nail Busby personally if she'd only played nice with Billy and agreed to put out for him. But she just couldn't do it. The mere thought turned her stomach. Becoming a whore was no part of her job description. Hell, if she had done it and been the one to nab Busby, the sleazy tactic would almost certainly come out at his trial, and then how would she be known?

Special Hooker Abra Benjamin, not special agent.

She'd have to hope that Byron would toss a little credit her way when he got his kudos.

The way the winner of a best director Oscar would thank his production assistant.

Or she could take satisfaction in the simple fact that she'd helped put a bad guy away.

Only where the hell was the joy in that? Where were the promotion, the power, the big bump in pay? The ability to buy just one of the dozen outfits she'd seen in Recoleta that she genuinely would like to own. Who knew Buenos Aires offered such terrific clothing?

Before she started either to cry or beat the snot out of a perfect stranger, Abra decided to get something to eat. The Argentines were big on beef and she thought chewing through a steak might prove therapeutic. Maybe she'd even have a beer with her meal. The concierge at the hotel had told her about a place where American ex-pats hung out: Casa Bar, on Rodriguez Peña 1150. Her iPhone gave her directions and she headed that way.

The place turned out to be a sports bar, insofar as it had a March Madness college basketball game on big-screen TVs. She didn't mind. It felt kind of good to be back among an American crowd. She placed her order, got a frosted pilsner glass of Coors as a starter, and waited for her meal. She was actually engaged in watching the game, NC State versus Villanova, when a young guy stopped at her table.

"Wendy Wasserman?" he asked.

She looked at him. Took her a beat to remember her cover name.

"Yes," she said.

He was a nice-looking kid, maybe early twenties, possibly Cuban-American.

His voice and manner were definitely American. He was smiling, but not hitting on her. She was too old for him, a thought that almost sent her back into a tailspin. He extended an envelope to her.

Before accepting it, she asked, "Who sent this?"

"A guy at the bar gave me twenty bucks to hand it to you. Don't know what's in it, didn't ask. But the guy didn't seem too creepy or I wouldn't be doing this."

"Just creepy enough?" Abra asked, taking the envelope.

"Well … if he's asking for a date, I'd give him a pass. You can do better, I'm sure. Enjoy your stay in B.A., *señorita*."

The kid left, having perked Abra right up. Saying she could do better. Calling her *señorita* instead of *señora*. His description of the guy who'd tipped him for the delivery could have fit Billy Midnight. She wondered if the SOB was watching her right now from some dark corner of the room.

She opened the envelope and took out the card. Sonofabitch. It was from Billy, and she was still in the running to nail Busby. The note on the card gave her the time and place where her *services* would be required. Abra knew she could check with the concierge at the hotel to ask if it was a real address in a good location. The note said she could also pick up an envelope with her payment inside at the front desk.

Without trying to spot Billy, if he was still there, Abra took her pilsner glass in hand and raised it in a salute.

Capitol Hill — Washington, DC

Edmond Whelan strolled through the empty corridors of the Capitol to the suite where his nominal boss, the house whip, had one of his offices, the place where Coleman Carter brought recalcitrant members of the GOP caucus to either cajole or intimidate them into doing the leadership's bidding, i.e. voting the way they were instructed to do.

More often than not, rank-and-file members were marched out onto the floor of the House and did just what they'd been told. Democracy in action. Well, that was the way things had gone in the good old days.

Customs started to change with Patti Grant's first election as president. Conservative representatives couldn't stand her even when she was still a Republican. Her point of view, one of moderation, was supposed to have been consigned to the party's scrap heap long ago.

Once she became a Democrat, the conservative resistance became open warfare. From the time of the Reagan presidency, party defections went in only one direction: Democrats became Republicans. The very idea that a sitting president could reverse that course was both heresy and a terrifying precedent.

The Grant administration had to be destroyed, never to rise from its ashes.

Of course, after True South had been founded and had become a viable third party, many a conservative had moved on from the GOP, exiting stage right. Those defectors didn't think of themselves as traitors. They were simply drawing closer to the flame of the true faith.

After the new party opened shop, it made life considerably harder for Carter Coleman. He couldn't impose party discipline on his most conservative members. If he pushed too hard, they could simply tell him to take a hike and move over to True South. If anything, their voters would applaud the change.

As the big brain behind the tandem of Peter Profitt and Carter Coleman, the pressure was on Ed Whelan to save the day. Ideally, he'd subvert and destroy True South. There wasn't room for two right-wing parties in Washington. It wouldn't be long before open warfare broke out between them. Each would attack the other for either insufficient purity or boneheaded extremism.

Leaving the Democrats to look on and giggle into their white wine.

As they continued to win one presidential election after another.

Good God, Ed Whelan thought, two terms of Jean Morrissey following the same number for Patti Grant and the new nanny state might last a century. He wanted no part of that or of the downfall of the GOP.

It was time for him to get out of government and into a think tank. Work from outside of the party structure. Lock up a long-term position with a fat paycheck and start planning the resurgence of a *sane* political right. The New Republican Party? That was why it was so important for him to get his original thesis back. He had to hide his own errors to secure his future. He couldn't let anyone see how many times he'd been wrong. He'd definitely learned from his mistakes, and he felt certain he knew what to do next.

Well, he knew what to do until a heavy hand fell upon his shoulder just as he put his key into the door of the whip's office suite. He jumped in fright, and a squeak of alarm escaped him. Turning, he saw Capitol Police Captain John Creedy staring at him.

Like he was someone who'd sneaked in off the street.

"Mr. Whelan, sir, haven't you been told?" Creedy asked, his voice cold.

"Been told what?" Whelan asked.

The big cop stared at Whelan, as if he was only playing innocent.

Whelan held his hands out to his sides, showing he had nothing to hide.

Creedy's expression changed to one of disgust. He thought it was a shitty thing to do, the speaker and the whip leaving their dirty work to him. Nonetheless, he sucked it up and delivered the bad news to Whelan.

"Your services here are no longer required, sir."

Whelan blinked and his ears began to ring.

As if he knew he had to compensate, Creedy raised his voice. "You've been fired."

"Who … who told you that?"

"Representative Coleman. The speaker was with him at the time I was informed. Your personal belongings have been packed up and will be delivered to your residence. I was told to ask for your office keys the next time I saw you."

He held out a large, calloused palm.

Whelan was dazed but didn't hesitate. He handed over a ring of keys.

"Would you like me to escort you out, sir?"

The former echo of the whip found enough self-respect to straighten his spine.

"I know the way," he said.

Creedy watched him go, followed, but allowed a buffer of several feet.

The chill March air should have cleared Whelan's head as he stepped outside but all it did was make him shiver. He started down the steps of the Capitol, needing a moment when he reached the sidewalk to recall how to get home. He'd arrived in a taxi, but he decided to walk back. The distance was almost four miles; he hoped inspiration might strike somewhere along the way. As things stood, he saw his publishing contract and any chance for a major think tank job vanishing. The phrase, "Don't back no losers," may have originated in Chicago politics, but as a point of view it was also held dear in Washington.

Nobody in town liked a loser much less rewarded one, and he'd just been fired from his job by two of the most powerful men in Congress.

The thought popped into Whelan's head that Union Station was nearby.

Maybe he should go step in front of a train.

He didn't have the resolve to do that. Instead, he mentally catalogued the bars that lay between him and his front door. Drinking himself into oblivion would be a better choice. He headed off, his eyes glazed and his gait wobbling.

He never noticed Eugene Beck following him.

The White House — Washington, DC

Tall Wolf thought the president seemed pretty chipper for someone who might be booted out of office in the coming week. He took the hand Patricia Grant extended to him and shook it gently and looked at her closely. She smiled at him with a gleam in her eye.

"What's the matter, Mr. Co-director, do I have some spinach stuck between my teeth?"

"No, ma'am, your teeth are perfect."

"Didn't start out that way. A fair piece of money from my parents and the dedicated work of an orthodontist who knew his stuff got things moving in the right direction. A little more work in Hollywood put the polish on, so to speak."

"Yes, ma'am."

With his substantial height advantage, Tall Wolf didn't have any problem seeing he was alone with the president. He hadn't expected that. She noticed him checking out his surroundings.

"You were expecting someone else to be here?"

"I was told Mr. McGill also wanted to see me, ma'am."

"He does. He's upstairs in the residence waiting for you. I just wanted a few minutes of your time, before you see Jim. Is that all right?"

"Whatever you want, ma'am."

"Good. Please take a seat." She gestured to the guest chairs placed in front of her desk. Tall Wolf waited until she sat before he did the same.

"How may I help, Madam President?"

Patricia Grant asked Tall Wolf if he'd seen or read about her Committed Capital announcement.

"Both, ma'am."

"Good. As a spin-off, the board of CC has decided to award a hundred scholarships to incoming college freshmen who choose to major in math, science and technology. These will be full-ride funding: tuition, fees, room and board and education-related travel and lodging. The *quid pro quo* will be that each recipient will promise to work in the United States for ten years. If they start a company, it must be based here and the people they hire must be their fellow Americans."

"I like it," Tall Wolf said with a smile. "Who else knows about this, ma'am?"

"Other than the people directly involved, you're the first."

Tall Wolf didn't hide his surprise.

"I hope you don't mind, John. I wanted a candid reaction."

Tall Wolf told the president about the idea he and his cousin had to start a major Native American university on the Northern Apache reservation.

Patricia Grant beamed. "I think that's brilliant. I hope you'll let me be part of your fundraising effort."

Tall Wolf allowed that they might find room for her.

The president laughed. "The particular reason I asked you to see me is I want to make sure every American student will be eligible for Committed Capital scholarships. I want you to help me reach out to the children of the people who got to this country first."

"Before there even was a country, as such," Tall Wolf said.

"Exactly. I know you have your own job to do, but if you could put together a list of people for me to contact, individuals you hold in high esteem, I'd appreciate it."

"Of course, but if I may ask, why me?"

"I told Jim what I needed. He recommended you as a starting point. Now that I've heard about your plans, I'm glad he did."

Tall Wolf was pretty happy himself.

McGill met Tall Wolf at the door to his hideaway. The White House head butler, Blessing, was on hand to take the visitor's drink order. McGill recommended the White House ice tea and Tall Wolf went with the suggestion. The two men chatted for a few minutes, McGill hearing about Tall Wolf's meeting with the president, before Blessing returned with the drinks.

Once they were alone, McGill said, "How do you feel about the way things went in California?"

Tall Wolf told him about his follow-up visit with Mira and the fact that one embryo was still missing.

"Damn," McGill said. "I hate loose ends."

"Ms. Kersten indicated the embryo she doesn't have is the one she wants most."

McGill made the correct assumption who the male contributor was.

Tall Wolf confirmed his guess.

McGill said, "So it's not just a loose end, it's the grand prize. All those other potential kids are just orphans in the storm. I'm thinking less and less of this client as time goes by."

Tall Wolf replied, "A peril of the private sector. You don't always get to work for the righteous."

"Yeah, I seem to remember things being the same way when I was a cop. How about you? Everything copacetic at the Office of Justice Services?"

"I had to lock up an old man I truly admire not too long ago. There's a chance he might even be my grandfather. The woman who was my estranged grandmother tried to have me killed and came to a bad end."

McGill gave a soft whistle. "Other than that, everything's okay?"

Tall Wolf laughed and took a hit of his ice tea. "Yeah, pretty much, once my fiancée and I figure out how we can get married and be together while living and working in two different countries."

"Sounds like someone will have to relocate, but I'm sure you've already thought of that. Meanwhile, back here in DC, I'm tied up for the immediate future. I'm going to be at the president's side for the duration of her trial in the Senate. Some of the prominent pundits suggest that this is going to be the quickest case in U.S. history, but once something like this gets started, things have a way of setting their own pace."

Tall Wolf nodded. "You never know who's going to want his or her moment in the spotlight."

"Right. Being a footnote in history isn't much fun if you can manage a paragraph or even a whole page you can call your own. Anyway, my hope is you can take time away from your other duties and catch the SOB who grabbed the embryos in the first place, find the missing one as well. Even if we don't like the client, the bad guy shouldn't get away clean. We need to discourage him from continuing his wicked ways."

Tall Wolf said, "That was my plan, too. I told Ms. Kersten I'd keep on, but not as someone working for her."

"Right, if she benefits, it will be incidental to our main goal. Please keep in close touch. I want this one to turn out right. If anyone gets in your way, let me know about that, too. I have certain connections."

Tall Wolf smiled. "I'll bet you do."

The two men stood and shook hands.

"May I ask a question?" Tall Wolf said.

"Sure."

"Why didn't you turn to your partner, Ms. Sweeney, for help with this?"

A sad smile formed on McGill's face. "She gave me the news when we touched down on our flight from L.A. As far as police work goes, public or private, she is now officially retired."

Tall Wolf thought about that for a moment.

"But if you weren't available and I needed to speak with someone?"

McGill nodded. "Sure, if you need to know something, give Sweetie a call."

He gave Tall Wolf the phone number.

Washington, DC

Edmond Whelan had plodded across the better part of the National Mall and veered toward Foggy Bottom on his way to Georgetown when a thought struck him that both organized his mind and energized his body. As bleak as things may have looked for him, he still had one last opportunity of which he might avail himself.

He could get even with the SOB who had stolen the original version of his masterwork.

He'd been wrong in thinking Mira had taken the document. It was only natural, he supposed, to suspect a former spouse who was a political strategist for the other side. The current state of politics in Washington practically demanded that he think of her first as someone who would want to bring him down. You threw in the fact that they'd both decided that living together had become a waste of time and, bingo, who else could have robbed him but Mira?

She'd told him who else and, brother, did that name make sense.

Thomas Winston Rangel, his mentor. The man who had made the introductions and greased the way for him to become a power behind the scenes in Congress. His patron, in effect.

All of the old hands who'd held seats in the House and Senate when Rangel had given him his start had long since retired or lost their jobs in subsequent elections. The institutional memory of who had sponsored Ed Whelan's rise to prominence had vanished. Now that the time had come for Whelan to suffer for his failings, Rangel didn't want anyone to recall who had launched the one-time golden boy.

Only there remained documentary evidence of the Rangel-Whelan connection: Ed Whelan's treatise. With Thomas Winston Rangel's fingerprints literally all over it. Worse than that, so were Winston's marginal notes. He'd both praised Ed's ideas and taken a number of them several steps farther. Some of their combined notions had worked brilliantly. Others had been unmitigated disasters, all the more so for the tactical flourishes Winston had added.

The old man must have felt for some time that Whelan was going to get the axe, and so he had to distance himself from his one-time protégé. Whelan didn't think T.W. was still active in the troughs of political skulduggery; the guy had to be older than Original Sin, but as long as he was still breathing, he would want to protect his legacy.

That would mean he had to retrieve the laudatory notes he'd made on Ed's treatise.

He'd have had to hire out to get the job done. If he'd been careful about it, he would have had his thief simply destroy the document, turn it to ashes. But Ed would bet he'd want to read the comments he'd written all those years ago. Find a way to rationalize all his mistakes so he could continue to think he was still the smartest guy in town.

Looking to his left, Ed Whelan saw a taxi pull to a stop at a red light. On impulse, he pulled a back door open and jumped in. He gave the cabbie Winston's address in Virginia, and as the light turned green away they went.

Leaving Eugene Beck, trailing half a block behind, completely taken by surprise.

But not without being able to see the name of the cab company and the number of the vehicle.

The White House — Washington, DC

The Co-director of Office of Justice Services was also caught off guard.

As John Tall Wolf left McGill's Hideaway and the door closed behind him, he heard a jazz tune start to play. McGill must have turned it on. The music sounded familiar to Tall Wolf, but he couldn't place the name.

Blessing was waiting in the corridor to see Tall Wolf out of the building.

Tall Wolf asked the head butler if he knew what the piece of music was.

"It's 'Take Five,' sir, commonly attributed to Dave Brubeck but actually written by Paul Desmond. I do believe that is The Brubeck Quartet playing, though."

Tall Wolf smiled. It was clear you didn't get to be head butler at the White House by letting any grass grow under your feet. As an impish test, he thought he'd see if he could push things just a step further.

"You know when that recording was made?"

The butler cocked an ear; Tall Wolf listened with him.

"Definitely The Brubeck Quartet. So I can only think it's from their *Time Out* album which was recorded in 1959." They started walking down the hallway and the head butler added as a bonus tidbit, "'Take Five' is the biggest-selling jazz single ever."

Tall Wolf smiled and asked Blessing if he had any plans for his retirement.

That brought the head butler up short. After a moment, he admitted, "I try not to think of that, sir."

"Sure, after working for the president, what could compare?"

Blessing gave Tall Wolf a look, not as a polished professional but as a man.

"You have something in mind?"

"My cousin and I are thinking of starting a university. It occurs to me we're going to need a first-rate faculty. What would you think about teaching a bunch of kids on an Indian reservation in New Mexico?"

For just a moment, Blessing looked stuck for an answer. He could only ask, "What would I teach?"

Tall Wolf said, "Understanding and committing to excellence. How about that?"

A twinkle appeared in Blessing's eyes. Before he could answer, though, a beep sounded. The head butler took a smart phone out of a pocket and read a text message.

Back in professional mode, he looked at Tall Wolf and told him, "If you have the time, sir, the White House chief of staff would like to speak with you."

"I've just spoken to Mira Kersten," Galia told Tall Wolf once he was seated in her office with the door closed behind him.

"Yes, ma'am."

"Ms. Kersten told you about the embryo that's still missing, I understand."

"She did."

"But did she tell you whom she feels sure stole Edmond Whelan's dissertation?"

Tall Wolf said. "She did, Thomas W. Rangel. I have to admit I'm not familiar with the man. I thought about asking Ms. Kersten for a briefing, but I decided doing my own research would provide a more objective picture."

Galia said, "I can tell you what you need to know. Rangel was Whelan's mentor, his introduction to the conservative leadership in Congress. Mira is sure Rangel stole Whelan's precious pile of political misjudgments."

"Whelan isn't the hotshot he thinks he is?" Tall Wolf asked.

Galia sketched a mirthless smile. "He's had his moments, but he swings and misses more often than he hits home runs. T.W. Rangel was thought to be retired for some time now, but I've had word from someone who knows that he's back in the game. He's more politically dangerous than Whelan ever was but … well, you're not interested in the political consequences here."

"Not at all," Tall Wolf said.

"What's relevant to you is that Mira feels Whelan will do with Rangel just what he did with her."

"Drop in for an unexpected visit?"

"Yes, and sooner rather than later."

"But Whelan didn't steal the embryos himself; he hired out. Why would he approach Rangel directly?"

Galia gave Tall Wolf a look, expecting him to see the reason quickly.

He did. "Because it's personal, and maybe he doesn't see Rangel as a physical threat."

"Exactly. On the other hand, we've come to think that the threat against Mr. McGill's life is likely represented by a former member of our military, Eugene Beck, who has special forces training. He's seen as very dangerous."

Tall Wolf said, "Ms. Kersten told me she thinks Beck has a score to settle with Whelan, might possibly even do him in."

That was news to Galia and she didn't like hearing it second hand.

Nor did she want Whelan to die. She told Tall Wolf as much.

"I trust you'll do what you can to prevent that."

Tall Wolf said, "Only up to a point for someone like Whelan."

Still, he understood that, politically, it would be much better for Whelan to live and stand trial for the crimes he'd committed.

He asked Galia, "So do we both think there's going to be a party at Mr. Rangel's house?"

Galia nodded. "That's the way I see things. Whelan's almost certain to go there. Beck's a good possibility, too."

"What I don't understand," Tall Wolf said, "is why Whelan would want Mr. McGill dead. The president's husband has no real power in government. He doesn't make policy. He doesn't appoint anyone to an important job. He can't veto legislation."

Galia smiled again, this time with feeling.

"You're absolutely right. At the beginning of President Grant's first term, my biggest worry was that Mr. McGill would meddle, stick his nose where it didn't belong and cause me endless headaches."

"Instead, he saved your life," Tall Wolf said.

"Yes, he did, and I've come to have feelings for him I'd never have thought possible. So you can imagine how much he must mean to the president. Losing him would effectively end Patricia Grant's presidency. She might remain in office or she might resign. If she stayed, though, going through the motions would be the best she could do."

Having talked to the president less than an hour earlier and gotten some small measure of the woman, Tall Wolf had his doubts about that. He thought Patricia Grant might become an avenging angel if she lost a second husband to political violence. Of course, the White House chief of staff might have insights he lacked.

Tall Wolf said, "In any case, it would set a terrible precedent, assassinating a presidential spouse in the hope of destroying an administration."

"Yes, it would. Without going into specifics, there's good reason to believe Beck is capable of killing a so-called hard target."

Tall Wolf only nodded. He understood he'd just been told the man had killed other people.

"Do you understand what I'd like you to accomplish, Mr.

Co-director?"

"Bring in the whole shebang of them, if I've got my Irish right."

"You do."

Tall Wolf got to his feet. "If you'll give me Mr. Rangel's address and your phone number, I'll head right out."

"I can offer you armed back-up," Galia said, clearly wanting him to take it.

Tall Wolf shrugged. "Who ever heard of an Indian with a side-kick?"

Galia frowned mightily.

"Okay," he said, "I'll take Leo Levy as my driver. He carries a gun. If we need more help, I'll call."

J. Edgar Hoover Building — Washington, DC

FBI Deputy Director Byron DeWitt was working late when he got a call from the National Police of Uruguay in the person of Captain Antonio Calvo. The news Calvo had to share amounted to winning the exacta at the Kentucky Derby. Or so it seemed at first. Calvo told DeWitt that the National Police had arrested an American for entering Uruguay illegally, using a fake Canadian passport.

That alone was enough to make DeWitt's scalp tingle.

Careful not to get ahead of himself, DeWitt replied, "And this person is someone who might be of interest to the FBI?"

"Only if you and your people are still looking for one of your congressmen named Philip Brock. Your notice to Interpol says you are."

DeWitt wanted to shout in jubilation, but he thought it best to play things cool. "Yes, we are. Will you please detain him until we can arrange for extradition?"

"We would be happy to do that," Calvo said. "I feel you should know, however, that Señor Brock is already claiming status as a political refugee. He says he is … *momentito.*"

DeWitt overheard Calvo confer with someone on his end.

"Cómo se dicé ..." How do you say ...

Calvo returned to the call. "Yes, Señor Brock says he is being *framed* in the matter of planning an assassination of your president."

"I'm sure he does," DeWitt said. "He'll have the opportunity to defend himself in court. Philip Brock has a lot of money; he'll be able to afford the best defense lawyers."

"Yes, he has already told us you would say that. He says he is rich, but not so rich as your president, and your countrymen will demand that someone must pay for the crime no matter how much money he has."

DeWitt intuited what else Brock might have told the National Police. "Let me make a guess here, Captain. Mr. Brock has also suggested he should be able to put up an enormous sum of money as a bond to be allowed to remain free in your country."

"Exactamente. I have recommended that this not be allowed, but my word is not the final one, and if you are familiar with our courts and government in Uruguay, you know we are not swayed by money."

"Of course," DeWitt said, "I'm sure you have great respect for the rule of law. If, however, anyone in your legal system were to be inclined to give Brock the benefit of the doubt, you should remember that he used a false passport to enter your country. A man of his resources might obtain another one to leave Uruguay. The FBI has already discovered he traveled from Costa Rica to Panama using a New Zealand passport."

There was another brief conversation on the Uruguayan end of the call.

"We did not know this," Calvo said, returning to DeWitt.

"Here are a couple more things you should pass along to your superiors, Captain. The FBI also strongly suspects Mr. Brock murdered a United States senator and a diplomat from Jordan who was stationed here in Washington. Philip Brock is one seriously dangerous man."

The off-phone conversation in South America was longer this time and a loud female voice seemed to dominate it. DeWitt regretted that he'd never studied Spanish, but hearing a strong woman speak gave him an idea to keep in his hip pocket.

When Calvo came back on the line, he said, "Please be assured I will pass this information along. What you say will be taken into serious consideration. I have something more to tell you: Señor Brock has told us of the whereabouts of another fugitive you are looking for."

It was all DeWitt could do not to let himself get a woody.

"Tyler Busby?" he asked in a soft voice.

"*Sí.*"

"Busby is also in your country, Captain?"

"As fate would have it, yes. Señor Brock thought he would give us Busby, hoping to distract us from himself is our guess. He approached an undercover officer, not knowing who she was. He asked her to take a message to the police for him."

DeWitt laughed audibly. Shit-birds of a feather flocked together, even when they had the whole world to use. The deputy director said, "You see what I mean about Brock being tricky, Captain?"

The captain asked, off-phone, what tricky meant. The female on his end told him and then she came on the phone. "This is Lieutenant Silvina Reyes speaking."

The woman had a lot of American tonality in her English.

"You've lived in the United States, Lieutenant?"

"For many years, yes. My father was a diplomat at the United Nations. Mr. Brock approached me on a street in Punta del Este, a wealthy neighborhood here in Montevideo. I was posing as a nanny. He asked me to go to the police for him. We put a watch on him and arrested him as he was trying to board the ferry to Buenos Aires."

DeWitt said, "Sure. He scoots out of your country until the uproar over Busby's arrest blows over and then he comes back when things are quiet. If anyone from your police talks to him then, he just says he was an upstanding guy doing what was right. If you didn't know any better, he might get a commendation from your government, solidifying his place in your country."

Silvina said, "And if he feels uneasy when he comes back he just runs and hides somewhere else."

"Exactly. Please allow me to give you a bit of advice about Tyler Busby. His money makes Brock's look like chump change. You know what I mean?"

"I do."

"He also has powerful friends around the world, people in governments that have no love for the United States. If push came to shove, they might give Busby asylum. He wouldn't like living in those places, but it would be better than a super-max prison here."

"Might these friends even fly him out of our little country clandestinely, if he was given the chance to remain free on bond?" Silvina asked.

"I know it sounds melodramatic but, yes, something like that is a possibility," DeWitt told her.

"I'll tell you what, Mr. Deputy Director. I will talk with my father. He will know much more than I do about how the upper reaches of my government might feel about all this, and about what foreign nations might do to assist Mr. Busby. I will get his opinions and forward them to the top of the National Police chain of command."

"Thank you, Lieutenant. Please include this in your report. The United States will be very grateful if Uruguay, lawfully, extradites both Busby and Brock to us."

"I will mention that, yes."

"You'll have the time to do everything you need to do?"

"We have learned there is an infant and a new mother in Mr. Busby's house. We have decided to wait until morning to make the arrest."

DeWitt was surprised to learn that Busby had, what, acquired a family while he was on the run. Still, he didn't know if that would be enough to … he had another idea. A risky one. He'd have to consult his own experts before moving on it. But now he was glad the Uruguayan police had given him a window of opportunity.

"Thank you, Lieutenant, and please give my thanks to your Captain. I'm very happy to have heard from both of you."

"De nada," Silvina Reyes said.

Great Falls, Virginia

"The bitch says she's not going to testify," House Whip Carter Coleman said.

T. W. Rangel, ear pressed to the phone in his home in Great Falls, winced. Coleman had delivered his message at the top of his voice. Apparently, Speaker Peter Profitt, also looped into the conference call, shared in the discomfort, saying, "Moderate your tone, Carter. If you keep shouting, the NSA won't need a wiretap to overhear us."

A moment of silence followed as all three men considered whether Profitt's comment, intended as a joke, might have an element of truth to it.

"You think they'd dare do that?" Coleman asked in little more than a whisper.

"I'm wondering myself, now that I've brought it up," Profitt said.

Rangel weighed in with his best assessment. "It's likely they're still vacuuming up everybody's calls. But they'd never use anything against either of you gentlemen."

"Why not?" Coleman asked.

"Peter?" Rangel said, wanting to see if he had one apt student.

Profitt proved equal to the challenge, "Because, Carter, if the NSA were to incriminate you and me, our esteemed colleagues in Congress would take umbrage. Whittle the NSA's budget down to pennies on the dollar. They wouldn't have the money to shop at Radio Shack."

"Didn't that place go out of business?" Coleman asked.

Both Profitt and Rangel sighed. The speaker said, "Yes, they did, but the point is we don't have to worry about being bugged. Just try to keep your voice down."

At a much lower decibel level, but still suffused with emotion, the Whip said, "We're screwed without that Renshaw bitch's testimony. We have less than forty-eight hours until we put the president of the United States on trial and it looks like we'll have to stand around with our dicks in our hands. I don't know about you, Mr. Speaker, but that ain't gonna play well in my district."

"The gentleman from Oklahoma has a point, T.W.," Profitt said.

Rangel reassured them. "You're both worrying needlessly. Before Joan Renshaw ever emerged from her coma, your House of Representatives impeached the president. You did so the same way that you intended to try her, on a lava bed of emotional animus."

Neither politician attempted to rebut Rangel.

"Having Ms. Renshaw wake up and claim she conspired with the president was manna from heaven, and having her recant is still a gift."

"How's that, T.W.?" Profitt asked.

He had his own guess but he wanted to hear from the man himself.

Knowing just what the Speaker was thinking, Rangel obliged him. He had to show he was worth the not-so-small fortune he was being paid. "You call Ms. Renshaw as a witness. If she reverses herself again and testifies on your behalf, she's your new best friend, an icon of courage and unbreakable character. If she denies she was working with the president and never told you otherwise, you play your investigator's recording of her saying otherwise and ask one simple question: 'Who got to you, Ms. Renshaw?'"

Profitt knew the answer to that and didn't mind supplying it. "Galia Mindel."

"Just so," Rangel agreed. "Once that's done, the trial becomes about the White House chief of staff as much as the president. Handled properly, we can neuter the president and destroy her number one political operative."

Coleman, playing catch-up, said, "Maybe we even find some criminal offense against ol' Galia. Put the pressure on the president to disown her, maybe even have the attorney general prosecute."

Profitt added, "The icing on the cake would be to get that damn Jean Morrissey in on the dump-Galia game by starting a narrative that she has to do that or she'll never have a chance of being elected president."

Rangel was pleased to see his students were exploring some of the more obvious ploys of the strategy. He was about to offer a more subtle variation when he was jarringly distracted by hearing his doorbell ring. He'd have to answer it himself; he'd given Roosevelt the night off. The cook and the maid had already gone home so they couldn't help out either. He was alone in the house.

"Excuse me for a minute, gentlemen," he said. "Someone's at my front door. I'll take a look and be right back."

Rangel put the call on hold. He didn't need to open his door to see who had come calling. A camera looked down at anyone who arrived at his threshold. Rangel pulled up the view on his laptop computer. At a glance, he had no idea of who the fellow was: A bald pate was the first thing he noticed. But then the visitor's eyes, nose and jawline registered in his mind.

The man then looked up, directly at the camera, and Rangel knew who he was.

Edmond Whelan.

Good God, had he found out who had stolen his treatise?

The question answered itself. Of course, he had.

It would be a disaster if Profitt and Coleman learned what he'd done, so he told them he had to go and broke the connection with them.

Then Rangel asked himself: "Where the hell did I put my gun?"

The answer to that eluded him, and Whelan began banging on his door.

The White House — Washington, DC

The conspirators in Great Falls and on Capitol Hill didn't need to worry about the NSA monitoring their call. The intelligence agency was more or less hewing to the recent Supreme Court ruling that it didn't have the authority to conduct the universal collection of phone calls, emails, texts and malicious gossip over backyard fences. There were moments, of course, when a sense of urgency demanded reversion to the old methods, but in general the NSA spooks tried not to put themselves crosswise with the Supremes.

As Rangel and company had accurately divined, Galia Mindel was their chief worry.

She knew it, too. That was why when Rangel was away for a metrosexual spa day and his cook and maid were sent out on errands Roosevelt had allowed a technician to enter Rangel's house and bug his phone system, his office and his bedroom — in case he talked in his sleep, not to record any amorous activity.

Rangel didn't fornicate at home. He went to a discreet establishment in the District for that. Galia was still looking for a way to, pardon the verb, penetrate that den of … well, she didn't really care to know the fine details of what went on there. But she did want to know what people talked about under that roof.

That, however, was a problem to solve for another day.

It both gratified her and sent a small chill down her spine to become a co-equal target with the president for the other side. Well, they'd soon find out how dangerous she was if someone tried to put her in a corner. A recording of the Rangel-Profitt-Coleman conversation would make its way to Ellie Booker when the time was right.

Maybe another copy would arrive on Vice President Morrissey's desk. Wouldn't she love it to hear that the boys on the right had a plan to intimidate her? Galia chuckled. She was sure Jean could kick the withered asses of all three of those bastards, even if they came at her in a bunch.

As a last resort, and purely for spite, she might send a copy to James J. McGill.

Give him the chance to break a few noses for real.

Shortly before Galia decided to execute her counterattack, she would have the bugging equipment removed from Rangel's house, leaving no trace of how the recordings were made and preserving Roosevelt's position within the enemy camp.

Buenos Aires, Argentina

Special Agent Abra Benjamin looked at her reflection in a full-length mirror, unsure of the presentation she should make. She knew how to dress for the office. How to dress for a formal dinner. How to dress for a date with a guy who ... damnit, wouldn't remind her of Byron DeWitt. But she was uncertain about how to dress for her debut as a high-priced hooker.

A display of cleavage was a given, but just how much was a matter of debate. Too little and she wouldn't look the part; too much and she'd look cheap. The same question applied to how much leg to show. A hemline above the knees, sure, but nowhere near a minidress. That would not only be déclassé but also, God help her, inappropriate for someone her age.

She decided to go with a happy medium in both cases. She needed to get Busby to look at whatever his preferred anatomical feature was. That and keep his eyes off her hands. Her fingernails were the only giveaway. She had the face and the figure for a high-end, if slightly mature, call girl, but her nails, though neatly trimmed and polished, were too short for a courtesan. She could have gotten extensions or overlays, but she wanted to keep her hands suited for punching, gouging, poking and shooting. She'd be carrying her gun in her handbag. A pair of flat, rubber-soled shoes, too.

She'd kick off her spiked heels if she had to beat feet.

Abra had finally arrived at a look that was acceptable, if not personally pleasing, when her cell phone chimed. Byron DeWitt was calling; she'd just been about to call him. Tell him she was on her way to nab Busby and would have her phone off until she'd cuffed the bastard.

She'd been looking forward to hearing Byron's surprise when

she informed him she'd found their target. Only the SOB had to spoil her fun. Damn him.

He didn't even say hello. Only: "We've got him, Abra. We've got Busby."

"*What?*" She couldn't believe it. "You've arrested him?"

"No."

"Somebody else arrested him?"

"No."

"Then what the hell are you talking about?"

She knew it was impolitic to talk to her boss that way but didn't care.

For his part, DeWitt didn't seem to notice. "We know where he is right now."

"So do I." She gave him the address in Punta del Este. "Busby's pimp set me up with him. Apparently, he likes Jewish girls."

To his credit, the deputy director said, "Well, good for you, Special Agent. That was fast work."

"Yeah. You should see how I look. I'm going to knock Busby's eyes out. Then when he's blinded, I'll cuff him and call the local cops."

She was hoping Byron would fix on the comment about how she looked. Maybe ask for a peek on FaceTime. He didn't. He addressed her mention of the police.

"About that: Don't contact the locals."

"Why not?"

"I don't want to get into that right now. I'll be sending an extraction team."

He gave her a number to call.

"What? Why?"

"Because, Special Agent, you are going to expedite Mr. Busby's return to the U.S."

Christ, Abra thought, Byron was telling her to kidnap the guy.

"Are you sure about this?" she asked.

DeWitt responded indirectly. "I'm going to resign soon, Abra. My slot will be open for someone deserving to fill."

It was easy to read between those lines. Who could be more deserving than the special agent who brought Tyler Busby back home to face justice?

"That's good enough for me," she said.

J. Edgar Hoover Building — Washington, DC

FBI Deputy Director Byron DeWitt felt only slightly guilty about what he'd just ordered Special Agent Abra Benjamin to do. If things went wrong, he'd take the brunt of the blowback, but Abra would get scorched, too. Might well lose her job, and then she'd have to devise a whole new future to build.

He was sure she'd see that, too, and soon. Once the initial excitement of thinking she might leapfrog to the upper reaches of the FBI organizational table wore off. Still, she'd do everything she needed, up to and including burning down Montevideo, to get away with Busby in chains.

Thinking about the capital of Uruguay being put to the torch, DeWitt felt bad about betraying Captain Calvo and Lieutenant Reyes. The FBI had a reputation for running roughshod over other police agencies, foreign and domestic, and much of it was deserved. DeWitt had always tried to play nice, but he couldn't take the chance that a small country in South America might give Busby the wiggle room he need to wind up in, say, Beijing.

If the Chinese wanted to, they could allow Busby a fair amount of freedom within their borders. He might even live like a member of the politburo. Twit Washington with photos of himself enjoying the high life. That would immediately cause both domestic and international turmoil.

It was impossible to believe the U.S. would go to war with China over Busby, but relations would grievously suffer, and if American ships or aircraft had close encounters with their Chinese counterparts, bloodshed might easily ensue. Once that dam had been breached …

DeWitt didn't like to think what might happen.

Or some deep thinker in the CIA might decide the thing to do was assassinate Busby. Show Busby, the Chinese and the rest of the world that no one was beyond the reach of the United States. Succeed or fail, something like that might also lead to a far greater conflict.

So DeWitt had decided to take his chances with offending tiny, non-nuclear Uruguay.

He'd send flowers and chocolates if Montevideo got upset.

As if bringing in Busby wasn't enough, DeWitt still had Philip Brock to consider. He was already under the lock and key of the Uruguayan National Police. The deputy director wasn't quite ready to stage a raid to put his hands on Brock. But he'd be damned if that prick was going to skate away free either.

DeWitt picked up his phone again. He called the embassy of the Hashemite Kingdom of Jordan. Speaking to only one intermediary was necessary before the ambassador came on the line.

"Mr. Ambassador," DeWitt said, "I apologize for calling you so late on a weekend."

"For matters of importance, sir, I am always available to my country's American friends."

"Mr. Ambassador, within the past hour, I was informed by the National Police of Uruguay in Montevideo that Congressman Philip Brock has been arrested for entering that country on a false passport. I immediately requested that Brock be held as a person of interest in the planned assassination of President Grant.

"What I need to tell you now, sir, is that the FBI strongly suspects and is developing evidence to show that Mr. Brock also killed United States Senator Howard Hurlbert and your own personal physician, Bahir Ben Kalil."

The ambassador took a moment before asking, "How strong is your evidence, sir?"

"Persuasive enough that Mr. Brock fled the United States using a false passport."

The ambassador asked, "And you personally, sir, do you believe that Brock killed Ben Kalil?"

"I do. I called not only to share that information but also to inform you that Brock has told the Uruguayans that he is a political refugee, a man being framed by my government. That is simply a lie. Still, Brock has offered to post a huge sum of money to be allowed to remain free in Uruguay. My police contact there told me that it is at least a possibility bail will be granted.

"The FBI has urged the Uruguayans not to do this. Brock might find a way to run and hide. Senior U.S. officials will be talking to their counterparts in Montevideo in the morning. It would be helpful, sir, if Jordan would add its voice to ours in this matter."

The ambassador paused before saying, "I will contact Amman."

"Thank you, sir. That's all I can ask."

Breaking the connection, DeWitt added, "But it's not all I can hope for."

Ideally, the Uruguayans would send Brock back to the U.S. with no muss or fuss … but snatching the bigger fish, Busby, from right under their noses might make them cranky. It was possible they would even release Brock out of spite. DeWitt wouldn't blame them if they did.

He just hoped he'd prepared adequately for that possibility. The late Bahir Ben Kalil had been a close friend of the ambassador, as well as his doctor. The dead Jordanian doctor was also the twin of Dr. Hasna Kalil. DeWitt had met her when her brother's body had been found.

Ostensibly, a physician who worked with the charitable organization Doctors Without Borders, Hasna Kalil was rumored, if not yet proven, to also work with terrorist groups in the Middle East. It was said she used her surgical skills to extract information from prisoners: operating on them without bothering to use anesthesia.

DeWitt was counting on two things now. One, the Jordanian ambassador was already in contact with his nation's capital. Word would be passed to their embassy in Montevideo. Even if the Americans acted badly, the Jordanians had done nothing wrong. They could ask for Brock to be surrendered to them to stand trial for the murder of one of their prominent citizens.

If the Uruguayans honored that request, the FBI would agree to share its evidence against Brock with the Jordanians only if they would agree to send Brock back to the U.S. to stand trial for conspiring to assassinate Patricia Grant.

Two, on the possibility that the Uruguayans might be steamed enough to honor neither the U.S. nor the Jordanian request for extradition, the ambassador would contact Dr. Hasna Kalil, have her and an assortment of her jihadi colleagues on hand in South America. They could snatch Philip Brock when the Uruguayans freed him. Let Brock discover how much pain a vengeful sister with a medical degree could inflict on the man who'd killed her twin brother.

A small part of DeWitt was rooting for that outcome.

Not that anyone could blame him if that was what happened.

All he'd done was make a call to the embassy of a friendly country.

Great Falls, Virginia

Though he was far from any sort of martial artist, Edmond Whelan managed to kick T.W. Rangel's front door open. It wasn't all that sturdy. People in that Great Falls neighborhood had little reason to fear home invaders. Further aiding Whelan's break-in, the lots on which the houses in the area sat were large and densely landscaped to ensure privacy.

The only immediate concern Whelan had was Rangel's burglar alarm system. Whelan estimated he had 30 seconds to disarm it before it signaled the security company that something was amiss. At that point, a call would be made to the homeowner. If he or she didn't report in a convincing tone that all was copacetic, a security company car would be sent and the police would be notified. In a place like Great Falls, the private and public guardians of the well-heeled would race to see who could come to the rescue first.

Whelan wouldn't have the time to retrieve his treatise, much less give Rangel the beating he deserved. Fortunately, from their past acquaintance, Whelan knew the security code for the alarm. The old bastard had delegated the chore of fingering the keypad to him many a time. Assuming Rangel hadn't changed the numbers recently. Say shortly after he'd had Whelan's property stolen.

Whelan's concern about the alarm vanished when he heard his former mentor rummaging through his nearby office and cursing about his lack of progress. With good reason, Rangel wasn't counting on anyone else saving him. The old alarm code hadn't been changed.

Rangel's complaints grew louder and more desperate as he looked for ... what? His old army Colt .45 semi-auto? The fucker had worked a desk job at the Pentagon in the early Vietnam War era. He had made one three-day trip to Saigon. He'd had more to fear from VD than the VC during his 72-hour tour of duty.

Still, if Rangel put his hands on the weapon that would seriously change the complexion of the night's events. Whelan thought he should have gone home to get his own firearm before setting out for Virginia. With a bitter taste in his mouth, he felt he was getting all too good at recognizing his mistakes a beat too late.

He dashed into Rangel's study as two things happened.

Three, if you counted the gunshot.

Somebody moving far faster slipped past him.

Rangel finally found his old sidearm and with a huge smile said, "Ha!"

He pointed the weapon at Whelan with every intention of firing it.

The gun did fire, but, intent on Whelan, the old man completely missed seeing the guy who grabbed his wrist with one hand and grasped the barrel of the weapon with the other. The second intruder shoved the barrel upward, causing the trigger guard to break Rangel's index finger as the shot went into the ceiling. Rangel screamed in pain, holding his damaged right hand against his chest with his left hand. The man who'd taken the weapon pushed Rangel down into his desk chair.

Whelan was about to slip away when the gun was again pointed at him, a moment before the man holding it even looked at him.

Whelan froze in place. The man turned his head and smiled.

"Good choice," he said. "You know who I am? Just nod if you do."

Whelan nodded.

"Who's this old fart?" He pointed his free thumb at Rangel.

"His name is Thomas Winston Rangel."

"Is he anybody important?"

"He likes to think so."

"What's he do?"

"He thinks for people who aren't smart enough to do it for themselves."

"Isn't that what you do, too?"

A moment of honesty overtook Whelan. "Used to. I got fired today."

Despite his pain, Rangel managed to laugh at his former protégé.

Whelan said, "Do me a favor and shoot him first, will you?"

Eugene Beck sighed and told Whelan, "See, that's how you got in trouble, talking like that. What do either of you dipshits know about killing people?"

Punta del Este, Uruguay

Special Agent Abra Benjamin's push-up bra was annoying the hell out of her as the taxi in which she was riding pulled into the semicircular driveway of the address she'd been given, but she still spotted an anomaly. A woman just up the street was pushing a baby buggy. Hell, as fancy as the thing was, they probably called it a perambulator. Fit right in with the flossy neighborhood. What didn't fit to Abra's eye was the woman steering Junior down the block.

She was a bit too lean and fit. The spring in her step belonged to an athlete not a nanny. Abra read her immediately for what she was: a cop. Maybe someone working an angle of her own, not what her boss had told her to do.

The taxi driver announced the fare in English. Abra paid him and added a substantial tip. The guy hadn't ogled her in the rear view mirror, hadn't made any wisecracks about her appearance. From what she could tell, he'd taken her to her destination without going out of the way. His thank you even sounded genuinely grateful about being tipped well.

"Would you mind if I ask you something?" Abra said.

"What is that, *señora?*" His English was pretty good, too.

"In your country is it common for a woman to be out walking her baby at night."

"I saw her, too," he said. "No, it is not common in this place."

"You think she's a cop?"

The driver thought about it. "The police presence here is more . . ."

Abra made a guess as to the word the driver wanted. "Straightforward?"

"I was going to say honest but, yes, I like your word. Is it a problem for you, if she is the police? If so, we can come back in ten minutes. No extra charge."

"No, that's all right, thank you."

They both turned their heads as the woman pushing the buggy passed by the driveway. She must have noticed the idling taxi sitting in front of the house, but she didn't look their way. That in itself struck Abra as suspicious.

She asked the driver, "You think, maybe, she could be the lookout for someone doing something they shouldn't?"

He shook his head. "No, she is the police."

"Yeah, I think so, too."

Just what the hell she needed, Abra thought, a snooping cop.

She said to the driver, "You have a cell phone?"

"Yes, *señora.*" He gave her his number without even being asked.

"If you're still on duty," she said, "I might need a ride later."

"I work all night. It would be my pleasure."

Abra exited the taxi just in time to see an Asian woman with an infant in her arms open the front door of the house. "Are you having trouble with that driver?" she asked in English.

"No," Abra said. "Just took a minute to get the right money to pay him."

The taxi pulled out of the driveway.

The baby turned to look at Abra, staring at her wide-eyed. Cute kid.

The woman holding the infant said, "And you have also been paid, correct?"

"Yes, I have."

Satisfied that all accounts were current, the woman opened the door wide.

"Then come in, please. My husband is already in bed waiting for you."

Abra stepped inside, telling the woman, "Nice to meet you, too."

Great Falls, Virginia

"That was some slick driving, Leo," John Tall Wolf said. "My compliments."

Tall Wolf and Leo had spotted the car that pulled into Thomas Winston Rangel's driveway about a mile out from the man's house.

Well, Leo had noticed it first.

He'd said, "That ol' boy ahead of us, he's up to something, and I don't think it's throwing toilet paper into people's trees."

"How can you tell?" Tall Wolf asked.

"He spends more time looking left, right and behind him than he does at the road ahead."

"Aren't you supposed to stay aware of what's going on around you when you drive?" Tall Wolf asked.

"Absolutely, but you know how many people do that?"

"Not enough?"

Leo laughed. "Hardly any. Way too many people flick a glance up ahead and then get back to their text messages. Some of the old-school types just read a magazine or newspaper while they drive.

That boy ahead of us, he's been trained. He's staying alert to his environment. Only problem is, he's fallen into a pattern. Three beats to each side, a pause, three beats up front, a pause, and three more beats to the rear view. It's almost like he's listening to music and moving his head and eyes with the tempo."

Tall Wolf said, "If I'm not mistaken, Leo, you've been changing lanes in that same time signature."

"Sure have. But I'm ziggin' when he zags. As far as he knows, we're invisible."

"That's one fine trick."

"Well, when you're out on a race track, the last thing you want is for the guy ahead of you to know when you're gonna make your move to pass him. The sumbitch might run you into a wall if he knows your coming."

"Excellent point, but how do you know that driver up ahead, while he might have had some training, isn't just out on everyday business, some normal activity?"

"I've been doin' this a while, Mr. Tall Wolf. You just watch and see where this fella is headin'. Then you'll know I'm right."

Leo was. The car ahead of them turned into Rangle's driveway. Never knowing he'd been followed and observed.

The White House — Washington, DC

"What are you thinking?" Patti Grant asked McGill.

The president and her henchman were having a quiet dinner in the family dining room.

"I'm just reviewing the biographical profiles of first ladies I've read."

"Oh, really?"

"Yeah, I wanted to remember what they did when their spouses were in a tight spot."

"Anything inspirational?"

"Not so far. Jackie Kennedy would buy a new hat and Lady Bird Johnson would gather wild flowers. I don't think either of those things will work for me."

"You need something more manly?"

"I'd still like to flatten a few noses. I'd even let you and Galia compose a top ten list and see if that lifted my spirit and yours a little."

"Your little jaunt to Los Angeles wasn't emotionally satisfying?"

McGill sighed. He told Patti about Mira Kersten calling off the investigation and then discovering the one embryo she really wanted was still missing. He said, "It's not the first time I've wanted to smack a client, but it's an impulse I try to restrain when I'm working for a woman."

"Maybe I could do it for you," Patti said.

McGill gave his wife a look and then laughed. "I could give you a refresher course in Dark Alley, but if we did that the next thing you know you'd be challenging members of Congress to duels."

The president grinned but then shook her head. "A tempting idea, but if I got that ball rolling, it probably wouldn't be long before we'd have a *Duel of the Week Show* on TV. Some customs are best left departed and gone."

McGill put his fork down. "You know, by the time Jean Morrissey takes her oath of office, you and I will be ready to blow this pop stand."

Patti laughed. "Pop stand? Does anyone still say that?"

"I do. How about we ask the waiter for a doggy bag? If any of this stuff still looks good in the morning, we'll fry it up for breakfast."

Patti said, "All right. So what shall we do now? Go to bed and read?"

"I'm with you on that first part. We'll go to bed. Then we'll see what happens next."

"Are you trying to seduce me, James J. McGill?"

"You bet, but give me a nudge if I start to fall asleep before things get good."

"It's all good with me, sailor."

McGill smiled. "Now that you mention it, I do recall things that way. Promise me, though, that you'll do that one special thing

I like best."

"I know just what you mean."

With one voice, they both said, "Turn off the phone."

Punta del Este — Uruguay

"Turn off my phone, will you?" Tyler Busby said. "I forgot to do it."

FBI Special Agent Abra Benjamin had entered the bedroom with her purse over her shoulder and closed the door. She'd seen Tyler Busby, the world's most wanted man according to the FBI, lying on his back in bed. She'd kept a straight face and started to plan how she might kidnap him.

Turning off the phone was a good start. Abra said, "Sure."

A wireless home phone sat on a nightstand next to the bed. Busby could have reached it with ease, but he wanted her to do it. Asserting his dominance. That or he was one really lazy son of a bitch. Might be both.

She lifted the phone from its charger, hit the mute button and put it back.

"Turn your cell phone off, too," he said.

"Already done," she lied.

"Good. Then we're ready to start."

Busby flipped back the duvet and top sheet that had been covering him. He was naked and erect. Smiling, now, too. Like he was proud to show himself off, wanting to impress her. Abra had to admit he wasn't in bad shape for an old guy.

She was also sure that wasn't a kosher wiener. Pharmaceuticals had to be involved. Chemicals to which no rabbi would ever give his stamp of approval. Still, Busby was proud of his display and did everything but ask Abra, "So what do you think?"

Neglecting to provide the hoped for compliment, she only asked, "What do you like?"

"You name it, I'll try it," he said, but there was a whining note in his voice. He was annoyed that she hadn't complimented him.

She realized a real hooker would have been more solicitous, pun intended.

Not wanting him to raise any kind of a ruckus, Abra said, "Well, with that thing of yours, I suppose we could play baseball."

Busby loved it, laughing loudly. "Right, I've got the bat and the balls."

She thought he could have come up with a better line, but smiled anyway.

Abra heard footsteps outside the bedroom door move off.

The indulgent wife making sure all was going well?

"How about role playing?" Abra asked. "You into that?"

"Why not?" Busby said. "I'll be the sultan; you'll be my newest concubine."

"We can do better than that." Abra sat on the edge of the bed, facing him. She undid two buttons exposing more of her breasts. "How about this? I'll be the boss of a mattress factory, and you'll be a job applicant, looking to fill the opening for … a quality-control manager."

Busby nodded; he was interested. "That's imaginative. What are my qualifications for the job?"

"Well, you'll have to tell me, now won't you?"

"I've taken a different woman to bed every night for the past five years."

"Well, aren't you the fickle boy?" For just a second, Abra wondered if that could possibly be true. "Relentless, too. Didn't you ever want a day off?"

"No, ma'am, I'm the hardest worker you'll ever see."

Getting into playing the job-seeker, Abra thought.

"Well, I'll concede you are experienced," she said. "Now, I want to see how perceptive you are. Take a good long look at me." She undid another button. "Now, close your eyes and describe how you see me, how you'd imagine me … well, anyway you'd care to."

Busby closed his eyes and rested his hands on his abdomen.

If the smile on his face meant anything, he'd started to fantasize, but Abra didn't let him get far. She slipped her handcuffs and her gun out of her purse. She snapped the cuffs over Busby's wrists and had her gun pointed at him by the time he opened his eyes.

Busby looked startled and said, "Is this part of —"

Abra raised a finger to her lips to shush him.

"Okay, we're still playing roles here, only we're not pretending anymore. I'm Special Agent Abra Benjamin of the FBI. You're Tyler Busby, fugitive, and now you're under arrest. How's that for a night you'll never forget?"

Abra wouldn't forget it either.

Not after she heard the clank of the bedroom door locking.

Busby smiled up at her. "My wife did that, bolted the door remotely. You see, I like to make video recordings of all my encounters, and my wife likes … well, to maintain quality control."

Abra thought: *Shit. Life is never simple.*

To top everything off, Busby was still hard.

Proof positive that his hard-on wasn't natural.

Abra decided if worse came to worse, she'd shoot it off.

Great Falls, Virginia

Beck liked the layout of T.W. Rangel's office and kept his little confab right there. He had Whelan and Rangel seated next to each other in a pair of wing chairs while he perched on a corner of Rangel's desk. Beck was amused by the fact that his lack of decorum seemed to upset the old man as much as being held captive at gunpoint.

"All right," he told his two prisoners, "who wants to tell me how the three of us came to be here together? Mercy points will be given for whoever cooperates the most."

"More," Rangel said.

"What?" Beck asked.

"You're addressing two of us. The comparative form, not the superlative, is the one you want. More not most."

Whelan pointed at Rangel and said, "He's a stickler for proper grammar. I'm more interested in what mercy points are, and do they extend so far as to include amnesty?"

"You mean a get-out-of-jail-free card?" Beck asked. "Probably not. Mercy means you're dead before you know it. Lack of mercy means being gut shot, living long enough to wonder if hell could be any worse." He turned his attention to Rangel. "Did I get all that right, Professor?"

"Might we at least know *why* we have to die?" Rangel asked.

Beck said, "That's a reasonable request. Mr. Whelan over there has to go because he tried to blackmail me into killing James J. McGill."

Rangel turned a look of amazement on his former protégé.

"You really did that?"

"That bastard over there with the gun wouldn't cooperate," Whelan said, figuring if he was going to die there was no need to be polite. "It's not like he hasn't killed plenty of people already."

"Hey," Beck objected, "the only people I've ever killed were targets selected by your government and mine."

"You work for the government?" Rangel asked Beck.

"Indirectly."

"That's even more interesting."

"I thought so, too, but look where it's got me."

"Gotten," Rangel corrected.

Whelan said, "He really can't help himself. You should just shoot us both now."

Rangel held up his hands. "No, don't. Not yet anyway. He hasn't answered my question." Turning to Whelan, Rangel said, "I didn't mean why did you use coercion on this man; I meant why did you choose to target McGill?"

Beck said, "That's one of the things I want to know, too. From everything I've seen of the man, he seems like a stand-up guy."

Whelan put things in the simplest terms he could, telling Beck, "You see who your enemies are; I see who mine are."

Beck shook his head. "Hey, we're all Americans here, aren't we?"

"And yet you're perfectly willing to kill me," Rangel said. "Why would you do that?"

The assassin sighed. "You committed the worst mistake anybody can. You're in the wrong place at the wrong time. You're collateral damage."

Rangel took the news with surprising grace. "That's comforting to know. I'm not undone by a fault of my own but as a matter of mere circumstance."

Whelan shook his head, telling Rangel. "You're not getting off that easy, you bastard. We're both here because you stole my treatise."

Beck's jaw fell open. He looked at Whelan and said, "Wait a minute. I thought your ex-wife took your papers. That's why you brought me into this mess."

Whelan's expression turned hang-dog. "I thought she did it, but she told me who it really was." He pointed at Rangel again.

"Is that right, Professor?" Beck asked.

Rangel looked defensive. "I was trying to preserve my reputation."

Beck said, "You two assholes are giving me a headache." Turning to Whelan, he asked, "Were you actually trying to accomplish something by wanting me to kill McGill?"

Whelan stiffened his spine and admitted, "I was hoping to weaken the president."

Rangel shook his head. "So wrong. I don't know what I ever saw in you. Look at how Patricia Grant bounced back after her first husband was killed. She went out and *became* the president. Twice. McGill is not the target, Galia Mindel is and ..."

Rangel fell silent, looking as if he'd just experienced an epiphany. "My God," he said, "how could I have been so foolish?"

Before Whelan could tell Rangel about all the mistakes the old fart had made or Beck could get around to shooting the both of them, a cylindrical object, measuring 5.25 inches in length and 1.73 inches in diameter was thrown into the room. Beck knew the precise dimensions because he'd used the M-84 stun grenade himself.

He'd had an angle on the doorway to the office but he had

neither heard nor seen anyone approach the room. He reacted to the reality of the threat without wondering about any whys or wherefores. He leaped from the desk, covering his eyes with one arm and slammed sideways into the two seated men. They all went over in a pile as the flash-bang detonated.

The grenade produced a bang of 180 decibels, capable of causing deafness, tinnitus, loss of balance and disorientation. The flash created a light of more than one million candela within five feet of detonation, far more than enough to cause momentary blindness. The effects were intended to be temporary, but there was a risk of permanent injury or even death.

None of that prevented Beck from wrapping an arm around the neck of what felt to him more like Whelan than Rangel and pressing his gun to the side of the man's head. When he thought he heard footsteps coming on the run, Beck called out, "On the chance this prick means something to you, whoever the hell you are, you better give me the time to recover and the chance to get the hell out of here."

Problem was, he couldn't see shit out of his right eye, and the left one resolved the world only to the point of being a blur.

"You don't shoot at him or me, I won't shoot you," a voice replied.

"Who are you?" Beck asked.

"The Co-director of the Office of Justice Services, Bureau of Indian Affairs."

"Bureau of Indian Affairs?"

Unspoken but clearly implied was the question of what the hell the BIA had to do with anything.

John Tall Wolf said, "I know. Thing is, I freelance for other people. I overheard you mention James J. McGill's name. How about I give him a call?"

Beck had a moment of doubt but then he smiled. "You can do that?"

"Uh-huh," Tall Wolf said.

"Okay, do it. If he needs any convincing, tell him if he doesn't come, I'll kill this prick."

He jabbed Whelan's jaw with the Colt, producing a yelp.

Tall Wolf wasn't impressed. "I don't think he gives a damn about him. I'll just extend the invitation."

The White House — Washington, DC

McGill and Patti had turned off any and all phones that might disturb them. They'd even left a do-not-disturb message with Blessing. Short of the launch of hostile ICBMs, they were to be left in peace and quiet. Things were good right from the start for the First Couple and just about to get really good when the lights in the bedroom began to brighten.

Lumen after lumen was added. For several moments, husband and wife tried to ignore the fact that the ambience of the room was changing from intimate boudoir to hospital operating room. Yes, nobody had intruded personally. No one had broken phone silence. But the word was being passed nonetheless.

McGill said, "Deliver us from evil."

"Amen," Patti added.

"My guess is the interruption is for you."

"Mine, too, I'm sorry to say."

She rolled over to her bedside phone, touched a single key and said, "What is it?"

Blessing said, "My apology, Madam President. Your lawyer, Mr. Collison, is on hold for you. He says it's imperative he talks with you right now."

McGill was listening closely and heard the name of his wife's chief defense lawyer in her upcoming trial in the Senate. He gave her a nod and said, "Take it."

Repressing a groan, the president said, "Put him on."

McGill got up to use the bathroom, grabbing his phone off the night table as he went. He turned it on just in time to hear his call tone. The ID screen showed John Tall Wolf's name. McGill closed the bathroom door behind him and tapped the answer button.

"Is that you, John?"

"It's me," Tall Wolf said. "I've got the guy who was supposed to kill you."

"*Supposed* to kill me?"

"He says he never intended to do it."

"It was just a passing notion?" McGill asked.

"He says someone was trying to coerce him but it didn't work."

"How can we be sure of that?"

"Well, he's holding a gun to the guy's head right now. You might remember the captive's name, Ed Whelan. The guy with the gun, Eugene Beck, says he'll kill Whelan unless he gets to talk to you in person. I think Beck is serious, but I don't think Whelan would be a big loss."

McGill heard a voice in the background say, "Hey!"

"Mr. Whelan disagrees with my evaluation," Tall Wolf said. "How would you like me to handle things?"

McGill said, "Maybe between Whelan, Mira Kersten and Eugene Beck, we can finally get some kind of resolution to this case. Where are you?"

Tall Wolf told him. Then he added, "Hold on a minute."

McGill heard some muffled voices speaking. Tall Wolf must have obstructed his phone's speaker somehow. Then he came back. "I just negotiated a point with Mr. Beck. I told him before you enter the room, he puts his weapon on the floor and kicks it to me. He's agreed."

"The Secret Service will approve of that. So do the president and I. See you soon."

What worried McGill for the moment was telling Patti he had to go out.

Talk about the ruination of what might have been a beautiful night.

He used the facilities, splashed water on his face and slipped into his clothes in his dressing room. When he returned to the bedroom, he saw his wife was sitting up and had her presidential face on. Romance was definitely out of the question, not solely because of him.

She said, "Yes, thank you for calling. You did the right thing. I'll see you at eight in the Oval Office. Goodbye."

McGill gave Patti the moment she needed to organize her thoughts.

She led with the headline: "Joan Renshaw has recanted her accusation that I put her in Erna Godfrey's cell to kill her."

For a split second, McGill was ready to cheer. Then he realized there had to be a catch, and a heartbeat later he even knew what it was. "Somebody threatened Joan."

Patti nodded. Let McGill continue to analyze.

"They're going to say *you* threatened her."

"Not personally, of course," Patti said, "but I had it done."

"Is there any evidence of a threat?" McGill asked.

"A bouquet of flowers with a note."

"That no one saw delivered, I'll bet."

"Exactly."

"What are you going to do?" McGill asked.

"Get Galia out of her bed. Talk with her in the Oval Office in fifteen minutes."

McGill wanted to ask if Patti thought Galia had authored the threat, but he knew even between the two of them some questions were better left unasked.

Patti took advantage of McGill's silence to ask, "Why are you dressed?"

"John Tall Wolf grabbed the guy who was supposed to kill me."

"That's wonderful."

"He wants to see me."

"Tall Wolf?"

"No, the alleged assassin. He wants to tell me his side of things."

Patti frowned.

McGill said, "What?"

"If I didn't have to speak to Galia immediately, I'd go with you."

McGill laughed, thinking Patti was as different from his first wife, Carolyn, as she could be. He surprised himself by saying,

"Maybe you should see it. Bring Galia along."

Patti got out of bed and kissed McGill. Gave him a taste of what he'd be missing that night. "No, what I have to say to Galia can't wait, and is best said just between the two of us. But you do make me so happy."

McGill said, "I have a few more ideas on that subject, if we ever find the time."

Punta del Este, Uruguay

"You're in trouble now," Tyler Busby told Abra.

He was still handcuffed but had rolled on his right side. SOB was *still* hard. He was enjoying the hell out of things. The situation must have been more exciting than any fantasy game he'd ever played. Nobody would ever have told him how much fun he could have playing the damsel in distress, waiting for his heroine to arrive and save him.

Abra stood at an open window, gun in hand, looking out on the street below. She'd been splitting her attention between watching Busby and hoping to see the woman with the baby buggy whom she thought was a cop. Even at the risk of embarrassing herself, Abra wanted to call out for help. But the old saw pertaining to the subject looked to be true.

Anytime you needed a cop, you could never find one.

"Won't be long now," Busby said with glee.

Abra had been thinking the same thing herself. That cold Asian broad should have come charging in by now. If that was her style. For all Abra knew, though, she might have a way to vent some kind of incapacitating gas into the room. Abra might wake up to find the Busbys at a whetstone, sharpening their cutlery, getting ready to serve up filets of Abra.

As if he could read her mind, Busby began to giggle.

She whistled a shot past his ear, close enough to make his head snap back, his laughter stop, and his damn erection wither like a vampire exposed to sunlight. Shooting the thing was going to be a lot harder now, but that made Abra smile.

Busby shouted, "Ah-lam, hurry, she's going to kill me!"

Abra thought she very well might do just that. She sure as hell wasn't going to go down alone. She focused her attention on the bedroom door. Until a feminine voice from outside called out, *"Oye. ¿Qué está pasando?"* Hey, what's going on?

Abra turned and looked down. She saw the nanny with her buggy.

The special agent yelled, "I'm an FBI agent, trying to arrest a fugitive. Christ, do you even speak English?"

"Damn right I do," came the reply.

Abra thought she heard a Texas twang.

"Are you a cop?"

"I am."

"I need help fast. Call for backup."

"I got all the backup I need right here," the cop said.

She pulled an M-4 carbine out of the buggy and ran for the front door.

Abra thought to yell, "Hey, what about the baby?" Only she realized there was no baby. Not down on the street anyway. But the door to the bedroom flew open and there at last was the hard-looking Asian woman.

She had a baby with her.

Holding the squirming kid up in front of her like a shield.

Advancing on Abra like she meant to cut her heart out.

The Oval Office — Washington, DC

Chief of staff Galia Mindel entered the room looking as rumpled and apprehensive as the president had ever seen her. Even in the wee hours of a primary campaign trip when an election was too close to call, she hadn't looked like this. Worse, the kind of fear in Galia's eyes wasn't the kind that could be shrugged off with a handy rationale.

"We might lose this primary, but we'll win the next three. The nomination and the White House are going to be ours."

Galia had used those very words, and Patti Grant would never forget them.

Now, all Galia had to say was, "How bad is the trouble we're in?"

The president gestured Galia to a chair opposite the love seat where she sat.

She didn't want her desk between them now.

This was a woman-to-woman, one-old-friend-to-another conversation

The president said, "That's what I want you to tell me."

"Did anyone kill Joan Renshaw?" Galia asked. "I didn't have the time to check."

"Not that I know," the president said. "Joan did, however, recant her accusation that she was acting as my agent when she killed Erna Godfrey."

Galia figured out the reason for the disavowal even faster than McGill had.

More to the point, she figured out how the change of heart applied to her.

Galia shook her head and said, "Wasn't me."

The phrasing was deliberately vague. Galia had not arranged the delivery of any threat to scare Joan into being truthful. She had also not specifically commented on the subject. If the president was ever required to respond under oath she could honestly say that she and her chief of staff had never spoken of the situation.

Continuing in the same elliptical fashion, Patricia Grant asked, "Any ideas?"

As to who might have frightened the the opposition's only witness.

"Not at this time," Galia responded.

"Any worries?"

That this might come back to bite us.

Galia thought about it. "Meaning no disrespect, ma'am, I think that's more my concern than yours."

I'm the logical person to fall under suspicion.

"Whatever the other side thinks, let see if we can get to the bottom of this first," the president said. "I'm not going to have anyone in my administration impugned."

Especially you; I need you.

Galia nodded. "Thank you, ma'am."

The president stood and the chief of staff also rose.

"If anyone tries to consume my presidency, Galia, I want them to choke on it."

"Yes, ma'am."

"I also don't intend to let anyone sue my caterer."

I've got your back.

Punta del Este, Uruguay

Special Agent Abra Benjamin moved to her left as the Asian woman holding the baby moved to her right, closer to the bed. Abra was trained in Krav Maga, Hebrew for contact combat, a discipline originated by Imre Lichtenfeld. Developed in Israel, it borrowed from boxing, wrestling, judo and aikido. The first principle of Krav Maga, if a fight could not be avoided, was to end the fight as quickly as possible.

By winning it, of course.

That meant counter-attacking immediately or even attacking preemptively. The primary way to assure victory was to strike your opponent's most vulnerable points: eyes, throat, groin, knees and so on. In case you were overmatched, it was also important to look for avenues of escape and objects that might come to hand and be used to attack or defend.

The problem facing Abra at the moment was that none of her training had instructed her on how to deal with a sociopath using an infant as a human shield. The kid, too young to have a tooth in his head, was squalling almost as if he knew the woman holding him was fully prepared to sacrifice his life to win this little set-to.

As Abra flashed through a list of possibilities of how she might land a blow or kick that would disable the woman without hurting the child, a gruesome thought occurred to her. The woman might use the kid as a projectile. Throw the little beggar at her and attack as Abra reached out to catch him.

Something along that line must have occurred to Tyler Busby, as well. He was kneeling on the bed behind the Asian woman, his hands still bound at the wrists. He called out in a panicked tone, "Ah-lam, what are you doing? Jonathan is our son."

The woman was the kid's *mother?* Abra asked herself.

Retreat was not a Krav Maga technique, but Abra took a step back in horror.

"He is but one child," Ah-lam said. "If we survive, we can make others."

"He's *my* son, goddamnit!" Busby roared.

Ah-lam turned her head, as if to look for an attack from her rear.

Just a glimpse of her Gorgon's expression froze Busby.

While still pinning the billionaire with her basilisk stare, she threw her arms forward and let her son go. He flew through the air, shrieking in terror, and Ah-lam turned and followed, less than a heartbeat behind. She intended to strike while Abra had her hands full.

Only Abra didn't catch the kid so much as propel him back the way he came. As Mom charged forward, little Jonathan sailed over her head going the opposite way. Ah-lam couldn't stop herself from sparing a glimpse at her shrieking child doing his imitation of a shuttlecock. When she did, Abra struck.

Not with a punch or a kick. She lowered her head and charged. Drove the top of her skull into Ah-lam's solar plexus. It was an unorthodox blow to be sure, but it followed an old martial art maxim: strike a soft surface with a hard surface. The breath exploded from the Asian woman's body and she jackknifed backward, colliding with Busby, who had plucked his son from the air and deposited him on the bed.

Busby looped his manacled hands around his wife's throat and pulled her hard against him. She didn't have the strength to resist and he would have crushed her windpipe in a matter of seconds if not for the barrel of an M-4 carbine being inserted into his ear.

The cop who'd been pushing the buggy had arrived at last.

"Let the lady go," Lieutenant Silvina Reyes told Busby.

He released the pressure on Ah-lam's throat without hesitation and she collapsed in a heap at his feet.

Abra said to Silvina, "I wouldn't be surprised if the woman has some kind of weapon on her."

"She usually carries a knife," Busby said.

"Then you will very carefully and gently get down on your knees and search her," Silvina instructed Busby. "Remove anything nasty and toss it over into that far corner. You understand me?"

Busby nodded.

Sparing a glance at Abra, she asked, "You're really FBI?"

Abra was also keeping her eyes on Busby and Ah-lam. "Yes." She nodded at Silvina's assault rifle. "Is that your standard duty weapon down here?"

Busby found a knife and tossed it into the corner.

Silvina told Abra, "No, the rifle is not standard, but I couldn't fit anything bigger into the buggy. And if you are FBI, please don't tell me you walked into this room unarmed."

Abra inclined her head to the Beretta on a table near the window.

"I put it down when I saw the baby. Didn't want to take any chance I might hit junior by mistake."

Silvina liked that, and little Jonathan, having had enough excitement for one night, rolled over onto his stomach and was quickly falling asleep. Silvina smiled at him.

"With luck, he won't remember a thing," she said.

"I was going to arrest Tyler Busby and take him back to the United State," Abra said.

Silvina replied, "After observing all of Uruguay's extradition requirements, of course."

"Yeah, sure. Did I forget to mention that? Anyway, with the woman and the child involved, it's more of a mess. They're all yours, if you want them."

Silvina had spoken with her father. He'd told her there were those in the national government who loved *los estados unidos* and those who were not so kindly disposed. His considered opinion was that Busby would be returned, eventually.

So the young police lieutenant, who was working on her own time, made an executive decision. "I'll tell you what, Ms. FBI, let's take your naked countryman and the other two to your embassy. Your government can pay for their room and board while my government decides if they should travel north."

Abra nodded her head and extended a hand.

"Special Agent Abra Benjamin."

"Lieutenant Silvina Reyes."

They shook on the deal.

Montevideo, Uruguay

While the government of Uruguay had a well-deserved reputation for honesty, corrupt individuals labored within its precincts just like any other place. Desperate and possessing a keen eye for flawed personalities, Philip Brock, congressman and fugitive, spotted what he considered his last chance for freedom in the person of Candelario Gonzales, the head jailer of the police lockup where he was being held.

Gonzales was an otherwise thin man with a large belly overhanging his belt. Clearly, he liked to indulge at least one kind of appetite. One look in his eyes told Brock the man had other cravings as well. Before Brock was shoved into his cell, he managed to both observe the deference the other guards showed Gonzales and to whisper a simple message to him.

"One hundred thousand dollars, half up front."

He delivered the message in Spanish so there would be no confusion.

Gonzales' only immediate response had been to cast a quick, reptilian look at Brock. For several hours, Brock sat alone in his tiny cell thinking he had failed. He was sunk. He would be returned to the United States and would stand trial for conspiring to kill the president. There was no way around it. His attempt to throw Tyler Busby to the wolves and save himself had failed.

How the hell could he have known that goddamn nanny was really a cop?

Still, he might simply have made an anonymous call from Buenos Aires. That would have been the safe way to hand Busby over to the feds. Only he'd wanted the pleasure of peeking out his window and seeing Busby hauled away. That would have been a gleeful memory to last a lifetime. Now, he was going to spend the rest of his life alone in a supermax prison cell.

If the prosecution didn't find a legal justification to execute him.

After hours of languishing in despair, Gonzales stepped into Brock's cell, alone.

In English, he said, "Fifty thousand now. How?"

Trying not to get his hopes too high, Brock said, "I give you the name of the bank, an account number and a password. I speak into a phone for voice recognition. The money is then available to wire into the account of your choosing."

Gonzales stared at him, as if searching for a lie.

"And the other half?" he asked.

"Once I'm out of the country, we do another transfer."

"I should trust you?" Gonzales asked.

"Travel with me, if you want. Once I'm somewhere safe, though, it would be better for me to make you happy than have you want to lock me up again."

Gonzales showed no expression, but Brock thought the man saw the sense in what he'd said. "I may be back or I may not," Gonzales said.

The chief jailer made Brock wait an hour, no doubt hoping that uncertainty would make his prisoner more pliable. Gonzales told him, "All of the money now."

Brock shook his head and said, "Half. The rest when I'm safe."

"I could torture you. Make you scream until your heart or your mind gives way."

"Then you'd get nothing. The voice recognition system works only when a person is calm. If there's stress from fear or pain, it locks the account. It's a security feature."

Gonzales scowled and left again, not promising to return.

He did come back, though. Opened the door and gave a brusque gesture. "Come."

Brock got off his concrete bunk and stood. He was unsure what fate he'd meet outside the cell: freedom, torture or extradition. He hesitated, and that made Gonzales smile. The jailer grasped the edge of the door and raised his eyebrows inquisitively.

Perhaps you'd like to remain where you are, señor?

No, that was the last thing Brock wanted. He hurried out of the tiny cell. He was no sooner across the threshold than Gonzales grabbed him by the back of his neck. Now, Brock was scared. People who'd been bought off didn't treat their benefactors that way.

But Gonzales whispered to him, "We will be taking a short ride to my bank. It is closed for business, but a door will be left unlocked. You will contact your bank. You will be so happy to be free, your voice will all but sing."

Brock tried to assess what he'd been told. He wouldn't have expected Gonzales to have the necessary contact at a bank to arrange the scenario. Or the sophistication to come up with such a plan in the first place. But what other choice did he have but to play along? Go back to his cell? No thanks. They stepped through the doorway out of the back of the lockup. A car with its motor running waited for them.

The lure of freedom was too strong for Brock to resist.

Even so, he asked, "What happens after you get the first half of your money?"

Gonzales said, "A helicopter flying very low takes you to Argentina. Not Buenos Aires, but a small town near there. You will wait in a safe place a day or two and then you will get me the second half of my money. After that, you may come or go as you wish."

"I'll need some documentation to travel," Brock said.

Gonzales opened a rear door of the car. He took a small dark blue object out of a pocket.

"Your passport, *señor*."

A forged American passport in the name of Darren Anderson, but with a photo of Brock affixed to it.

Brock snatched the passport from Gonzales' hand. For the first time, he felt as if he might truly get away. He asked the jailer, "Aren't you coming with me to Argentina?"

Gonzales shook his head. "I am leaving you here. I can not say I trust you, but you would be a fool to betray me. Fate allows a man only so many misdeeds. Then it bites him right on l*a cula*." His ass.

Brock thought, yeah right, you superstitious moron. But he kept a straight face. Nodded gravely. He got into the car, pulling the door shut before anyone could change his mind. The driver pulled away and the sense of relief Brock felt made him shiver.

So close to disaster and now …

He noticed that an interior light in the car was on. He saw two 8x10 glossy photographs on the seat next to him. Head shots. When it registered whose likenesses he was looking at his stomach knotted. The first picture was of Bahir Ben Kalil, his one-time friend and co-conspirator in planning the assassination of the president. Brock had killed him so there would be one fewer person to implicate him if things went wrong.

The other photo was of Bahir's twin sister, Hasna Kalil, a surgeon.

Rumored to be a terrorist interrogator able to inflict unimaginable pain.

Scrawled across her photo was an inscription: *The doctor will see you soon.*

Brock screamed in terror. He would have jumped out of the moving car but both of the rear doors were locked. The privacy screen between him and the driver did not yield to repeated pummeling. Tears formed in Brock's eyes as he realized Gonzales had been bargaining with someone besides him. No doubt someone who could pay cash in advance.

The jailer's story was meant only to pacify him, usher him eagerly into the death trap.

Brock intended to start kicking at a door when he heard a soft hiss. A bittersweet aerosol began to fill the rear of the car. Brock began to feel heavy-headed. He realized to his horror that he was being sedated. He gave up fighting and gulped as much of the gas as he could, praying for an overdose.

His only hope now was that he'd never wake up again.

Great Falls, Virginia

Special Agent Deke Ky of the Secret Service whispered to McGill, "The guy's unarmed, but I still think this is a bad idea, you talking to him."

The two men stood just outside Thomas Winston Rangel's office where Eugene Beck awaited his promised meeting with McGill. Elspeth Kendry was already in the room with her eyes and her Uzi on Beck. John Tall Wolf had told McGill and Deke he'd stunned Beck with a flash-bang grenade and had disarmed him.

Tall Wolf said, "The man has no weapons on his person. I even took his shoes and belt off him. But he is whipcord lean and solid muscle. When he's up and running at full speed, I expect he's both strong and quick. He absorbed the effects of the stun grenade with as little damage as anyone I've ever seen."

"And you want to talk with this guy?" Deke asked.

"He wants to talk to me," McGill said.

"He surrendered his weapon to me as promised and allowed me to search him, once he looked out the window and saw Mr. McGill step out of the car," Tall Wolf said.

"And he told you he just wants to talk, John?" McGill asked.

Tall Wolf nodded.

McGill told Deke, "He just wants to talk."

Without offering a word of rebuttal, Deke's look said, "Yeah, bullshit."

McGill told him, "Let's get into the room before Elspeth shoots him."

"If she doesn't, I will, if anything goes wrong."

Allowing Deke and Tall Wolf to precede him, McGill entered the room where Beck was waiting. He had no trouble picking out the only dangerous character. Not the old guy. Not the guy with the shaved head who McGill realized was Edmond Whelan. No, the former Air Force near special ops man was a couple inches shorter than himself, about six feet tall. A sleek one-seventy-five, give or take five pounds. He had short sandy brown hair, symmetrical features. Probably had a nice smile when he cared to show it.

Of course, the fact that Beck was the only one not wearing shoes or a belt and Elspeth had her Uzi pointed at him also made the identification process easier.

"Mr. Beck, I'm Jim McGill. I was told you'd like to speak with me. I've also been told you planned to kill me, so you'll have to understand if I don't extend my hand to you."

Beck smiled, and it did make him look like someone you'd want for a neighbor.

"That's all right, sir, in your position, I'd be careful, too. But that's one of the reasons I wanted to see you. So I could tell you I never had any intention of doing you any harm. It was that sonofabitch over there ..." He pointed at Whelan. "He's the one who tried to get me to do the job."

"Well, now," McGill said, "that's interesting."

He had no doubt Galia would be able to do something with that tidbit.

Rangel watched the byplay like a crow waiting to consume roadkill.

He was looking for angles to play, too.

"Yeah," Beck said, "I was planning to blow him off, but the prick put a billboard up in the town where I live, threatening to expose me if I didn't play along."

"Play along with killing me, Mr. Beck? What would give him that idea?"

The man sighed, "Well, the truth is, I have killed a few people. Eight to be exact. But I did all that working for a company with a contract from the Department of Defense. People in the know decided my targets were enemies of the United States. Folks who hailed from the Middle East and Southwest Asia. Jihadis, bomb-makers and such."

"Okay," McGill said, "let's take what you say at face value. How'd you go from that to stealing embryos from a fertility clinic?"

"Well, sir, the truth is that job held an element of personal interest for me."

"What's the element?"

"I'll get to that later, sir. Right now I just want to make sure you understand that even while I was being pressured I never made a move against you. I'm sure your Secret Service people can tell you I never appeared on their radar as anything but a name."

McGill looked at Elspeth.

Feeling his gaze but never taking her eyes off Beck, she said, "We should talk about this later, privately, sir."

McGill said, "All right."

"There's something else you should know, Mr. McGill," Beck said.

"What's that?"

"If I had tried to kill you, and especially if I succeeded, I was going to be the next one to go. I'm sure there's someone waiting out there to pop me."

Beck stared at Whelan. All eyes, save Elspeth's, followed his lead. Whelan refused to look at anything but his feet.

Beck continued, "The man who hired me to ace all those guys overseas, his name was Nicholas Wicklow. Poor fellow had himself a fatal traffic accident not too long ago. Without him to testify, my guess is there's no way to prove I was working for my country while I was busy shedding other people's blood. That's another of the reasons I wanted to talk to you. You seem to be real good at getting to the bottom of things. My bet is Nick Wicklow had some help dying."

McGill arched his eyebrows and said, "You're asking to become a client of mine?"

Beck's smile returned. "Only informally. Depending on how things turn out, I may not have much money to spend."

"Is that it, Mr. Beck? You have any other reason for wanting to see me?"

Beck's expression turned mischievous. "Well, I was wondering if you or anyone else noticed that one of those embryos I stole is missing."

"We did."

"And it gnaws a little bit, doesn't it, not being able to wrap things up neat?"

"It does."

"How about we make a bargain? You do something for me and I'll tell you where that embryo is. Otherwise, it probably won't ever be found. Well, not for a lot of years anyway."

McGill asked, "What do you want?"

"Well, sir, I have to admit to doing some studying on you. Like I said, I never intended, nor did I make, any move against you. But I was curious. Intellectually, you know. What would it have been like if I went the other way? You are one impressive man, sir. Beat the hell out of U.S. senator on a basketball court and got away with it. Took down a big blowhard in front of his whole damn militia on the National Mall. Stood off half the LAPD right there on TV."

McGill had a feeling where Beck was going.

So did Deke and Elspeth.

"You want to see how you'd do against me. Is that it, Mr. Beck?"

"It is, sir. Nothing serious. Just see which of us might knock the other on his ass first. I'm some years younger than you but, right now, after dealing with that stun grenade, my ears are still ringing and I've got spots of light dancing in my eyes. I'd say that's a fair handicap. What do you think?"

Deke and Elspeth answered as one, "No!"

But McGill said, "Mr. Beck, I've been wanting to bust someone's nose for a while now, and I think yours will do just fine."

"Here or outside, sir?"

"Right here, right now."

Once again the Secret Service chorused, "No!"

Deke added, "I'll shoot him."

"We need Mr. Beck for his testimony against Edmond Whelan," McGill said. "It's all right if he knocks me down. Won't be the first time."

"I bet it'll be the first time in a long while, though," Beck said merrily.

McGill told Deke, "Okay, if he knocks me down and tries to keep going then you can shoot him."

Beck nodded. "That's fair."

Elspeth gave a small shake of her head, possibly in disgust with McGill, but she told Beck, "Nobody's joking here, asshole. You don't stop when we say, you're dead."

Deke added, "Both of you step back. Maybe you're just standing in a zone of stupidity right now."

McGill grinned. So did Beck. But they both moved away from each other. Reaching a distance of fifteen feet, with a working margin of five feet on either side, they stopped and sized each other up. Measured the other man's posture for balance, took notice of hand positioning. Tried to see which hand or foot might be more likely to be used for a first strike.

Then Beck started to whistle. McGill didn't recognize the melody but it sounded country to his ear and was in 4/4 time. In time with his tune, Beck shuffled forward. McGill stayed where he was, shifting his weight from right to left and back. As Beck cut the distance between them in half, he went up on the balls of his feet and his open hands, held palms forward, moved out in front of his chest, as if to gesture the sentiment, "Hey, wait a minute now."

Beck didn't stop …

Until McGill began to hum, just a bit louder than Beck's whistle.

His musical selection had a jazzy sound and was in the rare 5/4 time signature.

It threw Beck off-beat, made him stutter step, try to find his rhythm again.

Beck tried whistling louder, but McGill just upped his volume, too. The musical dissonance started to aggravate Beck. Started messing not only with his physical balance but his emotional harmony, too. McGill saw it and grinned at Beck, letting him know he'd messed with the wrong guy, and that was always a bad mistake.

When McGill began bobbing his head back and forth to his music, Beck couldn't restrain himself. He lunged forward, hoping to catch McGill smack on the mouth as his head came forward. Come it did, but McGill smoothly stepped off at a 45-degree angle to his right. He used his right hand to push Beck's punch aside. Then he grabbed Beck's wrist with his left hand and yanked him forward. Beck came to an abrupt stop when McGill's right elbow, moving like a scythe, swung around and connected with Beck's jaw. Cut him down like ripe wheat.

Deke and Elspeth jumped in to cuff Beck. Fight over.

Rangel and Whelan looked at McGill and then each other.

They both silently wondered if the president's henchman hadn't just delivered a message to them almost as blunt as the one he'd given to Beck. *You want to play rough, we'll play rough.*

Elspeth said to McGill, "I thought you wanted to break his nose."

McGill said, "A bit of misdirection. Should I hit him again?"

Deke spared a glance at Whelan and Rangel and said, "Probably wouldn't be good for your public image."

Tall Wolf stepped over and said to McGill, "That was 'Take Five' you were humming, wasn't it?"

McGill smiled and nodded. "You know it?"

"Blessing told me all about it," Tall Wolf said.

"Yeah, funny the things that can save your backside in a fight," McGill said. "Thing is, though, you use whatever works."

CHAPTER 11

Sunday, March 29, 2015, The White House — Washington, DC

The day dawned bright but the temperature was right at the freezing mark. The First Couple chose to stay in bed and pick up where they'd left off the night before. It was time for brunch before they'd showered and dressed. At the dining table, McGill raised a glass of orange juice and offered a toast to Patti. "Here's to us, kiddo."

"Come what may," she added.

They touched glasses and drank.

"You want to start or should I?" Patti asked.

McGill knew she meant recounting their respective adventures.

They'd held off until now in the interests of marital bonding.

"Ladies and presidents first," McGill said.

"I was going to keep this strictly to myself, but this morning I feel like sharing with you. Galia told me without directly saying so that she wasn't the one who intimidated Joan Renshaw into recanting her accusation that I'd plotted to kill Erna Godfrey."

"Okay," McGill said, "assuming Galia didn't have her fingers crossed that must mean someone else did."

Patti nodded and the look in her eyes conveyed a silent plea.

McGill told her, "Wouldn't work, having me find out who really did it."

"I didn't think you'd be obvious about it."

"Even if I was a phantom, people would want to know where the info came from. A crowd will be looking for the answer to start with, but if it takes a long time there'll be one persistent guy or gal who will make it their life's work. You really want someone dogging us the rest of our lives?"

"Well, if you put it that way."

"I do. There's another investigation that I was recruited for but won't do."

He told his wife Beck's story of the death of Nicholas Wicklow. "That has to be a federal investigation, strictly by the book. If Edmond Whelan is involved in it, that's a big deal. If Whelan set up Beck to die after he made a run at me, that'll be headline news, too."

Patti shook her head. "My God, this job can be just awful. But there is the occasional ray of sunshine. I got a phone call while you were in the shower."

"Someone told you the cherry blossoms will bloom early this year?"

"Even better. We've got Tyler Busby."

McGill smiled and offered a brief round of applause. "That's wonderful. Where was he? Who nabbed him? Is he on his way back here wearing chains?"

"Special Agent Abra Benjamin nabbed him by posing as a hooker he solicited."

McGill laughed. "Money can't buy you love."

"Benjamin and a Uruguayan policewoman took Busby to our embassy in Montevideo. It was the local officer's choice of where to dump Busby so we're in no diplomatic difficulty there. We might have been, though, because the FBI had a kidnap team waiting in the wings for Busby. That would have caused a fuss."

"You think?" McGill asked.

"I do, and there was also a bit of unfortunate news from Uruguay. They had Philip Brock under lock and key, too."

McGill seized on the operative verb. "Had?"

"He was in a local police lockup awaiting a decision on a bail application, and then he just vanished. So did the fellow in charge of the place. He was an unhappy man who was facing a divorce proceeding that was going to cost him pretty much everything he had plus a big chunk of his pension."

"Please tell me Brock's disappearance wasn't the FBI at work," McGill said.

"No, it wasn't."

"So maybe Brock is on the run again or it's yet another mystery for someone else to solve."

"I'm beginning to think you're happy delegating these things."

"You bet. How about you?"

"I'll be glad when we move on to new things."

"So you don't want to hear about the guy who challenged me to a fight last night?"

Patti took McGill's chin in hand and used it as a swivel to examine his face.

She found no bruises, lacerations or stitches.

"Well, the good guy obviously won, so go ahead and tell me the story."

White House Chief of Staff's Office

On that Sunday, Galia Mindel was in her office. There was no other place for her to be when the president was one day away from being tried by the Senate. McGill rapped on the door and entered when given permission.

"Sorry to intrude, Galia, but I have a bit of news."

She gestured him to a chair. "Sit."

McGill did and told her of his brief clash with Eugene Beck.

"That sounds risky," Galia said.

"Life can be like that, but it turns out he's not a bad guy. Never tried to kill me, and he kept his word. Told me where Mira Kersten's missing embryo is."

"Don't keep me in suspense, please. I have one or two things to do before tomorrow."

"Sure. That embryo is presently *in utero.* More specifically, it is being carried internally by a Ms. Mary Lee Emberton, Eugene Beck's special lady friend."

Galia said, "What, the guy couldn't do the job himself?"

"Unfortunately for him, no. Beck caught the mumps as a kid and the illness left him sterile. When Edmond Whelan brought the job of stealing the embryos to Beck, he saw the list of who the fathers involved were. Turned out one of them was a favorite movie star. He talked it over with his honey. She was at the right point in her cycle and liked the idea, too."

"She's a recipient of stolen property," Galia said.

McGill nodded. "Maybe, but recovery would be problematic at this point, and while a frozen embryo might be considered property, a growing fetus likely wouldn't. There might be an element of kidnapping here, but I'll leave that with King Solomon. I'm done with this case. I just wanted to let you know what happened. If I get any calls from Mira, I'm going to forward them to you since you were the one who brought me in on this."

Galia sighed. "All right, I'll handle it."

McGill added, "Mira lied to me. She said she didn't know who had stolen Whelan's treatise, but she pointed her ex-husband right at Rangel. Technically, she might not have known Rangel was behind the theft but she certainly could have pointed out to me, too, that Rangel was a likely suspect. Why didn't she? I don't even

McGill saw Galia's face fall. He'd added concern to a heavily burdened woman. Telling Galia her one-time protégé was likely up to no good. He didn't feel good about it.

"Anything I can do for you, Galia? Short of talking to Mira again."

She shook her head. "I'll find out what's going on."

"Tomorrow's going to go okay, isn't it?" McGill asked.

"With the Senate? Yes. I've got all the Democratic votes we need and then some. Tomorrow will be political theater, nothing more."

"So what's the problem?"

She shrugged. "I just have the feeling something bad is going to happen." After a pause, she added, "Like we're coming to the end of something."

McGill shrugged. "If that's so, we'll go down fighting."

CHAPTER 12

Monday, March 30, 2015, McGill Investigations, Inc. — Georgetown

LAPD Detectives Zapata and MacDuff took a taxi to McGill's office straight from National Airport after flying all night. Despite spending six plus hours in coach seats much too small to accommodate their bulk in comfort, the two cops were in an agreeable if not convivial mood. They even deigned to shake McGill's hand.

"So this is it, huh?" Zapata asked, looking around McGill's inner office. "I was expecting something, I don't know, more impressive."

MacDuff added, "The neighborhood's real nice but, yeah, I thought it'd be more plush, too."

McGill told them, "Adjust your expectations. This is your future after you retire from the job. Unless, of course, you work security in a discount store."

The two West Coast dicks looked at each other and Zapata asked, "You saying you're offering us a job?"

"No, I'll leave that pleasure to someone else."

MacDuff said, "Lieutenant Proctor told us you said something about opening a shop in L.A."

"I might. I'm waiting to see if the guy who'd run the office gets final clearance from his rumored fiancée.

MacDuff and Zapata found that bulletin worthy of a snort.

Until McGill added, "He's a deputy director of the FBI. He might be marrying the vice president of the United States."

They thought McGill was kidding them until he said he wasn't.

To dispel the idea that he wasn't just any PI, he'd arranged to have Eugene Beck delivered by federal marshals from Virginia. McGill and his visitors made the transfer of custody on the sidewalk in front of his building.

"Try not to lose him in the airport," McGill told the LAPD detectives. "Eugene, play it straight; you know what your testimony back here will be worth to you."

"What's that mean?" Zapata asked.

He and MacDuff were looking at the prisoner's battered face. It looked like a giant bruise with eyes, and the guy's jaw was wired shut. "What'd you do?" MacDuff asked. "Run him over with a truck?"

McGill shook his head. "He challenged me to a fight."

Zapata said, "If we tuned up somebody that bad, we'd lose our jobs."

"To answer your earlier question, Detective, Mr. Beck will be testifying in a number of federal proceedings right here in Washington. He's a key witness. His testimony and other considerations will be taken into account when it comes time to decide his fate."

MacDuff said, "So we don't get to keep him, is that it? This is all just play-acting here."

"Lieutenant Proctor and I thought it was worth observing the niceties; you two get credit for the arrest and Eugene knows he's probably going to do a year or so in a California lockup. As to keeping Mr. Beck on a more extended basis, don't count on it. If Eugene comes through with what he's promised and otherwise behaves himself, I might give him a job in my L.A. office."

Beck grinned, insofar as he could.

Zapata and MacDuff looked exasperated. There was just no pleasing some people.

United States Senate — Washington, DC

President Andrew Johnson's trial in the Senate lasted more than two months. President Bill Clinton's trial lasted five weeks. The trial of President Patricia Grant was done in less than a day. The only witness called to testify was Joan Renshaw. Washed, coiffed and dressed presentably, Ms. Renshaw appeared to be in relatively sound health and her responses to questions were on-point and lucid, if not always entirely rational.

They were damning to Congress as an institution as well, according to most media accounts.

Q. Ms. Renshaw do you know why you were first arrested and held in custody?

A. I do.

Q. What was the reason?

A. I was accused of plotting to kill President Patricia Grant.

Q. Without speaking to your innocence or guilt in that matter, do you have any personal feelings about the president?

The hoped for answer by the prosecution was no.

A. I hate her.

Q. Why is that?

A. She took the man I loved, Andrew Hudson Grant, away from me.

Q. Were you and Mr. Grant engaged to be married?

A. No.

Q. Was there a less formal but still specific understanding between the two of you?

A.I just knew. He was going to marry me, until she came along.

Q. So, to be clear, that's the reason you bear ill feelings toward the president?

A. Yes.

Q. Has Patricia Grant ever done anything else to harm you personally or professionally.

A. No.

Q. Turning to your transfer into a jail cell in which the late Erna

Godfrey was housed, were you placed in that cell with Mrs. Godfrey by the president's directive with the foreknowledge that you would kill Mrs. Godfrey and then receive a presidential pardon for that crime and any other crimes you may have committed?

A. (Witness paused before responding and smiled) Maybe. I've told two different stories so far. In one I was working for the president and in the other I wasn't. But as a matter of fact Erna Godfrey was the only person I hated more than Patti Grant. She killed Andy Grant. I had a plan to win him back, but she put an end to that when she killed Andy. I had a plan and that bitch ruined it.

Q. Which of your answers is the true one, Ms. Renshaw?

A. Depends on who you are. The people who impeached Patti Grant and are trying her here today have their own reasons for hating her as much as I do. That's why we're all here. For them, for me, for us, there's only one answer: She's guilty. For everybody else ... well, fuck them.

As there were no other witnesses called, the Senate recessed for an extended lunch and caucuses among those who would cast their votes. That result followed strict party lines: the GOP and True South delivered 50 guilty votes (the four senators absent due to their incarceration on pending charges were not permitted to vote); the Democrats and the sole Cool Blue senator provided 45 not guilty votes. (Senator Randall Pennyman, Democrat, GA, subject of a federal arrest warrant, was still unaccounted for.) As a two-thirds vote was required to convict, President Patricia Grant was vindicated. In terms of the law, anyway. As a matter of public opinion, the debate was just beginning.

The Oval Office — Washington, DC

The four people sitting that evening in the Oval Office chose not to open a bottle of champagne to celebrate. They looked ahead to the final year of Patricia Grant's presidency, trying to work out how to make some small measure of progress for the people who sent them to Washington. Galia said, "Madam President, a flash poll says your henchman is the most popular public male figure in the country."

"You're making that up," McGill said as he sat next to his wife.

Galia shook her head. "It's true. In a question asking women in the United States who they would want sitting next to them at a critical moment in their lives, you were number one."

Patricia Grant took McGill's arm and said, "I'm not lending him out."

"Stop it, both of you," McGill said. "If I remembered how, I might blush."

The fourth person in the room, Vice President Jean Morrissey, changed the subject. "I don't know if it will mean anything politically in the short term, but I'm getting married."

The First Couple beamed and Galia joined them in saying congratulations.

"Byron DeWitt, I assume," the president said.

"Yes, ma'am. He proposed this morning, said we ought to remember this day for something happy."

"Isn't it customary for the fellow asking for a lifetime contract to offer a ring in compensation?" eagle-eyed McGill asked.

Jean said, "He did that, but he underestimated my ring size. Couldn't get it over my hockey knuckles."

Everyone laughed and Galia said, "Being married will help your run for the White House."

"Byron mentioned that, too. I had thought of it, but I said yes because I wanted to be with him in any case."

"I hope I won't be too big a drag on you, Jean," Patti Grant said.

"Madam President, I'd like you to campaign for me every chance you get. I'm sure I'll have different ideas on some issues, but I'll never run away from you. You were the first woman to hold the office and I can't imagine anyone doing better, especially considering the opposition you've faced."

"Thank you, Jean. Hearing that from you means a great deal

to me."

"There is one thing I have to tell you, though, that I will be doing differently."

The vice president looked at each of the others in turn. She saw that the president and McGill didn't know what was coming. Galia, though … damn, if she didn't have the inside dope.

"I won't be running as a Democrat," Jean said. "I'll be running for the nomination of Cool Blue. If I win that, I'll run on their ticket. Darren Drucker and Putnam Shady are putting the wheels in motion to get the nominating process up and running."

"As someone who's changed parties myself, I can't object," the president said. "Nor do I see having any problem campaigning for you, Jean."

"Count me in, too," McGill said. "I hear I might do well attracting the women's vote."

The vice president said, "Thank you. I'm sure you will, sir,"

"You made this decision at least a little while ago, didn't you?" Galia asked. "You held off telling anyone until the trial in the Senate was over. So you wouldn't alienate any Democrats."

"I didn't want to make your job or anyone else's harder," Jean said.

Before the chief of staff could respond, her cell phone trilled.

"You didn't think to turn your phone off, Galia?" the president asked.

"I'm sorry, Ma'am, I … I'm still a bit on edge. May I take the call?"

"Go ahead. It's probably just a telemarketer."

It wasn't, not from the look that crossed Galia's face.

Fear, anger and compassion all fought for and found places on the chief of staff's face. "Yes, of course. I'll have an attorney for him on hand within the hour. Tell him not to say a word to the police or anyone else."

Galia had everyone's attention as she clicked off.

"That was Mary Louise Roosevelt," Galia told them. "She's the wife of one of my … people. The ones who help me stay on top of things."

"One of your spies," McGill said. "And he's in trouble with the police?"

"Elias Roosevelt works for Thomas Winston Rangel. Rangel has accused him of stealing a stamp collection worth more than a million dollars. Don't ask if Elias did it. He didn't. I'd trust the man with my grandchildren."

Jean said, "Is there any way Rangel could have guessed Mr. Roosevelt was working for you?"

Galia said, "I really don't see how."

"Maybe it just dawned on him he was worthy of being snooped on," McGill said.

Before that point could be debated, the president said, "I assume the lawyer you'll be sending out shortly is first rate."

"Yes, of course," Galia said.

McGill told her, "That might be the giveaway Rangel hopes to see. Mr. Roosevelt likely can't afford top-end representation on what Rangel pays him."

Galia's face sagged and then hardened. "I don't care. I'm not abandoning him. He's one of my people."

"None of us think you should leave him hanging," the president said. "We'll work this out. Mr. Roosevelt will get the representation he needs."

Galia said, "There's more."

"What?" McGill asked.

"I decided long ago that if something like this ever happened I'd shut down my whole … group of people. If I do that, Madam President, you might have to go through your final year in office blind, so to speak. We'll likely have no advance word on what the other side might be planning."

"Maybe that's what T.W. Rangel himself has in mind," Jean said. "He might need to get knocked on his ass."

McGill smiled inwardly. He thought a Morrissey administration might be something you'd buy a ticket to see. He said, "Rangel should be worrying about the accusation Edmond Whelan has made against him, claiming that Rangel stole his treatise, but as far as I know it hasn't turned up yet. Not in Rangel's possession anyway. So —"

Galia picked up the thread. "If Whelan hears from the big money men on the conservative side that the only way he'll get the best lawyers in town to defend him is to drop the accusation against Rangel, that's just what he'll do. T.W. Rangel will feel like a geriatric Superman and come after —"

"You, Galia," the president said. "The other side has taken their best shot at me and failed."

"And they're probably still digging for dirt on me," the vice president said.

McGill held up a hand. "Let's get back to all that in a moment. Seems to me Rangel is fishing. If Mr. Roosevelt isn't a stamp thief, Rangel is using that allegation in the hope Roosevelt will have something he can use to buy his way out of trouble. 'Hey, boss, how about I tell you how I've been working for Galia Mindel all these years?"

"He'd never do that," Galia said.

"Okay," McGill said. "That's point number one. Number two is, even we can't foresee any attacks that might be coming this way, can we hit back hard?"

Galia nodded. "I've got the goods on just about everyone in town."

The thought encouraged Galia so much that she laughed.

She told the others, "There's a clause in most publishing contracts. It says the publisher can sell the rights to a book it has purchased to a third party. The publisher who was going to bring out Edmond Whelan's book, *Permanent Power,* got cold feet at the last moment. Someone started a rumor that Whelan had doctored the manuscript to make himself look more prescient and efficient than he really was."

The president said, "We won't ask who started those rumors."

Galia only grinned. "Another publisher, with a different political point of view, picked up the property for a song. Imagine how

Whelan and the opposition leadership in the house are going to look if *Permanent Power* comes out just as Whelan goes on trial for conspiring to kill Mr. McGill."

Possibly without even noticing what she was doing Galia began to rub her hands together in glee. McGill liked Galia's idea, but he had a cautionary point to make.

He said, "That would hurt the other side all right, Galia, but it will also make them come after you even harder. You know that, right?"

In three-part harmony, like they'd sung in the same choir for years, Galia,Patti and Jean said, "Just let them try."

ABOUT THE AUTHOR

Joseph Flynn has been published both traditionally — Signet Books, Bantam Books and Variance Publishing — and through his own imprint, Stray Dog Press, Inc. Both major media reviews and reader reviews have praised his work. Booklist said, "Flynn is an excellent storyteller." *The Chicago Tribune* said, "Flynn [is] a master of high-octane plotting." The most repeated reader comment is: Write faster, we want more.

Contact Joe at Hey Joe on his website: *www.josephflynn.com*

All of Joe's books are available for the Kindle or free Kindle app through *www.amazon.com.*

The Jim McGill Series

The President's Henchman, A Jim McGill Novel [#1]
The Hangman's Companion, A JimMcGill Novel [#2]
The K Street Killer A JimMcGill Novel [#3]
Part 1: The Last Ballot Cast, A JimMcGill Novel [#4 Part 1]
Part 2: The Last Ballot Cast, A JimMcGill Novel [#4 Part 2]
The Devil on the Doorstep, A Jim McGill Novel [#5]
The Good Guy with a Gun, A Jim McGill Novel [#6]
The Echo of the Whip, A Jim McGill Novel [#7]
McGill's Short Cases 1-3

The Ron Ketchum Mystery Series

Nailed, A Ron Ketchum Mystery [#1]
Defiled, A Ron Ketchum Mystery Featuring John Tall Wolf [#2]
Impaled, A Ron Ketchum Mystery [#3]

The John Tall Wolf Series

Tall Man in Ray-Bans, A John Tall Wolf Novel [#1]
War Party, A John Tall Wolf Novel [#2]
Super Chief, a John Tall Wolf Novel [#3]
Smoke Signals, a John Tall Wolf Novel [#4]

The Zeke Edison Series

Kill Me Twice [#1]

Stand Alone Titles

The Concrete Inquisition
Digger
The Next President
Hot Type
Farewell Performance
Gasoline, Texas
Round Robin, A Love Story of Epic Proportions
One False Step
Blood Street Punx
Still Coming
Still Coming Expanded Edition
Hangman — A Western Novella
Pointy Teeth: Twelve Bite-Sized Stories

You may read free excerpts of Joe's books by visiting his website at: *www.josephflynn.com*.

CPSIA information can be obtained
at www.ICGtesting.com
Printed in the USA
BVOW09s2207021117
499361BV00013B/215/P